With love and thanks to **Mike Griffiths** for his knowledge of Cornwall and conversations with the Coastguard, and to **Jenny Griffiths**, whose friendship has endured over time and an ocean.

Dear Reader,

I have four great *Scarlet* books to get you in the holiday mood this month! To start with, Judy Jackson's Canadian heroine suddenly finds her life whirling *Out of Control*. Then Stella Whitelaw takes *her* heroine to Barbados where nothing (and no one) is quite as it seems! In Kay Gregory's novel, Iain and Phaedra play out their involving story against a dramatic Cornish backdrop. And, last (but by no means least!) *will* Jocasta be *Betrayed* in Angela Drake's latest *Scarlet* romance?

You will notice that each of these authors has been published in *Scarlet* before and we are delighted to see their names back on our list. One of the things that makes *Scarlet* so special, I believe, is the very individual style each of our authors brings to her writing. And, of course, they also offer us a wonderful variety of settings for their books. It's lovely, isn't it, to be able to enjoy visiting a different country without having to leave home?

So, whether you're reading this book on a train, a bus or a plane, sitting at home or having a well earned vacation – I hope you'll enjoy *all* the *Scarlet* titles I have chosen for you this month.
Till next month,

Sally Cooper

SALLY COOPER,
Editor-in-Chief – *Scarlet*

About the Author

Kay Gregory was born and educated in England. Shortly after moving to Victoria, Canada, she met her husband in the unromantic setting of a dog club banquet. Since 1961, Kay and her husband have lived in the Vancouver area, and they have two grown sons who frequently return home to commune with the contents of the family fridge!

At various times, Kay has cohabited (more or less willingly) with dogs, hamsters, gerbils, rats and ferrets . . . currently down to one neurotic dog. Over the years, Kay has had more jobs than she can count: everything from packaging paper bags (the bags won and she lost the job!) to running a health food bar, cleaning offices and working as a not-very-efficient secretary.

As the author of twenty plus romance novels, Kay says: 'Writing books is definitely the best job I've ever had and one I don't intend to change. Selling my first long contemporary novel (*Marry Me Stranger*) to *Scarlet* was one of the most exciting things that has ever happened to me.' *The Sherraby Brides* was published early in 1997 and we are now delighted to bring you Kay's latest *Scarlet* romance.

Other *Scarlet* titles available this month:

SWEET SEDUCTION – Stella Whitelaw
BETRAYED – Angela Drake
OUT OF CONTROL – Judy Jackson

KAY GREGORY

HIS FATHER'S WIFE

Enquiries to:
Robinson Publishing Ltd
7 Kensington Church Court
London W8 4SP

First published in the UK by Scarlet, 1997

Copyright © Kay Gregory 1997
Cover photography by J. Cat

A copy of the British Library Cataloguing in
Publication data is available from the British Library

ISBN 1-85487-959-6

Printed and bound in the EC

10 9 8 7 6 5 4 3 2 1

PROLOGUE

Phaedra stretched her arms above her head, spreading her fingers to catch the wind, laughing as tendrils of dark hair whipped around her cheeks. Her grey, second-hand overcoat rode up to uncover bare knees above bulky grey socks, but she scarcely noticed the cold as she inhaled the fresh winter scent of the sea and listened to the waves dashing up the sand to collide with the tall black rock she had moments ago claimed as her castle. It had taken her ages to climb to the top, cautiously at first, afraid of slipping, and then with confidence once she knew she would reach her goal.

School was out. Tomorrow would be Christmas. And for two whole weeks there would be no one to taunt her about coming from the big house called Chy an Cleth and thinking she was somebody special.

Phaedra didn't think she was special. She knew she was the housekeeper's daughter. That wouldn't have mattered if she'd had even one good friend at school to take her part. But she was quiet, clumsy at games, and she didn't know how to make the others in her

1

class understand that she wasn't stuck up just because she didn't talk a lot. The teachers were nice though. She liked her teachers. *They* understood that she would have talked if she'd known what to say. One day she might even be a teacher herself – if she didn't decide to be an actress or an astronaut.

Far below her on the sand, waves were licking at the front of her castle. They were her subjects, those waves – because she was no longer plain Phaedra Pendenning of Chy an Cleth, but Amphitrite, Queen of the Sea. She extended her arms, laughing delightedly as a wave, higher than the rest, crashed against her throne and splashed her feet. Oh, she did love the holidays, and Christmas. And the sea, and . . .

'Phaedra!'

She started, brushing the hair off her face as a familiar and beloved voice shouted up to her from the sand.

'Iain!' she cried, teetering on the edge of her perch. 'Iain, you're back.'

'And just in time, from the looks of it,' the young man on the beach roared back. 'Phaedra, are you out of your mind? Come down at once.'

'Why? Why don't you come up? It's fun. I'm Amphitrite. You can be Poseidon.'

'Who the hell's Amphitrite? No, never mind. Just stop being her and come down. At once. Can't you see the tide's coming in?'

Phaedra looked around her. Oh. She had been so busy being Queen of the Sea she hadn't noticed. Iain was right. Her castle was almost surrounded by swirling sea.

'All right,' she called back. 'I'm coming.'

Oh dear, she was going to get wet. Mummy would be cross and say she'd catch her death, and didn't she know they couldn't afford to send her coat to the cleaners every time she got it covered in sand or mud?

They could afford it, of course. Mr Trebanian would get her a new coat if she asked him. Only Mummy wouldn't let her ask. Mummy was funny about asking Mr Trebanian for things. Phaedra didn't know why. He was a bit grumpy sometimes, and very strict with Iain, who was his son, and with Joan, his daughter, who went her own way and didn't seem to notice her father's strictures. But he was nice to Mummy, and nice to her. Phaedra sighed. It made no difference. There would still be trouble if she went home with her coat covered in sand and seaweed.

'Phaedra,' Iain called. 'I said come down at once.'

Oh no. She'd been dreaming again. 'Here I come,' she shouted, and sat down to swing her legs over the edge.

Easing her feet down the rockface, she scrabbled with her walking shoes for a solid footing. It was harder going down than coming up. She found a place for her feet, but now there was nowhere to put her hands. She gripped the edge, hanging on. The rock was awfully cold and scratchy. She wished she hadn't left her gloves at home.

Another big wave sent a shower of spray around her ankles. It must be getting deeper down there.

'Phaedra? What's holding you up?'

She moved her hands in a futile search for something substantial to grip. 'I'm stuck,' she screamed, as another spurt of spray drenched her legs. 'Iain, I'm stuck. I can't get down.'

Above the sound of the waves, Phaedra heard a stream of words Mummy would have scolded *her* for saying. At one time she would have scolded Iain too, but he was nineteen now, and she was only ten.

'Hang on,' he shouted. 'I'm coming.'

Phaedra hung on. There was nothing else to do. She didn't feel like Amphitrite any more. She just felt scared. And then Iain was behind her, his hands on the rock beside her, guiding her down.

'I can't . . .' she whimpered.

'Yes, you can. It's easy. I know about rock climbing. I promise I'll be right behind you if you slip. Come on, put your hands here. Right. Now move your left foot down a few inches. Good. Now your right one. That's it.'

Slowly, inch by inch, with Iain's cold breath mingling with the wind on her neck, they made their way down until both of them were clinging to the rockface only inches above the waves.

'It's too deep,' Phaedra said, fear snaking in her tummy. 'Iain, my coat –'

'It's not too deep for me.' Iain's voice wasn't calm and gentle any more, and she didn't much like the sound of it. 'OK, my feet are on solid ground. Keep still.'

Phaedra kept still, and in a moment his hands were around her waist, and she felt herself being plucked from the rock and dumped face down across his shoulder. As he carried her to dry land, she could hear the slosh of the sea against his boots.

When they reached the bottom of the path up the cliff, he dumped her on the ground, turned her around and raised his hand in a motion whose intent she recognized immediately.

'Don't!' Phaedra cried. 'Iain, don't smack me.'

She knew she wouldn't feel much through the thick cloth of her sodden coat, but her feelings, already balanced precariously between fright and relief, had taken a quick turn in the direction of bruised. She started to cry.

'Oh, for God's sake,' Iain muttered, dropping his arm. 'I wouldn't hurt you. And if I did, you'd damn well deserve it. Do you have any idea what might have happened to you if I hadn't turned up? Here.' He handed her a handkerchief, and when she turned to take it, still sobbing, she saw that his jeans were soaked to the top of his thighs.

She wasn't a good swimmer. Not yet. If he hadn't been there to rescue her, she might have drowned.

'Oh, Iain,' she cried, throwing her arms around his waist and burying her face in the folds of his heavy wool jacket. 'Oh, Iain, I'm sorry. I didn't mean to get stuck. But I wanted to be Amphitrite, and . . .'

'Who *is* Amphitrite?' he interrupted.

'She's Poseidon's wife. He's the God of the Sea, and she's his – his goddess, I think. Is that right?'

'I suppose so. It's *your* mother who used to be so keen on all that Greek stuff. In any case, you had no

5

business climbing that rock. You could have drowned, you idiotic little dreamer.' He bent down, tipped her face up and wiped her eyes with the handkerchief. 'Come on now, don't cry. I'm not really angry. You scared the hell out of me, that's all.'

'Because you didn't want me to drown?' She had to be sure.

'Of course I didn't. What would Chy an Cleth be without Phaedra?'

'Mr Trebanian's,' she said. 'And then yours.'

Iain laughed. 'I'm glad to see you have a prosaic streak about you after all. Life's not easy for dreamers. People always want you to follow *their* dreams instead of your own.'

Phaedra didn't know what he meant, and she had no idea what 'prosaic' was. But she was glad he was glad.

'I do love you, Iain,' she assured him.

'And I love you,' Iain said lightly.

He took her hand, and they walked together up the path to Chy an Cleth to face the inevitable wrath of Phaedra's mother.

CHAPTER 1

'What?' Iain roared. He smashed a fist on to his desk and leaned over the speakerphone, the better to concentrate on his caller's next words. 'He did *what*?'

'Got married. Your father. This afternoon.' The bombshell was delivered in the composed, carefully modulated tones of a man who is used to smoothing ruffled feathers.

Iain drew a long, rasping breath as he fought for control of his temper. 'Yes. That's what I thought you said. Is his – *bride* anyone I know?'

'Indeed she is. He married Phaedra.'

'Phaedra! Did you say *Phaedra*? Phaedra Pendenning?' Iain gave up the battle to keep his voice down, and his secretary stuck her head round the door to see if he was shouting for her. He waved her away.

'Angus? Are you still there?' He laid his palms flat on the desk and bent over the speakerphone as if he meant to smash it.

'Certainly I am.' The voice was still maddeningly composed. 'I thought you and Joan ought to know.'

'Yes. Of course. Thank you.' This was his father's

7

old friend he was shouting at. And Angus was attempting to do him a favour. Iain lowered himself deliberately into his chair and curled his fingers around its black leather arms. 'Joan is in the States. Anton's touring again and she went with him.'

'Ah. I dare say that had something to do with your father's decision to remarry. You know he always gets upset when he reads about his son-in-law in the papers.'

Iain closed his eyes. 'Are you trying to tell me that impossible old man who calls himself my father has married Phaedra Pendenning just because my sister married a dancer?'

'No, no. Wait a minute, Iain. Wait a minute. I think there's more to it than that.'

Iain raised an arm and pressed the tips of his fingers to his temples. 'So I assumed.' He drew another long breath and rapped out, 'The one I'd really like to get my hands on is young Phaedra. Angus, you're the family solicitor. You know Father as well as any of us. Why didn't you put a stop to this nonsense before it got off the ground?'

'Iain, you know very well there is absolutely nothing anyone can do once Charles Trebanian gets a notion in his head.'

'True.' Iain flipped the pages of his appointment diary. 'All right. I'll get down there as soon as I can. Obviously it's time I found out for myself what's been going on.' He scored a red line through the following day's appointments. 'I hope you're not going to tell me the happy couple have already left Cornwall?'

'Left?'

'On their *honeymoon*,' he explained, with a sneering emphasis on the last word.

'Oh, I see. I'm afraid there won't be a honeymoon. Your father's health – his heart, you know – has deteriorated considerably since the last time you were here. It's been almost two years, hasn't it?'

Iain heard the note of polite reproach in the ageing solicitor's prim voice. His lips tightened. 'There hasn't been much point in my going down to see him, Angus. The past three times I put in an appearance, he tried to throw me out within an hour of my arrival.'

'He didn't succeed though, did he? And you would insist on arguing with him, Iain. You know he can't bear to be thwarted.'

'Neither can I,' Iain said shortly. 'Thanks for phoning. I'll be in Porthkelly tomorrow.'

'I think that *would* be advisable,' agreed Angus. 'I'll look forward to seeing you.'

Iain switched off the phone before he was tempted to express his opinion in words too forceful for the straitlaced solicitor's elderly ears. His father's old friend was a decent, conscientious soul, but there were times when his relentless unflappability was enough to drive a sane man to murder.

Picking up his favourite silver pen, Iain tapped it sharply on the edge of the desk. What the devil had got into his cantankerous old misanthrope of a father this time? It was three years since Joan had married Anton Vanilos, star of the Ida Byrd Ballet Company. Surely the old man wasn't still brooding over that. And even if he was, why marry Phaedra? Unless . . .

Ah. Iain dropped the pen and leaned back in his executive chair. Did he begin to see a glimmer of light?

Yes. Of course. He should have made the connection from the start. His father would think it hugely amusing to repay his children for not allowing him to run their lives by acquiring a young and spritely wife as his new heir . . . A young wife who ought to be locked up and fed on bread and water for a year. No. On second thoughts, maybe not bread and water. Turnips. He seemed to remember she'd hated those the most.

Swearing softly, Iain stood up and went to stare out of the window at the busy accountants and secretaries scurrying along Cannon Street far below. When, five minutes later, he turned back into his expensively appointed suite in the Trebanian Advertising Corporation's London office, he was wearing the small, grim smile that invariably sent his employees scuttling off on imaginary errands across town.

Phaedra Pendenning. Little Phaedra. He wouldn't have thought it of her. She'd been such a funny, dreamy little girl . . .

A little girl who had obviously grown into a self-centred, grasping young woman. Iain hooked his thumbs into his pockets and scowled at the phone on his desk. He didn't like women who married men for their money. He'd been caught that way once himself – and if Phaedra Pendenning thought she was getting away with this without suffering the unpleasant consequences she had coming to her, then the little gold-digger was in for a surprise.

Phaedra was slicing strawberries when she heard the sound of knuckles rapping sharply on the front door. She jumped, and jabbed the point of the knife into her thumb. Who could be calling at this hour? And why didn't they ring the bell like everyone else? Nobody ever arrived at Chy an Cleth before lunch. Mr Trebanian – no, *Charles* – would she ever learn to call her husband by his first name? – didn't like visitors in the morning. And what Charles Trebanian didn't like, he didn't get.

The knuckles became a fist, pounding impatiently.

Sucking her thumb to stanch the flow of blood, Phaedra hurried into the hall. Lemon-scented polish only partly masked the pervasive smell of age as she paused at the bottom of the steep, Georgian staircase in order to adjust her eyes to the shadowed antiquity of her surroundings. Dark beams supported the ceiling, a modern telephone squatted on a carved Elizabethan chest beside a Chinese mahogany chair, and the only light came from two narrow, lead-paned windows set on either side of a heavy oak door that had so far survived more than two centuries of buffeting by the weather.

It would certainly survive this current assault, Phaedra decided, as she creaked her way across the uneven surface of the floor – especially on a day like today when the wind was resting, and the only clouds were the colour of dull pearls.

The pounding ceased abruptly.

Cautiously, unsure of what she would find on the other side, Phaedra opened the door – and heard the soft hiss of her own indrawn breath.

She might have known. *Should* have known.

The rays of the warm June sun fell harshly on the face of the man who stood at the top of the granite steps with his hands thrust into the pockets of a conservative custom-made suit that in some way accentuated the hint of muscle and raw physical strength concealed beneath the cut of the grey cloth.

He was staring with a peculiar concentration at the new electric doorbell he'd just ignored, and he paid no attention to her at first, which left Phaedra a moment to study him unobserved.

At thirty-six, Iain's features had acquired a hard virility, a toughness, that hadn't touched the youthfully handsome face of the daring, impatient young man she had admired so much as a child. The obstinate jaw, the full, sensuous mouth and the nose that was a little off centre were exactly as she remembered them though.

The eyes were not. When he finally turned them on her, she saw that they were dark with a savage contempt that held no trace of the kind, casually tolerant looks he had thrown the way of the quiet little girl he had known as the housekeeper's daughter. The look he was delivering now was anything but kind. As for tolerance – she would have sworn he'd never heard the word.

'Hello, Iain,' Phaedra said. She knew why he was angry, but that didn't mean she meant to stand here being glared at. 'Won't you come in?'

'What?' For a moment she thought he meant to hurl her bodily out of his way. Then he seemed to recollect himself, and went on in a quieter, but no less dangerous tone, 'Yes. I believe I will. Why have you changed the locks, Phaedra? Afraid I might sneak in and do you the harm you so richly deserve?'

'No.' Phaedra leaned against the doorframe, refusing to be intimidated. 'Mother says Mr Trebanian insisted on having them changed after your last visit. He said he didn't want you getting the idea you could come and go as you pleased.'

Iain gave a snort of a laugh. 'As he also told me never to darken his door again, that wasn't hugely likely, was it?'

'I don't know. You're here now darkening his door.'

'Did you think I wouldn't be?' He took a step forward and stood over her, blotting out the sun.

Phaedra stood her ground, gazing into the hard glitter of eyes that at one time had enchanted her. Iain's closeness, and the faint warm scent of his body, brought back memories she thought she'd forgotten – memories that were having an effect on her quite different from the one she suspected he intended. But she wasn't afraid of him. Never had been, never would be.

'I didn't think about you at all,' she said, skirting the truth. 'Your father tells me you haven't been near him in two years.'

Iain didn't answer. Instead he put his hands on her shoulders and moved her aside, kicking the door shut as he stepped into the hall.

Phaedra waited for him to remove the big hands that were sending unexpected ripples down her arms. But he didn't, and when the hard intensity of his gaze caused her to drop her eyes, he placed his knuckles under her chin and tilted her face up.

'You've grown into quite a beauty, haven't you, little Phaedra?' he murmured, turning her head to catch the light beaming through the two small windows. He was silent for a moment during which Phaedra wanted to move, but found she couldn't. 'No, perhaps not a beauty. There's too much of the gypsy about you, and your mouth's a shade too wide. But if you tidied up that straggling mess of hair, and wore something more flattering than that grey and white sack you have on, I think I might begin to understand how you managed it.'

Phaedra found the will to twist her chin from his grasp, at the same time adjusting her white tie belt and smoothing her hands awkwardly over the fabric of her simple print frock. Not that Iain's opinion of her appearance mattered. Why should it?

'Managed what?' she asked, feigning indifference. If only she *could* be indifferent to Iain.

'To entrap my father, of course.'

Phaedra moistened her lips. They felt dry. It was strange that on the outside her body had turned cold, because inside she was burning with a sensation that was totally new to her – caused, she was certain, by an almost uncontrollable urge to slap the contempt from Iain's jeering face.

No. She gripped her hands together. She would *not* allow Iain's atrocious behaviour to affect her own. *He* had some small excuse for acting like a barracuda looking for lunch. She hadn't. Besides, from the glint in his eye, she had an uncomfortable feeling he might appreciate the excuse to retaliate.

As soon as the thought occurred to her, she rejected it. Iain wouldn't stoop to violence. It wasn't his way.

'I didn't entrap your father,' she said quietly. 'His proposal came out of the blue.'

'I'm sure. Encouraged, no doubt, by considerable batting of those alluring dark eyelashes. Add to that your sexy wriggle of a walk, and I'd say dear old Dad didn't stand much of a chance.'

Phaedra bit her lip. She *mustn't* allow Iain's barbs to provoke her. 'What would you know about my walk?' she asked. 'You haven't seen me since I left for college – and that was nine years ago.'

'Hm.' Just for a second, she thought she saw a flicker of doubt in his eyes. Then he said, 'I happened to remember,' and took his hand from her shoulder.

Oh, he did, did he? That surprised her in a way. But she was willing to bet his memories were very different from hers.

15

She had been just eighteen at the time. Her suitcases, three rigid brown relics of her mother's honeymoon, had been wrestled down from the attic, packed, and lined up neatly by the door that September morning.

As she came down the stairs, feeling smart and sophisticated in her new black trouser suit, she heard raised voices coming from the library.

'I told you why I didn't go to Bolan's. It's the family bank. I won't have you owning me, Dad. This is *my* dream. *My* business. I've worked in advertising from the day I left college. I know what I'm doing, and I don't want you breathing down my neck.'

Iain's voice, of course. As usual, he was at odds with his father, this time over the issue of the financing for his new advertising company. He had always said he would break out on his own once he learned the fundamentals of the business. Now that he was doing it, Charles Trebanian, determined to wield a measure of control, was insisting that Iain should finance the new venture through Bolan's Bank in London. Three generations of Trebanians had been directors of Bolan's. Predictably, Iain was determined to look elsewhere for financing.

Phaedra, hovering uncertainly in the hall, understood his point. She wished they would stop quarreling, though. It was months since she'd seen Iain, and she had so looked forward to his visit. But the atmosphere in the house had been venomous from the moment he'd put his elegantly shod foot through the door.

16

Charles, confronted anew with the fact that he couldn't bend his son to his will, had started out by bringing up the red rag of Iain's unfortunate marriage to Rosie Sharpe.

Poor Rosie had been dead for three years, but Charles never failed to rub his son's face in the disaster of that match made out of youthful stubborness and Iain's desire to thumb his nose at his father.

'You don't know what you're talking about, boy.' Charles' voice now, rough with anger and aggression. 'What do you know about business? If you'd done what I told you, and gone to work for Bolan's instead of getting yourself mixed up with this advertising nonsense –'

'We've been through that, Dad. Repeatedly.'

'I know that. Obstinate young jackass. But if you must make a fool of yourself, at least do it with good, solid backing. Bolan's –'

'I'm not dealing with Bolan's.'

'Now just a minute . . .'

A door slammed. Phaedra, attempting belatedly to remove herself from the line of fire, began to edge back up the stairs.

'Phaedra? Have you been listening?'

She turned with her hand on the bannister, glad of its oaken support.

Iain, in a khaki shirt, and looking disturbingly militant, was standing in the middle of the hall with his hands on his hips.

'Me and everyone within a radius of five miles,' she answered. 'Why do you always fight with him, Iain? I know he's bossy, but if you tried to be a bit more diplomatic –'

'Diplomatic! If by that you mean obsequious –'

'Not obsequious, no. But –'

'Phaedra, don't meddle in things you know nothing about. How I handle my father is my business.'

'But you don't handle him. You just antagonize him.'

'That works both ways.' Iain frowned, and took a step in her direction. 'Why the sexy suit? Are you going somewhere?'

Sexy? Iain thought she was sexy? Phaedra dropped her eyes and ran a hand over the smoothness of the bannister. It came away smelling of her mother's favourite lemon polish. 'Yes. I thought you knew. I'm leaving for college in an hour. Manchester. I only came down to say goodbye to your father.'

'Then say goodbye to him. I didn't mean to scare you away.'

'You didn't,' she said quickly. 'I was leaving because my timing seemed off.'

The hard lines drawn around his mouth softened perceptibly. 'It was, wasn't it? How are you getting to Manchester?'

Without quite knowing why, she took two steps back up the stairs. 'I'm catching the train from Exeter.'

'And how are you getting to Exeter?'

Phaedra glanced down and saw that he had one lightly tanned hand curled around the newel post.

'Mr Trebanian said he'd order a taxi for me.'

'He needn't bother. I'll drive you.'

'Oh, you don't have to do that.' She took another step backwards. 'You're not leaving until tomorrow, are you?'

'I should.' He darted a malevolent look at the closed library door. 'But I promised your mother I'd stay.'

'Yes. She told me. I'm glad you promised.'

Iain raised his eyebrows. 'Are you? Why?'

'Because I think it'll be hard on her at first.'

'What will?'

Phaedra shook her head at this prize example of masculine obtuseness. 'Because I've never been away from home before. She'll worry about me.'

'Ah.' His dour expression lifted. 'All the same, I'm sure she can spare me to drive you to the station. She'll be glad to know you're safely on the train.'

Phaedra didn't doubt it. So why was she hesitating? 'Well,' she mumbled, when she could think of no good reason to refuse. 'If you're sure it's no trouble . . .'

'Of course I'm sure. It'll get me away from Bolan's one-man tank corps in there.' He gestured at the library. 'Among other things.'

Oh. So that was it. Iain was looking for an excuse to escape his father. When she still hesitated, he said, 'Go on. Say your goodbyes. I won't eat you on the way to the station.' He stood politely aside to let her pass.

She giggled. 'I didn't think you would. I'd be awfully hard on your digestion.'

'Only on my digestion?'

Was that some kind of not-so-subtle innuendo? As Phaedra hurried past him, she caught a hint of the warm man-scent of his body, and felt a peculiar sensation that had something to do with the hairs on the back of her neck – as if Iain's eyes were boring directly into her spine. She stumbled, righted herself, and walked the rest of the way to the library with her shoulders squared and her arms swinging like a soldier's on parade.

Behind her, Iain gave a low, teasing whistle, but she managed not to stumble again.

In the library, Charles was pouring himself a whisky. 'Stubborn young fool,' he muttered as she poked her head round the door.

Phaedra was inclined to agree about the stubborness, but all she said was, 'I've come to say goodbye, Mr Trebanian. Iain's very kindly said he'll drive me into Exeter.'

'Hmm. He has, has he? First sensible idea he's had since he left home.' Charles put his glass on the copy of *Country Life* he kept on the sideboard in lieu of a mat. He held out his hand. 'Goodbye then, young Phaedra. Make the most of your chances. Don't be a fool like my son. Or my daughter.'

'Oh, I will,' Phaedra assured him, deliberately ignoring the remarks about his family. 'Thank you, Mr Trebanian. Thanks for everything. If ever I can do anything to repay you –'

'Maybe you can,' Charles grunted. 'Maybe you can. If that boy of mine ever learns to see sense.

You're a good girl, Phaedra. Your mother made a fine job of you. Better than I made of my two.'

'Oh, you mustn't say that.' She was embarrassed. 'Iain and Joan are —'

'Idiots,' Charles finished for her.

Phaedra gave up and went to find her mother.

Just over an hour later, Iain's old, but still proud, Austin-Healey pulled on to the main road to Exeter from a narrow B road bordered by hedges trimmed with early autumn gold.

They didn't talk much. They had known each other too long for talking to be obligatory, and both of them were absorbed in their own thoughts.

Iain seemed intent on the road, but from the two small lines narrowing the space between his eyebrows, Phaedra guessed he was brooding over his argument with his father. For her part, she was thinking how strange it was to be leaving Chy an Cleth – and wondering if Iain had meant it when he'd said her suit was sexy.

When they reached the station, she told him there was no need for him to see her on to the train. But he only shook his head at her as if she ought to know better, tucked one of her suitcases under his arm and, hoisting the other two, strode towards the ticket counter without wasting time on an answer.

Phaedra trotted after him. 'Hey, I can buy my own ticket,' she objected, when she saw him take out his wallet. 'You don't have to —'

'I know. I want to.'

He stood squarely in front of her, blocking her way, and there was nothing she could do except take the ticket he handed her and pretend to be suitably grateful. She wasn't grateful. His generosity made her feel like a poor relation. Or the housekeeper's daughter.

They waited on the platform in silence as other travellers jostled them and a gust of wind blew a blizzard of empty cigarette packs, used tickets and discarded chocolate wrappers around their ankles.

When the train pulled in with a hiss and a squeal of brakes, Iain threw Phaedra's suitcases on to the rack of a first-class carriage and jumped out to hand her on board.

She turned in the doorway to face him. But instead of shaking her hand or waving a careless goodbye, he startled her by lifting her back on to the platform. She was just opening her mouth to ask him what he thought he was doing, when he tipped her face up and dropped a quick kiss on her lips. His mouth lingered just long enough for her to taste peppermint toothpaste mixed with the flavour of rich coffee. When the engine growled and someone in uniform shouted a warning, Iain lifted her back on board and slammed the door.

'Goodbye, Phaedra,' he called, as the train drew away and she leaned out of the window to wave. 'Be good. Don't forget us.'

Phaedra put a hand to her mouth to hold in the feel of his lips, and waited until he was no longer even a speck in the distance before she sat down. The grey seat felt firm against her back.

Forget them? Forget Chy an Cleth? And Iain? As if she ever could.

He was standing too close, trapping her. The cold white wall felt hard against her back. They stared at each other, eyes locked in a battle that ended abruptly when Phaedra moved her hand to push an irritating strand of hair out of her eyes.

'You're bleeding,' Iain said, lifting her wrist to glare accusingly at the crust of dried blood forming on her thumb.

'You startled me, playing Big Bad Wolf at the door. I was slicing strawberries and I pricked myself. It's all right now.'

'If I ever decide to play Big Bad Wolf, I promise you'll be the first to find out.' He spoke in a low, flat baritone that sent shivers that weren't all apprehension down Phaedra's spine.

'Thanks for the sympathy,' she said.

'It's not sympathy you're in need of,' Iain replied. 'It's –'

He broke off suddenly as a quavering but none the less demanding voice called from across the hall, 'Phaedra? What's going on out there? And where the devil are my pills?'

'Well, well. The dulcet tones of your devoted bridegroom,' Iain murmured. 'Better hop to it – *Stepmother*.'

Phaedra, already hurrying towards the drawing-room, stopped in her tracks to look back at the man who was following closely on her heels. Stepmother?

Dear Lord, she *was* his stepmother. This gorgeous hunk of glowering machismo was, officially, her stepson.

By the time she reached the partially open door with Iain right behind her, her wide mouth had split into a grin, and she was trying desperately not to burst out laughing.

Somehow she didn't think her new stepson was in any mood to appreciate the joke.

'Ah, there you are. Where are my . . .?' A thin, silver-haired man with a big nose and a head that seemed too large for his frail body stopped talking abruptly and collapsed into a worn black leather chair. Only the gentle ticking of the grandfather clock in the corner broke the silence that followed as fierce grey eyes beetled malignantly at Iain.

Phaedra held her breath. Her eyes flicked over the familiar room with its heavy gold draperies and solid dark furnishings which did nothing to relieve an atmosphere heavy with Victorian gloom. Even the gold brocade loveseat and settee had managed to absorb the general oppressiveness of Charles Trebanian's favourite room. Eventually her gaze settled uncomfortably on a sturdy roll-top desk set to catch what light there was from the narrow windows. It was better than watching the staredown taking place between the two glowering men.

Seconds passed, and neither Iain nor Charles Trebanian said a word. Then, when the air in the room had become so highly charged Phaedra expected it to explode at any moment, Charles completed his inspection of his son and leaned his head against the back of his chair. Just the hint of a smile curled the too-thin line of his lips.

'So,' he said, 'yesterday's little ceremony did bring you out of the woodwork. I thought it might. Well? What do you have to say for yourself? Not a damn thing you can do about it, you know.'

'Short of having you declared incompetent, no, I don't suppose there is,' Iain agreed.

'Wouldn't wash,' the old man retorted with a snort. 'Angus Cooper knows I'm in my right mind.'

'I'm sure you are. At your age, you'd have to be *out* of it to turn down the chance of bed– ah, *wedding* Phaedra.'

'Young whippersnapper,' Charles growled. But Phaedra could tell from the way he threw back his narrow shoulders that he was delighted his son believed she was sharing his bed.

'Won't you sit down?' she said to Iain, avoiding his eye and speaking in her frostiest tone. 'Lunch should be ready soon. Please help yourself to a drink. Here are your pills, Charles.' She bent down to pick up the plastic container that lay beside her husband's chair on an ancient but good Turkish carpet.

Charles took the pills with a grunt. Iain said nothing as he crossed to the carved Chippendale drinks cabinet, but Phaedra saw his eyebrows go up. As she left the room, she could feel his gaze on her back.

All right, she thought. All right, Mr High and Mighty Iain. You want a sexy wriggle, I'll give you one.

Without allowing herself time to reconsider, she raised her hands to shoulder height and began to mince her way across the floor, swaying her hips in an outrageous parody of seduction. She felt the dress he had called a grey and white sack swish around her knees like the silk it wasn't.

Neither of the men behind her said a word, but when she reached the door she heard an unmistakable chuckle.

It didn't come from Iain, but from the irascible old man whom – was it only yesterday? – she had taken for better or for worse.

'Oho. Bet that was for your benefit, boy,' Charles chortled as she was shutting the door.

Phaedra groaned and didn't wait to listen for Iain's answer.

The big, old-fashioned kitchen with its tiled red floor and gleaming copper pans welcomed her with the rich, spicy odour of melted cheese mingled with freshly baked bread – familiar smells that soothed her jangled nerves. Grateful for the respite from tension, she slumped over the old oak table and bowed her head.

It had been so much worse than she'd imagined. At the back of her mind she had hoped Iain wouldn't find out about the marriage until Joan and Anton were back from their tour. But she might have known old Angus Cooper would spill the beans.

If only she could have explained everything to Joan first, asked her advice when she came on her next flying visit. Iain's sister would take her father's marriage in her stride, but she would also appreciate the difficulty of explaining it to Iain. She saw him whenever she was in England, and understood him as Phaedra no longer did.

Joan, flighty as she was, would have known how best to break the news. She had never cared much about Chy an Cleth herself, but she knew how much it meant to her brother.

As a free spirit with little interest in a two-hundred-year-old house on the wild north coast of Cornwall, Joan had always dreamed of escape from Porthkelly. Marrying handsome, rootless Anton, who danced like an angel and was rarely in England for long, had been the perfect answer to her dream.

Charles had never seen it that way, and he continued to regard his son-in-law's chosen profession with a deep and abiding suspicion.

'Stockings,' he had been heard to mutter. 'No self-respecting man wears *stockings* on the job.'

'They're tights, Father.' Joan had laughed at him. 'Not stockings. Anyway, why should you care?'

'Because you're my daughter,' Charles answered, and that had been the end of that. He refused to attend the wedding, and Iain had given Joan away.

Iain. Phaedra picked up a clean knife and finished slicing the strawberries. Iain was a different matter. Iain loved Chy an Cleth. Even after that first major confrontation with his father, when he had married Rosie Sharpe and left to seek his fortune in London, he had always come back to Porthkelly when he could. The confrontations had escalated, as they

27

were bound to given the temperaments of those two self-willed men – but still he had come back. Until the last time.

Phaedra spooned clotted cream into a blue pottery bowl and lifted a warm cheese flan and freshly baked bread from the oven. Her mother had heard most of that last battle. As usual, it had started with Charles telling Iain the obvious – that he had been a fool to marry Rosie – progressed to the way his son made his living, and ended with Iain telling his father it was his own damn business how he chose to live his life.

Charles had so wanted his son to be a banker like himself, to follow his father, grandfather and great-grandfather into Bolan's. But Iain had insisted on going into advertising, a profession that he said still had some life in it.

According to Esther Pendenning, that disastrous row two years ago had ended with Iain slamming his fist into the wall and roaring that he had been president of his own agency for seven successful years, and couldn't his father get it into his head that he had no intention of going into banking? Ever. He had added, for good measure, that *his* children would be given the freedom to make their own choices and their own mistakes.

Charles, who had been a lot stronger in those days, had roared back that Iain didn't have any children, or a wife either for that matter, which he might have had if he'd married Allison Cooper, the daughter of his old friend, Angus, instead of that little tramp, Rosie Sharpe, who had only married him for his money.

Esther said Iain had left then. 'Probably because his father was dead to rights about Rosie,' she'd observed, with a shake of her head. 'She did marry Iain for the money she expected him to have. Only he was too young and too infatuated to see it. He hasn't been back since that day.'

Well, he was back now, Phaedra thought glumly. And if she wasn't mistaken, the three of them were in for a horribly fraught day.

She picked up the flan and a salad, along with the strawberries and cream, and made her way down the passage to the dining-room. She liked the dining-room. It wasn't as dark as the rest of the house. Some long-dead Trebanian, who obviously loved the sea as much as she did, had installed long windows along the wall facing the cliffs. On a day like today the sparkling glass surface of the ocean stretched for miles. Not that she had time to stand around admiring it. The doctor said it was important for Mr Trebanian – Charles – to have his meals on time.

Five minutes later, when she had finished setting the table with the heavy Trebanian silver, Phaedra stuck her head round the drawing-room door to announce lunch.

The two men were talking, she noted at once. That was something, even if Iain was frowning and strumming his square-tipped fingers on the wooden arm of the loveseat. Charles, ominously, was grinning.

'Lunch is ready,' Phaedra said.

Iain turned slowly, his heavy-lidded gaze travelling over her with an insolent appreciation that would have made her blush if she'd been a blusher. Only when he had finished his leisurely appraisal did he stand up and bend to help his father out of his chair.

Charles brushed him off. 'Haven't lost the use of my legs yet, boy. There are still a few things I can do for myself. Walking's one of them.'

'But not the only one, I gather.' Iain cast a meaningful glance at Phaedra, who was hovering tensely in the doorway.

She pursed her lips. The truth of this unreal situation would have to be made clear to Iain without delay. It wasn't, strictly speaking, his business, but she couldn't have him thinking she shared his father's bed. She wasn't sure why it mattered, but it did.

Her chin was tilted at an unnaturally elevated angle as she led the slow procession across the hall and along the passage to the dining-room.

The moment they were seated at the long mahogany table that Phaedra had rubbed to a glossy dark shine, Iain turned to her and said peremptorily, 'Now perhaps you'd care to tell me your version of this idiotic liaison. I've heard my father's.'

'Then you obviously know all there is to know.' Phaedra slid a slice of flan on to a plate. 'Salad?'

'Thank you. Then I take it you agree with Father. He tells me you succumbed to a sudden mutual – shall we say, *attraction*.'

Phaedra glanced quickly at her husband. He was grinning. Evilly.

Manipulative, troublemaking old devil. She sighed, and handed a plate to Iain. So Charles had no intention of telling his son the truth. That meant *she* would have to. Soon. But not now. Not in front of a husband who, for reasons of his own, was determined to stir up dissension.

Charles was enjoying himself, and he didn't take opposition well. If she contradicted him now, he would lose his temper and his blood pressure would shoot up. Precisely what Dr Polson had told him to avoid.

No, she would have to wait until later to explain the precise nature of her marriage.

'Just salad and some bread for you, Charles,' she said, succumbing to a disgraceful urge to pay him back. 'Doctor's orders, you know.'

'Damn the doctor. Worse fool than my son here. Did you make that flan just to torment me?'

'No,' she admitted. 'I made it because I've given up trying to persuade you to follow a diet.'

'You mean you've given up trying to make what's left of my life a living hell? Thank God for that.'

'Don't be ridiculous,' said Phaedra.

All the same it was true. There wasn't much point in depriving Charles of the things he enjoyed most when his failing heart would soon put an end to all enjoyment. She bent her head so he wouldn't see the sudden moisture in her eyes.

When she looked up, Iain was watching her as if he suspected her of putting arsenic in his lunch. But all he said was, 'No turnips today? How disappointing.'

31

His voice was as bland as blancmange but she wasn't deceived. 'You remembered,' she said. 'How flattering.'

'Who could forget? You threw a whole plateful of them at me once.'

'I didn't!'

'No, but you tried to. I'd told you to stop whining and eat them.'

'Phaedra didn't whine,' Charles objected.

'Not much, I agree. But one could always count on turnips to produce a snivel or two.' Iain eyed the delectable collation on his plate, and added condescendingly, 'I see you've grown into an excellent cook, Phaedra. My father chose well.'

Charles took the plate she handed him, and chuckled. 'I know quality when I see it, boy. Unlike you.'

'Oh, I can recognize quality. In a cook.'

'Too bad you never learned the difference between a tramp and a lady then, isn't it?' Charles snapped. 'Phaedra does a lot more than cook.'

'I'm sure she does,' Iain drawled. 'But a lady? Hardly the word I'd have used. By the way, my wife was not a tramp.'

'Course she was, and everyone in Porthkelly knew it. Tell me, how many men did she take up with before she did you the favour of getting herself killed?'

'We've been over this before, Father. Many times. Rosie didn't do me any favour by drowning.' Iain's mouth was a tight-lipped gash across his face. 'She had her faults, but I was working on them.'

'Course you were. Never could admit you'd made a mistake. That one married you for the money she thought I'd give you – and you know it.'

'She was my wife,' Iain said quellingly. 'Just as Phaedra is yours.'

To Phaedra's surprise, Charles gave one of his snorts and let the matter drop.

She bit into a slice of crisp cucumber. How cold Iain made his marriage sound. 'Rosie had her faults, but I was working on them,' he had said. *He* was working on them! What incredible arrogance. Yet he hadn't been arrogant, or cold, as a boy. He'd been all fire and passion and action, and she'd watched him from afar and dreamed dreams.

Charles, never silenced for long, turned to Iain now and said pointedly. 'Been twelve years since Rosie died, hasn't it? Allison Cooper's still alive and married to her man.'

'I imagine she would be. She was always besotted about Gavin.' Iain buttered a fresh piece of bread.

Phaedra, tuning out the two men's barely civilized sparring, quietly got on with her meal. What did Iain mean by that crack about her not being a lady? She was – had been – the housekeeper's daughter, and then the housekeeper, but that didn't put her any further down the social scale than Rosie Sharpe – whom she had just heard Iain firmly defend – even though everyone knew she had been with another man the day she died. His boat had capsized in a freak storm and drowned them both.

Loyalty was a good quality in a man, though . . . admirable, really . . .

'Phaedra? Are you going to answer me?'

Phaedra looked up. What had Iain asked her in that hard, biting voice he had adopted from the moment he'd stalked through the door? She hadn't been listening.

'I'm sorry, I didn't hear you,' she said.

'Really? And I thought you'd forgotten how to dream. I asked where your mother is? Surely you haven't turned her out now that you're lady of the house?'

Phaedra looked from Iain to Charles, then back again. What was the point of dreaming when her favourite dream had turned into a disappointing nightmare in a suit. And hadn't her husband explained *anything* to Iain? What on earth had they been talking about before lunch?

'Mother began having trouble with her arthritis about a year ago,' she said. 'As you would have known if you'd troubled to keep in touch. The doctor said it would only get worse if she didn't stop work.'

'I see. So of course she stopped.'

'No, she refused to. She said she couldn't leave Charles to the care of a stranger, and that she'd been with him for too many years to desert him when he needed her the most.'

'Fine woman, your mother,' said Charles, in a voice that, for him, was unusually gentle.

Phaedra believed he meant it. She smiled at him. 'Yes. She is.' Turning back to Iain, she went on,

34

'Dr Polson called me – I was teaching in Kent at the time – and said I had to make my mother see sense.' She shrugged. 'The only way I could do that was by offering to look after Mr Trebanian – I mean, Charles – myself. So I moved in here, and Mum moved to a flat in the town.'

Iain put down his knife and fork. 'Why?'

'Why did she move?'

'Yes. You lived here together quite amicably until the day you left for college. Why couldn't she stay?'

'I didn't throw her out, if that's what you mean.'

'No,' Charles put in, tapping his knife annoyingly on the edge of his plate. 'I did. Esther wouldn't stop working. Didn't know how to, I suppose. Bit of polishing here, some "I'll just shake those mats out" there. Had to kick her out for her own good. Fond of Esther. Always have been.'

'I see.' Iain, balked of another reason to criticize, picked up his knife, then laid it down again. 'So, Phaedra, are you telling me you left your job teaching – what . . .?'

'History.'

'History – to look after my father?'

'Yes. But I have lots of help. The nurse comes in twice a day. I do the housekeeping.'

'I see. Landed yourself quite a plum as a reward for your sacrifice, didn't you?' He touched a napkin to his mouth and leaned back.

With resentful fascination, Phaedra watched the fine cut of his suit pull across the breadth of his shoulders. 'Indeed, I did,' she said sweetly. 'Although I don't know if your father sees himself as a plum.'

Charles coughed into his glass of water. 'Maybe I don't. Got myself a tomato though, didn't I?' The look he gave Iain was sheer provocation, and if Phaedra hadn't been so irritated with the younger Trebanian herself, she would have felt justified in telling her husband to stop behaving like a silly old goat.

Besides, it wasn't just a matter of Iain. Dr Polson said Charles hadn't much time left. It wouldn't be kind to spoil his gleeful enjoyment of an essentially harmless joke . . .

Iain was shaking his head, but to her amazement his lips had twitched up in something like amusement. So he *hadn't* quite forgotten how to smile. In a way she wished he had, because he was devastating enough when he was scowling. A full dose of his smile would almost certainly be lethal.

'Yes. Your bride is undoubtedly – a tomato,' he agreed. The glance he threw Phaedra was enigmatic. All the same it sent shivers down her spine. Rather pleasant shivers considering the source.

She stood up hastily and went to make the coffee.

It wasn't until mid-afternoon, after her husband had gone for his nap, that Phaedra found herself alone with Iain again.

Charles and his first wife, Helen, had built a rockery at the bottom of the narrow garden above the cliff. It was as good a place as any to enjoy the sun and the fresh salt breeze blowing off the sea. If she was lucky, it might also blow away the tension that had been growing inside her from the moment Iain knocked on the door. She was just bending down to remove a renegade stalk of crabgrass from a patch of windblown forget-me-nots, when Iain's deep voice behind her drawled, 'How very tempting. A suitable retribution, in the circumstances. What a pity I'm not at liberty to apply it.'

Phaedra dropped the crabgrass and straightened so fast she almost overbalanced. 'Keep your hands off me,' she snapped, whirling to face him. 'Anyway, what are you talking about? I haven't done anything I'm ashamed of.'

'Haven't you?' Iain was standing on the lawn halfway between the rockery and the conservatory that his grandfather had added to the back of the house. As he moved towards her he started to unbutton his jacket.

'No, I haven't,' she said. 'Why did you come back, Iain? Because if you just came down to make trouble –'

'That's exactly why I came. To make trouble. For you.'

Phaedra watched his dark hair lift in the breeze, noted the grim line of his mouth and the way he stood with his hands in his pockets and his legs set aggressively apart. She didn't think he'd have much of a problem making trouble.

'Why?' she asked. 'I can understand you being angry I married your father. You think I did it for his money – and the house –'

'And didn't you?'

He wasn't going to believe her whatever she said. But she had to try. 'No. Not directly. And even if I had, there's nothing you could do about it. So what's the point of blowing down here like a storm cloud and getting us all upset?'

'So far I haven't upset anyone but you. Which was precisely my intention. My father, whatever he may say, is delighted to have me available for target practice again.'

That was true enough. She hadn't seen Charles so animated in months. 'I know he is,' she said. 'Don't spoil it for him.'

'I haven't spoiled anything. As you have both pointed out, there's nothing I can do about your marriage. I can, however, keep an eye on you. Make sure you don't bleed him dry –'

'I don't *want* his money.' Phaedra gripped her hands at her waist, surprised at how husky her voice sounded. 'Whatever you may think, I do love your father, Iain.'

Iain narrowed his eyes. With his back to the sun, and thin clouds dimming the light behind him, he looked darker and less civilized than he had within the confines of the house. He made Phaedra think of all the old Cornish legends – of smugglers and wreckers and fierce, proud men of the sea.

But Iain was no man of the sea. 'Love?' he said, sounding like the cynically modern man he really was. 'You expect me to believe you married my father because you love him?'

'No, because that's *not* why I married him.'

'I suppose I should be grateful for any small crumb of honesty you throw my way. But somehow I'm not.' He removed his jacket and slung it over his shoulder.

Phaedra looked away. She couldn't stand it when he spoke to her like that, and she couldn't stand that cold, aloof look on his rugged face. Should she tell him the truth? Now? He would have to know some time. She turned back to the rockery, pretending to search for more weeds. In his current mood, would he want to believe her? At the moment he was convinced she was nothing but a little schemer out to steal his inheritance – or, more accurately, his house. It was the house that mattered to him, and if he hadn't come back . . .

If he hadn't come back, his father might have died without ever seeing him again. And it was true what Iain said. However disgraceful his reasons, Charles *was* delighted to see his son.

She had to remember that.

Supposing she told the truth and Iain did believe her. What then? He was so proud, had always been so tough and independent. How would this high-powered, self-willed man take the news that the girl he thought of as little Phaedra had done him a favour he might never be able to return? Would he confront Charles and get him over-excited? Maybe it would be better *not* to tell him, at least until . . .

39

'Well?' Iain interrupted her increasingly muddled musings. 'Do you plan to enlighten me? Or are you still trying to come up with a suitable lie?'

'What do you mean by that? What lie?' There was another weed down there. Clover. She rather liked clover . . .

'You have assured me you didn't marry my father for love, or for his money. So why *did* you marry him? You haven't left yourself many options, you know. Unless you plan to tell me you married him for sex.'

She had to look at him then. He was smiling, but there wasn't so much as a glimmer of humour in his eyes.

'Don't be absurd. You've no right to make fun of your father,' she told him.

'I'm not making fun of him. He may be in his seventies, but that doesn't mean —'

'No, it doesn't,' Phaedra agreed quickly. 'But he's ill. You've seen how fragile he is. Iain, the doctor says . . .'

She stopped. How could she tell Iain that his father probably wouldn't live out the year?

Two seagulls circled overhead, squawking, and the sound of the sea besieging the cliffs below added a timeless rhythm to the moment. Phaedra watched the knowledge of his father's mortality dawn slowly in Iain's eyes.

'You're telling me he's going to die, aren't you?' he said, with a harshness that made her wince.

He cares though, she thought. Whatever he says, he *does* care. It's in his voice, in the line of his mouth, even

40

in the way he holds his head. In spite of everything, he loves that controlling old man he's fought against from the moment he first learned to talk. Oh, Iain . . .

She started to reach for him, wanting to give comfort, then hastily snatched her hand back. He wouldn't accept sympathy from her, wouldn't admit he needed it.

'Yes,' she said. 'He doesn't have much longer.'

Iain turned his head away and stared out over the sea. His profile gave no hint of what he was feeling, but Phaedra knew him well enough to know he felt more than he wanted her to see. There was nothing she could do to help though, nothing she could say to ease his pain.

After a while he said, 'Why didn't you tell me?'

'Your father didn't want me to. Perhaps I would have anyway in the end, but . . .' She bit her lip. 'We were only married yesterday. It was too soon to go against his wishes. And I didn't know . . . I mean, you hadn't been home for two years.'

'Are you trying to tell me you thought I wouldn't be interested?' The moment of vulnerability had passed. He was in charge again and furious with her.

'I had no idea what you might feel,' she said honestly. 'The man I used to know would have cared. But I hadn't seen him for nine years. All I knew for sure was that you hadn't once been to see your father since I came to look after Chy an Cleth.'

'Phaedra . . .' Iain swore and took a step forward.

Not sure what he meant to do, Phaedra automatically stepped backwards. When her right heel collided with the rockery, she stumbled, causing the heel of her left foot to sink into the recently watered earth. Seconds later, in spite of waving her arms in a frantic attempt to keep her balance, she found herself inelegantly planted on her backside surrounded by a riot of flattened flowers.

Afterwards she was never sure whether Iain had made any attempt to catch her before she fell. What she *was* sure of was that he found her predicament vastly entertaining.

'Charming,' he murmured, holding out a hand to help her up. 'Phaedra Among the Forget-me-nots. I begin to see why Father found you so irresistible.'

Because she had no choice unless she wished to lose even more of her dignity, Phaedra took the proffered hand and allowed him to pull her to her feet.

In the same instant the sound of a throat being cleared noisily made both of them swing towards the house.

Charles was leaning on his stick on the front steps of the conservatory. His head was poked forward and his eyes were bright with anticipation. Phaedra groaned silently. She knew that look. Thank heaven she'd landed in a rockery instead of a bed. Not that Charles would have minded. She had a feeling he was only waiting for them to make the next move in a particularly bad bedroom farce.

Her husband, as usual, was bent on stirring up as much trouble, drama and embarrassment as could be wrung from an already impossible situation.

CHAPTER 2

Phaedra dropped Iain's hand as if it had scorched her skin. Which made no sense, because his grip had been firm and reassuring, not threatening in any way.

Charles, watching them from the steps of the conservatory, snapped, 'Iain! Why are you picking my wife out of the flowerbed? Unhand her at once.'

Iain, looking impassive, said, 'No need to draw your sword, Father. She's already unhanded and all yours.'

'I fell,' Phaedra said, unnecessarily.

'Hah. At your age you ought to be able to stand on your own feet. Want me to lend you my stick?'

Oh, be damned to the both of them, Phaedra thought. But in a way she was tempted to laugh. Iain was doing a masterly job of hiding his irritation, but it was none the less obvious that he would very much like to consign his exasperating father to outer space. Charles, on the other hand, having settled on an attitude which he knew was bound to infuriate his son, looked healthier and more lively than he had in weeks.

'Mr – Charles, what are you doing up this early?' she asked resignedly. 'You know you're supposed to rest for another hour.'

'Not with that young troublemaker about, I'm not. Never know what he'll get up to. I'll say one thing for him though – always had an eye for a pretty girl.' He shot Iain a look of blatant one-upmanship. 'Beat you to it this time, didn't I, hey?'

He really was impossible. Once again Phaedra wanted to laugh.

Iain didn't. 'I have yet to lay my eye, or anything else, on somebody else's wife,' he said, taking a firmer grip on the jacket over his shoulder. 'And I'm not likely to start with a stepmother who has only just outgrown the braces on her teeth.'

Swine! I'm twenty-seven years old, Phaedra wanted to shout at him. And I've never worn braces. But she held her peace. There was nothing to be gained by allowing him to provoke her.

Charles scowled at his son. 'You be careful, boy. Remember, I'm still your father.'

'I'm not likely to forget,' Iain muttered.

'Huh. See that you don't.' Charles waved his stick at them and shuffled sideways. 'Now then, Phaedra, I'm waiting for my tea, so don't you waste your time hobnobbing with my ungrateful young offspring out there.'

Phaedra shook her head. Charles spoke as though Iain were no more than a callow teenager. Was that what he really thought of the son who had long since left boyhood behind to become a dynamic, domineering and exceptionally successful *man*?

Charles hobbled back into the house. 'He's up to something,' Phaedra said. 'I wonder what.'

'So do I. Tell me . . . exactly how ill *is* my father?'

Phaedra hesitated, and Iain added drily, 'I realize the average doctor in his right mind may not be all that anxious to save his misbegotten life – but . . .' He paused, and when he spoke again it was in a harsher, less superficial vein. 'Why in hell isn't something being done? An operation –'

'He's too old. Apart from which, he won't hear of it. He says any surgeon who wants to practise his carving skills can do it on the Sunday joint and not on him.'

A smile flickered across Iain's face and vanished. 'That sounds like Dad. And of course you haven't tried to persuade him to change his mind.'

'What?' Phaedra stiffened. 'Are you suggesting –?'

'I'm suggesting that the sooner he is out of the picture, the sooner you'll get your hands on his assets. It's a simple enough equation, wouldn't you say?' He raised his eyebrows in cynical enquiry.

'Oh! How could you?' Rage bubbled briefly in the pit of her stomach. She choked it back, remembering that Iain had every reason to be suspicious of her motives. 'Please don't think I feel that way about Mr Trebanian,' she said quietly. 'I know he's cantankerous and bossy. He always has been. But he's been good to me. It was his generosity that kept Mother and me from – well, from ending up on the dole. Mum was always funny about accepting his help, but any time it was for my benefit she broke down and accepted in the end.'

'So I noticed.'

Phaedra sighed. What was the use? Iain would never understand. But she had to try anyway. 'You know my father left us before I was born,' she said, twisting a strand of her hair around her thumb. 'If Mr Trebanian – Charles – hadn't paid my way through university, I wouldn't have been able to go. So you see, if there was anything, *anything* I could do to make him well, I would have done it. I told you I love him, and I meant it.'

'Yes.' Iain nodded distantly. 'You also said that wasn't why you married him. A pretty little speech, Phaedra, my sweet, but I'm afraid it just doesn't ring true.'

His face seemed to hang in the bright summer air like a dark, derisive mask. Phaedra stared at it in frozen disbelief until the coldly cutting words penetrated sufficiently to spur her to action. She wanted to slap him. But that would be unfair as well as childish.

In the end, all she could think of was that she had to get away from him before she made a fool of herself.

Spinning on her heel, she swallowed a sob and ran blindly for the door which Charles had deliberately left open.

'Phaedra . . .' She heard Iain's shout as she ran across the hall and up the first flight of stairs. But she didn't stop running. Only when she reached the sanctuary of her small, white-panelled bedroom beneath the eaves did her frantic need to keep running subside. She collapsed against the door, breathing hard. When her eye fell on the narrow bed with its daffodil-sprigged quilt, she closed her eyes.

Lord, how often had she lain there in the dark, listening to the voice of the ocean and dreaming of that loathsome man who had just accused her of the most venal of motives for her marriage? Only in those days the man had been a boy – a boy who had made a point of treating her with kindness . . .

Phaedra flung herself into a yellow brocade armchair beside the window.

How could he? How could he believe she would want to hasten Charles's death? Oh, she'd realized he was bound to misunderstand in the beginning, but, dammit, he'd known her all her life – if you didn't count the last nine years. And she'd already explained . . .

Abruptly Phaedra stopped digging her nails into the arm of the chair. Damn. She gazed distractedly at a painting of a Victorian street scene she had bought on a day trip to London.

Damn, damn, damn. The point was, she *hadn't* explained. All she had done was admit the precarious state of Charles's health – to which Iain had reacted with shock and a veiled concern. Was it all that surprising he had lashed out, automatically thinking the worst of her? She had known he was likely to see her marriage as self-serving, yet somewhere along the line she had lost sight of that dismal reality. What, unless she got on with telling him the truth, was Iain supposed to think of her marrying his father?

Phaedra leaned her head against the back of the chair and listened to the sea smashing against the rocks. She loved that sound, though sometimes it was a warning of disaster. On the night Iain's sister had been born, she'd been told the waves had roared halfway up the cliff.

Esther Pendenning had always said that if Helen Trebanian hadn't died giving birth to Joan when Iain was only four, things would have been different. Iain might have grown up gentler, less cynical, more willing to tolerate mistakes. As it was, he had become hard, self-sufficient and ruthless in pursuit of his own ends. At least on the surface. Esther swore he had a vulnerable side, but if that was the case Phaedra had seen no sign of it today.

She stroked the slick fabric covering the chair, remembering how her hand had felt in his. Comforted. Safe. As perhaps the child who had been Iain had never felt. For as long as she could remember he had been locked in mortal combat with the father who either ignored him or tried to bend him to his will.

Esther said that Charles, heartbroken by the loss of his wife, had spent most of his time in London immediately following her death. Instead of helping his bewildered young son to come to terms with his confusion and grief, he had travelled home only on occasional weekends in order to lay down the law – or so it must have seemed to the little boy. Charles didn't particularly like, or understand, children, but he had done what he thought was his duty. As far as he was concerned, Joan and Iain had a roof over their heads, a housekeeper to see to their needs, and discipline judiciously, if sporadically, applied.

Iain, naturally headstrong and independent, had quickly learned to resent the paternal visits that meant an instant curb on his freedom to do as he liked. Esther had done her best, but she had been young in those days, and admitted it had been a simple matter for the motherless boy with the winning smile to charm her into letting him get his way more than he should.

Then Iain had been packed off to school, and Esther had married Francis Pendenning. The marriage hadn't lasted. Even before Iain returned for his first long holiday, Francis had left for greener pastures in the form of the buxom barmaid from the Spotted Dog. Phaedra had been born six months later, and Esther hadn't left Chy an Cleth again until the doctor insisted she retire.

A gull landed on the window sill, tapping its beak on the glass and jolting Phaedra into an awareness of the passing of time. She glanced at her watch. Oh dear. Charles was still waiting for his tea – and Iain was probably waiting to scalp her. Why hadn't she stood her ground and made him see the truth?

'You're a fool, Phaedra,' she said out loud as she levered herself out of her chair. 'It's no wonder Iain thinks you're after Chy an Cleth.'

The gull put its head on one side and gave up waiting for a handout. Phaedra paused for a moment to watch it fly away, soaring gracefully over the points of light dancing on the calm summer sea. It looked so peaceful out there. Peaceful as her heart was not. But soon the sea would soothe it. It always did.

Twenty minutes later she wheeled the tea-trolly into the drawing-room.

'Where's Iain?' she asked, sensing his absence even before she took time to scan the room.

'Out,' Charles said. 'In a rare old temper too, if you ask me.' He slapped his palms on the arms of his chair.

Phaedra wasn't surprised. 'Where did he go?' she asked wearily.

'To see Angus Cooper. And your mother, so he said.' His gaze slid to the willow-pattern teapot. 'Why? What do you want him for?'

He *was* up to something. She was sure of it.

'Nothing really,' she said quickly. 'Charles, why didn't you tell him why I married you?'

'Not sure why you did. I asked you, you said "yes". What was there to tell?'

'Plenty, and you know it. You could have told him about the hotel, for a start.'

'Hm. He wouldn't have liked that.'

She shook her head. 'No, and you didn't mean him to like it.'

''Course I didn't. Would have served him right though. Shown him who's in charge.' Charles nodded, pleased with himself.

Phaedra frowned. 'Would you really have sold Chy an Cleth just to spite him and Joan?' She had asked him that before they were married, but maybe now the answer would be different.

'To spite them? No, to teach my son a lesson. Joan too. If that fancy man of hers thinks he's getting his hands on Chy an Cleth –'

'But Anton doesn't even *want* it,' Phaedra objected. 'Iain does.'

'Well, he's not getting it. It's all yours.'

She debated for about the hundredth time the advisability of telling Charles what he probably already guessed – that the moment Chy an Cleth was hers, she would deed it back to Iain. At least that had been her intention before he'd come home.

She poured the tea and handed a cup to Charles. Had her devious husband been aware that she might not be so anxious to part with her old home once she saw what kind of man her childhood idol had become? Or had he assumed that once the estate was hers she would want to keep it? Plenty of women would react in exactly that way.

She wasn't one of them.

'The house isn't mine yet,' Phaedra blurted. 'You may change your mind –'

51

'Haven't time to change it,' Charles said testily. 'That old fool Polson said I should get my affairs in order before I found myself sitting on a cloud strumming a harp. A harp. Me. I ask you. Rather stoke the damn fires.'

He looked so disgruntled that Phaedra couldn't help laughing. 'Don't worry,' she said. 'Play a couple of notes, and they'll send you right back down here to haunt us. I've heard you singing dirges in the bath.'

'Cheeky piece, aren't you?' Charles snorted. 'Time you learned your place, my girl.'

She knew he didn't mean it. He had never succeeded in intimidating either her or her mother. Which was probably why he was fond of them in his way – and why most of the time the two of them returned his affection despite his chronic ill-humour. Esther maintained he still missed his Helen. Sometimes, when her mother spoke of Helen, Phaedra thought she heard a kind of wistfulness in her voice, as if she wished someone had cared that way about her.

Francis Pendenning had never cared. He had taken his barmaid and disappeared completely from their lives. Esther had been too proud to pursue him for support, and Phaedra had no interest in the man who had deserted her mother. She had never tried to find him and never would.

'More tea?' she asked. 'Some sugar, perhaps?'

'Think I need sweetening, do you? Hah. You'll find out when I'm gone. Just you wait.'

Phaedra shook her head at him and smiled re-proachfully. It wasn't easy being married to a man who regarded his own demise as a goad with which to prod his errant family into line. Even so, hopelessly dictatorial as he was, when the time came she knew she would miss him.

'I need some more water for the tea,' she said, jumping up and hurrying from the room.

She refilled the kettle, refusing to let herself think about Chy an Cleth without Charles. But she couldn't stop herself thinking about Iain.

What would he say to her mother when he saw her?

There had always been a bond between him and Esther. But if he made the mistake of hinting that Phaedra might be a gold-digger out for what she could get, it was entirely possible her mother would spring to the defence of her only child by telling him exactly how the marriage had come about. If that happened, they were in for quite a scene when Iain returned.

But not in front of Charles, who would probably enjoy it. Any scene Iain made would be in private.

It was a warm day, but all at once Phaedra felt cold.

Esther Pendenning lived in a flat on the second floor of a Spanish-style building perched at the top of the steep, cobbled street leading down to Porthkelly harbour. Phaedra had once told her that the pink balconies and decorative brick arches looked totally out of place among the centuries-old cottages that gave the town its character. Esther didn't care. She liked her flat's modern warmth as well as its proximity to the shops.

Today she had been cleaning out cupboards – Phaedra would be cross if she knew – and she had to admit she did feel a little weary. She glanced at her kitchen clock with the big black numbers that were easy to see. Four o'clock. Yes, she had definitely earned herself a respite. With a sigh of relief, she hitched up her blue summer skirt and plumped her stocky body into one of the two deckchairs she kept on the balcony.

Esther closed her eyes, contentedly fanning her face with a straw sunhat. In a minute she would light a cigarette.

Her moment of peace didn't last long. Just as she was reaching for the lighter she had left handily on the plexiglass table beside her chair, she heard the slap of footsteps marching across the courtyard. A visitor? Surely not for her at this time of day. She leaned forward to part a screen of nasturtiums and geraniums growing in wooden tubs set along the balcony's wooden railing.

'Iain!' she exclaimed when she saw the man in the grey suit smiling up at her. 'What a lovely surprise! I didn't know you were home.'

'I'm not for long,' he called up to her. 'But I couldn't leave town without seeing you.'

'Well, I should hope not. Come along up.'

Esther heaved herself out of her deckchair, no easy feat these days, dropped her cigarettes behind a plump yellow cushion, and stopped in front of a small mirror hanging in the postage-stamp hall. She gave her pale blonde hair a quick swipe. At least that wasn't yet showing signs of age. More than could be said for the rest of her, even if Angus Cooper had called her round face 'pleasantly plump' only the other day. Angus said things like that.

Esther fastened the top button on her white blouse and went to open the door to the young man she had successfully raised to adulthood without his either breaking his neck in the course of some forbidden escapade, or driving his father to break it for him.

Oh. She made a quick mental adjustment. *Not* such a young man any more. There were lines on his face that hadn't been there two years ago – and he looked tired, as if life's burdens were getting him down.

'Tea,' Esther said at once. 'That's the thing. You'll have a cup, won't you, dear?'

'I'd love one. I'll make it, though. You're supposed to be taking it easy in your retirement, Pendy.'

Pendy. Iain and his sister had called her that since they were children, but hearing it now, from the lips of this craggy-faced man, caused a lump to form in her throat. She hadn't known how much she'd missed Iain's vitality and teasing these last two years.

'Hah,' she said brusquely. 'That'll be the day. And what do you know about making tea, I'd like to know?

Iain grinned. 'I'm not helpless. I've lived on my own for God knows how many years, and I *can* manage tea, I promise you.'

'This I have to see.' Esther lowered herself on to a chair beside the gate-legged table fitted between the fridge and the window, and propped her chin on her hands.

'You're too old to be living on your own,' she said to Iain's back as he moved competently around her small kitchen, taking down china cups and saucers and putting the kettle on to boil.

He smiled at her over his shoulder. 'On the contrary. The only time I tried living with somebody else, I was far too young.'

'Rosie? Yes, you were young. But age wasn't the trouble there. Rosie was. And you know you only married her to spite your dad. I often thought you two deserved each other.'

'Perhaps we did,' Iain agreed without rancour. He poured water into a squat yellow teapot, waited a few moments, poured out the tea, added milk and handed her a cup. He took his own cup and went to stand by the window.

'Is something worrying you, dear?' Esther asked. She knew exactly what was worrying him, but she doubted he'd tell her without prompting.

'Not really.' Iain's reply was as uncommunicative as he could make it. She knew that tactic of old.

'Rubbish. I've known you too long not to know brooding when I see it. You're upset about your father's marriage, aren't you?' She'd known he would be. Couldn't really blame him either. But she wished he'd felt able to admit it.

'Not at all. I hope they'll be very happy.' Iain swallowed a mouthful of tea. When Esther said nothing, he laid his cup on the sill and asked grudgingly, as if he'd rather be talking about the weather, 'How do *you* feel about it, Pendy? Phaedra's your daughter.'

'Yes, of course she is. And you needn't sound so accusing. As to how I feel – well, Phaedra has always done what she thought was right. She's a dreamer, but a very practical one once she's made up her mind. I couldn't stop her, Iain.'

'But you *would* like to have stopped her?' He lowered his head like a bull about to charge.

'I wish it hadn't been necessary for her to marry Charles, yes.'

Iain frowned, and she knew her answer had planted a seed of doubt in his mind. She couldn't tell him the truth, because Phaedra had asked her not to, but she didn't want him thinking unkindly of her daughter.

As for that foolish marriage, no, she didn't like it. If it had been a real marriage, she couldn't have borne it – for a great many reasons. One of them being that if the young man glaring at her from the window had seen fit to visit Porthkelly a bit more often, her daughter might still be single and available.

If only her joints had held up a bit longer. If only she hadn't agreed to let Phaedra take over the house-keeping for Charles. It had been selfish of her, she knew that. Phaedra had said it would only be tem-porary anyway, and that she could do with a break from the little hellions at school. But Esther knew she had let herself be persuaded too easily because she liked the idea of having her daughter nearby. It had seemed such a sensible arrangement at first . . .

'What do you mean, *necessary*?' Iain, still looking bull-like, was massaging his neck with his knuckles. 'You did say necessary?'

Esther nodded. 'Yes, I did.'

She knew what he was thinking, but there was nothing she could say to enlighten him. He would just have to wait until Phaedra was ready to explain.

When she saw he was about to ask more awkward questions, Esther said quickly, 'Have you seen Angus? It's been a year since his Meg died, but he's still not used to being on his own.'

'Yes, I've seen him,' Iain said. 'Now, about this marriage –'

Esther didn't want to talk about the marriage.

'I saw a very good programme on ancient Greece last night,' she announced, pretending she hadn't heard him.

Iain had always known when it was useless to push a point. 'Are you still interested in Greece then?' he asked resignedly.

'Well, not as much now as I used to be. I loved reading about all those gods and goddesses when I was young.'

'I remember.' Iain made an attempt to look interested.

After about twenty minutes of not talking about anything in particular, he picked up his cup, went to pour more tea, then changed his mind.

'I'd better be going,' he said. 'Thanks for the tea. Chy an Cleth isn't the same without you, Pendy.'

'Count your blessings. You could have lost a lot more than one worn-out old housekeeper.'

Iain tipped his head to the side. 'And what does that cryptic remark mean?'

'Nothing.' Esther smiled blandly.

'Worn out, my eye.' Iain snorted. He crossed the room and dropped a dutiful kiss on her forehead.

A minute later she heard him running down the stairs.

Esther sighed. Iain was doing a fine job of hiding his resentment but, knowing him as she did, it was easy to guess how much he must be hurting inside. He'd survive, of course. He was born to survive, that one. But she hoped Phaedra would soon tell him the truth.

After pouring herself a cup of tepid tea, she went back out to the balcony, rescued her cigarettes from under the yellow cushion and lit up with a murmur of relief.

Ahh. That was better. She breathed deeply, allowing the smoke to fill her lungs, then exhaling with slow contentment. But as she took a second blissful puff, a movement in the courtyard caught her eye. Glancing past the tubs of bright flowers, she saw that Iain had come to a stop by the brick archway leading to the street. He had his back to her and his shoulders were bowed as if they bore the weight of all the world. After a while he raised his right arm, pressed his fingertips to his forehead and held them there.

How well she remembered that gesture. It meant he was trying to suppress a temper that was spinning out of control because somebody or something was refusing to bend to his will. He had learned the gesture from his father.

Esther took another quick puff of her cigarette and closed her eyes. When she opened them again the courtyard was deserted.

CHAPTER 3

Iain glared down the street at a couple of tourists heading for the Spotted Dog, and took a swing with his fist at the pink bricks of the ornamental archway. The contact bruised his knuckles, momentarily taking his mind off more pressing problems. Unfortunately, the relief was short-lived.

What on earth had Pendy been talking about? Count your blessings, she had said. What blessings? Thanks to the scheming of his father and *her* damned daughter, he had lost the one certainty in his life. Chy an Cleth. He tugged irritably at his tie, loosening the knot and unfastening the top button on his shirt. Bloody hell. Devoted as he was to Pendy, she had the most infuriating ability to hold her tongue when it happened to suit her.

As for her daughter . . . He rammed his hands into his pockets, feeling the muscles in his jaw stretch and tighten as he made his way across the uneven cobbled street. As for Phaedra, he'd like to . . . What *would* he like to do to that conniving little witch if he had the chance? He could think of a number of options, some a lot more pleasurable than others. He scowled at a daisy growing between the cracks in the pavement.

Phaedra had stolen his birthright, no doubt of that. But in the years since he had last seen her she had turned into the most seductive, beguiling creature he had ever had the misfortune to lay eyes on. Even in her grey sack of a dress . . .

Rosie, who had made a point of flaunting her figure in leather and lace and every glittering, shiny fabric known to woman, could never have held a candle to Phaedra Pendenning in grey cotton.

He supposed he had recognized that, subconsciously, since the day he had driven her to Exeter to catch the train to college. Yet in the intervening years he had married and been widowed, and only occasionally thought of the young girl he had impulsively kissed on a windy station platform one long-ago September afternoon.

Phaedra was no longer a girl, but that didn't stop the unwanted memories from coming back to stab him in the gut.

He continued on his way up the hill, head down, oblivious to the curious stares of passing tourists.

Damn it, he had to forget that kiss had ever happened. Forget the taste of her lips, the feel of her adolescent body in his arms. She was – what? – twenty-seven now. Her body was a woman's body, full, and curving in all the right places. As his randy old father had pointed out. Not, thank God, that Charles was able to take advantage of those curves. Iain slowed his pace briefly. Why should he give a damn what the old man did with Phaedra? What ought to matter was that very soon he wouldn't be doing much of anything.

Iain's scowl had deepened by the time he side-stepped a suspicious brown pile on the pavement and crested the top of the hill.

Below him Chy an Cleth, his House of the North, stood sentinel above the ocean as it had for over two hundred years. Today that ocean was airforce blue and calm, but he knew all too well how quickly that could change. He lifted his head, inhaling the smell that came back to him at odd moments in cities all over the world, whenever he thought of Cornwall and the house he had always called home.

Soon, because of a father who had given away his inheritance, and a woman without a conscience who had taken it, Chy an Cleth would no longer be his. And the wound that cut the deepest, with a painful precision that drove him to dreams of unspeakable revenge, was that the same woman had once been the little girl who said she loved him.

So much for love. So much for promises. He should have learned by now that love was a myth invented by hopeless optimists and foolish dreamers – and that promises were worth only as much as the pretty, scheming witches who made them.

'Thanks, Rosie,' he muttered at a low-flying seagull. 'You did your level best to cure me, didn't you? But it looks as though the lesson didn't go far enough.'

The seagull shrieked in reply. Iain shook a fist at it, and turned in the direction of the house that, until yesterday, had been the one immovable anchor in his life.

Fifteen minutes later, when he strode into the drawing room, he had his chairman-of-the-board face firmly fixed in place.

From now on he would need that face more than ever. Because Trebanian Advertising was all he had left.

Charles was sitting in his chair, looking expectant. His new stepmother had her back to him, and was busy pouring pre-dinner drinks. She turned when she heard him come in, and promptly slopped some rather expensive sherry on to the carpet. Iain shook his head and draped himself casually in the doorway.

Phaedra bit the inside of her lip and searched his face for some clue as to what had passed between him and her mother. He returned her look dispassionately, with a very faint curl of his lips.

'How was Mum?' she asked, handing the sherry to her husband, who waved it away muttering that she'd already wasted enough, and what the hell was wrong with decent whisky?

'She seemed very well,' Iain said. 'Considerably better than I expected from what you told me.'

There was an edge to his voice she didn't like. Was he trying to suggest that there had been nothing wrong with her mother in the first place?

'I wasn't lying,' she said. 'My mother *does* have arthritis.'

'Did I suggest she hadn't?' He crossed to the drinks cabinet and poured himself a whisky.

Phaedra sank on to the gold loveseat. 'No, I just thought —'

'Don't. It only confuses things.' He held up his glass and twirled it against the light.

Phaedra reminded herself that this was Iain, and that Chy an Cleth was his beloved home. But it didn't help. In the end, and because throwing cushions, vases or her husband's pills wasn't her style, she stood, straightened to her full height, still holding Charles's rejected sherry, and stalked past Iain in dignified silence.

To think she had actually been making excuses for the man. That was one mistake she wouldn't make again.

Tight-lipped, she moved around the kitchen putting the finishing touches to the evening meal. When, not long afterwards, she announced dinner, no further reference was made to Iain's visit with her mother.

The only one who seemed ready to enjoy the meal thoroughly was Charles, who, in between mouthfuls of plaice, amused himself by directing gibes about advertising at Iain. Every now and then he put down his knife and fork to watch for a reaction.

To his evident disappointment, there wasn't one. Iain concentrated on his food with businesslike appreciation and responded to his father's barbs with the occasional half-smile or nonchalant shrug.

Phaedra, seeing her husband's growing frustration, began to worry that he would work himself

up to an attack. But just as she was about to inter-
vene, the phone rang shrilly in the hall, making her
jump. She hurried to answer it, glad of the chance to
escape, if only for a moment.

The call was from Iain's office.

He laid down his napkin and strolled unhurriedly
to take it. When he came back he ignored the two
pairs of eyes fixed on him with undisguised curiousity, and carried on methodically with his meal.

It wasn't until the last green pea and the last
mouthful of flaky potato had been consumed that
he placed his knife and fork neatly together, swallowed a mouthful of water and said, 'I'm sure you'll
both be devastated to learn that I have to leave for
London within the hour.'

Phaedra fixed her gaze on a patch of orange sun-
light on the wall.

Charles said, 'What's the matter? Agency gone
bankrupt?' and gave a cackle that made him sound
like a stage witch.

'Nothing like that.' Iain flicked a speck of dust off
his sleeve. 'Just a small emergency with one of our
accounts. I have to fly to Paris in the morning.'

Phaedra was astonished to feel a twinge of disappointment. 'Paris?' she said. 'But you can't –'

'Certainly I can.' His tone was condescending. 'But
don't imagine I won't be back to see what you're up to.
I wouldn't advise you to start getting ideas –'

'Ideas . . .?' She picked up her glass, saw that it
was empty, and filled it to the brim from a crystal jug.
'If by that you mean –'

'I mean I expect you to take care of my father and his house,' Iain interrupted her brusquely. 'And I do not expect to find out later that you've been making unnecessary jaunts to the bank. I won't have my father bankrupted while he's still in a position to make use of his money.'

'Phaedra's my wife. Watch how you speak to her,' Charles snapped.

'Oh, I'll watch her,' Iain replied. 'Never doubt it. Now if you'll excuse me . . .' He pushed back his chair and stood up, with an ironic little bow to Phaedra. 'I'm sorry I can't do further justice to your most excellent meal. But I know you, of all people, understand that business comes before pleasure.'

Phaedra stood up too, swallowing the bitter taste in her mouth. 'And what do you mean by that?' She planted both hands on her hips, tired of his thinly veiled insinuations and determined to make him spell it out.

'You're not stupid, Phaedra,' Iain replied. 'Merely acquisitive, as I see it.' He touched his fingers to his lips and blew her a kiss. 'Goodbye, Stepmother.' Then turning to Charles, he said, 'Goodbye, Father. I'll be back as soon as I've settled this business in Paris. Look after yourself.'

Phaedra wasn't sure, but he seemed to speak the last sentence on a different level, as if he actually meant it. Because of that, she quite forgot to tell him not to be a jerk.

Charles, predictably, told him he needn't bother coming back.

Half an hour later, Phaedra stood at an upstairs window, watching Iain drive through the gates and on to the road. Very swiftly she came to the conclusion that the advertising business Charles despised so much must be doing quite remarkably well.

Iain's old Austin-Healey was a thing of the past. These days he drove a late-model Porsche.

The following morning, when Nurse Clemens came in to see to Charles, Phaedra took the opportunity to walk into town for a quick visit with her mother.

The moment she knocked on the door, she heard a thump, and then something that might have been the slamming of a drawer. When Esther finally let her in, her nose was immediately assaulted by the reek of smoke.

Phaedra sighed. 'Mum, you've been smoking again,' she accused her.

'Last one,' Esther said promptly. 'Couldn't waste it, now could I?'

Phaedra didn't see why not, but she knew there was no point in saying so. Her mother's smoking was a worry. She was often short of breath, always promising to quit, but somehow she never got around to it. In Esther's mind tomorrow, or next week, was soon enough.

Phaedra followed her out to the balcony, where the smoke was dissipated by the fresh June breeze coming from the south.

'What did Iain have to say for himself?' she asked, as soon as the two of them had settled into their deckchairs with cups of coffee.

Esther pulled down the hem of her skirt. 'Not much,' she said vaguely. 'He seemed a bit grim.'

'He is a bit grim. More than a bit. He didn't say anything about the wedding then?'

'No. When I asked him how he felt about it, he said he hoped you would both be very happy.' She leaned over and patted Phaedra's hand. 'To tell you the truth though, dear, I got the feeling *he* wasn't happy.'

'You didn't tell him?'

'Tell him why you married Charles? No, I didn't. You asked me not to. Besides . . .' She adjusted the cushion at her back. 'He's going to find it difficult enough to cope with what you've done for him. Best he doesn't hear it first from your mother.'

'I suppose so. If he hears it from anyone,' Phaedra muttered.

Esther coughed. 'What do you mean?'

'Oh, Mum. He was such a swine the whole time he was home. I'm beginning to think I should have let Mr Trebanian sell the house.' She dropped her chin on to her chest and glared at the star-shaped splatter left by a visiting seagull.

'If Charles Trebanian had wanted to sell his house, he would have done it,' Esther said firmly. She threw her daughter a look that was hard to interpet. 'If you ask me, he had something else in mind.'

'What, marrying me? Why should he care about that? Nothing's changed except my name. I'm still his housekeeper.'

'From what you've told me, he married you so Joan and Iain wouldn't have any grounds to fight his will –

after he agreed to leave the house to you instead of selling it to that Peter Sharkey so he could turn it into some fancy, over-priced hotel.'

'He did. I don't believe they would have fought it though. Joan doesn't care about Chy an Cleth, and Iain –'

'Iain would have been too proud. I know. Don't you think Charles knows it too?' Esther picked up her cup, took a thoughtful sip of coffee and set it back in the saucer with a clink. 'The point is, Charles has always wanted everything cut and dried. In his mind, marrying you was probably a kind of insurance. Except . . .'

'Except?' Phaedra stretched, breathing in the scent of the harbour which was particularly pungent this morning. Fish, dead weeds, and the sea.

'I don't know.' Esther shrugged. 'If all he wanted to do was punish his children for going against his wishes, he could have sold Chy an Cleth and been done with it. But he didn't.'

'No,' Phaedra agreed. 'He didn't.' She glanced idly at her watch, did a double take and jumped to her feet. 'Oh dear. I didn't realize it was so late. Nurse will be ready to leave in a few minutes.' She gave her mother a hasty hug and turned to go.

She was thoughtful as she puffed her way back up the hill. It was true Charles could have accomplished all he wanted without marrying her. But then he wouldn't have had the satisfaction of seeing his children's consternation at what he'd done. Not that he'd got much satisfaction out of Iain – and Joan didn't even know about it yet.

Phaedra gave up. There had never been much point in trying to make sense of the Trebanians, and she wasn't about to waste her time now. She had enough to do looking after Charles.

If only he wasn't so fond of causing trouble. She sighed, and quickened her pace as she saw Nurse Clemens getting into her car.

A week passed with no word from Iain, and Phaedra began to breathe more easily. Then Charles took a turn for the worse, and she stopped worrying about Iain in order to concentrate all her energies on his father. But it wasn't until a cool, drizzly morning in early July that her concern became something akin to panic.

When the nurse arrived as usual for her visit, Phaedra had the door open before she had a chance to ring the bell.

'Oh, I'm so glad you've come,' she cried. 'He's had an awful night, Nurse, and he's terribly weak this morning. He couldn't even get out of bed.'

'Best not to try then,' said Nurse Clemens, who smelled comfortingly medical and antiseptic as she marched briskly across the hall and up the stairs.

Phaedra was right behind her when she bustled into the big, dark bedroom with the pale pink wallpaper that had darkened to plum over the years. Charles refused to have it changed because his Helen had chosen it long ago. Today the air in the room was heavy with medicine and sickness.

71

In the middle of a huge four-poster bed, the small, wasted figure of Charles appeared lost and insignificant. But when Phaedra approached him she saw that his eyes were bright with resentment, sparkling with malice in the pale, sunken face.

'He should be in hospital,' Nurse Clemens said, after carrying out a brief examination. 'I'll call Dr Polson.'

'Like hell you will.' Charles' blue eyes shot fire meant to singe.

The nurse turned to Phaedra for support. 'Mrs Trebanian, you must make him understand –'

'I do understand,' Charles snapped, in a voice that was surprisingly robust. 'You want to put me away in the damn hospital so you can get on with killing me off at once.'

'Mr Trebanian! We want to help you, not –'

'You can help me by getting the hell out of my house.'

'Now, Mr Trebanian –'

Charles struggled up on his elbows. 'And don't you "now" me, Nancy Clemens. You can't put me in the hospital against my will. Phaedra, show her out.' Exhausted by this show of authority, he gave them a final ferocious glare and sank back on to the pillows. A moment or two later his eyelids fluttered briefly and then closed.

'Don't worry,' Phaedra whispered to the nurse. 'I'll take care of him. He'll sleep for a while now.'

The two of them left the room, and Nurse Clemens hurried down the stairs to put through a call to Dr Polson.

'Doctor will soon fix things,' she said confidently.

'Yes,' Phaedra agreed, with less confidence. 'Yes, I'm sure he will.'

As soon as the nurse left, she picked up the phone to make a call of her own. But there was no answer at the number she called. She sighed. That left her with only one alternative.

'Mr Trebanian?' repeated a chirpy woman's voice when she was eventually put through to Iain's secretary. 'Yes, he's back, but I'm afraid you can't speak to him. He's – um – in a meeting.'

So much for Iain's promise to check on his father the moment he returned to England. Phaedra watched the rain, which was coming down hard now, smash against the windows and break into big, transparent stars. 'I'm afraid I *must* speak to him,' she said. 'It's rather urgent.'

'I'm sorry. He's not available. If you'd like to leave your name . . .'

Phaedra managed not to grind her teeth. The woman Joan called 'Iain's overpaid dragon lady' was a very effective guardian of his time. 'I'm Mrs Trebanian,' she snapped. 'His stepmother.'

'*Stepmother*!' the woman exclaimed. 'I had no idea –' She broke off abruptly as someone in the background snapped a word Phaedra hadn't heard before but whose meaning was abundantly clear.

A moment later Iain came on the line.

'Phaedra? What the blazes do you mean by calling me at the office? I have an important meeting in precisely five minutes, after which –'

'I think you'd better cancel it. Your father's very ill. He should be in hospital, but he won't go.'

There was silence on the other end. When Iain spoke again, his tone was quieter but no less authoritative. 'Of course he won't go. Trebanians don't die in hospitals. Arrange for round-the-clock nursing at once. And don't even think about sparing expense. Do you understand me?'

Phaedra gripped the receiver and resisted an urge to throw it at the wall. 'Of course I understand you. But don't you think he'd be better off in hospital?'

'Not if you do as I tell you. Good nursing is what he needs, and what I expect him to get. And I don't care if it takes every damn penny you were planning to spend on yourself.'

'What?' Phaedra took the phone away from her ear and stared into the receiver with tears of rage stinging at her eyes. 'Iain, are you *daring* to suggest I'd even think of depriving your father of decent care just so – so –'

'So you can spend his money on luxuries for yourself? Yes, the thought had crossed my mind. Now don't let's waste any more time. You get the ball rolling in Porthkelly, and I'll be down as soon as I can get there. Have you called Joan?'

Phaedra was still fighting to catch her breath. Of all the ignorant, arrogant, despicable swine, Iain Trebanian had to take the prize. But she would tell him that later. Right now she didn't have the time.

'No,' she said coldly. 'I tried, but I haven't been able to reach her. I'll leave it to you to track her down

74

– since you obviosuly need something to think about besides all those fairy tales you've been spinning about wicked witches scheming against your father. Whom I happen to love, by the way. Good-bye, Iain.'

She hung up before he could respond and hurried back upstairs to check on Charles. To hell with Iain. She had someone more important to think about.

Charles was still sleeping. In repose, his features were softer, less malicious, reminding her of the crusty benefactor who had put her through college without any expectation of personal reward. How sad, how very sad, that he had shown so little of that side of himself to his own children.

She bent over the bed to smooth the thinning grey hair off his forehead.

Dr Polson arrived a few minutes later. After one look at Charles, he agreed that, in the circumstances, round-the-clock nursing would be easier on his patient's heart than forcing him into hospital against his will.

Within the hour, a small blonde nurse had been installed in Charles's room, and Phaedra went to call her mother.

'I'll be there right away,' Esther said.

She was as good as her word. Ten minutes later, puffing a little, she was standing in the small cloak-room off the hall, closing her battered umbrella.

'Oh, Mum. You needn't have hurried,' Phaedra protested. 'He's still asleep.'

'Good. Can't cause any trouble that way, can he? Let's have a look at him.' Esther spoke gruffly, and when Phaedra tried to help her up the stairs, she shook her off. 'I'm not an invalid,' she protested. 'Just a little stiff in the joints. I can manage.'

Charles opened his eyes when he heard her sensible brown shoes thumping across his carpet.

'Esther.' He smiled weakly. 'Knew you'd come.'

'Well, of course you did. We go back a lot of years, you and I.' Esther's voice was unusually hoarse.

'So we do. Come closer, so I can see you.' Charles held out his hand.

Esther sniffed and accepted it with an odd, jerking motion. 'Not much to see any more,' she muttered, sinking into the chair beside his bed.

'Nonsense. You're still a good-looking woman. Almost as pretty as my nurse here.' Charles waved his free hand feebly at the diminutive nurse, who was sitting in an armchair with a heap of lumpy pink knitting in her lap. She giggled uncomfortably.

Esther shook her head. 'Charles, you shouldn't say things you don't mean.'

'Do mean it,' he said. 'Always thought so. Sorry, Esther. Sorry . . . Wish I'd realized – but it was too late, wasn't it? You and I, we . . .' He drew a long, rasping breath and dropped her hand.

The click-clack of the nurse's knitting needles broke the silence, and Phaedra, watching her mother's face, saw Esther close her eyes as if she couldn't bear to see her old employer in such straits.

'He's fallen asleep, Mum,' she whispered.

76

Esther started. 'Yes. Yes, I know.' Her eyes opened again and rested with a kind of reluctance on the feeble figure lying in the bed. 'He was so big, you know, so handsome when I first knew him . . .'

She didn't seem to expect an answer, and when none was forthcoming, she bent forward and dropped a kiss on the old man's bloodless lips.

He moaned softly and said, 'Helen.'

Esther's shoulders slumped, and she murmured something inaudible and stood up.

'You don't have to leave,' Phaedra said softly. It was important to say that. Something was going on here that she didn't understand.

'No, it's . . . it's all right. His children will be with him soon. Look after him, Phaedra. I . . .' Esther threw a last agonized glance at Charles and stumbled from the sickroom, holding on to her side as if she had stitch.

Phaedra waited a few moments before she followed.

Her mother was halfway down the stairs, clutching the bannister with both hands.

'Mum?' Phaedra said. 'Mum, are you all right?'

Esther turned to look up at her. Although she made no sound, tears were streaming silently down her face.

'Mum?' Phaedra repeated. She couldn't remember ever having seen her mother cry.

Esther raised a hand, shook her head wordlessly and continued on to the bottom of the stairs. She took each step carefully, as if she were a very old woman.

'Go back to Charles now,' she said to Phaedra when she finally reached the hall. 'Tell him . . . No. Just take care of him. Please.'

Her voice was higher, less certain than usual, and something about it stopped Phaedra from arguing, or pleading with her to wait. She watched, frowning, as her mother walked stiffly across the hall to collect her raincoat and umbrella from the cloakroom. Only after Esther had opened the door and let herself out into the rain was she able to shake off her paralysis and move.

'Mum, you shouldn't be out in this weather,' she cried. 'Not with your arthritis the way it . . .'

She reached the front door without quite knowing how she got there. But just as she pulled it open, Angus Cooper's old Fiat skidded to a stop by the gate.

Angus *skidding*? Phaedra's mouth dropped open as she watched her mother close her umbrella, shake it, and climb sedately in beside her old friend.

Still rubbing her eyes, Phaedra went back into the house.

Just under three hours later, Iain's Porsche slammed to a stop on the gravel.

As she went to meet him, Phaedra became aware that the line of her mouth had gone rigid with animosity. She didn't care. Iain was the last person she wanted to see or speak to.

Unfortunately, in this situation, she had no choice.

'How is he?' Iain called, ignoring the rain and

springing out of the Porsche with an agility that would have been impressive if Phaedra had been in any mood to be impressed. He was still wearing his executive suit. Did he ever take it off, she wondered, or was it supposed to be some kind of power symbol? If it was, it worked. He did look formidable, more than a little intimidating and, yes, she had to admit it, disturbingly sexy – for a stepson.

'Your father is not in any pain, but he's very weak,' she replied woodenly. 'Dr Polson says he mustn't be upset.'

Iain gave her a sharp look and strode towards the house, oblivious to the rain streaking down his face. 'Are you suggesting I'm likely to upset him?' he demanded.

'I expect you upset a lot of people,' Phaedra said, standing aside to let him pass. 'Just be considerate.'

He stopped so close to her that their bodies were almost touching. She could smell the steamy dampness coming off his clothes. 'I'm always considerate. But you're right about one thing, Phaedra. It will give me great pleasure to upset *you* – when I have the time.' On that inauspicious note he swung away from her and sprinted up the stairs.

Phaedra, whose limbs had gone annoyingly numb, bit back the abusive words she was longing to hurl at his back. Briefly, she considered leaving him alone with his father and the nurse. But she didn't altogether trust him not to agitate Charles. In her husband's weakened state, that could too easily be disastrous.

In the end, but slowly, she followed Iain up to the bedroom.

He was bent over the bed when she walked in. The nurse was tactfully busying herself at a table bearing an arsenal of pills.

Iain's face was in shadow, but his voice, when he finally spoke, was low and less abrasive than usual.

'Hello, Father,' Phaedra heard him say. 'You didn't have to go this far to get my attention.'

'Hmm. Damned impudence.' Charles's breathing was laboured, but that didn't stop him adding irascibly, 'You never should have married that Rosie girl.'

'I probably wouldn't have if you hadn't told me I couldn't,' Iain admitted. He turned his head slightly as Phaedra coughed into her fist, and when their eyes met, she thought she saw the beginnings of a smile.

Charles waited to regain his breath, then muttered, 'Is that so? And I suppose you'd have gone into the bank too if I'd had the sense to tell you not to?'

'No. That was different. I've always been interested in advertising.'

'Have you, now.' Charles' bony fingers plucked at the sheets. 'Well then, we'll see which one of us has the last laugh. Won't we? I've left everything to Phaedra, you know.'

'Yes, I know.' Iain glanced across the room to where she was standing near the door. Although the look in his eyes was unreadable, it made her take a hasty step backwards.

'It's all you deserve, boy. You know that, don't you?' Charles rasped.

'I suppose it is,' Iain agreed. He straightened to his full height. 'I should have kept a closer eye on Phaedra.'

Phaedra took another step backwards and hit the doorframe. She noted the small, hard smile on Iain's lips and the subtly aggressive thrust of his chin. Damn him. He knew she wouldn't cause a scene in Charles's sickroom.

'Hmm.' Charles seemed to know it too, and she guessed he regretted that he wouldn't be given the opportunity to witness the trouble that would inevitably result from his machinations. Yet when he spoke again he only sounded tired. 'You do that, boy. You do that . . . watch young Phaedra . . .'

When she looked again he was asleep.

Iain shoved his hands into his pockets, looked her over laconically, and said, 'Well? Which part of you shall I keep my eye on first?'

Phaedra turned her back on him and went downstairs to see to supper.

It wasn't that Iain made a noise, or called attention to his presence in any way, but Phaedra knew he had come into her kitchen. She put down the potato she was peeling and swung round to find him standing by the door.

Their eyes met in mutual appraisal before she turned deliberately away and went back to peeling potatoes.

'Phaedra . . .' He came up behind her, put his hands on her shoulders and turned her to face him without effort. 'Phaedra, how long has Dad been like this?'

The top of her head came just to his chin and his spicy breath was lifting her hair. Phaedra gulped and tightened her grip on the peeler.

Iain glanced at it, raised an eyebrow and let her go. 'Well?' he said.

She reached behind her, eyes steady on his face. The peeler clanged into the sink. 'Charles has been ill for some time,' she replied. 'He took a turn for the worse yesterday – as you would have known if you'd come back to see him as you promised.'

Iain thrust out his jaw. 'If it's any of your business, I went straight from Paris to New York, got back late last night and intended to come down tomorrow. Have you done what I told you?'

'What you *told* me?' She couldn't keep the sarcasm from showing.

'Yes.' He ignored it completely. 'I said you were to engage nurses around the clock. Have you done it?'

'Yes, I've done it. I'm his wife, Iain. I care about him. Unlike you, I've been looking after him for over a year. Once I realized there was no way he was going into hospital, of course I arranged for nurses to come in. What else could I do?'

'Not much. I hope you didn't find it too painful.'

She hated the contempt in his eyes. Hated his taunting insinuations, hated everything about him. But Charles, who had been her mentor and was now her husband, lay ill and perhaps dying upstairs. This was not the time or the place to engage in a war of words with his son.

'I was glad to do it,' Phaedra said, and turned her back on him.

She knew he was still behind her as she picked up a small potato and began to scrape it. There was a kind of magnetism about Iain that couldn't be ignored, even when he didn't move or speak. Fleetingly, she felt his hand on her neck. Then he said something she was just as glad she couldn't hear, and left the kitchen without another word.

Phaedra leaned over the sink and tried to make the bees in her stomach stop buzzing. When they wouldn't, she put a hand to her neck where Iain had touched it, and took half a dozen deep, relaxing breaths. That, eventually, did the trick.

Later, when it was time to eat, she laid a cold supper on the dining-room table, loaded a plate for herself and went upstairs.

'You two go and eat,' she said, walking purposefully into Charles's bedroom. 'It's all on the table. I'll stay with my husband.'

The nurse put down her knitting and looked hopefully at Iain, who was sitting by his sleeping father's bed.

'Ever the dutiful little wife,' he murmured, stretching as he rose to his feet. 'Come along, nurse.'

The nurse needed no second urging. She jumped up with such eagerness that her pink knitting tumbled on to the floor.

Iain stood politely aside to let her go ahead. Phaedra watched them leave and wished the little blonde joy of him.

Half an hour afterwards, when they came back, the nurse's pretty bow of a mouth was turned down at the corners. Iain looked frankly bored.

Phaedra waited until he sat down, then went across the landing to the room that had always been his. Quickly, in case he reappeared, she made his bed. It was still covered by the black and red quilt he had chosen as a teenager.

Briefly, as she crushed the soft cotton in her hands, she allowed herself to remember him as he had been then – reckless, laughing, casually kind to the quiet little girl who adored him.

Strange how life, and time, could change a man for the worse.

As soon as she had finished the dishes, Phaedra went back upstairs, meaning to spend the evening with Charles. But she found Iain still sitting on the hard chair beside the bed, reading his father the news from the daily paper.

Charles was looking at his son with an expression she hadn't seen before, and didn't particularly trust. It wasn't affection, yet nor was it out-and-out antagonism.

Phaedra frowned. Even now, in his affliction, she had a feeling Charles was plotting something.

She hesitated, wondering if she ought to make her presence known, but when neither man paid the slightest attention to her discreet shuffling, she quietly closed the door and went away.

An hour later she was sitting in the cramped room that had once housed the Trebanians' ancestral library and that these days was dedicated to the watching of television. Charles didn't approve of what he called 'Entertainment for the mindless', but he conceded there was suffcient value in the news to permit the installation of a small, hard-to-see set in the least comfortable room in the house. A programme on birds was the feature of the day. Phaedra was watching it without really seeing it when Iain came in to tell her his father was asleep. He said the night nurse had suggested they should use the opportunity to catch up on some sleep.

'Yes. All right.' She clicked off a nestful of cheeping finches and stood up. 'I made your bed.'

'Thank you. It might have been awkward if you hadn't.'

Phaedra blinked. 'What does that mean?'

'Mostly that I didn't expect to share yours.'

She switched off the light so he couldn't see her face. He would probably be delighted to know just how much she longed to hit him.

'It may surprise you to learn that I didn't expect it either,' she said lightly. 'You mustn't take my name too seriously, Iain. Mother may have been into Greek mythology when I was born, but I'm sure it never occurred to her that one day I might marry her employer. She certainly wouldn't have equated your father with Theseus – or thought of you as Hippolytus.'

'I'm relieved to hear it. He came to an unfortunate end, didn't he?'

'Mmm,' murmured Phaedra, beginning to enjoy herself. 'When he rejected the advances of his father's wife, she killed herself – something I don't plan to do, by the way – and left a letter accusing him of raping her.'

'And did he?' Iain's voice was very low and much too close to her ear.

She hurried into the hall. 'No, but his father, Theseus, believed the lie, and got *his* father, Poseidon, to send a useful sea monster to scare Hippolytus' horses as he drove his carriage along the shore. It was smashed to pieces. Then Theseus discovered the truth, and father and son had a lovely wallow being reconciled. It was too late, though. Hippolytus still died.'

'You say that with a most unseemly relish,' Iain remarked. He touched a hand to her cheek. 'The stepmother's name was Phaedra, as I remember.'

Was that amusement she heard beneath the natural resonance of his speech? Or was lack of sleep making her fanciful?

'Yes,' she said. 'But it was all Aphrodite's fault. She *made* Phaedra lose her heart to Hippolytus. So you see, you needn't worry. It would take more than one of Aphrodite's spells to make your stepmother fall in love with you.'

She *hadn't* been imagining Iain's amusement. Even in the dim lighting cast by the brass lamps clinging to the walls, it was impossible to miss his smile.

'Oh, you don't have to convince me,' he said softly, when they parted at the top of the steep staircase. 'I'm sure you know better than to cast your lures at a man who enjoys excellent health and has no intention of leaving you in possession of his estate.'

Phaedra sucked in her breath and counted to thirty. When she replied, it was merely to say frostily, 'Goodnight, Iain,' before she took the second flight of stairs up to her room.

Hard as it had been to keep from decorating that handsome face with a few well-placed scratches, she knew she would only regret it if she allowed him to provoke her into losing her temper. That was probably exactly what he wanted. And it was a luxury neither of them could afford. Not with a desperately ill Charles asleep in the room across the landing. Nor could she allow herself the satisfaction of telling Iain the truth. In his current frame of mind, that would probably provoke an even more disturbing row.

Half an hour later Phaedra fell asleep, thinking of all the unpleasant things she would like to do to Iain. Then she dreamed about him.

But her dreams were not unpleasant at all.

It was lucky she'd forgotten them by morning, because Charles's health had deteriorated to the point where she had no time to dwell on dreams.

Halfway through the afternoon, just as she finished clearing away lunch, Phaedra heard wheels screeching down the driveway. Wiping her hands on her blue denim skirt, she hurried into the hall in time to see a young woman dressed all in black and carrying a shiny black raincoat sweep through the door and pause dramatically in the centre of the floor. When she fluttered her hands, the scent of gardenias wafted through the air.

'Joan!' Phaedra cried. 'You came. Oh, I am so glad to see you.'

'If it isn't the new Mrs Trebanian,' Iain's sister replied with a grin. 'It's good to see you too.' She shook her head. 'I couldn't believe it when Iain told me you'd married Dad.'

'You don't mind?'

'Of course not. Why should I? It's you that has to live with him.'

Not for much longer, according to Dr Polson. Phaedra tried to smile and failed miserably. 'Thanks,' she said. 'I was sure you'd feel that way. All the same, it's nice to have it confirmed.'

Iain, who had been with Charles, appeared at the top of the stairs looking unusually delectable in a soft black pullover and grey tailored trousers. So he *did* occasionally abandon the suit. Phaedra eyed him with a mixture of approval and irritation as he sauntered down to meet Joan.

When he reached the bottom step, he paused, frowning. 'Joan? What have you been bathing in? Eau de Harlot?'

'Is that any way to greet your sister? It's a very expensive scent and Anton likes it.' Joan tossed her head, causing an unruly curl to escape from her sleek black chignon. She held out her arms. 'Come and say hello properly. Then you can tell me all about Dad. He's going to be all right, isn't he? He always is.'

Iain, looking resigned, dutifully embraced his sister and gave her a perfunctory peck on the cheek. But when he stepped back, for the first time in years Phaedra saw something like consternation on his face.

In a moment she understood why.

'Did you say Anton?' he demanded. 'Not – you didn't bring him with you?'

'I couldn't. He's still touring. And there's no need to look at me as if you suspect me of packing my pet python. Anton's my husband, and I'm fond of him.'

'Dad isn't,' Iain said succinctly.

'No. No, I know he isn't. He's always been totally unreasonable about Anton's dancing. Iain, how is he? You haven't said.'

'You didn't give me a chance. He's not well. You'd better go up and see for yourself. But I suggest you wash that smell off yourself first or you'll have him threatening to put you in a brothel.'

'Pig,' said Joan, wrinkling her nose at him. 'It'll do him good to smell something that isn't medicine.' She trotted off up the stairs, leaving Iain and Phaedra standing in the hall gazing after her.

'I'm glad she came,' Phaedra said. 'Dr Polson says – says he doesn't think it's going to be long now.'

'Long? Before all this is yours, you mean?' Iain sounded so bitter and scornful that Phaedra flinched.

'No,' she said making up her mind. 'That's not what I mean.' It was now or never – and, with luck, Charles would be occupied with Joan for the next little while.

'There's something I have to tell you,' she began. 'You may not want to hear it –'

'If it concerns my father, I most certainly do want to hear it.'

'It does, of course. The thing is . . .' She paused, searching for words with which to tell this man she no longer knew that she had married his father, not for her own sake, but for his.

She made herself look him in the eye. 'I married your . . .'

The sentence was never completed. Before Phaedra could get the words out, a strangled cry came from the top of the stairs. Seconds later, Joan, her face the colour of white ash, came tumbling into Iain's waiting arms.

'Dad,' she gasped. 'He's still conscious, I think. He even grunted at me. You know the way he does. But – oh, Iain, the nurse says . . .'

Iain and Phaedra didn't wait to hear what the nurse had said. They were already on their way up the stairs.

CHAPTER 4

Charles was awake, as Joan had said, but something about him had changed. At first Phaedra wasn't sure what it was. Then she realized it had to be his eyes. They were softer, misted, as if already he had left for a place where breath came naturally, joints moved easily and pain was no more than a memory. There was a strange, sweet smell in the room.

Joan, unused to seeing her father laid so low, moved to the end of the four-poster and stood holding on to it, gazing down at him in dark-eyed disbelief. Iain and Phaedra drew up straight-backed wooden chairs and took their places on opposite sides of the big bed. The moment they sat down, Charles reached out to grasp Iain's right hand. Then he turned to Phaedra, and when she took his other hand his skin felt so brittle she was afraid it would break.

'Father . . .' Iain's voice was rough as he bent over the frail old man, 'You've got to –'

Charles moved his head on the pillow. 'Nonsense. Only one thing I've got to do – now.'

91

They waited, puzzled, as he drew their two hands across the bed until the tips of their fingers were touching.

'Take her,' he whispered.

Neither one of them moved.

'Take,' Charles said again, with hoarse urgency

Iain met her eyes briefly, gave a shrug, and wrapped his firm, blunt fingers around her palm.

This seemed to satisfy Charles. He gave a sigh and allowed his arms to fall back on to the covers.

Reluctantly, resenting her instant awareness of Iain's touch, Phaedra studied the stern features of the man on the other side of the bed. His skin had darkened, but otherwise his face gave no hint of his true feelings. Perhaps he had none. Sometimes, lately, she had wondered if he still had the capacity to feel.

Iain tightened his grip, but he was looking at his father and seemed not to know the pressure hurt. Yet when she gave a little gasp, he frowned and laid her hand quite gently on the sheet.

Embarrassed, unsure of what was happening, Phaedra turned to Charles for an answer. What was it he wanted of her and Iain? He had looked so ill when they came in, but now . . . Puzzled, she leaned forward to study him more closely.

Oh, no. He *couldn't* be. Surely not. She blinked her eyes rapidly and looked again. Dear Lord, he *was*. She hadn't been dreaming . . .

Charles, her supposedly helpless husband, was grinning. Actually *grinning*. No other word could accurately describe that triumphant flash of teeth in the sunken face.

Had she really been fool enough to think he was letting go gracefully, slipping peacefully into a better and kinder world?

She might have known Charles would never let go.

'Told you,' he whispered looking straight at Joan, who was straining to catch his every breath. 'Chy an Cleth. Not – yours. Not – prancing fancy man's either.'

Joan shook her head. 'Dad, it doesn't matter. Anton's not here. You have to get well . . .'

'No.' Charles turned to look at Phaedra, then at his son, and said in a voice that was weak but still bitingly clear, 'No. Damned if I have to. Had enough. Going to find – Helen. You'll see. You'll all see. Oh, yes, you . . .'

He took a long, shuddering breath, gave a last feeble, 'Hah,' and closed his eyes.

Minutes passed. Nobody stirred. Phaedra's gaze remained fixed on her husband's hands lying on the sheet with the palms turned upward. Ivory on white. So thin and veined they were . . .

Footsteps brushed softly on the carpet, and the nurse, who had been hovering unobtrusively in the shadows, moved to the side of the bed. She felt for a pulse, then said quietly, 'He's gone. I'm sorry.'

Still no one said a word, and after a while she added with a puzzled frown, 'He went very peacefully. He – he even seems to be smiling.'

Phaedra understood her bewilderment.

Charles was indeed smiling. But it wasn't the calm, peaceful smile of one who has accepted the inevitable. It was the gloating, celebratory smile of a man who has scored his final victory, and enjoyed every jubilant second of the battle.

Charles Trebanian had left this mortal coil happy in the conviction that he'd won.

Just *what* he had won, Phaedra wasn't yet ready to consider.

It rained all through the service in the ancient stone church on the cliff where generations of Trebanians had been baptised, married and, eventually, dispatched to a happier, and no doubt drier world.

Afterwards, when the brief ceremony was over, the small group of mourners shuffled off to Chy an Cleth to drink a last toast to the man all of them had known, but only a few of them had liked.

Angus Cooper, Charles's bespectacled solicitor and friend, was genuinely overcome. So were Esther Pendenning and her daughter, both of whom were wiping away tears.

It was harder to tell how Charles's children were taking his passing. Joan kept glancing at her watch. She had a plane to catch that evening, back to the husband her father had so despised. Iain moved among the guests with the stone-faced courtesy of a man who was used to entertaining clients and saw no reason why emotion should interfere with the efficient running of what he appeared to look on as just another social obligation.

Watching him, Phaedra couldn't make up her mind whether she felt sympathy or irritation. In a way she wanted to comfort him, but he seemed not to need comfort. In another way, she wanted very much to shake his steely control and oust him from the dominant role he had automatically assumed from the moment his father's spirit had left his body.

Iain had made all the arrangements, treating Phaedra as if she were no more than the house-keeper's daughter. And she had been too confused and distraught to care much. Why should she? Iain was a Trebanian, handling Trebanian affairs. She had loved his father, but never in the way a wife loves her husband. It was right that Iain should be in charge. Besides, it came naturally to him. Being in charge always had.

Phaedra was heading for the kitchen to make more tea when Angus Cooper waylaid her in the hall.

'Your mother,' he said anxiously. 'Is she all right?'

'All right?' Phaedra stared at the dapper little man with the sweet smile. 'Yes, I think so. In the circumstances. Why? Did she say something?'

Angus shook his head. 'No, no. But when I offered to drive her home she said she'd rather walk. Something about wanting to be by herself.'

Phaedra glanced round the room, surprised. 'Has Mum gone then? She didn't say she was leaving.'

'She seemed – overcome. I don't think she felt up to goodbyes. But she shouldn't be walking in this weather.'

'Yes,' Phaedra agreed. 'I mean no. No, she shouldn't. Don't worry, Mr Cooper. I'll give her a call in a minute and make sure she made it home all right.'

Angus nodded, not entirely satisfied, as she could tell from the way he furrowed his forehead.

Phaedra shook her head. So many things had been happening lately that she hadn't fully taken in how much time Angus spent hovering round her mother. Was something going on between them? How odd if that were true. Somehow she'd never imagined . . .

At that point her thoughts skidded to a halt. Peter Sharkey, whose offer to buy Chy an Cleth had precipitated her wedding to Charles, was bearing down on her, wearing a face-splitting beam. Did he think Charles's death was cause for celebration?

She made a dash for the stairs before he had a chance to make eye contact.

Five minutes later, when it dawned on her that she couldn't spend the afternoon skulking in the rather chilly bathroom, she made her way cautiously back down to the kitchen. To her relief, there was no sign of Peter. Thank heaven. She didn't think she was up to handling him today.

Angus was talking to Letty Brown, who owned the Spotted Dog, when Phaedra walked into the drawing-room with the tea. Oh dear. He looked as anxious as a dog who'd lost its mistress. Giving him a quick smile, she went at once to the phone to call her mother.

'Mum? Are you all right?' she asked, when Esther answered on the first ring. 'Angus says —'

'Yes, yes, I'm fine. Don't worry, dear. Fond as I am of him, Angus is an old fusspot at times. I just need to be by myself. Charles and I — we went back a long way, you know. Over half a lifetime.'

Phaedra, hearing the break in her mother's voice, said gently, 'Of course. I understand. I'll call you tomorrow then, Mum.'

'Yes. Do that.' Esther hung up, leaving Phaedra blinking at an abruptly silent phone.

'Is she all right?' Angus, rimless glasses falling off the end of his nose, bustled worriedly over to join her.

'Yes, she's fine,' Phaedra said. 'At least she will be. Come and have another sherry, Mr Cooper.'

'Oh, I don't think so.' Angus pursed his mouth, as if she'd offered him a jug of smuggled rum.

'Oh, but you must.' Phaedra took his arm and towed him back to the drawing room. 'It's just what you need to warm you up.' She didn't add, 'And to stop you fussing.' But she thought it.

'Well, perhaps just one . . .'

'Of course.' Phaedra led him over to the sideboard where Iain was pouring drinks.

'How are you holding up?' Iain asked her, after Angus had accepted his sherry and gone back to talk to Letty.

Phaedra was touched. It was only a casual question, asked quietly and without pressure but, for the moment at least, he seemed to have forgotten she was

97

Phaedra the Witch and was treating her as if she were his friend.

'I'm all right.' She gave him a smile and sniffed discreetly. The sweet, ripe smell of alcohol was very much in evidence in this corner.

She was about to move away when a tall man with a scruffy red beard strolled up and, without a word, enfolded her in his arms.

'Hello, Lloyd.' Phaedra smiled shakily, and extricated herself as best she could from the bear-like embrace. 'It was nice of you to come.'

From the look Iain threw her way, she gathered he didn't see anything nice about it.

'Pleased to,' Lloyd said. 'You've been good to us. Bringing us those heaters for the cottage, lending us extra blankets. We'd never have survived the winter without them.'

Iain, with a lift of dark eyebrows, managed to convey that he wouldn't have regarded Lloyd's death from cold as any special loss.

'I'm glad I could help,' Phaedra said. 'Iain, have you met Lloyd.'

'Not officially.' Iain concentrated on pouring a drink and made no effort to greet the other man.

'Oh. Well then. Iain, this is Lloyd Davis. He's a sculptor. He and Jade – she's an artist – have been living in Portis Cottage near the harbour. Lloyd, this is Iain, Charles's son.'

'Pleased to meet you,' said Lloyd.

'How do you do.' Iain nodded briefly, but didn't trouble to hold out his hand.

Phaedra drew Lloyd away. What was the matter with Iain? Why was he suddenly behaving like a socially inept gorilla? Funerals had that effect on people sometimes, she knew. But she hadn't expected it of Iain.

'Jade's been looking for you,' Lloyd said, kindly ignoring his host's rudeness. 'She's over there talking to the dramatic-looking girl with all the makeup.'

'Iain's sister, Joan.' Phaedra took Lloyd's elbow and inched her way towards the two striking young women standing beside Charles's antique desk.

When she glanced back at Iain, she was relieved to see he was making an effort to be pleasant to Angus. Thank God for that small mercy, since he obviously saw no reason to make himself agreeable to Lloyd.

'Oh, Phay, I'm real sorry,' Jade cried as they came up to her.

Phaedra was about to say, 'Thank you,' when she found herself enveloped in another bear hug, this one involving yards of biscuit-coloured cloth smelling pleasantly of sandalwood. 'Real sorry,' Jade repeated. 'I liked your old man. Oh. Sorry, didn't mean to suffocate you.' She stepped back and tossed her long, blonde hair out of her eyes.

Phaedra laughed. It was the first time she'd felt like laughing that day.

A few minutes later, when she saw Angus move away from Iain and start to drift in her direction, she murmured something about fetching another cake from the kitchen, and edged her way out into the hall.

Angus was a dear, but his fretting was more than

she could cope with today. She wondered if her mother had felt the same.

'Phaedra!' A man's enthusiastic voice assaulted her as she stepped through the door.

Peter Sharkey again. Talk about out of the frying pan . . .

'Thanks for coming,' she called, and made another blind dash for the stairs.

Oh dear, Peter was going to think she had a bladder problem, although that was the least of her worries today. Angus might be a fusspot, but Peter was the shark he was named for.

By the time she came down again, the first guests were starting to leave. The rest soon followed, and within the hour the last awkward condolence had been mumbled, and Iain, Joan and Phaedra were finally on their own.

'That's that, then,' said Joan, closing the door on the last departing back. When nobody answered, she looked at her watch and exclaimed, 'Oh, my God. Look at the time. I'll miss my plane . . .'

'Keep that up and you'll be able to fly under your own steam,' Iain called after her as she shot up the stairs.

Ten minutes later, after giving Phaedra a hug, and Iain a misty-eyed kiss, she departed with a squeal of brakes to catch her plane.

Phaedra waited until her car was out of sight, then hurried up to the bathroom to wash away the day's residue of tears. When she emerged, feeling fresher but no less dejected and unfocused, she was surprised to discover she had the house to herself.

Good. Iain had probably gone into Porthkelly to be with friends. Assuming he still had any. Or even to the Spotted Dog to drown his sorrows – although that didn't seem much like him. It wasn't important. She could do with some time on her own, and anyway she didn't know what to say to him. They hadn't been alone together since Charles's death, and the matter of the inheritance was still unfinished business between them.

Joan had suggested Phaedra leave it to Angus Cooper to break the news to Iain that Chy an Cleth was his.

'He won't go all arrogant and flare his nostrils at Angus,' she'd explained. 'If he hears it from Dad's old friend, he'll have to sit on his pride and be civilized. In fact the best thing would be for Angus to wait until Iain's back in town. Then he can tell him the news over the phone.' She giggled. 'He'll probably take it out on Caroline, that overpaid secretary of his.'

Seeing the wisdom of this sisterly advice, Phaedra had smiled ruefully and agreed.

How quiet the house seemed now that everyone had gone, as if it too were mourning its master. Phaedra stood at the bottom of the stairs, running her hand along the bannister. Lord, what a day it had been. People had been kind on the surface, but she hadn't missed the curious looks and whispers that every now and then had erupted from behind the mask of good manners.

She knew most of the guests thought, as Iain did, that she had married Charles Trebanian for his money. But now, at last, the worst of the public scrutiny was over. A burden had been lifted.

Phaedra raised her head. She hadn't noticed the wind coming up, but now, all at once, it was shrieking down the chimney, rattling the windows and storming at the door. She lifted her arms, pretending she could feel it blowing through her fingers – and all at once she knew what she had to do.

Maybe out there, alone with the elements, she would start to feel human again – as she hadn't since the day she married Charles.

An old grey windbreaker hung on a peg in the cloakroom. She pulled it on over her black and white dress and, moments later, was battling her way on to the path above the cliffs.

The rain had tapered off, but the wind hadn't. It whipped around her head until every last pin was shaken from the long hair she had been at such pains to pile up only this morning. The flared linen skirt of her dress slapped so hard against her legs that her progress was slowed to a crawl. It didn't matter. She relished the challenge, needed it to clear her brain, which had been sadly befuddled of late.

By the time she had made her way around Porthkelly Bay to the far headland, she knew exactly what 'chilled to the bone' meant. Shivering, she moved to the shelter of a large boulder perched near the edge of the cliff, and stood under it listening to the thunder of the breakers. The sea was in a terrible rage today.

Holding tight to the boulder, Phaedra leaned over the edge, the better to observe the tumult below.

Just as she expected, nature was giving a spectacular demonstration of its power. The sight of the sea raging and roaring at the rockface like the bully it was, was one she had seen many times before. But it never failed to steal her breath with its frightening magnificence.

She forced some air into her lungs, but just as she was about to pull back something that didn't quite fit the landscape caught her eye. Phaedra pushed at the hair blowing across her face. Was she seeing things? No, maybe not. She looked again – and this time knew for certain that what she had seen was no illusion or trick of the greying light.

A man was standing down there among the rocks.

Iain hadn't gone into Porthkelly. Dressed in a bulky fisherman's jersey and well-worn corduroy trousers, he stood alone above the crashing waves, staring out to sea just as his ancestors must have done before him. To Phaedra's stunned gaze, in a way he seemed to belong there, a part of nature, at one with the savagery of the storm.

The suited executive might never have existed.

She started to back away, feeling herself an intruder in a world she had no part in. But at that moment he looked up and saw her.

He was too far away for her to be able to read his expression, but she noticed the instant tensing of his shoulders.

He didn't move.

Time passed, the waves went on pounding the cliffs, and after a while Iain relaxed his rigid stance and began to make his way steadily across the rocks to the steep path that wound up the cliff. Phaedra watched him with her heartbeat on hold.

Wind swirled around his head, lifting his hair and fighting him for every step he took. Yet he moved with the ease of one used to battling the elements and winning – like some wild Cornish storm god emerging from the sea to claim his own.

Except that she wasn't his own, Phaedra had to remind herself. Until a week ago she had been his father's wife.

The path ended only a few yards from where she stood, and when he reached the top of the cliff and came towards her she was finally able to see his eyes – and for no reason that made any sense, all at once she was tempted to turn tail and run. Yet she held her ground.

'Hello, Stepmother,' Iain shouted above the wind. 'Did you follow me? I'm surprised you were willing to take the risk.'

'No,' Phaedra replied, wishing he wasn't standing so close to her that she could see the salt crusted on his skin. 'I didn't follow you. What risk?'

The wind chose that moment to soften its assault, and his next words were chillingly clear.

'That I might not be able to resist the opportunity of tossing you over the edge.' He nodded at the jagged formations far below. 'Bereaved young widow, overcome with grief, decides to end it all. I'd get away with it, don't you think? Or do you suppose a jury might take into account that your husband could

104

have been your father and that you'd just inherited his rather comfortable estate?'

Not a god of the storm after all. Just a magnetically sexy and thoroughly unpleasant man. 'You really are a bastard, aren't you?' Phaedra said.

'Not that I know of. I believe my mother was married to my father. I have, however, been referred to as a heel, a jerk, a shark, a scoundrel and, my personal favourite, a slubberdegullion. I'd been involved in a bit of a dust-up at school on that occasion.'

Was he *laughing* at her? Only a few seconds ago he had threatened to toss her over the cliff. No, he couldn't be laughing. Either he was just being his usual obnoxious self, or he was taking out on her the fact that his father's death had affected him far more deeply than he was willing to admit.

If that was the case, he'd have to find another way to grieve. He wasn't the only one who missed Charles. If he did miss him.

'I'm not surprised you've been called a lot of names,' she said.

'Aren't you?'

Something about the quiet question unnerved her. She swallowed and took a hasty step backwards, forgetting in her confusion that the boulder was no longer behind her but that a sheer drop on to the rocks was.

'Phaedra!' Iain's shout competed with another blast of wind as his arm shot out to grab her around the waist. 'Are you out of your mind?' He bent his head until his nose was almost touching her face.

'Keep that up, and you won't live long enough to enjoy the fruits of my father's labours. What the hell's the matter with your brain?'

Phaedra decided she'd had enough. At some point during the day's proceedings she had actually wanted to comfort this abrasive man, had almost decided to explain about the inheritance at once, instead of following his sister's advice. But now all she wanted was to puncture his arrogance, then go somewhere quietly by herself where she could come to terms with the loss of the equally impossible man who had been her husband.

'I'm not interested in the fruits of your father's labours,' she snapped. 'But if you're so anxious to get your hands on them yourself, why didn't you just let me fall? A minute ago you were threatening to throw me over.'

Iain shrugged. 'I do have the odd chivalrous impulse. Misguided, I know. But on the whole, I prefer not to write my business deals in blood.'

'Business deals?'

'Mmm. I'm afraid I can't let you keep Chy an Cleth. But that shouldn't be a problem. You've already proved you can be bought.'

'Oh! How . . .' Belatedly, Phaedra came to the realization that Iain's arm was still around her waist. Did he mean he thought she . . .? No. No, not even Iain could think that. Not on the day of his father's funeral. 'Please take your hands off me,' she said, icily calm now. 'I'm afraid you're wrong about the price.'

'Am I?' He gave a hard little laugh that was carried away on the wind, and moved his hand to her elbow. 'I doubt that. But in fact I was talking about the house, not your other – assets, shall we call them?'

Phaedra gritted her teeth and pulled her elbow out of his grasp. 'Neither the house, nor my other *assets*, is for sale,' she told him. 'Now, if you don't mind, I'm going home.' Without waiting for his answer she began to hurry back the way she had come. The wind, behind her now, slammed into her back and practically blew her along the path.

Iain caught up with her just as she skidded on a patch of wet grass. 'Slow down,' he ordered. 'One slip and you'll be over the edge.'

'Which would solve all your problems,' Phaedra snapped, deliberately increasing her pace.

'I told you I like to solve my problems in my own way,' she heard him growl – just before her feet left the ground and she found herself sprawled across his shoulder.

'Put me down,' she gasped – and then, struggling for dignity in an impossibly undignified situation, 'If you don't, I'll have you up for assault.'

'Will you? In that case, perhaps I ought to make it worth my while.' He continued his progress along the path without breaking stride, as though she were no more than an old coat he'd brought along it case it rained.

'Put me down, please,' Phaedra repeated firmly.

Iain stopped to shift her weight. 'Say that again.'

'I said put me down.'

He didn't move.

'*Please*,' she said through her teeth.

'That's better.' He tipped her briskly on to the path. 'Now, are you going to walk at a sensibly circumspect pace? Or do we have to repeat that little performance?'

He meant it, she could tell. Just as he had meant it that day, seventeen years ago now, when she had stood at the top of a very steep rock dreaming she was Amphitrite while the sea crept up to surround her. Iain had been angry then too, but he had helped her down . . . and she hadn't climbed the rock again.

That was the trouble with Iain. He had an infuriating habit of being right.

'I'll slow down,' she muttered. 'You needn't worry.'

'I wasn't,' he assured her.

They walked the rest of the way home in silence.

The moment they reached Chy an Cleth, Phaedra said she was going upstairs to change. 'I suppose you expect me to make your supper,' she added ungraciously.

Iain propped himself against a solid oak beam and crossed his arms. 'Not unless you want to. We've both had a difficult day. I was going to suggest we sample the fare at the Spotted Dog. Not the most sophisticated of eateries, but it's the best Porthkelly has to offer.'

Phaedra eyed him doubtfully. 'Sophisticated? No, it certainly isn't that. How do you feel about chips and egg, or the farmer's plate?'

'I dare say I'll survive. What about you? We could drive into Bude if you prefer?'

Why was he was being nice to her all of a sudden? 'You want me to have dinner with you?' She frowned suspiciously as she shrugged off her dilapidated jacket.

'If you like. And provided you stop glaring at me as if I'm some particularly virulent species of woodworm.'

Unexpectedly, Phaedra caught herself wanting to laugh. 'Woodworm?' she repeated. 'Yes, that about covers it. But let's not do the Spotted Dog. I don't much feel like going out.' She hesitated. 'If you'll promise to stop being a jerk, I could whip us up some pasta – with fresh tomato sauce. And a salad.'

'Done. We'll call a truce for this evening.' He smiled – quite a nice smile considering its source, Phaedra decided with cautious approval. She also noted the lines of weariness beneath his eyes and the deepening grooves between his nose and his mouth. Was this proposed truce more a matter of exhaustion than a willingness to reform? It had been a long, arduous week. Although Charles was gone, he was still managing to make his presence felt.

'I'll go and get changed,' she said. 'My black and white's a bit much for home-cooked pasta.'

'Oh, I don't know. I thought I remembered you had a waist. And hips. It's nice to know I was right.'

Phaedra glared at him. 'Woodworm,' she said, and

marched upstairs without responding to the chuckle she heard coming from behind her.

Damn Iain anyway. Just when she was beginning to think she might be able to tolerate his company, he had to go and spoil it with that gibe about her figure. She usually favoured loose-fitting clothes. They were comfortable, and she didn't like advertising her curves. She'd never been quite comfortable with them because they seemed to give men the wrong idea. In college that had led to a lot of unsolicited groping. Later, she had tried to set a good example to her hormone-obsessed pupils. That was what she told herself anyway, though in her more introspective moments she wondered if perhaps she was using clothes as a subtle 'no trespassing' sign.

The truth of the matter was that although she sometimes went out with men, and enjoyed their company, she had never experienced the yearning and burning that had caused most of her friends to fall into bed with the first appealing pair of male thighs that came their way.

Jeans, Phaedra decided, peering into her antique wardrobe. Iain couldn't tell her those didn't fit. And a baggy black sweater on top would have to do.

Iain said nothing about her appearance when she found him in the library and told him she was about to start supper. Instead he followed her into the kitchen, where he pulled out a chair and settled himself astride it with his arms crossed loosely on

110

the back. As Phaedra busied herself with pasta and the dressing for the salad, he watched her movements with lazy approval. At least it looked like approval. She felt a vague sense of alarm.

After a while, and without being asked, he got up to open the bottle of wine she had put on the counter.

'For the cook,' he said, handing her a glass.

Phaedra nodded and accepted it gratefully. 'Do you want to eat in the dining-room?' she asked.

'Not particularly.' He hitched a hip on the corner of the table. 'For an intimate little dinner *à deux*, why don't we make ourselves comfortable in the kitchen?'

Intimate? Intimate was the last thing she wanted to be with Iain. She glanced at him quickly, but he appeared to be absorbed in a thoughtful appraisal of a row of copper pots. Of course. He only meant he wasn't in the mood for formality at the end of this very long day.

She threw salt and a bay leaf into boiling water and slid the pasta in to cook. After that she poured dressing over the salad in a wooden bowl and passed it to Iain with instructions to mix it in while she set the table.

He raised his eyebrows slightly, but did as she asked with an efficiency that took her by surprise.

So far the truce was holding up.

'Do you cook?' she asked.

'Only if I can't find anyone willing to do it for me.'

'Which I imagine you usually can,' she said drily. Iain might be arrogant, but he was undeniably attractive – and he was rich. He probably had women lined up at his door waiting to cook for him. She took a long serrated knife from a drawer and began a vicious assault on a loaf of French bread.

Iain eyed her warily. 'Usually,' he agreed. 'Not all the time. Do you always attack your bread with such ferocity?'

'What do you mean?' She stopped slicing and stared at him blankly.

'You're going at that unfortunate loaf as if it's a mortal enemy. Or your faithless lover.'

Phaedra turned back to the bread. 'I hadn't noticed,' she said. 'And in case you've forgotten, I was married to your father.'

'I hadn't forgotten. What's your point?'

'My point is that I don't have a lover.'

'I'm glad to hear it. That doesn't, of course, preclude lovers in the past.'

Phaedra narrowly missed slicing off her thumb as she whirled to face him. 'I suppose it doesn't. But for your information, there weren't any. That's what you wanted to know, isn't it?'

Iain smiled faintly and stretched his legs. 'It's hardly my business.'

'That's what I thought.' Phaedra took the bowl from his hands, slammed it on the table, and said, 'Let's eat.'

Iain cocked an eyebrow at her and stood up. He didn't comment on her sudden ill-humour, and as soon as the pasta was served the two of them took their places at the table.

They didn't speak much after that. Phaedra had no idea what he was thinking. Her own mind seemed to be not so much on the events of the day, as on his reference to her non-existent lovers. Her inexperience had never bothered her much before, but now, for no reason, it did.

There had been opportunities, of course – men who had been only too eager to introduce her to the pleasures of the bedroom. But none of them had ever quite measured up, and when it came to the point where the chaste kisses that were all she would allow were no longer enough, the friendships had ended abruptly.

Phaedra was only now beginning to suspect that at the back of her mind there had always been a boy with a slashing white smile who had been kind to a shy little girl.

Could that really be true? She stared into the rich, red liquid in her glass. No, it couldn't be true, because the daredevil boy who had captured her childish imagination had turned into the cynical, autocratic man who had spent the last week setting her teeth on edge and driving her to contemplate murder.

'I know the feeling, believe me,' she heard Iain saying softly. 'But I wouldn't advise you to try it.'

Phaedra started, then realized she was clasping her knife as if it were a dagger.

She gave a strained little laugh and put it down. 'Sorry. I was just – fantasizing.'

'Dangerous fantasies,' Iain said drily. 'I hope they don't involve me.'

'Hardly likely, is it?'

His lips quirked and she knew he didn't believe her.

'What about you?' she asked, anxious to change the subject, and seizing on the first topic that came to mind. 'Is there anyone – special in your life?' If he could ask personal questions, so could she.

'Special?' Iain's tone was acid of the quick-acting kind. 'No. I've made certain of that since Rosie. Why? One Trebanian fortune not enough for you?'

Phaedra paused with her fork halfway to her mouth. 'What did you say?'

Iain threw his napkin onto the table and leaned back. 'Sorry. I'm breaking our truce, aren't I?'

'You most certainly are.' She laid the fork carefully back on her plate. He wasn't a bit sorry. If he had been, he wouldn't be lounging there, smiling the self-assured smile of a man who believes he has a right to say anything he likes.

'For your information,' she said, 'one Trebanian was more than enough. And believe it or not, I miss him. He, at least, was a gentleman.'

'And I'm not? You're probably right. Would it help if I complimented you on your cooking?'

'I know I'm a good cook.' Phaedra smiled frigidly and pretended to concentrate on her pasta. When she looked up again, Iain was watching her, his eyes narrowed as if he didn't quite know what to make of her.

She didn't know what to make of him either. Was his abrasiveness only a shield for something deeper, some inner chaos he was determined to keep to himself? Did he, in fact, mourn his father's passing as much as she did?

'It's strange without him, isn't it?' she said, purposely offering him an opening. 'I keep expecting to hear his stick tapping on the floor.'

'Yes, it takes some getting used to.' Iain spoke without emphasis, leaving Phaedra as much in the dark as she'd been before.

'Do you miss him?' Perhaps he would respond to a direct question.

Iain stroked his jaw, unconsciously calling attention to the roughness of his five o'clock shadow. 'Miss him? That's hardly the way I'd put it.'

'How would you put it?'

'He was my father. I spent so many years fighting him for control of my own life that I suppose it became something of a habit.' He paused to examine his hands, then went on without visible emotion, 'It's hard to believe that's all over.'

And that's as close as he'll come to admitting his father mattered to him, Phaedra realized with a rush of compassion.

'He loved you,' she said. 'In his own way.'

The corner of Iain's mouth turned down. 'I suppose so. Unfortunately, his way wasn't mine. He thought love gave him the right to run lives. My mother, apparently, didn't mind. I did. Joan got around it by pretending to do as he said and then

115

going ahead and doing precisely as she pleased. I couldn't do that.'

'Wouldn't, you mean,' Phaedra said. 'You're as stubborn as he was.'

Iain inclined his head. 'As you say. Wouldn't. I gather he had better luck with you.'

'What?' She frowned. 'I don't understand.'

Iain lifted his right arm and waved it in a sweeping half-circle around the room. 'All this. The house. Your reward for obedience, I imagine.'

'Then you imagine wrong. Dammit, Iain . . .' She stopped. No. She was not going to rise to his bait. And she wasn't going to tell him the truth either. Not now, when he was lounging there, all mocking and contemptuous and cynical. Besides, anything she said was bound to lead to further dissension, and she'd had enough dissension for one night. Better leave it to Angus Cooper. He was good at coping with irascible clients.

'Yes?' Iain raised his eyebrows. 'You were saying?'

'Nothing. I'm going to do the washing up now. You can help if you like.'

He didn't trouble to reply, but when she began to carry dishes to the sink he stood up to help her clear the table. When she placed the clean plates in the rack, he picked up a towel and began to dry them.

So although at home he almost certainly had the dish-washing machine Charles had considered an invention of the devil, Ian *could* be helpful when it suited him – even if he did carry out the task in a

116

grim, uncommunicative silence. Perhaps that was his habitual way of working.

What would it be like to work *for* him? she wondered – then decided she wasn't anxious to find out.

It wasn't until the last dish had been put away, and she had said a cool goodnight and headed into the hall, that Phaedra took in how quiet the house had once again become. When a floorboard creaked behind her, she jumped, and in the next moment realization struck.

She was alone in the house with Iain. No Charles, no nurse, no Joan. Not that Iain would pounce, of course. But there was something so appallingly intimate about the current arrangement that she would have given anything to avoid it.

She swung round, feeling his presence behind her.

He was smiling – a slow, taunting smile that told her he was as aware of the situation as she was – the difference being that he didn't care.

'No,' he said, shaking his head gently. 'You needn't worry. I wouldn't dream of it, Stepmother.'

Phaedra lifted her chin. 'Neither would I. But there's been so much going on I didn't stop to think.' Not for the first time, she was thankful she wasn't given to blushing.

'About what?' Iain drawled.

'Joan's gone. I should have asked Mother to stay,' she replied obliquely. 'But it's too late now. She'll be in bed.'

'As you and I will shortly be.'

Phaedra gulped, and he added drily, 'Separately. I know you have a low opinion of me – it's mutual, by the way – but I have no intention of seducing my father's widow on the night of his funeral.'

So much for the truce. 'It's not that,' she began indignantly.

'Ah. Surely you're not going to tell me you're concerned about the proprieties? My dear Phaedra, we're not a couple of teenagers, and this isn't the nineteenth century. Do you really imagine anyone will care?'

'My mother . . .'

'Will think nothing of it. She trusts me. And presumably she trusts you – though I must say I can't imagine why.'

Phaedra curled her hand tightly around the bannister. As usual, the feel of the smooth oak beneath her fingers helped to calm her. He'd be singing a different tune when he learned of her plans for the estate. And if the truth made him feel guilty – well, so it should. Not that regrets or guilt were sentiments she associated much with Iain . . .

'Goodnight,' she said again. 'I hope your conscience doesn't keep you awake.'

He laughed. 'Why should it? Goodnight, Phaedra. I hope you get all the sleep you deserve.'

Not deigning to answer, and having little choice but to make the best of an absurd situation, Phaedra headed for the sanctuary of her room. She'd had enough of Iain. Maybe in the morning she would find a way to put him in his place.

But in the morning, when she stumbled, bleary-eyed, into the kitchen to make breakfast, she found a note in the centre of the table. It was from Iain, and it informed her, with characteristic terseness, that he had risen early and gone back to London.

CHAPTER 5

Iain was reading the statistical analysis on an up-coming presentation to a new client when Angus Cooper phoned to deliver the second bombshell.

He listened carefully, then picked up a gold paper knife in the shape of a sword and stabbed it into his blotter with intent to maim.

'Thank you,' he said. 'Tell Phaedra I'll be there tomorrow.'

Angus hung up with a relieved murmur. Iain extracted the knife from the blotter and wrapped his fingers around the hilt.

'Of all the insane' – stab – 'devious' – stab – 'manoeuvres' – stab. 'What the devil is she up to this time?'

'Did you call?' His secretary's bright red head popped round the edge of the door.

'No.' Iain waved her away.

As soon as he was alone again, he dropped the knife and pushed back his chair, gripping its soft leather arms and gazing grimly at a knot in the panelled wall. The statistical analysis could wait. What he had to do now was decide on his next move in this incredible mind game he found himself engaged in with Phaedra.

What *was* she up to? This latest move didn't make sense. People, especially people who hadn't a lot of money, didn't throw away inheritances for nothing. So – presumably the lady wanted something in return.

Iain tipped back his chair, propped a foot on the edge of his desk and steepled his fingers beneath his chin. Why? Why was Phaedra playing these stupid games? She was supposed to be a balanced, intelligent inspiration to the nation's young, not a devious manipulator of men. He closed his eyes, shutting out the light from the glittering fixture above his desk.

Phaedra. A soft name steeped in myth – the name of a dreamer and a lover. But this modern Phaedra, who had once been one of the few people he would have trusted with his soul, had obviously gone far beyond dreams. What could she possibly want that . . .?

Lord almighty! Iain dropped his foot back on to the carpet and sat up. Was that it? Was *that* what she wanted from him? It had to be. What else was there she hadn't got already? He picked up the paper knife and pointed it at the rubber plant his secretary tended each day with such devotion. It was only when he realized he was on the point of getting up to stab the unfortunate plant through the heart that he allowed his weapon to drop back on to the blotter.

No wonder the little witch was hell-bent on turning his life inside out. She knew what she wanted and meant to get it. Iain shook his head, his lips curling up in reluctant admiration. She was a worthy adversary. One of the best he'd come across in years. Too bad for her that he'd learned the hard way to spot guile and exploitation when he saw them. Phaedra and Rosie were two of a kind.

Someone in the outer office giggled. Iain frowned. Phaedra had giggled like that at one time. It was a sound that used to make him smile.

He strummed a furious tattoo on the edge of his desk, and went back to checking the statistics.

When the doorbell rang at eleven-thirty in the morning, Phaedra knew at once who it would be.

Angus Cooper had phoned to pass on Iain's message. He had also mentioned that the anticipated explosion hadn't happened.

'He took the news quite calmly,' Angus said, sounding both surprised and relieved.

Phaedra had been non-committal. She knew better than most how accomplished Iain could be at concealing his true feelings.

The bell rang again. She gave the tights she'd been rinsing out in the washbasin a quick squeeze and went to answer it, her heart beating an irritating drum roll against her chest.

'Hello, Phaedra,' said the man on the doorstep. He flashed her an ingratiating grin. 'How are you? Recovered from your recent loss, I trust?'

Damn. Not Iain, but Peter Sharkey, who wanted to turn Chy an Cleth into a hotel. It was bad enough that Iain was likely to land on her doorstep at any moment without adding Peter to the mixture.

Her heart resumed its normal steady pace. 'Hello, Peter,' she said without enthusiasm. What was the point of explaining to a man like Peter Sharkey that you didn't recover from the loss of a husband in less than a month? Not even when that husband had been more of a father than a mate.

'Can I come in? I'd like to talk to you.' His grin became positively beseeching.

Phaedra sighed. She didn't like Peter. He wasn't bad looking in a florid, thick-lipped sort of way, but she had never taken to his habit of speaking as if his voice had just been oiled, and she didn't much care for the way he looked everything over as if he was assessing its net worth. At the moment he was looking her over.

She stepped back reluctantly and waved him in. 'What do you want to talk about?'

'This house.' He sidled past her into the hall. Phaedra waited, deliberately not shutting the door.

'What about the house?'

'Isn't it too big for you all by yourself?'

'Perhaps.' It wasn't Peter's business that the house was no longer hers.

'That's what I thought.' He beamed. 'You know, of course, that I've had some success investing in local properties, turning them into quite profitable concerns –'

'Turning them into horrid modern monstrosities, you mean. The library was a lovely old building until

123

you bought it and converted it into a trashy department store. As for the old post office –'

'Now, now.' Peter held up his hand. 'You can't stop progress, Phaedra.'

'That depends on what you call progress.'

Peter cleared his throat. 'Yes, well . . . the thing is, with a few renovations I can see Chy an Cleth becoming quite a successful small hotel. Exclusive, you know. The sort of place that appeals to rich tourists who like a place to have character, but want all the latest conveniences along with it. For instance, I'd be inclined to leave the staircase as it is –'

'You'll leave everything as it is. I'm not selling.'

'Now, Phaedra, be reasonable . . .'

'I am reasonable. And if that's all you have to say to me, I'm afraid you're wasting your time.'

Peter shook his head with an exaggerated air of reproach. 'As if that could possibly be all I'd have to say to a pretty woman like you. Aren't you going to offer an old friend a cup of coffee?'

Peter wasn't an old friend. At one time they had attended the local school together, but he had teased her about coming from 'the big house' just as all the other children had. Phaedra eyed him glumly. On the other hand, her mother *had* brought her up to be hospitable . . .

'Why?' she asked eventually. 'We haven't much to talk about, Peter.'

Peter patted his carefully combed hair. 'Actually, there is something I'd rather like to discuss. It won't take long. Just a quick cup and I'll be off.'

Phaedra sighed. 'All right. Provided you don't discuss Chy an Cleth.'

'Of course not. This involves you, not the house.'

Oh God! Phaedra closed the door with her foot. That didn't sound much better. But she was committed now. 'We'll have it in the kitchen,' she said, leading the way without troubling to find out if he was behind her.

He was. 'I wouldn't want to be any trouble,' he said, following so close on her heels that his scented aftershave made her sneeze.

Liar, Phaedra thought. You couldn't care less.

Peter sat down at the table, wriggling his well-padded backside as if he was settling in for a long, intimate chat. Fleetingly, Phaedra was reminded of the evening when she and Iain had shared a meal in this same kitchen. But there was no comparing Peter with Iain.

Ten minutes later she set the coffee pot on the table, slapped down two earthenware mugs along with milk and sugar, and reluctantly pulled out a chair.

'Good girl.' Peter's gaze settled unabashedly on the swell of her full breasts that not even the baggiest of sweatshirts could conceal.

'I am not a girl,' Phaedra snapped, flipping her hair forward over her shoulders to spoil his view.

'Oh, I say –' Peter broke off as the front door slammed and heavy footsteps sounded in the hall. Seconds later they heard a man's voice swearing.

125

'Phaedra?' the voice shouted, coming closer. 'What kind of fool of a woman leaves her front door open in this day and age? Anyone could walk in and . . . Ah. I see anyone has. How very cosy. What's your business here, Sharkey?'

Reluctantly, Phaedra withdrew her attention from the cream swirling in her coffee.

Iain stood framed in the doorway, formidable in an almost-black suit. His dark hair had fallen across his forehead and, in the sharp morning light of the kitchen, his eyes were the colour of night. Lord, he was magnificent. Overbearing, and at this point highly inconvenient, but still magnificent.

'Well?' he said, when nobody spoke.

'Peter came to talk business,' Phaedra explained. 'I asked him to stay for coffee.' Not strictly true, but it wasn't up to Iain whom she chose to entertain.

'I see. What kind of business? Making porno flicks now, are you, Peter? Or is running an erotic phone service more your line?'

Peter blinked and swallowed half his coffee in one gulp. 'I say, no reason for you to talk like that, Iain. As a matter of fact, I thought Phaedra might be interested in selling the house. It's too big for one little woman –'

'Phaedra is not what I'd call a "little woman",' Iain remarked with deceptive smoothness. 'Rather the opposite, in fact. *Was* she interested in selling?'

'No. No, not at this time.' Peter gulped down the rest of his coffee and stood up, knocking over the empty mug in his haste. 'Have to be going. Thank

126

you for the coffee, Phaedra. If you should change your mind –'

'She won't be changing her mind.' Iain took Peter pointedly by the elbow and escorted him out into the hall.

Vaguely, Phaedra wondered what Peter had wanted to talk to her about. Now, with luck, she would never need to know.

The smart snap of the front door closing was followed by a brief silence. Phaedra waited, and seconds later Iain strode back into the kitchen as if he owned it. Which, come to think of it, he did.

'Sit down,' he ordered, pulling out a chair.

'I am sitting down.'

His hand tightened on the chairback, but after a short, startled pause the corner of his mouth twitched up in wry acknowledgement. 'So you are. Good.' He moved to the opposite end of the table and stood with his hands held loosely at his sides. For the first time since he'd blasted his way into the house he actually looked at her.

'All right – let's start with Sharkey,' he said. 'What possessed you to allow that little bottomfeeder in?'

Phaedra shrugged. 'Manners, mostly. You wouldn't know about those.'

'Oh, wouldn't I? In case you've forgotten, there was a time, not so long ago, when I had to teach you a few lessons in decorum.'

'Decorum? What kind of a word is that, for heaven's sake?'

'A good old-fashioned one.' He put his fists on the

table and leaned towards her as if he were conducting a high-powered meeting.

Phaedra sniffed as the bracing aroma of coffee wafted up her nose. Who the hell did Iain think he was? She had expected him to have trouble accepting what she had done with Chy an Cleth. But why should he care about Peter Sharkey? And what made him think he had the right to talk to her as if she were a child? *She* was the teacher, not him.

'You're hardly in a position to criticize,' she pointed out.

'Oh? What makes you think that?'

'Don't get me started. For one thing you have yet to say, "Good morning, how are you, Phaedra?" For another, most people have the courtesy to say goodbye before they leave.'

'Good morning, Phaedra. I can see you're very well. As for saying goodbye – what in hell are you talking about?'

He had no idea. He really had no idea. Phaedra linked her fingers tightly in her lap. 'The morning after your father's funeral,' she said.

'What?' Iain leaned towards her as if he couldn't believe his ears. 'I left you a note.'

'Yes. A very abrupt one.'

'What did you want? An engraved apology?'

Phaedra took a sip of her coffee and eyed him ingenuously over the rim. 'That would have been nice.'

She watched warily for signs of imminent explosion but, to her relief, he chose to sit down instead, hooking his arms carelessly through the rungs of the chairback.

Phaedra waited, and eventually a faint smile lifted the flat contours of his mouth. 'You know you're not going to get one,' he said. When she met his eyes without answering, he added on a softer note, 'I didn't think you'd care.'

'I didn't.'

'Well, then . . .?' He shrugged.

Phaedra said nothing, and eventually he went on as though she'd asked for an explanation. 'If you want the truth, I decided to leave on the spur of the moment – after I woke up and heard you sighing in your sleep in the room above me.'

Phaedra gaped at him. 'Don't tell me I sigh that loudly.'

'No, but it was a very – evocative sigh. It reminded me that all too close at hand my young and lovely stepmother was lying all soft and unchaperoned in her bed –'

'But you said . . .' Phaedra frowned, pressing her back against the chair to still the tremors running up and down her spine. 'You said it hadn't even crossed your mind.'

'It hadn't,' he agreed. 'When it did, I decided I'd better leave. I've rather passed the stage of respond-ing to my more mindless glandular impulses.'

Phaedra gulped back a gasp. Was he actively trying to hurt her feelings, or was he just naturally rude? He hadn't been in the old days. 'You needn't have worried,' she said. 'I'm happy to say *my* glandular impulses weren't involved – and I doubt if you'd stoop to using force.'

Iain tipped his chair back and propped an ankle on his knee. 'I doubt it too. But since I was awake and had a mountain of work piling up in town, it seemed as good a time as any to leave. I did mention that you weren't getting an apology.' He added the last sentence as if that made everything all right.

It didn't make anything all right, because what she had actually got was on a par with a slap in the face.

Why in the world had she married this hateful man's father in order to save an inheritance for him that she was fast becoming convinced he didn't deserve?

'What brought you down here, then?' she asked, gathering up the empty coffee mugs and carrying them over to the sink. 'Apparently you didn't come to thank me for Chy an Cleth.'

Iain didn't reply. Phaedra stared at the coffee rings in the bottom of the mugs, all scummy brown and depressing. She went on staring for some time.

When she could no longer stand the silence, and made herself turn around, she found Iain had moved over to the window. He was standing with his back to the light.

Mr Boss Man, Phaedra thought with a jolt of recognition. With his ankles crossed and his thumbs hooked into his belt, Iain was the very picture of the take-charge executive on a roll. Only the slight tensing of a muscle in his jaw convinced her he wasn't as calm as he appeared.

130

'Do you want me to thank you?' he asked.

'It's usual when someone gives you something you particularly want.'

He inclined his head. 'Very well. I thank you. Now tell me what you expect in return.'

'In . . .' She wiped uncomfortably damp palms down her jeans, then wished she hadn't because Iain's gaze dropped immediately to her hips. 'What makes you think I want anything?'

'People don't give away inheritances for no reason. Of course you want something.'

'I don't. What could I possibly want from you?'

He smiled, a slow, sensual smile that made him look like a tiger in pursuit of a snack. At any moment she expected him to start twitching his tail.

'Since you've assured me glandular motivations weren't involved,' he said, in a voice so soft it sent further shivers up her spine, 'I can only assume you're holding out for marriage. You see, I called on Angus Cooper this morning. He tells me my meddlesome father had our – shall we say *nuptials* in mind from the beginning.'

'Nuptials? *Nuptials!*' Did he have to keep using those stuffy words? 'You don't mean . . . Iain, he didn't . . .?'

Iain ignored her. 'Father always wanted me to march to his drum, and we all know how he felt about Rosie. But you were *his* choice, not mine. That made all the difference. Any woman *he* chose was bound to make a suitable bride.'

'How flattering,' Phaedra murmured, hating the

way he seemed to be blaming her for his wicked old father's scheming.

How *could* Charles have orchestrated this scene? Dammit, he was dead. 'It's not fair,' she muttered, not realizing she was speaking out loud.

'I agree,' Iain said. 'I suppose he thought that with Chy an Cleth at stake I was bound to fall smartly into line. That's what he promised you, isn't it? But when I failed to come up to scratch, you hoped bribery would bring me to heel.' He removed his thumbs from his belt and balanced a hip on the sill. 'It won't work, Phaedra. I've already told Angus I can't accept your donation.'

Phaedra closed her eyes and counted to twenty. If she opened them, if she so much as glanced at Iain, or caught even a glimpse of his cynically mocking mouth, she would undoubtedly start looking for sharp knives.

She had counted to fifty before she turned back to the sink. 'Why on earth should I want to marry you?' she asked over her shoulder, keeping her voice level only by a massive exercise of will. 'I already have what your father left me.'

'My father's estate is merely comfortable. Chy an Cleth, some good stocks – nothing exceptional. Trebanian Advertising is worth rather more. Surely a considerable inducement for a young woman in circumstances like yours.'

In other words, a young woman far beneath him on the social, monetary and every other scale. 'Perhaps,' she agreed. 'You forget, though, that there's one insuperable disadvantage to that scenario.'

'Oh? And what's that?'

'You. You come with the package.'

'Are you telling me you see that as a disadvantage?' Iain sounded honestly surprised.

Phaedra gripped the sink to prevent herself from spinning round to scratch his face. 'That's exactly what I'm telling you. I'm rarely attracted to men who imagine they're irresistible.'

'Is that so?'

She didn't move fast enough, had only just become aware that Iain had left the window, when she felt his hand touch her neck. A quiver, sharp and shocking, shuddered from the tips of her ears to her toes.

'Turn around, Phaedra,' Iain said.

She couldn't help herself. When his hands moved to her waist, she could only do exactly as he wished.

He held her lightly, edging her away from the sink. It should have been easy to break away. He was giving her every opportunity. Instead she reached backwards for the counter and held on to it, not breathing, waiting for what would come next.

Iain nodded, as if she had just confirmed his expectations, and slid his hands gently around her back. When he began to revolve his thumbs in a slow, erotic motion at the base of her spine, Phaedra gasped and reached up to clutch his shoulders.

'You see,' he said. 'You don't find this part of the package such a disadvantage. I didn't think you did.'

His eyes were gleaming at her through the haze of her own unsatisfied desire. Their dark light held her transfixed. She tried to move and found she couldn't.

133

Outside, the wings of a small bird flapped against the window. Then Iain transferred his hands from her spine to her hips, and she exhaled a long breath as partial movement returned to her limbs.

'Please,' she whispered, pressing her fists against his chest. 'Please . . . don't.'

He stepped back at once, and in that moment Phaedra would have run from the room. But Iain's pleased, I-told-you-so smile awakened her pride and made her hold her ground.

She leaned against the counter, her breath coming out in short gasps. 'Perhaps you aren't – altogether a disadvantage,' she admitted. 'All the same, I don't want to marry you. I don't even like you very much. Not any more. I did once.' She dropped her eyes and stared down at his expensive black shoes. 'That's why I married your father. So you wouldn't lose Chy an Cleth to Peter. And now that it's yours, I'm going back to my old teaching job in Kent. They've kept it open for me.'

If Phaedra had been looking, she would have seen Iain flinch and close his eyes. As it was, when she did lift her head, he was perched on a corner of the table with his arms crossed and his legs extended to their full, impressive length. Classic power pose, Phaedra thought, remembering her course in educational psychology. Iain was good at power.

'What do you mean, you married my father so I wouldn't lose Chy an Cleth?' he asked.

'Just what I said.'

'Are you deliberately trying to be obscure?'

'No.'

She hadn't meant to be ambiguous. But she could understand why he might think so. Sometimes she too had trouble believing in the events of that hot June afternoon which had ended in her engagement to Charles . . .

Peter Sharkey had called earlier in the day, and when she brought tea into the drawing room as usual, she had been startled to find Charles huddled in his favorite black armchair chortling like an evil old gnome.

'Mr Trebanian? What have you done?' Phaedra exclaimed. Knowing him as she did, alarm bells had switched on at once.

'Me? Done?' Charles slapped his hands on his knees. 'Nothing much. Just agreed to sell the house to young Sharkey. Now there's a fellow who knows where he's going.'

'You've agreed to *what*? Mr Trebanian, you can't sell Chy an Cleth.' When she laid the tea tray on the table beside him, as she did every afternoon, her hands were shaking so badly that the cups danced up and down in their saucers and milk splashed on to the embroidered linen cloth.

'I can, you know. It's mine.' Charles tipped his head back and looked up at her like a child who has just eaten all the cookies and knows he can't be told to give them back.

'But – why would you want to sell to Peter? You know what he'll do with it. And what about Iain? He's always loved this house . . .'

'Hah. Should have thought of that, shouldn't he? Joan, too. Teach them not to do what they're told. Joan would marry that fairy prince of hers. As for Iain – hussy he married was no better than a tart.'

'But –'

'No buts about it. Not only that. He wouldn't even take a decent, steady job. *Advertising!* How can I be proud of a son in *advertising*?'

'But he's done very well –'

'Course he has. Advertising! Telling lies, that's what my son does for a living. Easy to do well with lies.'

Phaedra tried a different tack. 'But you love Chy an Cleth. Iain does too. And Joan – well, Joan grew up here.'

'Too bad. It's going to young Sharkey.'

'Just because neither of them would jump through your hoops?' Phaedra put her hands on her hips. Damn this cantankerous old man.

'Hah! That's exactly why. Time those two found out they can't defy their own father and get away with it.'

'But, Mr Trebanian, you *can't* . . .'

'Can. It's my house. I can do what I like with it. Now, how about pouring my tea?' Charles peered at her from under bushy grey eyebrows, waiting to see how she would react.

Phaedra bent down, picked up the teapot and filled two delicate china cups with Earl Grey. 'Please,' she said, 'won't you reconsider?'

'Don't see why *you* should care. Not yours anyway.'

Phaedra winced. 'No, but I've lived here most of my life. I thought – well, that I'd always be able to come home. I can't bear the thought of Chy an Cleth being turned into a horrible Sharkey hotel.'

'Hmm.' Charles gave her a calculating look that instantly put her on her guard. 'All right, then. I'll leave the place to you. If you like.'

'Mr Trebanian! Don't be – you can't do that.' He didn't mean it, of course. But what could she say now? How was she going to make him see sense? Charles hadn't been well for some time, but that was no excuse for this kind of malice.

'Why can't I? Sit down, girl. Don't stand there quivering.' Charles waved her impatiently to the loveseat.

Phaedra perched on its arm as she searched frantically for an answer that might convince him. 'Even if you did leave the house to me, your will wouldn't stand up in court,' she finally announced with relief. 'Not if your children contested it.'

'Humph.' Just for a moment she thought he might concede defeat. But almost at once his brow smoothed out, and he said smugly, 'Would hold up all right if I married you, though. Heh? Wouldn't it?'

Oh, for heaven's sake! Was he losing his mind? 'I suppose so,' she reluctantly agreed. 'But that's not the point. You can't –'

'Why not? Too old to get down on my knees, but . . .' He leaned forward, seizing her damp palm in his dry one. 'Will you marry me, Phaedra

Pendenning? For worse, I expect. But you'll certainly end up better off.'

'*Mr Trebanian*. You're being ridiculous.' She tried to pull her hand away, but his grip was surprisingly strong.

'No, I'm not. Marry me or I'll sell the place to Sharkey.'

'But – you know you don't mean it?'

'Yes, I do. Never say anything I don't mean.' When she only sat, stunned, breathing in the faint odour of well-aged tweed jacket, he said testily, 'No need to gape like a fish. You needn't worry about *that* side of marriage. Not up to it these days. More's the pity.'

'Oh, I wasn't thinking – I mean, of course you are, but –'

'But nothing. Course I'm not. So you're quite safe. Marrying me won't change a thing. We'll go on as we have been, and when I die you'll get the house.'

'But I don't want the house. Iain does.'

'Hmm. Take your pick. Marry me, or let Sharkey have it.' Charles stuck out his lower lip, reminding Phaedra of an elderly infant who sees his mother weakening in her resolve not to let him have any more sweets.

Iain had once called his father a manipulative old satyr. She'd been shocked at the time. Now she was beginning to see what he'd meant.

'Why?' If she understood what was behind this incredible ultimatum, perhaps she might be able to change his mind.

'Because you're a good girl who does what she's told. Most of the time. That's why you're here, isn't it? To help your mother.'

'Yes, but she didn't tell me to come. Mr Trebanian, you *can't* –'

'Stop telling me I can't. You think about it.' He took a sip from his teacup and deliberately closed his eyes.

Phaedra poured herself a fresh cup, and thought about it. Her tea grew cold.

What, when it came right down to it, did she have to lose? Nothing, except the right to marry another man. And that wasn't an issue. What did she have to gain? The continued existence of her childhood home as she had always known it, and the peace of mind of Charles's only son – if Charles Trebanian stuck to his word, which he always did.

When he opened his eyes again, Phaedra said, 'Very well. I'll marry you. *Charles*.'

Charles let out a guffaw, and said he'd known she'd be sensible about it.

A week later they were married in front of a judge. Only Angus and Esther attended, and when the ceremony was over, Charles went straight to bed to sleep it off.

'So you see,' Phaedra said to Iain, who hadn't moved from his position on the table, 'I had no choice but to marry your father.'

'That may be true,' Iain agreed. 'Especially if you expected to inherit.'

Phaedra conquered a desire to stamp her feet and throw expensive china dishes. It wasn't hard, because what she really wanted to do was bury her head under the nearest cushion and howl.

'The point,' she explained wearily, 'is that if Charles left everything to me, and you contested it, his will wasn't likely to hold up. I told him that.'

'And offered to marry him? How very ingenious.'

'No,' she said, determined not to cringe as he drove yet another nail into the fabric of what had once been an unbreakable friendship. 'He said his will would hold up just fine if I was his widow. Or something like that. I told him not to be ridiculous. But in the end, when I realized he was serious, that he really meant to sell Chy an Cleth to Peter – I agreed. But only so I could give everything back to you.'

He wouldn't believe her, of course. But it had to be said. Should, perhaps, have been said weeks ago.

Iain shook his head as if he were fighting off a plague of invisible gnats. 'Don't you think my father would have guessed that? If it were true?'

She'd known he wouldn't believe her. Phaedra's shoulders slumped tiredly. 'I don't know what to think any more. A minute ago you told me that, according to Mr Cooper, Charles actually *wanted* us to marry. I suppose he could have got it into his head that if Chy an Cleth was mine –'

'I'd fall neatly in with his final and most creative attempt to run my life. Just so I could get my hands on my own home. God!' Iain raked both hands through his hair. 'Even from the grave that evil old man doesn't give up.'

Phaedra was appalled. No one ought to feel that way about their own father. She had never felt anything much about hers because he hadn't been a part of her life. But she had never hated him.

'Iain,' she said, 'even if that's true, I believe Charles meant it for the best. He loved us both in his way.' She spoke quietly, feeling defeated, hopeless. What was the use of trying to convince Iain that she had only his interests at heart? He would never accept that because he had already made up his mind.

When he didn't answer at once, she walked slowly back to the table and sat down.

Iain came to stand over her. There was a small rough spot on his chin where he'd used his razor too enthusiastically. 'Do you believe Dad would have sold this house to Sharkey?' he asked.

Was he, at last, seriously asking her opinion? Phaedra swallowed the lump in her throat and leaned away from him, desperate not to betray that his closeness was making the cleft between her breasts break out in beads of sweat.

'Maybe,' she said. 'Yes, I think he would have. If it was the only way he could think of to show you who was boss.'

He gave her a look so morose, so filled with disillusion, that she hastened to add, 'My mother says he wouldn't, though, and she knew him better than either of us. I don't know, Iain. He was manipulating me as much as you.'

Iain gave a kind of groan and lifted both hands to his face. Phaedra seized the opportunity to stand up and make a beeline for the door. When she turned around, Iain was staring after her as if she'd kicked him in the stomach.

'You know, of course,' he said in a constricted voice, 'that I can't accept this house as a gift. You must have realized I'd insist on buying it back.'

So he still thought she had married Charles for her personal gain?

'I knew you would *try* to buy it back,' she acknowledged. 'I also knew I wasn't going to sell it. It's yours, free and clear. I don't want it.'

Their eyes met and locked in a battle neither of them was willing to concede. When Phaedra refused to let him outstare her, Iain slowly shook his head. 'God help me. You mean it, don't you?' he groaned.

'Yes. I told you I did.'

He closed his eyes. 'OK. I think I'm convinced.'

'You should be. I've signed all the papers.'

'Why didn't you tell me? That everything I thought about you was wrong?' His voice was thick, as if swallowing a rather large crow didn't agree with him.

'I didn't know how. And then you were so rude and bloody-minded I didn't want to. In the end I decided to leave it up to Mr Cooper.' No need to mention Joan's involvement. Iain was wounded enough already.

He made a visible effort to look her in the eye. 'All right, I suppose I have to accept that. But *you* have to accept that I won't take advantage of your largesse.'

'My *largesse*?' Phaedra groaned, even though she'd guessed from the first that her gift would be a blow to his pride. 'You mean your stupid pride won't let you accept a gift from the housekeeper's daughter. Is that why you had to pretend I didn't mean it? That I deeded you the house for – for ulterior motives –'

'Don't talk rubbish.' Ian spoke without raising his voice. 'I don't care who you are. I couldn't accept such a gift from any woman.'

'Oh? And what if I were a man?'

'You're not a man. And no man I know would be fool enough to give away his house. Not unless he had a damn good reason.'

'Oh, so now I'm a fool.' She marched to the other side of the table and planted her fists on its cool surface. 'Well, I suppose that's better than a gold-digger.'

Iain rubbed a hand round the back of his neck. When he raised his eyes, he said, 'Yes. I suppose it is,' in a clipped tone that did nothing to help lower her blood pressure.

'Right, so does that mean you've finally got it into your thick head that I married Charles for you? Or partly for you? Because I couldn't bear to see my old home turned into one of Peter Sharkey's flashy monstrosities? I . . .' She paused for breath, and saw that Iain's fists were also balled on the table.

They glared at each other across the expanse of shaking oak.

'Phaedra,' Iain said. 'If you think for one moment . . .' He stopped, shrugged off his jacket and
slung it over a chair as if preparing to make the next
move in a power game that had suddenly become
serious. 'Now then. This is insane. What, exactly,
are we fighting about? Neither of us wants Chy an
Cleth to fall into Sharkey's hands. I want the
house. You say you don't –'

'I don't,' Phaedra said.

'Then why in hell won't you let me buy it from
you?'

It was a reasonable question. Why wouldn't she?
He wouldn't even notice the dent in his bank
balance. And she and her mother could use the
money . . .

'I can't,' she said. 'I'd feel as though I'd married
Charles for his money just the way you thought I
had. And you – well, you'd never be sure I hadn't
done just that.'

'And that would matter?'

He was frowning, but the anger was gone.

'Yes,' she said. 'It would.'

His eyes narrowed, and she remembered how,
earlier, she had succumbed without even token
resistance to the lure of his easy virility. All it had
taken was one brief, unsatisfying embrace. It
wouldn't do for Iain to get the idea that she cared
for him as more than a friend. An ex-friend, she
amended.

'I mean I prefer to make my own way in life,' she
explained. 'I wouldn't want you, or *anyone*, to think

144

that the only way I could do it was by enticing an ailing old man to leave me all his money.'

'Hmm.' Iain nodded. 'You know, in a crazy sort of way that actually makes sense.'

'I'm not crazy!'

'Aren't you? Then maybe I am. Because I'm not accepting the damn house from you.'

'It's not a damn house. It's your house. You love it.'

He shrugged. 'It wouldn't be the first time I've lost something I love. Eventually one learns to let love go.'

So dispassionate. So untouchable. This wasn't the impetuous boy she had adored with all her soul. But it was true he had suffered grievous losses. His mother, Rosie – even Charles. Had he really learned to turn off all deep feeling?

'You don't have to let this love go,' she said. 'I want you to have Chy an Cleth.'

'So you said. I don't care what you want.'

They stared at each other across the table, not angry now, but tense, wary, both of them unwilling to give an inch.

The grandfather clock in the drawing-room chimed the hour.

'It's time I made lunch,' Phaedra said.

'Not until we have this settled.'

She was still blinking at him, wondering what would come next, when he stalked round to her side of the table, took her by the wrist and said, 'Come on. If we're going to argue, let's do it in comfort.

Surely two reasonably intelligent people can come to some sort of sensible arrangement.'

He hadn't said compromise, Phaedra noted as he picked up his jacket and towed her out of the kitchen and into the drawing-room she had never much liked.

Just as they walked through the door, the clock gave a last resounding peal. Iain paused, then led her over to the settee and sat her down.

'What sort of arrangement?' she asked doubtfully.

He threw his jacket on to an elderly brocade chair and didn't answer. Phaedra watched as he rolled up his sleeves, eyeing the ropey sinews of his forearms with fascination. When she found she was breathing too fast, she said quickly, and mainly because she needed to remind herself, 'You haven't apologized yet.'

'Apologized?' He paused with a sleeve halfway up his arm. 'What are you talking about?'

'You called me a gold-digger.'

'Did I? I wouldn't have done if you'd explained what you were up to.' He finished rolling up his sleeves and went to open the drinks cabinet.

Phaedra glared at his ramrod-straight back. 'You,' she said slowly and precisely, 'have to be the most arrogant, ungrateful man I have ever met.'

'Thank you. I do my best.' Iain poured sherry into a long-stemmed glass.

Phaedra picked up a blue and white cushion, raised it above her head, then realized what she was doing and let it drop.

Iain poured a second glass of sherry, and said over his shoulder, 'Very wise. I might have been tempted to forget we're both grown up.'

'I wish you would. I may yet be tempted to forget it myself,' Phaedra told him. 'You have a way of reminding me how much easier it was to get my own back in the old days.'

Iain was half-turned towards her with a glass in each hand, but all at once he went still. 'Do you want to get your own back?' he asked.

'Yes. Frequently.'

'Hmm.' He crossed to the sofa and handed her a sherry. 'There's an easy way to do that. Surely it's occurred to you.'

'No. What?'

'You could tell me that the deal's off and you're going to sell Chy an Cleth to Sharkey. It would save us both a great deal of trouble.' He sat down beside her, put his glass on a carved Chinese end table, and draped his arm along the back of the settee. 'But you won't do that, will you?'

'I might.' Phaedra spoke sharply. His thumb was grazing her neck.

'And if I apologize properly?' He seemed more interested than concerned.

'Are you going to?'

'No. You should have told me what you meant to do with the house. Dammit, Phaedra, what was I supposed to think? But that doesn't mean I'm not touched – no, *overwhelmed* by your generosity. It's just that it takes some getting used to. No one has ever done anything like that for me before.' He touched her cheek, then withdrew his hand abruptly. 'I didn't – don't know what to say. But I wouldn't have called you a golddigger if I'd known.'

Phaedra couldn't bring herself to look at him. She didn't need to. There was regret, sincerity, and a kind of confused defensiveness in his voice that told her everything she needed to know.

This was as close to an apology as Iain would get. And it was enough.

'So – are you going to sell Chy an Cleth?' he asked.

Phaedra gazed into the rich amber liquid in her glass and tried to ignore the fact that if she moved her cheek just half an inch it would rest on the silken smoothness of his shirt.

'No,' she said. 'You know I'm not. But please don't get the idea it was only devotion to you that persuaded me to marry your father. It was more a matter of – of principle. Chy an Cleth by rights *should* be yours.'

'If you say so.' He spoke softly, close to her ear. 'That being so, and since we seem unable to come to an agreement, let's settle on a cooling-off period. In the meantime, I have a suggestion.'

'What's that?' Without thinking, Phaedra turned to look up at him.

His lips were parted in the small, killer smile that had been stirring her blood and disturbing her dreams from the moment he had returned to Porthkelly.

'I suggest,' he said, 'that until you come to your senses, we hire a reliable caretaker to look after the house.'

'I've already come to my senses.' Phaedra wished it were true. Almost as much as she wished Iain's fingers weren't oh-so-gently brushing her shoulder. When his smile broadened, she added grudgingly, 'All the same, it's not a bad idea.'

'Good. That's settled. Now, what was that you said about your senses?'

Phaedra swallowed. He was very close. She could smell the lovely, warm scent of his body. Surely a man who smelled like that couldn't be *all* discipline and business . . .

'Senses?' she murmured, as hers began to swim. 'What senses?'

'That's what I wondered. Why don't we find out?'

'What – what are you talking about?'

His hand was in her hair now, playing with it, winding it between his fingers. 'I'm talking about sealing our agreement with a kiss.'

Phaedra opened her mouth to say 'certainly not', but Iain cupped her cheek with his free hand and smiled, warmly this time. Then he removed her glass and bent his head so that his lips were only inches from her own.

Her mouth turned dry as dust, and she held her breath.

When the rhythmic, insistent beat of her heart became a clamorous call to surrender, she closed her eyes and waited for what would follow.

CHAPTER 6

Iain put his arm around Phaedra's shoulders, holding her loosely as he gazed at the sweep of dark lashes on her cheek.

She had grown into a lovely young woman, this bright, dreamy sprite from his youth. Her back felt warm through the crisp white cotton of her blouse, and she looked so ready and welcoming that he wanted to stretch her out on the sofa and get down to business at once. As if she were Gloria, who shared his bed now and then when it suited her.

Lately, Gloria had been beginning not to suit *him*. Maybe that was why Phaedra had turned into such a temptation – one he knew he ought to be resisting with every weapon that came to hand. Except now that he had her in his arms, he couldn't seem to bear to let her go.

He touched his cheek to the dark glory of her hair. Hard to remember she had been married to his father. Married for his sake, so she said. Or for a principle. It hardly mattered. Either way, she had offered him the gift of his home – and if he made the right moves now, in the next few seconds, he was certain she would offer him far more.

He wasn't going to make those moves – or, more accurately, he wasn't going to take them to their logical conclusion. If he did, he would be trapped – as irrevocably as he had once been trapped by Rosie.

His father had probably counted on him to think with his groin instead of with his head, just as he had in the past. But he was damned if he was going to fall in with this, the old man's final and most Machiavellian scheme. Phaedra might have been married in name only, but legally she had once been his stepmother. Now she was his father's leftover wife.

Iain ran a hand over her hair, thick, shining and smelling of raspberry shampoo.

Sweet, generous Phaedra. God, he was glad she hadn't, after all, grown into the venal young woman he had thought her. From the beginning that had been the part that stuck in his throat until it threatened to swell up and choke him – thinking that she, of all people, had betrayed him.

He should have known that Phaedra would never do anything to hurt him.

As he listened to the sound of her rapid breathing, and felt its warm whisper against his neck, she placed a hand on his chest, tentatively, as if she expected him to push her away. His muscles tightened instinctively. He couldn't have pushed her away if he'd wanted to.

Had he really been such a swine to her? He supposed he must have been. But in a way she had brought it on herself with her idiotic refusal to tell the truth. His bright little dreamer had developed a mind of her own along with her woman's figure – a mind that had led her hopelessly astray.

Iain smiled crookedly and stroked his knuckles across her cheek.

Phaedra gave a little murmur of frustration, and his smile softened. Her lips were so close he could almost believe they were waiting for his blessing.

He gave it then, knowing it was madness. The heat in his loins was sending an explicit message he could no longer ignore.

Within seconds he began to doubt his sanity. She tasted as sweet and inviting as nectar to a bee – but her kiss was diffident, inexperienced, a schoolgirl's kiss hinting at a passion only dimly understood.

She had meant it then, when she told him there had never been a lover.

Who would have thought it of a woman as desirable and passionate as he knew she was. He trailed a hand over her breast, then withdrew it with an oath when he felt her nipples harden. What *was* he doing? And how could innocence be such an aphrodisiac?

When the heat spiralled up through his abdomen, Iain groaned and tried to pull away. But Phaedra gave a little wriggle and wrapped her arms around his neck. He groaned again, allowing his tongue one last delirious exploration while he ran a hand across her rear and down her thigh. Then he said in a voice he barely recognized as his own, 'OK, bargain sealed. Let's cut to the next scene, shall we?'

152

'What?' she murmured against his mouth.

Hell! If she didn't watch it, if she kept on squirming like that, she was going to find herself flat on her back being divested of every scrap of clothing she had on. He even had an idea she wouldn't mind. But *he* would. Not now, but about fifty seconds after he'd done all the things to her that his body was crying out for him to do.

Lost in his own delicious agony, Iain didn't at once take in that Phaedra had stopped squirming and gone still.

'What did you say?' she whispered.

It took him a few seconds to regain his breath. 'Cut. I said cut.' He took her elbows and held her away, his arms going rigid with the effort. If he allowed himself to relax so much as a muscle, he was certain to give in to his body's clamouring and haul her back into his arms.

Hell! If only she'd stop looking at him like that.

'Iain,' Phaedra said, in a thin, childlike voice that shook as she tried to control it, 'don't ever do that again.'

'Why not?' he asked gruffly. He knew why not, but he asked anyway.

She refused to look at him, keeping her gaze fixed resolutely on the hands now gripped between her knees. 'Because I don't want you to.'

That wasn't strictly true, but he understood why she'd said it.

'OK,' he agreed. 'If I try to do it again, you have my permission to . . .' He paused. His permission to what? Slap his face? How ridiculously old-fashioned that sounded.

'Kick you?' Phaedra suggested. 'Where it hurts?'

'What?' Iain choked. He stared at her, seeking evidence his ears had deceived him.

She stared back. No, there was nothing the matter with his ears. Nor was there anything old-fashioned about Phaedra.

Some instinct of self-preservation propelled him on to his feet. But when he realized his arousal must be as obvious to her as it was painful to him, he collapsed back on to the sofa. Her knee brushed his thigh and he shifted up against the arm, waiting for her to raise her head and look at him.

When she did, her big eyes were wide and wary. Good grief, surely she wasn't afraid of him? Not Phaedra. The idea was ludicrous. And it irritated the hell out of him for some reason. His pain and frustration wore off, to be replaced by a quickly dampened flare of temper.

Dammit, the part of him she had threatened hurt already, and he hadn't done anything she hadn't wanted him to do. Oh, the kiss had been his idea all right, he took full responsibility for that. But he hadn't expected her to start squirming like a sexy little fish on a hook.

Not that he hadn't enjoyed it . . .

'Phaedra,' he snapped. 'Don't go all maidenly on me. It was just a kiss.'

'Yes. I know. Just a kiss.' She stood up and moved to Charles's old chair, and the lips that had melted so warmly beneath his looked as pale and cold as white marble.

Damn. Had he hurt her feelings as well as her pride? He hadn't meant to. Not this time, even though he knew he'd been doing it more or less routinely up until today. It was a habit he couldn't seem to break.

'Look,' he said. 'Let's go back to where you agreed that getting a caretaker wasn't a bad idea –'

'In a minute.' Phaedra straightened the collar on her blouse. 'First, I want to know why you kissed me.'

'Why, I – for heaven's sake, woman. I don't know. I think it had something to do with an apple and a snake in the Garden of Eden. You were sitting there, so guileless and reproachful – my little Phaedra, all grown up and looking as if she wanted to be kissed.' He shrugged. 'I did what came naturally, I suppose.'

'And then wished you hadn't.'

'Not exactly.' How could he tell her that by the time he'd come to his senses, he had mentally removed her blouse and was working on her underwear and jeans? 'Why? Is that why you threatened to kick me in a rather unkind place? Because I *stopped* kissing you?'

Phaedra sucked in her upper lip and smoothed a hand stiffly over the cracked leather of Charles's chair. 'Of course not.'

Iain, unable to resist, leaned forward and tilted up her chin. 'You know you enjoyed it,' he said, smiling to take the sting from his words.

'Are you laughing at me?' she asked reproachfully.

'I'm trying not to. I'm not at all sure laughter would be wise at this juncture. I have a healthy respect for that part of me.'

He saw a small movement at the upper left corner of her mouth. As he watched, it developed into a full-fledged, slightly shamefaced grin. 'I didn't mean it,' she said.

Iain spread his arms along the back of the settee and gave an exaggerated sigh of relief. 'Thank heaven. You had me quaking in my shoes.'

Phaedra giggled. 'Don't be a fool.'

Iain raised his hands in mock surrender. 'Does this mean it's safe to return to the subject of a caretaker?'

Some of the laughter died out of her face. 'Yes, of course.' She folded her hands in her lap in a gesture he found primly endearing. 'Chy an Cleth would be perfect for Jade and Lloyd.'

Iain frowned. 'Who the hell are Jade and Lloyd?'

'Friends of mine. Jade's American, but she's lived in England for years. You met them at the funeral.'

'Lloyd?' Iain stroked his jaw pensively. 'You don't mean that fellow with long hair and beads who looked like a refugee from the sixties?'

Phaedra made a clicking sound with her tongue. 'I suppose you could describe him that way.'

'What other way is there? And didn't his wife – lover – whatever she is, dress the same way he did, so it was impossible to tell which was the woman?'

'You're beginning to sound like your father going on about Anton. And Lloyd has a beard. Jade doesn't.'

Iain shrugged. 'Makes no difference. I certainly wouldn't trust either of them with the house.'

'Why not? Just because Lloyd doesn't dress in power suits and conservative ties, the way you do? You weren't so conventional in the old days.'

'Wasn't I?' Her judgement irritated him, although he couldn't have said why. But he was damned if he was going to let her win this round. He hadn't taken to that hairy creep who had grabbed her in an octopus-like hug. 'I suppose I must be feeling the weight of my years then,' he said, knowing he sounded stuffy enough to be his own grandfather. 'The point is, I don't want any middle-aged ragamuffins looking after Chy an Cleth. They'll have the place reeking of pot in no time. Or worse.'

'No, they won't. They both gave up smoking it years ago.'

'I don't care. They're not the kind of tenants we need. You must see that.'

'No, I don't see that. They're kind, friendly people struggling to support themselves with their art. She paints, he's a sculptor. And they're paying exorbitant rent for a horrible, pokey little cottage with no heat. If they came here Lloyd could fix up the conservatory as a studio. And –'

'I don't want the conservatory fixed up as a studio.'

'Why not? No one's grown anything in there for years.'

'No. I won't have it. We'll get a good, reliable person through the rental agency. Someone like your mother –'

'You're prejudiced,' Phaedra accused. 'Just because they're artists doesn't mean they won't take care of the house. Jade actually likes cleaning. She says pushing a Hoover gives her time to think. And Lloyd is good at fixing things –'

'I'll bet.'

'Iain! He unplugged the drains for us last year when your father threw a tantrum and dumped two full bottles of pills and his toothbrush down the lavatory. And he fixed our toaster, and laid new tiles in the main bathroom –'

Iain held up his hands. 'OK, OK. He's a genius with a tool kit and she's the Einstein of the Hoovering set. I'd still prefer someone with references –'

'You want references? Right.'

He sat back and watched, bemused, as Phaedra sprang to her feet and stamped across the room to his father's desk. Muttering under her breath – he distinguished the words 'fuddy duddy', 'fossil' and 'stuffed-shirt' – she rolled up the lid and rustled furiously through a pile of old letters and bills, eventually coming up with the remains of a lined yellow pad.

Iain eyed the jumble of papers without enthusiasm. He would have to go through that lot one of these days and sort it into 'rubbish', 'file' and 'fix'. Maybe he'd bring Caroline down to do it for him. If he asked Phaedra, in the mood she was in now she'd be more than capable of filing 'fix' under 'rubbish'.

He watched her pick up a pen and begin scribbling on the pad with sour-faced concentration. The moment she finished, she ripped off the top sheet and marched back to wave it under his nose. 'Here.' She flapped it at him, the movement of air fanning his face. 'Here's your reference. Satisfied?'

Iain glanced at it, took in her angrily scrawled signature, and sighed. 'Phaedra, I know you mean well –'

'Don't patronize me. I don't want your house, but at least give me credit for caring about it almost as much as you do.'

He regarded her flushed cheeks and sparking eyes with a mixture of impatience and admiration. She wanted to spit in his eye, that much was obvious. But she was managing to hold on to her temper. Although, as usual, she was certain she was right. No wonder she'd gone into teaching. But he wasn't a pupil in her charge, and he still didn't like the idea of that scruffy-looking fellow living in his house. If Phaedra thought that made him like his father – well, the old man hadn't *always* been wrong.

Phaedra rattled her 'reference' again, and he remembered that if it hadn't been for her, Chy an Cleth would now belong to Peter Sharkey. He took the paper from her and laid it on the sofa without looking at it.

'Look,' he said. 'Since I can't accept your gift, and you won't accept my money, we'll have to compromise.'

'Will we? I don't see why.'

'All right, *I*'ll have to compromise,' he snapped.

'We'll give your friends a month's trial. If they don't work out, we'll get rid of them.'

'Oh? What do you have in mind? Rat poison? Or a nice line in bombs or machetes?'

Iain shook his head and gave her a look that made her scoot briskly out of his reach. Good. He wasn't a violent man by nature, but there were times when he wished the caveman era hadn't ended. Especially when Phaedra Pendenning stood glaring at him with her chin pointed like an arrow, looking so bright-eyed and cocky and sexy that he wanted to grab her around the hips, haul her down on to his knees and kiss that tight little smirk right off her face.

He wasn't going to do it though. Glancing at his watch, he asked pointedly, 'Do you use that tongue of yours to sharpen knives?' She opened her mouth, but he carried on before she could get a word in. 'And speaking of knives, isn't it time you started thinking about lunch?'

Phaedra stopped smirking. He waited, enjoying the way the buttons on her blouse lifted with each indignant breath. But to his surprise and – yes, he had to admit it – disappointment, she didn't attempt to retaliate by telling him to do his own damn cooking. Instead, she tossed her head theatrically and stalked off in the direction of the kitchen.

Iain watched her leave. She stalked well. Those long legs of hers gave her an advantage. He stretched, and got up to follow, but when she stopped suddenly and turned to look over her shoulder, he only just had time to wipe the smile of weary admiration off his face.

What was the use of scoring points in this game of Aggravation they were playing when he suspected neither of them was going to end up a winner.

Phaedra folded her grey pleated skirt, laid it on top of her suitcase and looked around for the grey cardigan that went with it.

'You ought to wear reds and royal blues. Not that mousy old grey all the time,' a woman's voice said from behind her.

Phaedra straightened and sat down on her daffodil quilt. There was no mistaking that voice, or the sandalwood smell that always heralded Jade's arrival.

'You're a fine one to talk,' Phaedra said. 'I've never seen you wear anything but biscuit-coloured caftans or jeans with paint-spattered smocks.'

Jade laughed. 'Sure, but that's me. That's my style. You don't have a style.'

Phaedra thought about that. Maybe her friend was right. 'Don't I?' she asked.

Something in her tone must have alerted Jade to the possibility that her words could be hurtful, because she said at once, 'Hey, I didn't mean that the way it sounded. It's just that you're so – well, attractive. You ought to make the best of yourself, Phay.'

Iain had said something like that once. But she didn't believe it was her lack of style that had sent him hurtling so precipitately back to London once they had settled the matter of the care and protection of the house.

Over lunch that day he had reluctantly agreed that Jade and Lloyd could stay until Christmas. Immediately afterwards he had left on the pretext of urgent work in town.

Since then he had phoned only twice. Once to find out if Jade and Lloyd had actually moved in, and again to ask when Phaedra expected to return to her school. They hadn't talked for long on either occasion, and he had given no indication that he planned to be in Cornwall in the near future.

As Jade continued to prop herself in the doorway, Phaedra gazed through the window at the pewter-grey clouds gathering on the horizon. She didn't like the look of them against the ice blue of the chilly September sky. It was going to rain again. Dropping the lid of her suitcase over her pile of drab clothes, she turned round to answer her friend.

'There's not much point in attracting a bunch of giggling schoolgirls,' she explained. 'Besides, Miss Carter wouldn't like it. Neither would I.'

'Who's Miss Carter?' Jade hitched up her caftan and plumped herself into the yellow brocade chair.

'The Head. She keeps an eagle eye open for hanky-panky in the dorms. Not that she really needs to worry. Most of the girls are obsessively heterosexual by the time I get them.'

Jade grinned. 'I remember those days, and thank the Lord they're over. Are you really looking forward to getting back to teaching? Now that *would* be my idea of purgatory.'

Phaedra laughed. 'Believe it or not, I am. Just think, by tomorrow night I'll be miles away from the sea, surrounded by . . .' She paused as the sound of hammering started up directly beneath her feet.

'Don't worry,' Jade said. 'It's only Lloyd. The light fixture in our bedroom came loose.'

'Oh. Good. I mean it's good he's fixing it.' Phaedra bent down to snap the locks on her suitcase. 'There. That's that. Now all I have to do is – well, say goodbye to Mum.'

Jade nodded. 'You go on, then. I'll fix supper.'

'Thanks, but Mum's making Welsh rarebit. It was one of my favourites as a kid.'

Jade smiled her understanding. In Esther's eyes, her daughter would always be a child. All five foot eight of her.

Ten minutes later Phaedra, in jeans and a navy blue pullover, was ploughing her way against the ever-present wind along the cliffs. She had one final pilgrimmage to make before she saw her mother.

The wind had grown stronger by the time she rounded the headland and came to the big rock above the cove. She hadn't been here since the day of Charles's funeral when she had looked down to see Iain standing alone among the rocks, a part of the wildness from which she half-believed he came.

There was no sign of life down there today. Only the waves and spray dancing over the rocks. The spot where Iain had stood was invisible now behind the fine mist thrown up by the sea.

He was gone, her Iain. Gone from her life. For good. When, eventually, he came to his senses and accepted her gift of his house – or she came to hers and allowed him to salvage his pride by buying it back from her at a nominal price – she would have no further contact with the man who was the reason why, at the ripe old age of twenty-seven, she had never had a serious relationship.

For a long time she had refused to accept that shattering truth, had hoped the fire in her blood would fizzle and turn out to be no more than a belated attack of lust. Now she knew better.

The knowledge hadn't come to her all at once, but gradually, borne out by all the little reminders around the house. An empty chair at the table, an unused package of pasta, the smell of strong coffee in the morning – even the sight of turnips at the greengrocer's – brought back the memory of Iain's teasing laughter and all the past years they had shared.

She loved him for more than his body – had fought to save Chy an Cleth for love of the boy he had been.

For her there had never been anyone but Iain.

It wasn't the same for him. She understood that. He would never feel anything for her beyond mild attraction and an affection based on an old and fading habit. If she had meant any more to him than that, he wouldn't have gone rushing back to town.

Phaedra picked up a small stone and flung it at the rocks. He must lead a very glamorous life up there in London. A life into which she wouldn't fit. Not even if she changed her style of dressing. It would take more than reds and royal blues to hold Iain's interest for long.

Wrapping her arms around her chest to defeat the wind, Phaedra tore her gaze from the deserted cove and struggled back along the cliffs to Porthkelly.

By the time she reached her mother's house the pewter clouds were directly overhead and it was raining.

Esther, watching the downward droop of her daughter's mouth, reached automatically for a cigarette.

'Mum! You said you'd given up smoking.'

Quickly Esther pushed the package behind the bowl of fresh-cut purple dahlias Angus had brought her that morning from his garden. 'I have,' she said. 'Most of the time.'

'Oh, Mum!'

Esther sighed. Phaedra worried about her, she knew. But she did hate being nagged about her smoking. It was easier to pretend she meant to quit. At least it was as long as she remembered to keep her habit out of sight.

'I just wanted to get your attention,' she said defensively. It was partly true. Phaedra had been distracted and inattentive all evening.

The Welsh rarebit had been consumed with appreciation, the dishes put away, and now the two of them were sitting at the kitchen table talking desultorily, and listening to the rain splatter on the roof.

'You don't have to *smoke* to get my attention,' Phaedra said.

'Well, I have to do something, dear. You've been brooding all evening. Don't you want to go back to your job?'

'Oh yes,' Phaedra replied without enthusiasm. 'Of course I do.'

'But you don't really want to leave Porthkelly? Is that it?' Esther probed worriedly. She hoped that was it, but she didn't think so.

'I don't mind. Except about leaving you.'

Phaedra had always been a kind child, bless her. 'Is it Iain then?'

'Iain is in London.'

Esther reached for the cigarette package, saw Phaedra's eyes follow the movement of her hands, and changed her mind. 'So he is,' she said. 'Are you in love with him?'

'Oh, Mum!' Phaedra's smile quivered the way it always did when she wanted to conceal her feelings. Esther wasn't for one moment deceived.

'You are, then. I was afraid of that.'

Phaedra fidgeted with a corner of the mat beneath the dahlias. 'Am I that transparent?' When no answer was forthcoming, she said, 'Oh, all right. Yes, I suppose I am. In love with him, that is. I'll get over it.'

Would she? Would Phaedra get over it?

'Trebanians!' Esther muttered without thinking. 'They've always been the curse as well as the blessing of us Pendennings.'

Phaedra blinked, her wide mouth stretching in

166

surprise. 'Why? Why do you say that, Mum? Mr . . . I mean, Charles was always good to us in his way. He wasn't much of a curse.'

Esther shrugged, thought about the cigarettes, and fanned herself with an advertisement for a new muscle relaxant instead. 'No reason. I lost my train of thought.'

'But . . . you never do that. Your mind always goes in a straight line.'

Did Phaedra really believe that? Yes, perhaps she did. Children always saw their parents through a distorting mirror.

'I'm not getting any younger, you know,' she pointed out.

Her remark about the Trebanians had been unfortunate. There was nothing to be gained from dwelling on the past, no point in adding to Phaedra's problems. But she could see only too well what was happening.

History had a habit of repeating itself.

She didn't like history. Not any more. Phaedra might be able to lose herself in the real and bloody battles of other years, just as she had once lost herself in the myths and magic and legends of ancient Greece. But it was better to forget what had gone before. Better not to dream of myths and magic.

She had named her daughter for a myth that appeared to be taking on a lamentable aspect of reality.

Phaedra's head was bent as if she were studying the residue of coffee in her cup. 'What is it?' Esther asked sharply. 'Is there something else?'

'No. It's just that – I don't want you to grow old, Mum. You're all I have.'

There was a ring of such desolation in her voice that Esther wanted to kick herself. What was the matter with her, complaining about her age when her only child was leaving town tomorrow?

'I'll be around for a long time yet,' she said bracingly. 'You needn't doubt that. Besides, you have your friends. And one day there's bound to be a man who loves you.' She hoped that was true. Everyone needed someone. Especially when they were young. She knew what it was like to be alone.

'Not everyone gets married, Mum. Not any more.'

Esther thought of Francis Pendenning. Not with regret, but with a kind of nostalgia for the lost dreams of youth. 'And a good thing too,' she agreed. 'But *you* will.'

'Maybe.' Phaedra made an attempt at a smile that was almost painful to watch, and Esther got up to pack a box of home-made biscuits for her to take back with her to school. She knew Phaedra wasn't a child to be consoled with biscuits any longer. But she was a mother, and she didn't know what else to do.

If only Phaedra wasn't so obstinately independent. If only she would accept at least some of the money Charles had left her. Money wouldn't buy her happiness, but it would enable her to travel, to meet some nice young man who wasn't a Trebanian . . .

Fifteen minutes later she watched her daughter's slim figure disappear through the pink archway to the street.

'Poor girl,' Esther muttered. She plodded into the bedroom that the rental agency had called 'conveniently compact'. It was cold in the flat all of a sudden. She pulled a soft blue sweater out of a drawer, kicked off her shoes and sank on to the edge of the bed. Lord, she was tired . . .

When she caught sight of her reflection in the mirror on the door, she made a face. How old and flabby she looked. Not that there was anyone to look at her any more . . .

'Stop feeling sorry for yourself, Esther Pendenning,' she said out loud. 'There's always –'

As if on cue, the phone rang.

'Angus,' she finished, rolling her eyeballs at the ceiling as she reached for the receiver.

CHAPTER 7

'Bye, Miss Pendenning. Are you going home for half-term too?'

Phaedra nodded at the big, gangly girl with the glasses who was charging at the school's front door as if she were a battering ram expecting opposition. 'Yes, I am, Jennifer. And slow down, please. No running in the halls. Don't worry, your mother isn't going to leave without you.'

Jennifer grinned sheepishly. 'Sorry, Miss Pendenning. Have a nice holiday.'

'Thank you, Jennifer.' Phaedra watched, smiling as the big girl restrained herself with an effort and proceeded at a borderline jog. She had a special place in her heart for Jennifer Reilly, a school misfit as she herself had been. Jennifer was an enthusiastic, if unfocused, scholar, but she couldn't throw or hit a ball to save her life. As a result she suffered from merciless teasing about her clumsiness and size. No wonder she looked forward to the respite of half-term.

Phaedra wished *she* could feel that kind of enthusiasm for these holidays. But they wouldn't be the same this year. Charles was dead, her mother no longer lived at Chy an Cleth, and Jade and Lloyd were spending the weekend in London. The house would seem empty, full of ghosts. Her mother had said she could stay with her, but there was so little space in the small flat that Phaedra knew she would be an inconvenience. So, she guessed resignedly, would her unerring nose for smoke.

She sighed and went to finish packing her suitcase.

It was close to nine o'clock by the time she arrived in Porthkelly. Her suitcase wasn't heavy, but her mother had made her promise to take a taxi from the bus stop.

'Times have changed, Phaedra. Even in Porthkelly. It's not safe to walk alone in the dark,' Esther had fussed when she'd phoned the night before. 'And don't forget to call me when you arrive.'

Phaedra had promised she wouldn't.

As the wheels of the taxi spun off into the night, she leaned on the gate and gazed up at the dark bulk of the house massively outlined against the stars.

Chy an Cleth. Phaedra breathed in the blessed air of the only permanent home she had ever known. How she would miss it when the time came to hand it over to Iain. There had been a time, once, when he would have insisted it was as much her home as his. Not any more. Because of what she had done for him, Iain no longer wanted her in his life. He hadn't said so, but she knew it was the truth.

Phaedra sighed and started up the driveway, ready now to exchange the early winter chill for warmth and light.

She had almost reached the door before it came to her that something wasn't as it should be. There were lights on, not just in the hall as she'd expected, but in the dining-room and one of the bedrooms as well.

She hesitated, tightening her grip on the handle of her suitcase. Had Jade left the extra lights on by mistake? Or to deter would-be burglars? Or was a would-be burglar already in the house? She stared at the lighted windows and shivered slightly. It was colder out tonight than she had thought.

Now what? Should she return to the town and alert the police – undoubtedly what her mother would tell her to do – or sneak quietly in and confront what would probably turn out to be an empty house before whoever wasn't there had a chance to get away?

Phaedra wrinkled her nose as common sense came to her rescue. She was making a production out of nothing. There was nobody in the house. Jade had just decided to leave the lights on.

Taking a quick breath, she hefted her suitcase, climbed boldly up the steps and inserted her key in the lock. Of course there was no one in the house.

The door gave a small creak, and Phaedra flinched.

It was glaringly bright in the hall after the winter darkness outside. Bright, familiar, hospitable and – she gasped and put a hand to her throat.

A slim, red-haired woman in grey wool trousers and a mint-green blouse was swinging gracefully

172

down the stairs. Waiting for her at the bottom was a man.

He had his back to the door, and he was wearing hip-hugging jeans and a dark green, polo-necked sweater. Phaedra was used to seeing that particular back in a well-cut executive suit, but she would have recognized it even in a toga.

She closed the front door with a snap.

The red-haired woman saw her first, and paused with her foot on the bottom step.

Iain's shoulders stiffened when he heard the door, but by the time he turned to face her any sign of surprise had been erased.

'Hello, Phaedra,' he said, giving her the full benefit of his devastating smile. 'What brings you to Porthkelly?'

Phaedra swallowed. No one had a right to smile like that. It wasn't fair.

Their eyes met and she took a step forward. When he held out his hand, she wanted to hurl herself across the floor and into his arms. But the redhead coughed discreetly, and Phaedra guessed that Iain's arms had recently been otherwise engaged.

'It's half-term,' she said tiredly. 'Where else would I go? You didn't tell me you meant to be here.'

'I didn't mean to be here. Not until your mother phoned and said the house would be unoccupied because our oh-so-reliable caretakers were heading for the bright lights of London.' He put his hands in his pockets, causing his jeans to cling even more snugly to his hips, and gave her a look that positively dared her to make excuses for her friends.

Phaedra wasn't interested in making excuses that in her view weren't needed in the first place. Only one thing Iain had said held any significance.

She dropped her suitcase on to the floor with a thud. 'My mother? Did you say she knew you were coming?'

'I did. She thought I ought to be aware that our blessed tenants would be away.' He draped himself against the bannister, his back to the redhead, who was busily examining her nails. Pink pearl and long, Phaedra noted.

'Oh.' She digested that. 'But – didn't Mum tell you I'd be here?'

Iain picked a strand of red hair off his sleeve. 'Apparently not.'

'You must have known it was half-term.' Phaedra flexed her fingers. The suitcase had been heavier than she thought.

'To be honest,' Iain said with a shrug, 'it's been some years since I paid much attention to the vagaries of the school system.'

Phaedra frowned. That *sounded* reasonable enough . . .

But it was too much. She was tired, she was heartsick, as she hadn't allowed herself to be in weeks, and now she would have to spend the night with her meddling mother. Esther had undoubtedly meant well, but it was certain she hadn't counted on Iain's svelte redhead turning up.

'Aren't you going to introduce me to your friend?' she asked, covering her hurt with what she hoped was a smile.

'Yes, of course. Forgive me, this is Caroline, my secretary. Caroline, I'd like to introduce you to my stepmother.'

Damn him. Damn and blast him. Did he have to keep harping on that? 'Iain,' she snapped, attempting to put her feelings into words he couldn't fail to understand, 'I've had about enough . . .'

She stopped. Iain was grinning. And Caroline was biting her lip.

'I was teasing,' he said mildly. 'Caroline, this is Phaedra, whose son I most definitely am not.'

'How do you do.' Caroline came the rest of the way down the stairs. 'I hope Mr Trebanian and I aren't interfering with your plans.' She extended her long, beautifully manicured hand.

Phaedra eyed her narrowly. The woman sounded sincere. There was no malice in the blue eyes behind the expertly mascara'd lashes, no hostile edge to her voice.

'It's not your fault,' she said. 'Obviously my mother made a mistake.'

Esther had done nothing of the sort, of course. She had orchestrated this embarrassing mess single-handed and with the best of intentions. Wanting only to make her daughter happy, she had succeeded in making an already awkward situation worse.

'Oh dear.' Caroline was sympathetic. 'I am sorry. We'll try not to get in your way, though.

Mr Trebanian asked me to come down to help him organize his father's papers. We started on them just this afternoon.'

'You won't be in my way,' Phaedra said. 'I'll call a taxi and go to my mother's.'

'You'll do nothing of the sort,' Iain said. 'If there was any question of a taxi, I'd drive you. However –'

'You don't have a car. I'd have seen it.'

'We didn't fly down on my magic carpet. I brought the Bentley. It's in the garage. Which is entirely irrelevant because you're not going anywhere. Your mother will probably be in bed.'

'No, she won't. She's waiting for me to let her know I've arrived.'

'Then you'd better do it.' Iain, she could tell, was losing patience.

He was also right about the call to her mother. Averting her eyes from the two at the bottom of the stairs, Phaedra stalked over to the phone and dialled the number.

'I'm here, Mum,' she announced when Esther answered. 'At Chy an Cleth. But Iain's here too with his – um, secretary. So if it's not too much trouble, I think I'll stay with you?'

Esther had barely managed to mumble, 'Yes, of course, dear, but . . .' before Iain was grabbing the receiver from Phaedra's hand.

'Pendy,' he said. 'It's all right. Phaedra's staying here. She'll be over to see you in the morning. Don't worry, I'll look after her.' He hung up, then continued as if he'd done her a favour, 'That's settled then. Your mother is expecting you in the morning. She *was* in bed, by the way.'

Phaedra gaped at him, speechless. How could he, how *could* he expect her to stay in the house he was sharing with his girlfriend? Had he completely forgotten the kiss they had shared? The kiss that had shattered her self-delusions and awoken her to the knowledge that she loved him? Or had it meant so little to him that he had no way of understanding that to stay under the same roof with him and Caroline would be torture?

'I . . . the Spotted Dog,' she said in a strangled voice. 'I can stay there.'

'Oh, please,' Caroline said. 'You mustn't leave on our account. There's no reason why we should get in each other's way. Iain and I will be busy with his papers, and you'll be visiting your mother –'

'Of course she's not leaving,' Iain interrupted. 'We've finished our supper, Phaedra, but there's some leftover Chinese in the fridge. Why don't you help yourself? Then when you're ready you can join us for coffee.'

Just like that. As if her unexpected intrusion into his love nest was on a par with a visit from a kindly but dotty maiden aunt who wouldn't understand what was going on. Well, she wasn't dotty, and she knew exactly what was going on. But she couldn't let him guess how she felt, couldn't let him see her desperation. Perhaps it *would* be best to stay one night. She could always find somewhere else tomorrow.

'All right,' she said. 'Thank you.'

'Good girl.' Iain bent to pick up her case. 'You go and eat, then. Caroline will show you.'

'Do you want me to show you?' Caroline asked, as Iain disappeared up the stairs.

'No, thanks. I know where the fridge is.'

Caroline nodded. 'I thought you might.' She gave Phaedra the ghost of a smile. 'Mr Trebanian likes to give orders, but they're not always necessary.'

'No.' Phaedra started towards the kitchen. 'His father was like that.'

It wasn't until she was seated at the table, consuming a glutinous meal of soggy stir-fryed vegetables and rice that it occurred to her to wonder why Caroline called her lover 'Mr Trebanian'.

Kooky, she decided, swallowing another tasteless forkful of rice. Like something out of Dickens. Not that she cared about their sexual fantasies, or what went on behind their bedroom door. Why should she? What difference did it make?

She was wiping a teardrop off the edge of her plate when Iain came in to say the coffee was getting cold.

'Soya sauce goes better,' he said gravely, eyeing the teardrop. 'Want me to get you some?'

'No, thanks. I've finished.' She kept her gaze firmly on the remains of what had passed for her supper.

'Then come and have coffee.'

'I will in a minute.' If only he'd go away. He probably knew she'd been crying, but that didn't mean she wanted to give him a full frontal of her damp and swollen face.

178

Iain, as usual, took matters into his own hands. 'What's this?' he asked, coming to stand over her. 'Tears, Phaedra?'

She shook her head. 'No. I think I've got a bit of a cold.'

'Ah. I see. Tell me . . .' he snapped his fingers around her wrists and hauled her without ceremony to her feet '. . . have you given any thought to bringing this nonsense to an end?'

'What?' Startled, achingly aware of his touch, all Phaedra could think of was that if he didn't let go of her at once she was going to make a terrible exhibition of herself. The scent of his beautiful body was working a subtle and deadly magic on her senses.

'Are you going to let me pay you for the house?' he said, as if he were explaining the obvious to a child.

A sudden gust of wind rattled the windows. 'No. No thought at all.' Phaedra spoke with false lightness. 'When I give someone a present, it's for keeps.'

Iain dropped her wrists and curled his fingers over the back of the nearest chair. 'I'm not just "someone". And you can't equate Chy an Cleth with a box of cigars or a new book. A house isn't something you can gift wrap.'

'No. And I haven't tried to wrap it. It's yours, free and clear.'

Iain's mouth flattened briefly. 'All right. I suppose that's why we have your damned artist friends in residence. But come Christmas I want the matter settled.' He leaned forward until his nose was almost touching hers. 'By the way, do you have any idea why your mother didn't tell me you were coming?'

Phaedra tried to step back, but the table was in the way. She had never grown used to Iain's habit of changing the subject without warning. But she had known him too long to waste time making up stories there wasn't a chance he would believe.

'I think,' she said, her gaze on the soft, green collar of his sweater, 'that Mum hoped proximity would lead to –'

'Bed?' he suggested. 'How fortunate, then, that I brought Caroline.'

'Yes –' Phaedra nodded '– isn't it.' She closed her eyes and turned blindly in the direction of what she thought was the kitchen door. It turned out to be the fridge.

'Ouch,' she moaned, rubbing her head where it had connected with a hard chrome corner.

'For heaven's sake!' exclaimed Iain, grabbing her by the hips and marching her out into the hall. 'Don't tell me you're still running into furniture.'

'Not usually,' she said, fighting to catch her breath as the feel of his big hands sent desire rocketing up through her body, adding fuel to the fire already smouldering in her veins.

'Good. In that case I suppose it's safe to let you loose on the drawing-room.'

He released her, and she stumbled the last few steps on her own.

Caroline was seated on the settee, pouring coffee from a white china pot with a delicate design of gold leaves. That pot had been in use at Chy an Cleth for as far back as Phaedra could remember, but it seemed odd, wrong somehow, to see Caroline presiding over it.

She accepted a cup with mumbled thanks and sat cradling it in her hands as if its warmth could in some way help to dispel the air of tension in the room. When the clock struck, she and Caroline glanced at each other and looked away.

'We've made some progress with Dad's papers, as you can see.' Iain, who was still standing by the door, gestured at Charles's open desk.

A definite improvement, Phaedra saw at once. On one side of the desk top two neat piles of paper awaited Iain's attention or disposal. On the other, wooden pigeon holes bulged with statements, receipts, bills and the detritus of a lifetime of banking. A wicker basket on the floor was filled almost to overflowing.

So they really were dealing with Charles's papers. Iain and Caroline must be very close.

'It's been a long day,' Phaedra said, abruptly putting down her cup. 'If you don't mind, I think I'll go to bed.'

'Of course,' Caroline said at once. 'We won't be much longer either. Will we, Mr Trebanian?'

'Probably not,' Iain replied laconically. 'Neither of us slept much last night. Sweet dreams, Phaedra.'

'Goodnight,' she said, and scurried from the room.

Sweet dreams? When she was little, Iain had always said that to her at bedtime. This time he

181

probably meant it. Or maybe he didn't care that her bedroom was right above his.

So he and Caroline hadn't slept much last night . . . Phaedra stamped up the last few steps to her room and gave the door a vicious backward kick.

Not vicious enough. As she waited for it to close, she heard Caroline say, 'Goodnight, Mr Trebanian. I'll see you in the morning.' Her rather high voice carried perfectly.

Phaedra didn't hear Iain's response. Probably he was too busy hustling his secretary into bed to be bothered with putting up a smokescreen.

That night, Phaedra lay awake for some time listening to the rhythm of the sea and straining not to wince at every creak and groan of the old house that could conceivably have been made by a bed-spring.

When she finally fell asleep she didn't dream. Or if she did, her dreams were better forgotten.

In the morning, when she went downstairs, the smell of coffee met her in the hall. She followed it, humming loudly and slapping her slippers on the floor. If Iain and Caroline were breakfasting companionably in morning dishabille, for her own sake she meant to give them fair warning.

She needn't have worried. Iain, in jeans and a sweatshirt, was standing at the counter making toast. Caroline was nowhere to be seen.

'Good morning,' he said. 'Did you sleep well?'

'Very well. Did you?'

She couldn't keep the sharpness from her voice, and knew Iain had noticed it when he deserted the toast and said with a smile that made her want to scratch if off his face, 'Not as well as Caroline, I'm afraid.'

Did he have to rub Caroline in? 'Isn't she up yet?' Phaedra asked, disguising her hurt with a superior lift of her eyebrows. 'Would you like me to make you something more substantial than toast?'

'Oh, this is for you.' He flipped the toast into a rack. 'I heard you emptying the bath. Caroline and I have finished ours. She's already hard at work on Dad's papers.'

Round One to Iain. While Phaedra was trying to come up with a satisfactory answer, he went on, 'The old man never threw out a damn thing. I've found letters and receipts dating back almost sixty years. All of which have to be sorted.'

'You don't mind Caroline working on them alone?' Phaedra edged her way towards the table.

'Why should I? She's been working for me for years. A very competent lady, is Caroline.'

Phaedra didn't doubt it. Competent in more ways than one. 'I'm sure she is,' she said sweetly. 'Joan calls her your dragon lady.'

Iain shrugged. 'Unfair. Dragons can be useful at times. Here, eat your toast. Coffee's on the stove. I'm going to see how she's getting on.'

Phaedra watched him go, hating the thought of Caroline looking through her dead husband's papers. But Charles hadn't been a real husband. Iain, as his son, had every right to handle his father's affairs as he saw fit.

At least he hadn't burnt the toast.

Phaedra delayed as long as she could over breakfast. Her mother wasn't an early riser any more, and she didn't want to disturb her before eleven.

In the end curiousity, and sheer bloody-mindedness, got the better of her. This was still her house, since Iain had refused to accept it. Why *should* he and Caroline have it to themselves?

When she pushed open the drawing-room door, she found Iain standing beside Caroline with his hand lightly touching her shoulder and his cheek bent close to her hair.

They were studying what looked like a photograph.

Jealousy, black and unattractive, twisted deep in Phaedra's chest. Had she really married a man she didn't love for the sake of that dark-haired devil currently breathing sweet-nothings into the gracious Caroline's ear?

'Well, well,' she said brightly. 'Busy as bees, I see.'

Iain looked up as though he'd forgotten who she was. 'Oh. Phaedra,' he said, taking the photograph from Caroline. 'Off to see your mother now, are you?'

Iain wasn't a man she would ever have characterized as shifty. But the look in his eyes was definitely evasive. 'What's the photograph?' she asked, trying without success to forget the intimate little scene she had just witnessed.

'Nothing that would interest you,' Iain said. 'Just some people my father must have known.'

Caroline turned to look up at him, blue eyes wide and surprised 'But, Mr Trebanian, it's –'

'Just a photograph,' Iain said. 'So you're off now, are you, Phaedra?'

'You already said that. Yes, I'm off. In a while. After I've had a look at that photo you don't want me to see.' Iain's determination to be rid of her was enough to convince Phaedra that she wasn't going anywhere until she'd seen whatever it was he was trying to hide.

She crossed the room, held out her hand and said in her best schoolmistress voice, 'All right, hand it over.'

Iain's lips twitched. 'I'm glad I'm not one of her pupils, aren't you?' he said to Caroline. 'We wouldn't get away with much in her classroom.'

Caroline smiled. 'And a good thing too. I expect Phaedra's a very good teacher.'

Phaedra leaned over the back of Charles's chair. Did the woman mean it? She actually seemed to like her. But of course that was only because she didn't know about the kiss.

'Thank you,' she said, acknowledging the compliment. 'Yes, I am a good teacher. Iain, can I please see that photo?'

'I'd rather you didn't.' He spoke in the final tone of voice that had worked so well when she'd been a ten-year-old child who adored him. It had little effect on the twenty-seven-year-old woman she had become.

'Why?' she asked. Iain had always been fair. If there was a reason she shouldn't see his precious photograph, she might be willing to accept it.

'Because I don't want you to,' he said.

'That's not an answer.' She made a grab for the photo.

Iain held it above his head. 'Isn't it? All right then – because I don't want to see you hurt. Is that better?'

'Hurt? That doesn't make sense.' She was hurting already. What more could an old photograph do?

Impatience flared in his eyes, and Phaedra knew she'd won. 'Fine,' he said. 'Have it your own way. But don't say I didn't warn you.'

She held out her hand.

He gave it to her with a shrug, and, suddenly wary, she smiled and accepted it gingerly.

It was a black and white photograph, cracked diagonally across the middle, of two people standing against a background of flowers. The man had his arm around the woman's waist, and she was gazing up at him with a look whose meaning had been clear since the beginning of time. He was staring straight ahead, not looking at her. Behind them, unmistakable, was the Eiffel Tower.

Phaedra's smile wilted like a leaf in autumn as she studied the faces of the two lovers. For a moment the walls of the room slipped out of focus and dissolved. The photograph fluttered from her fingers.

The man in the picture was her dead husband, Charles Trebanian.

The woman was her mother.

CHAPTER 8

Wind gusted through the open windows of Esther's flat, flapping the curtains and rustling the pages of the well-thumbed Sunday paper on the kitchen table. She shivered, and dodged into the bedroom to fetch a cardigan. It was ridiculous what she went through to keep her daughter from finding out that she'd been smoking – especially as Phaedra always knew anyway, and if the smoke didn't kill her the cold would.

She shivered and wrapped her arms around her chest. If Phaedra brought Iain with her this morning, she would know her little strategem was working. Iain would be a good husband once he made up his mind to it. *If* he made up his mind. The trouble was, he saw only what he wanted to see. Just like his father before him.

Stifling a sigh, she went to put on the kettle. Any minute now, Phaedra would be here.

A blast of wind blew the newspaper on to the floor and set the clear plastic cover over the ceiling light rattling up and down in its frame. Muttering, Esther put her hand to her back and bent to pick up the paper. When she straightened, slowly, she decided she'd had enough of fresh air and stamped off to shut all the windows.

A light tap sounded on the door just as she had the last awkward catch wrestled into place.

Phaedra. She was here. Beaming a welcome, she bustled into the hall.

'Hello, Mum.' Phaedra spoke in a stiff little voice that instantly put Esther on her guard.

Oh, oh. Had her innocent attempt to play match-maker gone awry? Phaedra didn't look happy. And she *hadn't* brought Iain with her.

'Hello, dear. Lovely to see you. Aren't you going to give me a kiss?' Esther lifted her cheek.

'Yes, of course.' Phaedra bent down and gave her a hasty peck – not the enthusiastic hug she'd been anticipating.

'I've put the kettle on. Would you like tea or coffee?' Esther asked. No sense trying to find out what was wrong until both of them were well fortified with caffeine.

'Coffee, thanks.' Phaedra trailed into the kitchen and threw her jacket over the back of a chair. 'I'll make it.'

Esther sank down thankfully, watching her daughter as she took out the coffee-maker and set cups and saucers on the table. Her movements were listless, automatic, as if she were miles away and half-asleep.

This didn't look hopeful. Not hopeful at all. Phaedra had always been dreamy, but not like this.

'Is something the matter?' she asked, as the first aromatic drops sizzled into the pot.

'It's cold in here,' Phaedra answered obliquely.

'I know. I've just closed the windows.'

'Oh.'

Oh? That was all? Wasn't she even going to ask why the windows had been open in the first place?

'What is it, dear?' Esther asked anxiously. 'I don't mean to interfere, but –'

'Mum, don't. You know you *did* mean to interfere.' Phaedra didn't turn round. Her attention seemed riveted on the rapidly filling pot.

Esther eyed her daughter's drooping figure with misgiving. 'Yes, well, perhaps I did,' she admitted. 'But I only meant to help. I thought if you and Iain could spend some time together . . .' She broke off as a frightening thought came to her. 'Phaedra! He didn't – you didn't –'

'What? Sleep with Iain? Wasn't that the whole idea?'

'What?' Esther put her hands to her head to ease the instant throbbing in her temples. Surely this young woman with the bitter-sounding voice couldn't be the lovable little girl she had raised. She sat up straight and scooped a speck of dust from the corner of her eye. 'No, dear, it wasn't,' she said firmly. 'You're both adults, and naturally I trusted you not to do anything foolish. But you and Iain have always been such friends. I thought if you had a chance to talk things over, he would realize – well, that Charles was right.'

'Right?' Phaedra gripped the handle of the pot but she didn't turn around.

'Angus told me. That Charles wanted you and Iain to marry.'

'Oh. Yes. That's what Iain said. He didn't know his own son very well, did he?'

So cold, so passionless. Almost as if it didn't matter. Esther, still chilled herself, buttoned her cardigan up to the neck. 'No, I'm afraid he didn't,' she agreed. When Phaedra said nothing, she carried on, 'It's not impossible though, is it? There are worse things to base a marriage on than friendship.'

'Friendship? I expect you're right. Only Iain's not interested in marriage. Certainly not to me.'

'Why do you say that? Have you asked him?'

'Asked him to marry me?' Phaedra swung round so fast, still holding the pot, that a stream of coffee splashed on to the counter. 'Of course I haven't. He thought I gave him the house as a kind of blackmail. Not as effective as telling him I was pregnant, of course, but –'

'Phaedra! Surely you've told him it isn't true?'

'Oh, yes.' She poured coffee into the two cups on the table.

Esther breathed deeply, taking comfort from the familiar aroma. 'Didn't he believe you?'

'I think so. In the end. But it made no difference.'

'You can't be sure –'

'Mum! I can be sure. I *am* sure.' Phaedra slammed the pot down and slumped into a chair. 'You shouldn't have meddled. Iain came down with his secretary. And she's *nice*.'

'His secretary?' Esther fidgeted with her buttons. Oh, what she wouldn't give for a cigarette! 'But surely that doesn't mean –?'

'Yes, it does. She's gorgeous. They came down on Friday and she's staying with him. At Chy an Cleth.' Phaedra stared down into her cup as if it she expected it to divulge the meaning of her life.

'Oh. I see.' Esther swallowed a mouthful of coffee and tried not to choke. 'I am sorry, dear. If I'd known . . . But, of course, I didn't. I wanted to help.'

'I know.' Phaedra raised her head as if it weighed a ton. 'Mum . . .?'

'Yes, dear?'

'They – Iain and Caroline – were looking through Charles's old desk.'

Esther nodded. Phaedra wanted to change the subject. Perhaps it *was* best. For the moment.

'I suppose it had to be done some time,' she said. 'Not a task I'd look forward to myself. That was one place Charles never let me tidy.'

'Do you have any idea what he kept there?' Phaedra asked.

Esther had a feeling the question wasn't nearly as casual as it sounded. 'Bills,' she said. 'Receipts, I suppose. Old letters. Articles he cut out of the paper so he could grumble about them later. Anything he didn't want to throw away. Not that I ever really looked.'

'Photographs?'

'Perhaps. I know he kept photographs in those big leather albums in the library. The ones full of ancestors – and there are some of his wife, Helen, and of Iain and Joan when they were young. Why? Were you thinking of any photo in particular?'

Phaedra shook her head. 'Not really.' She swirled her coffee round the inside of her cup. 'You knew him for a long time, didn't you, Mum?'

'Charles? Yes, of course I did.' What was this all about? And why was Phaedra avoiding her eyes? 'I knew him all my life really, though I didn't start working at the house till I was twenty. He was different in those days. Softer.' Remembering, she started to smile – then saw Phaedra staring at her and quickly turned the smile into a grimace.

Phaedra lowered her eyes and said in funny, constricted voice, 'Yes, well, he would have been, wouldn't he? He was young.'

'That's true. Phaedra, what is it? Oh, my dear, don't – you're not crying . . .?'

'I'm all right.' Phaedra lifted an arm and swiped it across her eyes.

Esther bit her lip. Her child *wasn't* all right. She was desperately unhappy. And it looked as though her foolish matchmaking had only managed to add to that unhappiness. If only there was something she could do, or say, that would help. But all the old platitudes about there being other fish in the pond, and time being a great healer would only irritate. She knew. Her own mother had tried every one of them on her.

'Cake,' Esther said. 'I made a cake. Would you like some? It's chocolate.'

Phaedra sniffed, but her lip slanted up. As smiles went, it wasn't much. But it was something.

'Why not?' she said. 'It always worked when I was a kid, didn't it?'

Esther's answering smile was resigned. Phaedra always saw through her. But at least she was holding her head up, and her eyes had lost that dull, vacant look.

'That's my girl,' Esther said, and went to cut the cake.

Phaedra slipped into the house via the conservatory, hoping no one would see her come in. To her relief the hall was empty. But as she hurried up the stairs she heard voices coming from the drawing room, along with the the rustle and crackle of old paper.

So Iain and Caroline were still dealing with Charles's desk. She didn't think she could face them just yet.

The moment Iain had shown her that photograph, she had taken one look at his dark eyes flashing 'I told you so' and rushed from the room before he could say it. Her reaction had been instinctive, born of an unnamed fear she couldn't put in words.

It wasn't until she was halfway to her mother's that she allowed the full implications of what she'd seen to sink in.

Her mother and Charles. Her own husband.

Yet when she thought about it, it wasn't such an unlikely scenario. Esther must have been about thirty in the picture. By then Helen would have been dead for six years, and Francis Pendenning missing in action for two. Which would have made Iain about ten, Joan six, and she herself almost two.

It was all right. The dates were right. And packed away somewhere at the back of a drawer, she had her father's picture. Her mother had always told her she had the Pendenning mouth . . .

As her relieved breath drifted off on the wind, for a few glorious seconds Phaedra forgot all about Iain.

Imagine! Charles and her mother. What secrets had they been hiding all these years? Until today she would have sworn there had never been anything between them beyond comfortable familiarity and a lifetime of reserved, strictly platonic affection.

It was a strange thought. Strange that her mother might once have loved Charles, the man who had been her own husband. She supposed she ought to mind, but she didn't really. Her feelings about her mother and Charles were too mixed up with her feelings about Iain and the beautiful redhead he had installed at Chy an Cleth.

In the end she hadn't been able to bring herself to ask her mother directly about her relationship with Charles, and they had ended up eating chocolate cake and talking about school and the weather. After that they had gone to the Spotted Dog for lunch, and there, surrounded by old friends and acquaintances, there had been no opportunity for private conversation.

Phaedra was halfway up the stairs when Iain's voice stopped her in her tracks.

'Phaedra, is that you? Come on down when you're ready. I want to talk to you.'

'Why?' She took another step and paused with her hand on the bannister. 'What is there to talk about?'

Behind her she heard an exasperated groan. 'Are we back to that again?'

'Back to what?'

'Game playing. We've known each other too long for games, Phaedra.' He paused, then asked in a quieter, less assured tone, 'Have you seen your mother?'

'Yes, of course. She and Mr Cooper have gone into Bude to visit friends. They asked me to go with them, but I was tired.'

'At six o'clock in the evening?'

Did he *have* to sound so disbelieving? She turned to confront him, but he was smiling at her, and there was nothing worse than mild amusement in his eyes.

'I'm not very good company this evening,' she explained truthfully. 'And I think Mr Cooper wanted Mum to himself. I'm sorry if that upsets your plans.'

'What plans?' For a moment Iain looked mystified. Then his brow cleared, and he said, 'Ah. You mean *those* plans.'

Phaedra pushed at her hair. 'Yours and Caroline's,' she amended, attempting to speak naturally, and as if his plans for the evening were a matter of indifference.

Iain put a foot on the bottom step, his eyes shadowed in the dim light thrown by the wall lamps. 'I was lucky to find Caroline,' he said. 'She's one of the most versatile secretaries I've had.'

'Lucky indeed,' Phaedra gave a brittle little laugh as she turned away.

When she reached her bedroom, she slammed the door so hard that the Victorian street scene bumped against the wall.

Versatile, indeed. Yes, she just *bet* Caroline was versatile.

As for Iain – did he have to flaunt his tarts in front of her nose? Not, she supposed, that it was altogether fair to call Caroline a tart. Compared to Rosie Sharpe she was a princess. Which didn't make it any better. She was still *here*, at Chy an Cleth, with Iain.

Phaedra hung her jacket in the cupboard and went to gaze out of the window. A slow-moving barge was battling the whitecaps across the bay. What a day to be at sea, especially on the unpredictable north coast. She thought of Iain's Rosie, and sighed.

By the time she went downstairs again she had her hair pinned neatly on her head, and her emotions firmly hidden behind a smile. Iain had a right to bring anyone he liked to Chy an Cleth – and Caroline was none of her business.

She would hear what he had to say, have a quick bite to eat in the kitchen, and then make herself scarce so he and his lady-love could get on with what they'd come here to do.

Charles's desk, she was sure, was no more than a convenient red herring.

Caroline was sitting on the settee looking spruce in a green wool skirt and white blouse as she shuffled through a yellowing pile of paper. Iain, in jeans and a black sweatshirt, was perched on the arm beside her with his hand once again on her shoulder. But this time, instead of a photograph, the two of them were absorbed in rapt contemplation of a bank statement.

Iain looked up when Phaedra walked in, gave her a bland smile, and wrapped a lock of Caroline's hair around his finger. Caroline blinked, and he released it at once, allowing his thumb to graze the top of her ear.

Phaedra produced her best impersonal smile. 'What do you want to talk about?' she asked, attempting to sound breezy, but suspecting she merely sounded strained.

'That photograph you insisted on seeing.'

'Oh.' Phaedra thought about telling him the photo was nobody's business but her mother's, but something about his flat, inflectionless tone made her hesitate.

Caroline said, 'Excuse me. I have a phone call to make,' and disappeared into the hall.

Phaedra stared after her. 'Did I do something?'

Iain shook his head. 'I told her I wanted to talk to you in private.'

'And she didn't object? Found the perfect doormat, have you, Iain?'

'Don't be bitchy. Caroline is no doormat. If she was, she'd be no use to me.' He patted the settee beside him. 'Come and sit down.'

Phaedra chose a hardback chair with delicately curved legs, moved it a few inches from the wall and sat with her hands folded in her lap. 'What about the photograph?'

Iain propped an ankle on his knee and smiled, irritatingly unfazed by her manoeuvre. His air was casual. His eyes, when they met hers, were not.

'I'm not your brother,' he said.

'Oh, so that was it. 'No,' she agreed. 'I didn't think you were. Did you?'

'Not for a moment. Even my father, for all his delight in making trouble, would have drawn the line at marrying his own daughter.' He stretched his arms above his head and his sweatshirt pulled tight across his chest.

Phaedra swallowed. Was he serious? His small, come-hither smile made her wonder if he, too, was trying to make trouble.

She didn't mean to let him.

'Yes,' she agreed. 'Charles would certainly have drawn the line at that.' And a good thing too. Otherwise the instincts she was trying to suppress while she observed Iain's long body sprawled across the settee would not only be unwise, but illegal.

Iain lowered his arms and rested his hands on his thighs. Phaedra moistened her lips. God, he was gorgeous. She stood up, restless, unable to keep still. 'Is that all you wanted? To tell me what I already knew?'

'I wanted to set your mind at rest. But I see I needn't have worried.'

He was annoyed. She could tell from the way he was strumming his fingers on his thighs and looking at her as if he didn't like her much.

The photograph had disturbed him too, then. And he had expected her to be even more disturbed – which she was in a way. But she didn't want to talk about it. Not with Iain. Once she would have. Not any more.

Maybe that was at the root of his problem.

'I'm going to make something to eat,' she said. 'What about you?'

'Oh, I dare say Caroline and I will find some way to satisfy our appetites.' He leaned his head against the back of the settee. 'Don't worry about us.'

'I won't,' she said. 'Goodnight. I hope you sleep well.'

She didn't wait for him to answer, but as she was closing the door she heard him say softly, 'Oh, I'm sure I will. Eventually.'

Caroline was hanging up the phone when Phaedra reached the hall. 'Everything all right?' the redhead asked.

'Yes, of course. Shouldn't it be?'

Caroline flushed. 'Sorry. I thought you looked a bit pale.'

'Oh. Thanks. I'm all right.' Phaedra immediately regretted her rudeness. She shouldn't have snapped at the woman. It wasn't her fault Iain fancied her in bed. 'I am a bit tired, come to think of it. Have a nice evening with Iain.'

'But . . .'

As she hurried down the passage to the kitchen, Phaedra sensed Caroline's puzzled gaze on her back.

No warm smell of bread greeted her today. No comforting coffee. Only a carelessly wiped table, and a faint odour that she eventually tracked down to the dish rag draped across the tap.

Screwing up her nose, Phaedra carried it into the laundry room and dropped it in a plastic tub along with soap and bleach. Then she went back to the kitchen and made herself an omelette.

Afterwards, as she walked through the hall on her way upstairs, she passed Iain helping Caroline on with a black mohair coat. His hands rested familiarly on her collar. 'We've decided to have dinner in Bude,' he said to Phaedra. 'Sure you won't come with us?'

'You didn't ask me,' she pointed out.

'Didn't I? How neglectful of me.' He didn't repeat the invitation.

'Do come,' Caroline said. 'There's isn't much to eat in the fridge.'

'I made an omelette. Don't worry about me.'

Iain grinned. 'We won't. Come on, Caroline.'

'Well, if you're sure.' Caroline threw a backward glance at Phaedra as Iain appropriated her arm and drew her with him towards the door. She didn't look particularly animated.

Phaedra shook her head. If *she* had been going out with Iain, and anticipating delights of a more intimate nature to follow, she would have been glowing from every pore. And she wouldn't have asked another woman to come along.

The phone rang just as she was about to head upstairs.

'Good evening, Phaedra,' said Peter Sharkey's slick-as-oil voice. 'What a pleasure to have you back in town.'

'Thank you. I'm leaving tomorrow,' Phaedra said.

She wasn't, but with Peter it never hurt to keep your options open.

'Tonight, then,' he suggested. 'How about dinner in Bude?'

'No. Thank you. I've already eaten.'

'A film, then? Or –'

'Peter, I can't go out tonight. I . . . I'm not feeling well. Iain's looking after me,' she added quickly, before he could offer to play doctor.

'Oh. I'm sorry to hear that. Will you be coming home for Christmas?'

'No. Yes. I don't know, I suppose so.' Didn't the man ever give up? His persistence might have been flattering if she hadn't known he never made any move that he didn't expect to result in a profit for Sharkey Holdings.

'I'll call you at Christmas, then,' he said.

'Goodnight, Peter.' She hung up before he could suggest breakfast or lunch.

Tomorrow she would visit her mother in the morning, and maybe she *would* return a day early to school.

From now on, the pattern of her days was set.

School, visits to her mother, and perhaps the occa-sional solitary holiday somewhere warm. There were worse ways to get through a lifetime.

Phaedra was rubbing her eyes when she went down-stairs the next morning. She had passed a fitful night dreaming that Iain and Caroline were climbing up the outside of the Eiffel Tower while Charles floated above them strumming on a harp. Behind him came Esther with a butterfly net. Eventually, the scene shifted and dissolved into a wet, grey cloud that turned out to be the sea. Phaedra had awoken sweating, alone and afraid. There had been no moon to light the room with its gentle light, and she had lain in the dark for some time wondering if the dream was an omen of her future.

Just before she finally drifted into oblivion, she heard Charles's voice saying, 'Stuff and nonsense. I won't have it. D'you hear me?'

Phaedra heard him. But she didn't hear Iain and Caroline come in.

When she reached the kitchen, they were drinking coffee amidst the remains of toast and marmalade. Phaedra managed a morose 'Good morning' without looking at them, and went to pour herself a cup of coffee.

'Did you sleep well?' Caroline asked politely.

'Not particularly. Did you?'

'Oh, yes. Very well, thank you.'

Phaedra turned to look at her, expecting to en-counter a vision in creamy silk and lace, and prepared to feel resentful of anyone who could look beautiful in the morning. But there wasn't a lace panel or a silk frill in sight. Caroline was wearing a practical grey woollen dressing gown over a white, high-collared nightdress. With no makeup, and her hair neat but uncurled, she wasn't at all what Phaedra had expected of Iain's mistress in the morning.

Her surprise must have shown, because Iain said, 'What's the matter? Have you turned into one of those people who shouldn't be spoken to before they've consumed three cups of coffee and read the paper?'

Phaedra shook her head, as much to clear it as in answer to his question. 'No. I'd like to be, but life in a boarding school doesn't permit that sort of luxury.'

'I'm glad to hear it. Sit down.' He waved at an empty chair.

Phaedra took it reluctantly. She was having enormous difficulty pretending this was any normal morning. Iain was sitting directly across from her wearing beltless jeans and a plain white shirt he hadn't taken the trouble to do up. That tantalizing glimpse of flesh, surprisingly tanned for the time of year, would have been unfairly provocative at any time of day. First thing in the morning, and with his hair all dishevelled from sleep, he was an aphrodisiac no woman should be obliged to swallow without the relief of consummation.

Caroline, understandably, was reluctant to make further conversational moves, and Iain seemed disinclined to bother.

In the end Phaedra broke the silence by asking much too brightly, 'So what's on the agenda for today?' When two pairs of eyes looked at her, and nobody answered, she said, 'Are you hoping to finish clearing up Charles's desk?'

Iain tipped his chair back and extended his never-ending legs. 'We've pretty much finished. I expect we'll head back to town late this afternoon.'

'Perhaps Phaedra would like to come with us,' Caroline suggested. 'It would save her catching the train.'

Iain, looking none too pleased, said, 'What about it, Phaedra?'

Phaedra, astonished by the offer, wiped a damp hand down her jeans. 'No. No, thank you. My mother –'

'Would be delighted,' Iain muttered, as if he were talking to himself.

'Yes, but – you and Caroline. I'll be in the way.'

'Why should you be?' It was Caroline's turn to look astonished. 'You and Iain have known each other forever. At least that's what he told me.'

'Yes, we have. But – I don't understand.'

She was looking at Caroline, but an odd sound made her glance in Iain's direction. He had a hand over his mouth as if he were smothering a yawn.

She turned back to Caroline, whose blue eyes were soft with surprise.

'What's the matter?' Phaedra asked. 'Surely you didn't think – I mean, I wasn't born in the fifties. I realize you and Iain . . .' She stopped. It was no longer the fifties, but that didn't make it any easier to say, 'I realize you're sleeping with Iain, whom I happen to love.'

'Phaedra,' Caroline said carefully, 'I think – I think somehow you may have got the wrong idea.'

Iain made another odd noise, a kind of snort. Phaedra ignored it.

'What idea?' she asked.

Caroline fidgeted with the high cotton collar of her nightgown. 'Iain is my boss. That's all he is.'

'All?' Phaedra blinked at her, still not understanding.

'Yes. I'm his secretary, not his – oh dear.'

'What Caroline is trying to say,' Iain drawled, 'is that she wouldn't let me into her bed if I paid her. *Especially* if I paid her, I imagine.'

'But, I thought –'

'I know you did. I've told you before you think too much.'

Unexpectedly, Caroline started to giggle.

Phaedra, confused, out of her depth, and desperately embarrassed, didn't see anything to laugh at. She said so.

'Oh, Phaedra, I am sorry,' Caroline said, 'But honestly, can *you* see Mr Trebanian, London's bachelor of the year, settling for the occasional dirty weekend with a thirty-nine-year-old mother of three?'

'Whose husband happens to be a championship wrestler,' Iain put in drily.

Phaedra looked from Iain to Caroline and then back again. Iain, especially, seemed to find the joke hugely entertaining, and she did her best to join in his merriment. But when he got up and patted her condescendingly on the shoulder, she said, 'Excuse me,' and stalked regally from the room.

Once through the door dignity vanished. She raised her hands to her face.

For the first time in years, she was blushing.

CHAPTER 9

The interior of the Bentley was warm, almost steamy, as it purred up the M4 towards London. Yet its preoccupied occupants were as cool and remote as if they were on their way to a funeral. Only Caroline, in solitary possession of the back seat, showed any sign of animation.

Phaedra had tried to insist *she* should sit in the back, but Caroline had said firmly, 'No. After sitting beside Mr Trebanian all the way down from London, it's only fair you should get him on the way back.'

This ambiguous comment had earned her a black look from Iain and a harried one from Phaedra. But as Caroline was the passenger closest to the disputed back door at the time, she had gained custody without further opposition.

Iain switched lanes and overtook a procession of Volvos and Range Rovers wriggling with children and dogs. He meant to waste no time getting into London. Once there, he looked forward to unloading his unwanted cargo and returning to the peace and solitude of his flat.

He glanced at Phaedra, seated motionless beside him in her trim navy blue trouser suit. What in hell had possessed Caroline to include her in what would otherwise have been a relaxed and uneventful drive? Pendy's scheming had caused more than enough trouble as it was. He could have done without the company of her silent and sour-faced daughter on the drive back to town.

Yet, in spite of himself, when Phaedra had first arrived he'd been glad to see her.

She hadn't been glad to see him. And she'd been so prickly and rude to Caroline that he'd deliberately let her go on imagining his secretary was his lover. He wasn't proud of himself for that. No one liked being made to look a fool, and he knew Phaedra was more sensitive than most in that department – had been since her schooldays, although most of the time she hid it well. He'd felt sorry for her then. She didn't make it easy for anyone to feel sorry for her now.

When he'd followed her upstairs after she departed from the kitchen looking martyred, he had found her standing at her bedroom window with her long fingers gripped around the sill.

'Phaedra?' he'd said. 'Phaedra, don't sulk. It's not like you.'

'I'm not sulking.'

'No? Then why the vanishing act? And why won't you look at me?'

'Are you laughing at me?' she answered indirectly. 'Not that I'd blame you if you were.'

Just as he'd thought. It wasn't her fault really. She'd suffered too much from unkind laughter at school.

'I'm not laughing,' he said. 'Not any more.'

'You were, though.'

'Yes, I was. I wouldn't have if you hadn't treated poor Caroline so rudely – without the least justification, I might add.' When she didn't answer, he moved across the room to place an admonitory hand on her shoulder. She flinched, but didn't pull away. 'I know you jumped to the conclusion we were lovers. But even if that were true, we're both adults. Who I sleep with is hardly your business.'

'Of course it's not. And I don't *care* who you sleep with.'

Phaedra's neck stiffened so haughtily he would have laughed if he'd dared. 'Good,' he said. 'Then why all the drama?'

'I'm sorry.' She fell off her high horse so quickly he felt like a heel. 'I didn't mean to be dramatic. But I felt like an idiot, and it's been such a miserable weekend . . . I suppose I was overwrought.'

'I suppose you were. All the same, it did serve you right.'

'Did it?' Her head drooped with such uncharacteristic meekness that, without thinking, Iain took both her shoulders in his hands and began to knead them. Her muscles were knotted tighter than old Angus Cooper's ties.

The raspberry scent of her hair was in his nostrils and her bottom was curved softly against his

209

abdomen. He wanted her. Now, and without further conversation. But she flinched when he slid his hands down her sides, and instead of dragging her into his arms and giving in to his baser instincts as he longed to do, he fixed his gaze on the winter blue sky and went back to massaging her shoulders.

'Caroline's nice,' she said, a moment or two later.

'Yes. You know she had no idea what she'd done to offend you?'

'Hadn't she?'

'No. I had – but you were being such a snippy little witch I didn't see any reason to enlighten you.'

'Oh.' Phaedra pressed her forehead against the window.

Again Iain resisted the urge to drag her into his arms and kiss her silly. She seemed so lost, so woebegone. So unlike the quiet, self-assured young woman he thought he knew. Her shoulders felt sharper than the rest of her, tense and resistant to his touch. After a while, and knowing he wasn't being entirely fair, he said, 'I hope you've learned something from all this.'

'Don't lecture, Iain,' Phaedra said with a return of her usual spark. 'That's *my* job. And yes, I have learned something. That Caroline is a mother of three.' She lifted her head. 'How on earth did you coerce her into deserting her family for the half-term weekend?'

Iain felt a familiar flare of annoyance. Why did Phaedra always assume he'd used coercion or some kind of force? As if he were entirely without decent feelings.

'I didn't know it was half-term,' he reminded her. 'But as it happens, I offered her rather a lot of money and the chance of a weekend away from her children. Their grandmother, so Caroline says, is thrilled to have the little demons. I can't think why.'

For a moment he thought Phaedra was going to laugh, but if the thought crossed her mind, she dismissed it at once.

'What about Caroline's husband?' she asked. 'Is he thrilled?'

'Donald? He's working somewhere in the north. Why should he care?'

'I'd have thought that was obvious.'

'Why, thank you – if you mean what I think you mean.'

'I expect I do,' Phaedra said.

'Mmm. Then I have to tell you, reluctant as I am to admit it, there *are* women who don't find me irresistible. Caroline's one of them.' He stopped kneading and, taking her by surprise, spun her around until she was facing him. At once she lowered her eyes. When they reached the level of his navel she squeezed them shut.

'It's all right,' he said. 'It's only flesh. I'm not naked.'

'I know. Would you mind doing up your shirt?'

Iain laughed. He'd forgotten how inexperienced she was. Even so, this was surely carrying innocence too far. 'Don't be a prude,' he said, and bent to kiss the tip of her upturned nose.

She recoiled from him at once, her dark eyes enormous with shock.

Hell! He hadn't meant to scare her. Hadn't meant to kiss her for that matter. But he'd caught another whiff of that blasted raspberry shampoo, and she was standing there with her eyes closed, looking so damned kissable . . .

'It's all right,' he said. 'That wasn't a prelude to a serious pass. You'd know if it was.'

She nodded, still with her eyes closed. 'Yes. Yes, I suppose I would. Would you mind going away now?'

'Not at all. Can I take it, then, that you're not accepting my offer of a ride back to London?'

Phaedra hesitated. 'It was Caroline's offer.'

He resisted the temptation to shake her. 'Very well, then. Are you accepting *Caroline's* offer? It's up to you. Your mother tells me our artistic caretakers will be coming back tonight, but if you'd rather stay –'

'You want me to stay, don't you?'

Iain counted to ten. 'I want you to make up your mind. If that's beyond you, I'll make it up for you.'

'All right, I'll come,' she said promptly.

'Good. That's settled then.'

It wasn't good. Not in any way he could think of. He stood for a moment, observing the challenge in her eye with resignation. He knew she had only made the decision to travel with him and Caroline because he'd pushed her. Left to herself, she would have stayed behind. Not, he supposed, that it made a great deal of difference in the long run. Either way, by the end of the day she would be out of his hair.

212

He had left her bedroom then. He'd had to. The sight of her standing there, all soft and quivering and defiant, had been a temptation no decent man could be expected to endure for longer than a few painful seconds.

Once outside her room he leaned against the wall and wiped the heel of his hand across his forehead. It came away dripping with sweat. Damn. The sooner they got this business of the house out of the way, the better it would be for all of them – except his bloody father, who was probably up there in the clouds somewhere chortling with unangelic glee as he watched the results of his machinations.

Iain swore again, with feeling. Then, without stopping to put on a jacket, he went to move the car from the garage. The cold air stinging his naked chest brought a measure of relief to his heated skin.

Six hours later, as the Bentley neared the outskirts of London, Iain again felt the need for cold air.

Phaedra, seated next to him in her sensible navy suit, and with her hair piled neatly on her head, was still an impossible temptation. He decided raspberry shampoo ought to be banned.

'Won't be long now,' Caroline said cheerfully from the back. 'Are you sure it's no trouble to drop me off in Richmond, Mr Trebanian?'

'I picked you up there,' Iain replied. He had no patience for civilized pretences this evening. Caroline knew quite well he would drive her right to her mother's door.

'Yes, I know you did,' she said, 'but –'

'I said I'd drive you home. Let's leave it at that, shall we?'

'There's no need to snap. Caroline was only trying to be helpful,' Phaedra reproved him.

As far as Iain could remember, it was the first time she'd spoken since they left Exeter, but her intervention only served to heighten his ill humour. 'Caroline was not trying to be helpful,' he said. 'She was mouthing polite platitudes for the sake of having something to say.'

'Iain! It wouldn't hurt *you* to mouth a few polite platitudes sometimes. Caroline –'

'It's all right,' Caroline interrupted calmly. 'He's often like this. It's best just to ignore him.'

'He wasn't like this in the old days,' Phaedra said. 'He lost his temper sometimes, but he was always fair. And always polite.'

Iain tried not to grind his teeth. 'Would you ladies mind not talking about me as if I'm somewhere else,' he growled. 'I am, as a matter of record, in full possession of my hearing.' He swung the Bentley off the motorway with a savage flick of his wrist, throwing Phaedra and Caroline against their respective doors.

'Sorry,' he said, as Phaedra straightened stiffly and began to rub her elbow. 'I took that a little too fast.'

Phaedra glared at him and didn't answer.

Iain began to feel better.

Caroline, visible only from the chest up above a screen of clamoring hands and chocolate-covered faces, waved goodbye from the lamplit steps of her mother's terraced home.

Phaedra waved back enthusiastically. Iain, with a last bemused glance at the group jostling and shouting on the steps, shook his head and pulled the Bentley on to the road.

'No wonder Caroline was so keen to have a weekend away,' he muttered.

Phaedra frowned. 'They seem fairly normal kids to me. Don't you like children?'

'I haven't had the misfortune to be around them much. But memories of my schooldays lead me to believe they are vicious little beasts closely related to weasels.'

'Iain! You told me you quite liked school.'

'I did. I was head weasel.'

'Some weasel,' Phaedra murmured. When his head jerked sharply, she realized she had been gazing at his profile with the kind of dreamy admiration the lovesick adolescents in her class usually reserved for the new gardener's assistant.

'Thank you.' Iain inclined his head gravely.

It was too late to withdraw her remark, so Phaedra said instead, 'You used to like children. You were always nice to *me*.'

'Was I? But you were different. And anyway there was only one of you. For which, I suppose, I should be thankful.'

'There was Joan. You were nice to her too.'

'As she spent most of her holidays away, that wasn't difficult. I rarely saw her.'

She had to agree with him there. Joan had lived at Chy an Cleth and gone to a school near Bude, but she had had itchy feet even in those days. Whenever a school friend invited her home for holidays or weekends, she accepted. Phaedra had envied Joan her private school. Naively, she'd believed private school girls would all be too well brought up to pick on anyone who might be different. She knew better now.

'I suppose, in a way, I was more of a sister to you than Joan was,' she said, watching with her heart set on pause as a black-clad cyclist narrowly escaped annihilation between two cars.

'In a way. In other ways not.' Iain concentrated on his driving. 'Where did you say you were staying?'

'Near Marble Arch. The hotel's called The Rose Chiltern. It's right across the street from the Bear and Badger.'

'I haven't heard of it.'

'You wouldn't have. It's cheap.'

Iain's mouth turned down. 'The fact that Trebanian Advertising is solvent doesn't mean I'm totally out of touch with the needs of the less affluent.'

Phaedra made a face. 'Don't go all pompous on me, Iain. You'll be rid of me in a minute.'

'Hmm. So I will.' He removed a gloved hand from the wheel and patted the handiest part of her, which happened to be her knee.

Her stomach rolled over as it always did when Iain touched her, and she squirmed away from him until the door prevented her from squirming any further.

He laughed, and a few minutes later pulled the Bentley up to the kerb outside an unprepossessing four-storey brick house with a metal plate on the wall identifying it as The Rose Chiltern Hotel. Across the road the patrons of the Bear and Badger sounded as if they were working up to a fight.

Phaedra jumped out on to the pavement. 'Thanks,' she said. 'I do appreciate the lift.'

Iain leaned across the seat to look up at her. 'Don't you want your suitcase?'

'Oh. Yes, of course. I'll get it if you'll give me the key.'

'Ah, but I won't give you the key. Hold on a minute.'

Phaedra held on as Iain swung himself out of the car and strolled around to the boot, taking his time about it.

'Better check your reservation first,' he said.

'Oh, I'm sure it's all right.'

He glanced at his watch. 'I wouldn't count on it. It's nearly nine.' He put a hand on the boot and leaned on it, smiling implacably.

Iain's classic high-powered executive pose, Phaedra noted with a resentment that was fast becoming familiar. If only he didn't look so tough, and so sexy, in that damn suit. Other men would have chosen jeans for the long drive back to town. But then Iain had never been 'other men'.

She sighed. It was obvious he wasn't going to open up the boot until she'd checked her reservation, so she might as well give in and get on with it.

217

'Wait a minute, then,' she muttered.

Stupid thing to say. She climbed the three steps to the door and rang the bell. He had every intention of waiting until he had his way.

No one answered her ring. Somebody from the Bear and Badger shouted an obscenity. Phaedra shivered a little in the autumn chill and tried again. Eventually a shuffling sound started up on the other side of the door, and after a further wait it was pulled open by a stooped, middle-aged woman with a thin face full of teeth.

'We're full up,' she said in a mannish voice.

'I have a reservation –'

'Full up,' the woman repeated. 'No room.'

'Yes, I understand. But I have a reservation. My name's Pendenning.'

'Pendenning?' The teeth clamped together, then opened just enough to mumble, 'Ah. Pendenning. Tomorrow. Reservation's for tomorrow.'

'No, it's for tonight, I –'

'Trouble?' inquired Iain's voice from behind her. She felt his breath stirring her hair.

'Tomorrow,' the woman said to Iain. 'Her reservation's for tomorrow.'

'But I phoned this morning –'

'Full up,' the teeth repeated. 'Sorry. No room.' She started to close the door.

Iain moved Phaedra aside and put his foot in the rapidly narrowing aperture. The woman stepped back, and Phaedra caught a brief glimpse of stained, red-flocked wallpaper and floorboards that were badly in need of paint.

'Hmm. Fish for dinner,' Iain remarked, inserting his head through the opening. He touched a hand to his nose. 'Boiled, I should think. No, I'm afraid this won't do for Miss Pendenning. Come on, Phaedra.'

'But . . .' Phaedra began.

'I said, come on.' He took her elbow in a business-like grip.

The woman closed the door.

'Iain, you had no right . . .' Phaedra began.

'Maybe not. Not that it makes a difference. She had no intention of giving you a room. Besides, the place stank of fish. How on earth did you find it?'

'Mum stayed there years ago. It was probably all right in those days. She suggested it this morning when I went to say goodbye.'

How long ago the morning seemed now. Her mother had been so maddeningly pleased that she was driving back to town with Iain that she had been half-inclined to change her plans at the last minute. There was little to be gained from promoting false hope. In the end though, she had stuck to her decision.

Phaedra yawned. Lord, she was tired. As well as hungry. And to top it all off, she had nowhere to stay.

Something of her mood must have communicated itself to Iain, because his stern features softened marginally, and he put an arm around her shoulders and said, 'Don't look so glum. We'll have something to eat, and then I'll see you settled in a good hotel.'

'Iain, I can't afford your idea of a good hotel. I'd better go straight back to school.'

Iain tightened his grip on her arm. She waited, and after a moment he put his other hand under her chin and tipped her face up. 'It's late. There's no reason why you should go back to school until tomorrow. And you most certainly can afford it. My father left you money as well as my house. Don't pretend you've forgotten.'

'I haven't forgotten. But it's not mine. I –'

'Phaedra . . .' His voice hardened, and she guessed he had no tolerance for what he perceived as hypocrisy.

'What?'

'That money is yours. So unless you want me to kidnap you and drag you forcibly off to my flat, you will spend some of it on a decent room in a decent hotel where you will have some hope of getting a decent night's sleep. I have no intention of standing guard outside your door, and I don't propose to spend the night wondering if some man less entitled to the liberty than I am has taken the opportunity to kidnap you for himself. Do you understand me?'

Put like that, she did. 'You're not entitled,' she said, and then added curiously, '*Would* you worry about me?'

'Yes. I would. You have no idea what some of these fleabag hotels are like. You're a country girl, Phaedra. You don't know about life in the big city.'

'Manchester is big. That's where I got my degree.'

'Maybe so, but you lived in a residence there. It's not the same. Now will you stop arguing? Please. I'm hungry.'

'So am I,' Phaedra admitted.

'Get in then.' He gestured at the car.

Phaedra got in. Iain came up behind her and slammed the door.

'Where are we going?' she asked, as the Bentley eased its way along Oxford Street, which was surprisingly deserted.

'My club. It's convenient and they'll give us a good meal.'

Phaedra relaxed slightly. She had never been to Iain's club, but she knew it by reputation. Dignified, discreet, comfortable. Quiet. She was ready for some quiet after the endless thrum of traffic, the swish of tires spinning on concrete and the shouts of aggressive revelry from across the street. But as she leaned back in the seat and closed her eyes, her anything-but-quiet thoughts were of the silent man in the suit sitting beside her . . .

The *suit*. She sat up, gazing at Iain in consternation. 'Your club? I'm not suitably dressed. Don't they insist on skirts and fancy clothes?'

'They'd probably like to. But as you'll come as my guest, there won't be a problem. Besides, you look very presentable in those trousers.'

'Really?'

'Really. I wouldn't say so if it wasn't true.'

He wouldn't either. Iain was unflatteringly frank on the subject of her clothes. Thank God she'd decided to set an example to the girls instead of turning up at school in her jeans. 'Well, if you're quite sure,' she said. 'I don't mind being dropped off at a café.'

'Keep it up and I'll drop you off in Lost Luggage. Here we are.' He pulled the Bentley to a stop on a sidestreet just off Pall Mall.

Once inside the club, it wasn't long before the warmth and the stuffy opulence of this bastion of privilege began to work their Victorian magic on Phaedra's senses.

Iain settled her in a big leather wingback in the spacious lounge while he left to make arrangements for their meal, and as soon as he disappeared she gave a sigh of pure contentment and closed her eyes. Almost immediately, the tensions of the day began to fall away.

When Iain returned she was asleep.

'Hey. Wake up, sleepyhead,' he ordered softly.

Phaedra woke with a start to find Iain bending over her with his hands on the arms of her chair and his face mere inches from her own. He smelled of expensive whisky.

Still only half-awake, she said, 'You smell nice. Like your father.'

The pleasant smell was abruptly withdrawn as Iain said something concise and unprintable. Phaedra opened her eyes and sat up.

'Iain! Someone will hear you.'

'No, someone won't. We happen to have the place to ourselves.' His voice was clipped – and he looked very *big*, looming over her as she gazed up at him from her chair.

'Have I said something wrong?' she asked.

Iain was frowning, but he shook his head. 'What does my father have to do with anything?'

Oh, oh. She'd invoked the wrong ghost. 'I meant,' she said carefully, 'that you both drink – drank – the same kind of whisky.'

'I see.'

'No, you *don't* see,' Phaedra said, knowing her voice sounded overloud in the big, echoing room. 'Your father never – he didn't . . .' She paused as the murmur of voices reached them from the hall.

'I know that.' Iain ignored the voices. 'So you liked the smell of Dad's whisky, did you?'

Phaedra shrugged. 'It beat those cigars he used to smoke.'

'I suppose it did. But as I don't smoke cigars, I fail to see the connection.'

He was being difficult on purpose, she knew he was. Talk of his father always made Iain bad tempered. But she'd been half-asleep at the time, and there was nothing much she could do about it now.

As she tried to think of something – anything – that might turn the conversation in a less contentious direction, a svelte, expensive-looking matron in black silk strolled into the lounge on the arm of a tall, balding man in a dinner jacket. They were followed by a small man bearing a silver tray with champagne and two glasses.

Phaedra, in her navy blue suit from Marks and Spencers, tried to make herself invisible in her chair.

'Well?' Iain said, as if he'd her asked a question.

She pushed a loose pin back into her hair and made an effort to pull herself together. 'I was married to your father. A lot of things about you remind me of him. Is that what you want me to say? Iain, please . . .'

He held up a hand to cut her off. 'Let's go in to dinner.'

All right, if that was how he wanted to play it . . .

Phaedra started to rise, and he took her elbow to steady her. As she came to her feet, his thigh pressed firm and compact against her hip, transmitting instant lust to every pulse-point in her body. She froze until he started to move. Then she melted.

Lord, what this man could do to her normally sluggish libido. As he drew her across the thick carpet and out into the hall, she found herself leaning into his side, revelling in the feel of him, rubbing her cheek lovingly against the smoothness of his jacket . . .

Iain growled, 'Phaedra,' out of the corner of his mouth, and she remembered where she was and straightened up.

The uniformed guardian of the front desk put a hand to his mouth to hide a smile.

'That's better,' Iain said. 'I hope you're not going to fall asleep over the prawns.'

If he only knew! It wasn't weariness that had caused her attack of limp knees. 'Oh, I promise I'll wait until dessert,' she said sweetly.

Iain patted her discreetly on the rear and said, 'Good girl,' which only increased her frustration.

Phaedra's immediate impression of the spacious dining-room was of dark red tapestry walls, gilded chandeliers gleaming with a pale, cold light, and

224

acres of white linen set with crimson napkins and heavy silver. Two businessmen seated in a corner were the only other diners.

Phaedra felt very small and conspicuous.

A man with a long face whom she wouldn't have dared to refer to as a waiter led them to a prominent table near the velvet-draped windows.

'Do you always sit here?' she asked Iain.

'Yes. Don't you like it?'

'It's fine. Just a little – exposed.'

'Sorry. If I'd known you objected to being seen, I'd have got them to set up a table in the corner behind the potted plants.'

'There aren't any potted plants. And I don't object to being seen.' Phaedra was nettled. 'I just feel underdressed in this suit.'

'You're not underdressed. Take my word for it.' His eyes gleamed at her in a way that made her feel as if a hot poker were touching her nerve-ends.

'No,' she began. 'I meant –'

'I know what you meant.' He gazed pensively at her mouth.

Was her lipstick smeared? 'What are you looking at?' she asked suspiciously.

'Nothing. As a matter of fact, I'm trying not to imagine you "underdressed". You were a baby the last time I saw any part of you between your neck and your knees.'

Phaedra gaped at him. She hadn't expected such devastating honesty and she had no idea how to respond. 'Then maybe I should stop imagining

225

you,' she blurted, trying to suppress a vision of Iain
sprawled naked on her small bed at Chy an Cleth
with his arms and legs hanging over the sides. In
spite of her efforts, a giggle erupted from her
mouth.

'I'm glad you find the idea amusing,' Iain said.

She didn't think he was glad at all. But before she
could answer, the long-faced man came back to take
their orders. Phaedra asked for prawns, followed by
salmon.

Iain raised his eyebrows and ordered prawns as
well followed by something that sounded fattening
and Greek, and a wine that sounded French and
expensive.

'Why fish followed by fish?' he asked after Long-
face had left.

'I like fish,' she said. 'Although, strictly speaking,
prawns are crustaceans.'

'There speaks the dedicated schoolmarm. I think I
preferred you when you were worrying about being
underdressed.'

Oh, so they were back to that again. Now she was
sure that accepting this invitation was a mistake. It
had started out all right, but somewhere along the
line Iain had gone from being bossy to downright
suggestive. And she was tired of it.

'You're not a bit like your father,' she said crossly.
'I was wrong.'

'Aren't I?' Iain shot her a fishy look and picked up
a breadstick.

'No. He, at least, was a gentleman.'

Instead of replying, 'And are you suggesting I'm not?' or something that would have given her the opening she was looking for, Iain merely raised his eyebrows and said, 'So you've said before. He must have been the first one the Trebanians ever produced, then. And no doubt the last.' He waited as their prawns were placed in front of them, then picked one up and cracked it as if he hoped it would fight back.

Phaedra's mouth tightened with irritation as she watched his capable hands making short work of the prawn. If he wanted to maintain this aloof distance for the rest of their time together, that was up to him. She watched him crack another prawn. If those hands were as capable when occupied with . . . No. Oh, no. She picked up one of her own prawns and cracked it back. There was no point in thinking about Iain's hands. No point in envying a prawn. Even if he wanted to, Iain would never seriously touch her. He couldn't. That would be allowing Charles to win.

He snapped a breadstick in half and bit down on it, showing his teeth.

Phaedra watched in astonishment. Something was going on here, but she didn't understand what it was. In the end, because it was funny and she didn't know what else to do, she burst out laughing.

Iain wasn't noticeably perturbed. 'You should laugh more often,' he said.

'So should you.'

Still holding her gaze, he cracked the last prawn and bit into it with relish. 'Do you think so? I haven't found much to laugh about lately.'

227

'Haven't you? Why not? You're rich, successful in business and other ways —'

'What other ways, Phaedra?'

He sounded dreadfully cold. What was the matter with the man anyway? Why, whenever she was with him, did she so often get the feeling he was either about to explode, or to crack like ice in hot water? Whatever the reason, she'd had enough of it.

'Obvious ways,' she said. 'You don't look to me like a man suffering from sexual frustration.'

'Don't I? Looks can be deceptive.' He smiled pleasantly at Long-face as their main course arrived.

'Oh.' Phaedra was taken aback. Was he serious? His looks were of the magnetic kind that invariably attracted female attention. And in spite of his assertive, sometimes downright obnoxious personality, he wasn't without charm when he chose to use it. He was also a man one would trust instinctively in a crisis.

'Are you trying to tell me,' she asked, 'that if you stood on the pavement and whistled, women wouldn't come running from all directions?'

'I doubt it. Last time I stood on a pavement and whistled, I attracted a taxi, two poodles, an underage whore and a very boring lecture from a militant blonde who thought I was whistling at her.'

'And weren't you?'

'Yes. But I was only nineteen.' He didn't quite succeed in suppressing a grin.

It was infectious. In spite of herself Phaedra grinned back. 'Served you right,' she said smugly.

'Probably. But you can't have it both ways. You're the one who said I should stand on the pavement and whistle.'

'I didn't. I said you *could* stand on the pavement and whistle. There's a difference.'

'Maybe.' He refilled her glass, and then asked in a funny, flat voice, 'Would *you* come if I whistled?'

'Of course not.' She concentrated on her fish, pretending to check it for bones. 'Would you want me to?'

'Only if you were running to tell me you'd come to your senses about Chy an Cleth.'

'Iain, you promised not to bring that up again until after Christmas.'

'So I did. Well then, that lets out my sex life and my old home as topics of conversation. And presumably your sex life as well, since I seem to remember you told me you don't have one. What about our respective parents and their jaunt to Paris? That –'

'No,' Phaedra said.

'Not over salmon and moussaka? I see what you mean. So what does that leave us to talk about? Your job?'

He really was hopeless. 'Why not?' she said, smiling over-brightly. 'I'm covering the Social History of the Victorian Era at the moment. Want to hear about it?'

'Not if I can help it. Although I have heard that Victorian society wasn't as morally upright as it appeared on the surface. Are you going to teach *that* to your girls?'

'Of course,' Pheadra said. 'With suitable editing.'

'Ah.' Iain's eyes gleamed at her over the top of his glass. 'Tell me about the editing.'

'You're impossible,' she said. But Iain grinned again, and it was a nice grin, the one she remembered from her childhood, and in the end she did tell him a little about her job.

He was a good listener, and she found herself relaxing. Then she remembered that, according to her mother and all her friends, men liked to talk about themselves, so she asked him to tell her about his work.

Because Iain loved the world of advertising, Phaedra found herself caught up in his enthusiasm, and for a while it was almost as it had been in the old days, when they'd been friends, comfortably at ease in each other's company.

The mood lasted only until it was time to leave. As Iain took her arm to lead her down the steps to the lighted pavement, she looked up at him, laughing at something he'd said, delighted by the unexpected magic of the evening. And he didn't laugh back.

At once her own laughter died.

'We'd better find you a hotel,' he said gruffly.

'Yes.'

'The Dorchester?' he suggested.

'Iain! I was going to stay at The Rose Chiltern. The Dorchester is –'

'A step or two up,' he agreed, opening the door of the Bentley.

Phaedra climbed in and sat down. 'A step or two! Iain, I can't afford –'

He slammed the door so hard she was almost jolted off her seat.

'Phaedra,' he said, closing his own door more gently, 'we already had this conversation, and I don't want to hear any more about what you can, or cannot, afford. Do you remember what I said earlier this evening?'

Phaedra's heart began to beat ridiculously fast. She could hear the blood thundering in her ears. 'I think so. You said something about kidnapping me and taking me back to your flat.'

'Yes. Well, I meant it.'

She put a hand to her head. Why did she feel dizzy and light-headed? She hadn't had very much wine. Yet the dull drone of traffic had become music, and the lights cutting the shadows across the pavement were highways leading to the stars. *Was* she drunk? She didn't think so. Unless it was possible to be drunk on the look and sound and scent and feel of a man.

'Did you?' she said, leaning her head back against the seat and twisting to look at him. '*Did* you mean it? Because I'm not going to the Dorchester. I know it's a marvellous hotel. But I'm twenty-seven years old, and I'd rather go to your flat. But only if you insist,' she added belatedly.

Iain's face was half-hidden by shadows, but she could see his chest expand in the light from a streetlamp. When he released his breath he said, 'Do I have a choice?'

Phaedra began removing the pins from her hair one by one. 'Sure,' she said. 'You can let me out right here if you like.'

231

'I would like.' Iain slammed his hand viciously on to the dashboard.

'OK.' Phaedra reached for the door.

Before she could get it open Iain had switched on the engine. The Bentley lurched only once before it sped off down the street.

CHAPTER 10

Phaedra gripped the rail at the back of the lift and stared straight ahead at the blue and green parrots painted on the inside of the doors.

She was trapped. As they rose smoothly towards Iain's flat on the top floor of a gracious old building overlooking one of Mayfair's private squares, she wondered, bemusedly, how she had managed to get herself into this fix. Telling Iain she would rather go to his flat than to the Dorchester had been insane. True, perhaps, but still insane.

Iain, standing beside her, crossed his arms and bumped her with his elbow. She took a quick step sideways and huddled in the corner.

Worse than insane, that's what she was. Alone with him in his flat anything could happen. And probably would. At this moment he was looking at her with murder in his eye. But that didn't mean his instincts couldn't turn in another, more pleasurable, direction given the opportunity. And opportunity was exactly what she'd given him.

The uniformed custodian of the door had been in no doubt as to the reason for her visit. He had given her a poker-faced look when Iain hustled her across the lobby that told her exactly what kind of woman he thought she was.

The lift hummed to a stop, and Phaedra stepped out into the small foyer. In front of her loomed a solid white door with a gold doorknob. Iain came up behind her and inserted his key.

'Welcome to my parlour,' he said. 'I'd show you my etchings, but I don't have any.'

Phaedra glanced up and then away. He didn't look murderous any more. Just resigned as he deposited their cases inside the door.

'That's a relief,' she said, taking in a large, starkly lit room that totally destroyed her preconceptions of what the wealthy bachelor's lair was supposed to look like. 'You have some good oils.' She added that because it was easier to discuss art than to think about where she was going to spend the night. 'Who's the artist?'

'Stephen Lewin. You wouldn't have heard of him.'

Phaedra frowned. As it happened, she *hadn't* heard of Stephen Lewin. But she liked his style – mainly interior scenes using models dressed in period costumes. 'No, I haven't,' she admitted. 'But I'm interested in Victorian artists.'

'Are you? What a coincidence.' He spoke in a dismissive tone that set her teeth on edge. 'Well? What do you think? How does this compare to the Dorchester?'

234

Phaedra looked around the big, rectangular room. She couldn't answer him because it didn't compare with a hotel in any way. Furnished entirely with excellent antiques, Iain's flat reminded her of Chy an Cleth without a soul. At first she couldn't understand what was missing. Then it came to her that the room was without the normal clutter that went with the business of day-to-day living. Not a magazine or a cushion was out of place. Not a speck of dust lingered on the surface of the round mahogany table in front of the sofa, and there wasn't so much as a single leftover ash in the grate of the cold white fireplace. Fireplaces weren't supposed to be cold.

'It's very tidy,' Phaedra said at last.

'Yes. Mrs Crump knows I like it that way.'

'Mrs Crump?'

'My housekeeper. She comes in every weekday.'

'Oh. And who keeps it tidy on weekends?'

'I do. What is it with you Pendenning women? I do know a duster when I see one. Your mother seemed to think I was incapable of producing a decent cup of tea.' He walked over to the fireplace and stood with his back to it, not smiling, although she had an idea he didn't really mind that she and her mother thought he needed looking after.

'Did she really?' Phaedra said. 'I expect that's because she was so used to doing everything for your father. *He* certainly wasn't the domestic type.'

'No. Apparently not.'

Phaedra swivelled round to study him more closely. 'What are you not saying?' she asked.

He shrugged. 'Nothing in particular. Funny, isn't it, how one thinks of one's parents as asexual?'

'Oh.' Without thinking, she collapsed on to the gold brocade sofa facing the fireplace. And then wished she hadn't, because Iain was standing in front of it, unfastening the buttons on his jacket.

'What do you mean, "Oh"?' he asked with a sceptical smile. 'I know you ran away last time I brought the subject up, but don't tell me you haven't thought about that picture.'

'I didn't run away. Of course I've thought about it.'

'And what did you decide?'

'Decide?' She shifted to the very edge of the sofa and clasped her hands around her knees. 'There wasn't much to decide, was there? Obviously Mum and your father had a fling.'

'It looks that way, doesn't it? Do you mind?'

His eyes were fixed on her with such intensity that she was forced to look away. 'Why should I mind?'

'Children usually do. As I said, parents and sex aren't supposed to go together.'

She wished he would stop talking about sex. Yes, she had been startled by the picture taken in Paris, as well as shocked that the man with her mother had been Charles. But it wasn't her mother's sexuality that disturbed her now. It was her own.

Iain, standing casually in front of his empty fireplace with one hand resting on the mantel, was a breathtaking reminder that a delicious slice of life was passing her by.

She mustered a faint smile. 'I suppose you're right. I never thought about Mum in that way. Or Charles. Do *you* mind?'

He shook his head. 'My mother would have been dead for some years by the time that photograph was taken. In a way, it's a kind of relief to know the old man was human once – when he was young.'

'Of course he was.' Phaedra unfastened the top button on her jacket. Her mother had been human too. Still was. 'I wonder what happened,' she said.

'Apart from the obvious, you mean? Didn't you ask her?'

'No. I was going to, but in the end I couldn't. Mum looked so different – so happy – in that picture. I didn't want to revive memories that – well, that might make her sad.'

'Mmm. You're a surprising woman, do you know that, Phaedra Pendenning?'

'Am I?' She wished he would sit down.

As if he had read her thoughts, Iain took off his jacket, laid it over a chair and and came to sit beside her.

'Relax,' he said, when she fastened her top button again. 'I'm not about to seduce you.'

'You wouldn't get the chance.'

'Wouldn't I? Then why did you run the risk of coming here?'

Phaedra studied the intricate blue-and-gold pattern of the carpet. 'I didn't see it as much of a risk. But it's a good question.'

'I thought so. Are you going to answer it?'

She could feel his fingers in her hair removing one of its few remaining pins.

Why *had* she come here? She raised her head, looked into dark, questioning eyes, and all at once knew exactly why she'd come.

It was now or never. She might never know why her mother hadn't found permanent happiness with Charles, and God knows, *she* didn't expect permanent happiness with his son. But she wanted, just once, to know what had put that light in her mother's eyes.

She took off her jacket and tossed it on to the chair along with his. 'I came to seduce *you*,' she said.

Iain's nostrils flared. The faint smile lifting the edges of his mouth turned into a flat line of censure as he laid his hands on her shoulders and gripped them so tightly that she gasped.

'You don't know what you're saying,' he said. 'Behave yourself, Phaedra.'

'I'm not a child and I know exactly what I'm saying.'

She made herself face him directly, and their eyes locked in a battle they both knew only one of them could win. Far below them in the street a dog barked, and was answered by another. Iain swallowed. She could see the veins shifting in his throat.

'No, you're not a child,' he agreed, in an unusually husky voice. 'You were my father's wife. Which makes you off limits.'

Phaedra ran her tongue over her lips. 'And if I hadn't been your father's wife?'

'You'd still be off limits.' His eyes focused on her lips. 'Because you're Phaedra, and I don't want to hurt you.' As if to prove the point, he relaxed his grip and moved both hands to her upper arms.

'Why should making love with you hurt me?'

'Because it wouldn't be enough.' Once again his fingers pressed into her flesh. 'You'd want more. You'd want marriage and children —'

'Would that be so bad?'

'For you?' His fierce expression gentled and he let her go. 'No, for you it would probably be right. But not for me. I've been married once, and I know how quickly that hormone-induced obsession can turn into disappointment and regret. I'm not interested in going through that again. Especially not with you.'

'Oh.' Phaedra lowered her eyes so he wouldn't see the dampness in hers. 'Because of Rosie?'

'Yes, partly because of Rosie.'

'And the other part? The especially-not-with-me part. Is it because of your father? Because of Charles?'

A spasm of something that was either exasperation or anger flamed across his face and then was gone. 'No. It's because of you. I will not let that misbegotten old man use Chy an Cleth to manipulate me into a second marriage. And I will not betray your mother's trust, and my own self-respect, by offering you anything less. So you can forget all those romantic yearnings and find some kindly young fool who'll be willing to give you everything you want.'

239

Everything I want? But I only went you, Iain. Can't you see that? She didn't speak the words out loud, but she guessed he could read them in her eyes.

He shrugged and stood up. 'Come on. Time for bed.' He held out his hand.

Phaedra's eyes widened, and he said briskly, 'No, that doesn't mean I've changed my mind. I do have a spare bedroom. Two, as a matter of fact.'

'Yes, of course.' She accepted the proffered hand, and he pulled her up, letting her go the moment she was safely on her feet. 'Iain . . .?'

'Yes?' He had his back to her now and was making for a door in the far corner of the room.

Now that she had his attention, Phaedra couldn't think of anything to say. What *was* there to say, unless she told him what was in her heart: how she loved him, and how it didn't matter if he married her or not; how, whatever happened, she wanted their friendship to last? But she couldn't find the words. Didn't know how to break through the wall he had built around his feelings.

Then it came to her that although she couldn't breach that particular wall, there was another wall he might find it harder to defend.

She eyed his back, straight and square-shouldered, tapering down to the belt at his waist. Then her gaze swept over his hips, down the length of his thighs and across the tempting tautness of his backside. All male, all hard angles and muscle. And all vulnerable to the touch of a woman.

240

Iain opened the door on to a short flight of stairs. Taking a deep breath, she hurried after him as he paused with his foot on the bottom step.

It creaked.

She raised her hand, hesitated, then ran it with delicate provocation across his rear.

He swung round with an oath. She started back. But when she saw that his eyes had already turned smoky with desire, she lifted both arms and wrapped them around his waist.

Needles of fire punctured Iain's groin. The walls of the narrow stair-well shifted and turned upside down. He looked for the source of this incredibly sweet torture that was making him groan in agony and shudder with desire in the same breath, and found soft, dark hair trailing across his chest. Then he felt the touch of gentle fingers on his backside and breathed in the scent of raspberries that was Phaedra.

Clutching at the remnants of his sanity and control, Iain reached for the hands working their bewitching magic behind his back.

'Phaedra,' he growled, 'For God's sake. Don't you know you're playing with fire?'

'Mmm,' Phaedra murmured, 'I like fires. Don't you?' She moved her hips in voluptuous enticement.

Iain swore. 'What I like has nothing to do with it.' He caught her busy hands and snapped them away from the danger zone, holding her arms securely at her sides. 'What the hell do you think you're doing?' he demanded.

She lifted her chin and smiled sweetly, giving him just a glimpse of her teeth. Like a beautiful vampire seducing her midnight snack, he thought savagely.

'I want you, Iain,' she said quietly. 'Just once. Is that so much to ask?'

Iain closed his eyes. This was more than any man should be expected to endure. 'You had better believe it is,' he said. 'I won't do it, Phaedra. I've already told you why. But if you're looking for trouble, you're going the right way about it.'

For answer, Phaedra pinned herself as close to him as she could get while he still had control of her arms, and began to sway her hips from side to side in a slow, sensuous rhythm meant to drive him wild. She even began to hum a little tune, as if they were dancing on the grass beneath the moon instead of in this dimly lit stair-well – with bedrooms close at hand.

His arousal was instant. And devastating. He wanted to kiss her. Or kick her. He wasn't sure which. He did know that he was on the edge of losing what was left of his mind. Phaedra had to be stopped. Now. Had to learn she couldn't play dangerous sexual games and get away with it.

The only question that remained was *how* to stop her.

Anger, fuelled by frustration, came to his rescue.

'That's enough,' he said. 'That's bloody enough, Phaedra.'

She paused in her activities for less than a second, but the momentary relief gave him the will to do what needed to be done. In one furious movement he scooped her up, grabbing her beneath her squirming bottom, and carried her up the stairs to his bedroom.

Vaguely, through his rage and arousal, he heard her give a little cry that might have been fear. Or, more likely, anticipation. He didn't know, didn't care, which it was – any more than he knew what he meant to do with her now he had her.

Breathing heavily, he carried her over to his bed, dropped her on to the crimson brocade bedspread and turned her over on her stomach. He wasn't entirely sure why he did that, but he knew he couldn't stand the sight of her big, dark eyes gazing up at him in hope and bewilderment.

In that moment, confronted with the vision of Phaedra's navy blue bottom upended on his bed, Iain knew exactly what it was he meant to do.

But as he sat down heavily beside her Phaedra said, 'Iain . . .?' in a voice so low he could scarcely hear it.

In an instant he was transported back seventeen years, to the beach at Porthkelly. He heard again the endless swish of the waves, and over them the voice of a little girl who said her name was Amphitrite. *'Iain. Don't smack me.'*

With a groan, he lowered the arm he hadn't even realized he had lifted. *Was* he out of his mind? If he was, the woman on the bed had driven him there. And she *was* a woman, hadn't been a little girl for many years. Whatever was going on between them had to be dealt with by two reasonable adults – not by a teenage boy and a dreamy child.

He took Phaedra by her shoulders and turned her on to her back. 'Time to stop dreaming,' he said. 'You and I have some talking to do.'

She stared up at him, her gypsy hair wild on his pillow. 'You're angry.'

He nodded. 'I was.'

'But you're not any more?'

'I don't know what I am.' He tried to smile, but it wasn't worth the effort. 'I *can* tell you that if you ever try that again I'll be worse than angry.'

'Oh. You didn't like it.' It was a statement, not a question, and she looked so gloomy that Iain would have laughed if he hadn't thought his laughter would hurt her.

'"Like" isn't the word,' he assured her. 'You damn near drove me crazy.' He pulled at his tie. It felt unnaturally tight.

Phaedra brightened a little. 'Did I? I meant to, but . . .' She wrapped a tangled lock of her hair around her thumb and admitted ruefully, 'I haven't actually had much experience at playing Mata Hari.'

Iain did laugh then. 'Mata Hari you're not,' he agreed. 'But with practice, I'll bet you could have given her a run for her money.'

'Do you think so?'

She looked so damn young, lying there all wide-eyed and appealing – with her hand curled beside her head like a baby's.

'Yes,' he assured her. 'I do. But that's not what we need to talk about, is it?'

'I suppose not.'

'I've said it before,' he said, as patiently as he could, 'but I don't seem to have made myself clear. I'm fond of you, Phaedra. If you were anyone else, I'd be glad to oblige —'

'Oblige?'

He might have known she would force him to be specific. 'To take you to bed, then. But because you *are* you, I won't do it. It would be a betrayal. Of everything.'

She moved her head on the pillow. 'Yes. I do see.'

To his utter consternation, her enormous eyes began to fill with tears. Bloody hell! He couldn't stand it when women started crying. It made him feel helpless, and helpless was something he didn't care to be. That was one reason he and Gloria had lasted as long as they had, albeit on an intermittent basis. Neither one of them was given to embarrassing outbursts of emotion.

'Phaedra . . .' he said, picking up her hand and gently uncurling her fingers, 'Phaedra, I don't know what to say to you that I haven't said already. But the last thing I want to do is hurt you —'

'It's not your fault. You can't help it.' She turned her head to the side, and Iain felt a guilty relief that he could no longer see her eyes.

He laid her hand back on the bedspread. 'Can't help hurting you? No, I suppose not.' She sniffed, and he went on desperately, trying to lighten the mood, 'Look, you're crying all over my bedspread. Why don't I pour you a brandy . . .?' He stopped.

Phaedra had rolled to the edge of the bed. 'I don't want brandy,' she mumbled into the covers. 'I'm sorry about your bedspread.'

He reached for her, pulled her back towards him, and at once she tried to sit up. But he was in her way and she was so busy trying not to touch him that after a brief and fruitless struggle, she lost her balance and collapsed against his shoulder.

'It's all right,' he said. 'About the bedspread, I mean. It was a joke.' The scent of her was in his nostrils, and her soft hair was once again draped across his chest. He patted her back, not knowing what else to do. He must have been crazy to bring her here – should have let her spend the night as she'd wanted to, in some bug-infested hotel with drunks stumbling all over the halls and probably into her bedroom.

'Phaedra,' he said, patting some more. 'Phaedra, listen . . .'

She lifted a tear-streaked face. Her pale skin was all puffy and splotched with purple, and her beautiful eyes were rimmed with red. Iain felt as if someone had punched him in the stomach.

She tried to smile, and without forming any conscious intention, he gathered her into his arms and held her on his knee, cradling her tenderly against his chest. 'I'm sorry,' he said. He wasn't sure what he was sorry for, but he supposed it needed to be said.

In that he was mistaken. 'What are you sorry for?' Phaedra asked at once.

He had fallen in and out of temper too many times this evening, and he was getting tired of feeling out of control. Nor did he like the fact that his body was reacting predictably to the seductive pressure of her bottom on his knees. 'I'm damned if I know,' he snapped.

Her body seemed to harden like starched linen in the circle of his arms. He stroked the sleeve of her virginal white blouse, automatically seeking to soothe her, but she pushed him away and jumped up.

'Phaedra, for heaven's sake . . .' He broke off. She was already out the door and stumbling down the stairs in the sensible flat shoes that he now saw had left small, damp moons on his bedspread. His fault, that. He stood up to follow her down.

She was standing by the sofa, pulling on her navy blue jacket.

'Now what?' he asked wearily. 'Don't tell me you're about to throw a tantrum and walk out.'

She buttoned the jacket and smoothed back her hair. 'No. I'm about to walk out quite calmly and get your doorman to call me a taxi.'

Iain pulled off his tie and dropped it on to the floor. 'Mmm-hmm. And where are you going in that taxi?'

'To Victoria. I'm taking the train back to school.'

He looked at his watch. 'No, you're not. It's almost midnight. The trains don't run this late.'

'Then I'll wait till the morning.'

'In the station?'

'Why not?'

'Because I won't have it, that's why. Don't be an idiot, Phaedra.'

'I'm not an idiot. There's no reason I can't wait for the first train.'

'There's every reason. You don't know who you'll find hanging around there at this time of night. It's not safe. Now take your jacket off, I'll make you something hot to drink, and in the morning I'll drive you to the station.'

'No,' she said stiffly. 'You've done enough already.'

'What's that supposed to mean?' Iain felt his tenuous patience begin to crack.

Phaedra sniffed. 'You didn't want me here in the first place. And you only want me to stay now because you feel it's your duty to look after me. Well, I don't need looking after. I'm quite capable of taking care of myself. So thank you for dinner, thank you for putting up with me, and now I'm going to leave you in peace.'

Damn her obstinate hide! 'And how much peace do you think I'd have, wondering if some low-life was assaulting you in an alley behind the dustbins?'

'I said I can take care of myself. And anyway, why should you care?'

That did it! Iain forgot about patience, forgot that Phaedra was behaving with such uncharacteristic foolishness because, once again, he had hurt her, and replied with a harsh authority that brooked no opposition, 'Because I've spent half my life caring, that's why. And tonight I'm responsible for what happens to you.'

Phaedra opened her mouth. She was going to argue. Again. Giving way to the frustration he had been suppressing all evening, Iain strode across the room, pushed her hands out of the way and began to unbutton her jacket with short, angry movements.

'Hey!' Phaedra cried. 'You can't –'

'I can. I am. Just try and stop me.' He unfastened the last button, grabbed her collar and dragged the jacket down her arms and on to the floor.

'Iain . . .' she protested.

But Iain wasn't listening. All he could see, through the red rage in front of his eyes, was that this woman he had loved and protected since childhood was determined to do herself harm. Just to spite him. And the only way he could stop her was by taking away her clothes so she couldn't leave.

She was standing quite still now, surprised, perhaps, into making it easy for him. He reached for the button on her trousers, snapped it open and pulled down the zip. It wasn't until he had the trousers halfway down her thighs that she recovered enough to fight back.

'What the hell do you think you're doing?' she gasped, struggling to catch hold of his wrists as her clothing slid down to her knees.

'Undressing you,' he snapped. 'It won't be the first time. I told you you're not going anywhere tonight.'

'Iain! You've no right . . . I'm an adult, dammit.'

He straightened, leaving her trousers in an awkward heap around her ankles. 'Then stop behaving as if you're barely out of nappies.'

She glared at him, and drew herself up until the top of her head came to just below his chin. 'And you stop behaving like a Neanderthal. It's not up to you where I choose to spend the night.'

'Oh, yes, it is. This time it most definitely is.' He tipped her on to the sofa and knelt down beside her. In a moment her shoes were off, and the trousers had joined her jacket on the floor.

He was about to start on the next layer when he felt her fingers in his hair.

'Phaedra . . .?' He lifted his head. Too late.

She pulled, hard, as if she meant to have his scalp.

'Damn you,' Iain muttered, and made a grab for her wrists.

They tussled briefly before he was able to pry her loose, and by the time he succeeded his head was burning as if she had pulled most of his hair out by the roots.

He pushed himself on to the sofa, still holding her wrists, until he was lying half on top of her and half on the floor. Several buttons on her blouse had torn loose, and it gaped open to reveal a skimpy lace bra that barely covered the fullness of her breasts.

Iain had no qualms about looking his fill. As far as he was concerned, she had lost her right to modesty when she had refused the safe hospitality of his flat.

It was a while before he took in that she was making no effort to push him away, and that her nipples were pointed peaks against the lace. He lowered his gaze slowly to her waist. More lace, equally skimpy, over a flat stomach and softly curving hips.

Heat coiled painfully in his abdomen. His hands around her wrists were pressed against her thighs. Swallowing to dislodge a peculiar thickening in his throat, he raised his eyes at last to Phaedra's face.

She smiled, a sad, painful little smile that in another place, at another time, might have filled him with remorse. Tonight all it did was make him want to kiss her.

So he did.

The moment he let go her hands, she clasped the back of his head, holding him fast, returning his kiss with passion. Ready to burn already, Iain was barely conscious of her slender fingers slipping between their bodies, wrestling with the buttons on his shirt, until he felt her nails scrape across his chest.

He groaned. This was Phaedra. He mustn't . . .

She laughed and raised her long legs. Her toes teased the backs of his thighs.

And he was lost.

CHAPTER 11

Something wonderful was going to happen. She could feel it in her bones, in the warm, honeyed feeling liquefying her limbs, and in the spirals of pleasure swirling up and down her spine.

'Iain,' Phaedra whispered, pushing her hands up under his shirt, stroking the tough, smooth skin of his back, 'Iain, help me.'

She gasped as he took her nipple gently into his mouth, tasting, teasing intensifying her pleasure until she moaned. When she thought she could bear it no longer, Iain raised himself on his forearms and groaned, 'Help *me*, sweet Phaedra. Undo my belt.'

With shaking fingers, Phaedra did as he said, and the belt rattled on to the carpet. She touched the dark, silky hair on his chest.

Iain inhaled sharply and bent to kiss her again. She closed her eyes, savouring the taste of wine and rich coffee on his lips. As he lay over her, her hips began to move as if they belonged to someone else. She had no control, wanted no control.

Iain was breathing hard, and when he raised his head again she saw that his eyes were as glazed as she guessed her own must be. He slipped a hand under the waistband of her panties, slid them down until they too were on the carpet. Her bra followed, and, frantic now, not knowing what she was doing, Phaedra cried out and tried to pull him into her.

But suddenly, incomprehensibly, he sat up.

'Iain!' She held out her arms, desperate for him, needing him, wanting whatever it was that was going to happen.

'Wait,' he said.

And Phaedra waited, her body trembling with a need she didn't understand, except that she knew it could only be satisfied by this beautiful man she had adored for all of her life.

And, oh, he *was* beautiful. His clothes were gone now, and she could see him in all his virile glory.

He turned back to her, his flashing white smile making her put a hand to her heart to steady its frenzied beating. When she held out her arms, he lowered himself gently over her body, moving his hand in between her legs, stroking and tormenting until she cried out, 'Iain! Iain, please . . .'

He slid down her body, lowering his head, and again it was his tongue that drove her wild.

'Please,' she whispered, grasping his shoulders. She didn't know what else to say.

Iain raised his head, moved back up her body and murmured 'Phaedra, my own Phaedra' against her lips.

There was only a moment's pain and then he was a part of her, as she had always known he was meant to be.

The glory that was inside her exploded.

And it *was* wonderful.

Time passed. Stretched out on top of her, Iain gave one last ecstatic shudder. Phaedra arched her body to meet his, and he wrapped his arms around her, kissed her with exquisite mastery and, still holding her, rolled over on to his back.

'Iain!' Phaedra cried in warning.

She was too late. In a tangle of limbs and passion, the two of them thudded on to the carpet.

Below them, way below them, someone shouted and pounded on the ceiling.

Some time later, when breath was restored to her lungs, Phaedra giggled and dropped a kiss on Iain's lips. 'We've upset the neighbours,' she said.

'Bugger the neighbours.'

Phaedra blinked at him. It wasn't the first time she had heard him swear by any means, but there was something rough and raw in his voice now that frightened her a little.

Not knowing what to reply, she leaned over and nibbled at his ear.

Iain lay still, one hand on her rear, the other caressing her neck. After a while he said, 'We'd better get off the floor.'

He might as well have been suggesting that the board meeting should move to another room. Phaedra clambered off him and reached for her blouse. She had one sleeve on and was struggling to get her hand into the other, when Iain came up behind her and linked his arms around her waist. She stood still, and the blouse fell back on to the sofa.

As Iain lifted her hair and planted a kiss on her neck, she whispered, 'Thank you. Thank you, my love.'

His body tensed against her back, and almost at once he withdrew. When she turned to see what was wrong, he was already pulling on his trousers.

'Iain . . .?' she said. 'Iain? What's the matter?'

He gestured at her crumpled white blouse. 'Better get dressed. It's cold.'

Puzzled, Phaedra did as he said. It *was* chilly in the flat because Iain hadn't got around to turning on the heat. But it wasn't only the air that was cold.

Iain buckled his belt and shrugged on his shirt without troubling to do it up. Then, as she waited uncertainly, he moved in front of her, took her by the shoulders and pressed her down on to the sofa.

Phaedra gazed up at him, filled with instinctive foreboding. But he looked so desirable, standing there with his legs apart and his white shirt hanging loose on his hips, that instead of asking again what was the matter, Phaedra said softly, 'Now I know what I've been waiting for all these years.'

Iain turned his back on her and walked across to the window. In spite of the chill, he opened it, and cold air rushed into the room. Phaedra shivered and wrapped her arms around her chest.

He stood at the window for some time staring down into the quiet square. In the distance she could hear the occasional hum of cars along Park Lane, and the brisk slam of doors as late-night revellers returned to their homes.

When he finally spoke, it was only to say bleakly, 'I hope it was worth it?'

'Oh, Iain. Of course it was. How could you doubt it?'

'Easily, I'm afraid.' He still had his back to her. There was no emotion in his voice, just a cool acceptance of reality.

Phaedra clasped her hands and pressed them to her chest in an age-old gesture of supplication. 'You needn't. It was the most incredible, most wonderful experience of my life. I think I've always known it would be. And that it couldn't happen with anyone but you.'

Iain put his hands on the window sill and allowed his head to drop against the glass. 'Don't say that, Phaedra. You mustn't say that.'

'But it's true.'

'No. No, it's not true. Somewhere there's another man who will make you far happier than I can. Ever.' He spun round. 'You have to accept that. I'm sorry.'

Phaedra closed her eyes. Yes, he was sorry. She believed him. It was in his voice, in the lines around his mouth, and in his eyes. But he wasn't sorry enough to accept the love she had to give him.

'Do you *want* me to find another man?' she asked, making herself look at him, unable to believe that after loving her so beautifully he could be willing to pass her on to someone else.

He held out his hands, palms upward. 'Don't ask me that. I have to want it. For your sake.'

'Didn't you . . .? Wasn't it . . .? For you, I mean?'

'Wasn't it incredible for me?' Iain put his hands over his face, and after that his voice came out muffled. 'Yes. Yes, it was. Thank you.'

'You don't have to thank me.'

'I do have to thank you. I also have to apologize. I had no right, no business to do what I did. God knows, I never meant to.'

'Of course you didn't. But you had every right. I wanted you to.' She held out a hand and tried to smile. 'I want you to do it again.'

Iain lowered his hands and rammed them into his pockets. 'I know you do. So do I. But I'm not going to.'

'But Iain, why? I'm here. We've got the rest of the night together –'

'NO!' His answer came out on a roar. '*No*, Phaedra. It's bad enough I lost control once. I am not going to add insult to injury by doing it again. It wouldn't be fair. To you – or to me, for that matter. So please, just go on upstairs and make yourself at home in one of the spare bedrooms. Then in the morning I'll drive you to the station.'

Phaedra had known him too long not to recognize the finality of his words. Iain wouldn't change his mind. He had some crazy idea that because he wouldn't marry her, he couldn't make love to her either. And because of that the two of them were doomed to spend this night, and every other night of their lives, in separate beds.

She stood up, picked up her jacket and shoes and went to fetch her suitcase from beside the door.

Iain moved then. He crossed the floor silently on bare feet and took the case from her unresisting fingers. Phaedra, breathing in the scent of their love-making, looked up at him with a hope that was instantly crushed. There was no relenting in the darkness of his eyes. Nor would there be in the future.

Defeated, she turned away from him and walked across the room and up the stairs. At the top she hesitated.

'The one on the left is furthest from mine,' Iain said from behind her.

Phaedra squeezed back her tears and turned left.

Iain followed her and slung her suitcase on to the white, woven bedspread of the narrow room's single brass bed.

'Goodnight,' he said from the door.

Phaedra caught hold of the bedpost with both hands. 'Goodnight,' she said.

He looked at her without really seeming to see her. Then suddenly he was standing in front of her and his thumb was tracing the line of her cheekbone. Their eyes met, and he bent to kiss her, so fleetingly that when the door closed behind him Phaedra wasn't convinced she hadn't dreamed his kiss.

She slumped down on the bed and gazed without seeing it at the floor.

Some time later the floor came back into focus, and she saw that it was covered by a a thick red and gold rug. She fumbled for the buttons of her blouse, tugged it off along with her trousers, and slipped beneath the soft comfort of the blankets. She forgot about washing herself, forgot to turn off the light, forgot about everything except that she had first won, and then lost Iain. It had been both the best and the worst night of her life.

The best was over now. From this moment on all she could do was make the most of what was left.

It wasn't much to look forward to.

Hell! Iain flung his crimson bedspread to one side and fell on top of the blankets.

He thought about taking his clothes off, but rejected the idea as soon as it came into his mind. What was the point? The feel of the sheets against his skin would only make him think of Phaedra lying alone and unhappy at the end of the hall. Phaedra, who had lain with him on the sofa, but never in his bed.

Incredible, she had called it. Wonderful. Only with him, she had said. God, he felt like a heel. Groaning, he slammed his fist into the pillow. She had been so generous, so loving – had given him the gift that a woman could only give once. And what had he given her in return? He reached for the discarded bedspread, ran his hands over its smooth, satiny surface. The scent of her still lingered in its folds. He pressed it to his face.

Nothing. He had given her nothing. All he had done was take, whatever she might say. How could he have done that to Phaedra? How could he have been so lost to all decency as to take advantage of the woman he had once wanted only to protect?

'Because you wanted her, Trebanian, that's why,' he heard someone mutter out loud. 'Have wanted her since she was a kid of eighteen. And she was there, on her back, wanting you, offering herself . . .'

Damn. He couldn't just lie here, remembering.

Pushing himself upright, Iain swung his legs over the edge of the bed and sat holding his head in his hands. What could he do to make it up to her? Go to her room? Give her what she wanted? What *he* wanted? That was a laugh. How self-serving could he get?

He lifted his head. What was that he heard? Phaedra? Crying? No, he was imagining things. The only sound was the faint whirring of the anti-quated central heating fan. And there was nothing he could do for Phaedra now but deliver her to her train in the morning and, some time soon, get old Angus Cooper to see to the transfer of a large sum of money to her bank account. Enough to buy Chy an Cleth. She might not accept it, but with that done his obligation would be at an end. The house would be his, because she had already deeded it to him, and as long as he stayed away from Porthkelly during school holidays, there was no reason for him to see her again.

He put up a hand to block out the moonlight beaming through the window. Phaedra had grown from a dreamy child into a sensible young woman. She would soon come to accept that he wasn't the right man for her. God, if she only knew, he wasn't the right man for any woman. Certainly not a woman who suffered from an old-fashioned belief in happily-ever-after. Certainly not for Phaedra Pendenning.

He wouldn't marry again. Once was enough for any man who still had his brain intact. There were plenty of Glorias in the world, modern women who wanted what he wanted – bed with no strings attached, and no obsessive need to procreate.

Iain pulled off his shirt, hung it over a straight-backed wooden chair, and made himself get back under the covers. He would do neither Phaedra nor Trebanian Advertising any good by spending a sleepless night staring at the moonlight on the wall.

He closed his eyes, willing himself to sleep, and immediately Phaedra's face appeared in the darkness of his mind. And then Phaedra's body, soft, female, long limbs wrapped around . . .

He groaned and rolled over on his side.

In the morning, when his alarm went off, he was already wide awake, and Phaedra was moving about somewhere below.

Half an hour later, after showering and dressing, he followed the smell of coffee downstairs and found her frying eggs in the compact cubicle of his rarely used kitchen. She looked so fresh and pretty, and so damn desirable, that he wanted to shout at her to get the hell away from the cooker and into bed.

'I heard you get up,' she said, nodding at the counter. 'Coffee's ready. Or would you prefer tea?'

Iain scowled. 'Coffee's fine.' He lowered himself on to the padded bench in the corner beside the table. When the coffee continued to tantalize his nose while Phaedra went on cooking, he got up and poured himself a cup.

A minute or two later she placed a plate of eggs and toast in front of him. He eyed the yellow yolks with misgiving. After a sleepless night, and a shower that had done little to improve his sense of physical well-being and nothing to improve his disposition, Iain wasn't sure he could face anything fried. Especially anything fried and yellow.

'Is there something wrong with them?' Phaedra asked.

'No. No, they're fine.' He picked up his knife and fork. 'You shouldn't have bothered, though.'

'Why not? We have to eat. And I was up.'

'So I see. Did you sleep well?'

'Very well, thank you. And you?'

This was ridiculous. 'I had a rotten night,' Iain snapped, swallowing a mouthful of egg.

'Mm. You look a bit mouldy. Sort of grey around the edges,' Phaedra said.

Iain wished he had the energy to throttle her.

'Here's your paper,' she said, waving a headline about a particularly gruesome murder under his nose.

Iain took it. 'Aren't you going to eat?' he asked.

'I already did, thank you.'

She sounded so bright and alert he decided mere throttling wouldn't do the job. He glared at the paper because he knew he had no right to glare at her.

Phaedra sat down across from him, and he was aware that she was nursing a cup of coffee and that her navy blue suit looked as neat and crisp as it had the day before. But he kept his eyes on the paper, absurdly soothed by the grim details of the murder. He refused to look at her directly.

She certainly seemed to have recovered from her disappointment of the night before. It was as if the two of them had never lain together on his sofa and made love – that's what she would call it anyway – never, for a short time, known what it was to lose the world in each other's arms.

He would never forget it – didn't think she would either. Women didn't forget their first time, any more than men did. But he couldn't look at her now. If he did, he might see behind the calm and collected manner she was wearing like a cloak, to whatever was hidden behind that cool façade. He knew her too well to believe the façade was all there was.

Iain choked down his breakfast without tasting it, helped Phaedra put the dishes in the washing-up machine, and said briskly, 'Ready then? You won't want to miss your train.'

'No,' Phaedra agreed. 'No, I wouldn't want to do that.' He glanced at her, but her face was averted, and he couldn't tell if she was being sarcastic.

They drove to the station in silence. It occurred to Iain that driving with Phaedra was always a silent business. He couldn't complain that she indulged in idle chatter.

As he had done once before, he saw her to the doorway of her carriage. 'Thanks. Don't bother to wait,' she said. 'I hope you sleep better tonight.'

Was that a gibe? He looked at her sharply. If it was, it certainly didn't show. She was smiling as if she hadn't a care in the world. Iain experienced an overwhelming sense of *déjà vu*. The wintery sky vanished, and once again he was on the platform at Exeter on an autumn afternoon nine years ago. The only difference was that her suit that day had been black instead of navy blue.

'Phaedra,' he said, unable to keep up the absurd charade any longer. 'Phaedra, listen. If ever you need – anything – let me know . . .'

'Thank you. I won't need anything.' Her smile didn't falter.

'I meant – damn.' Suddenly he was standing on the step of the carriage. A whistle blew, doors slammed – and he dragged Phaedra into his arms where she belonged. How could he have thought of letting her go? He crushed her lips beneath his, feeling the soft, womanly length of her against his body . . .

Phaedra didn't try to push him away. She stood motionless, as if her limbs were made of ice, accepting his kiss but not responding. He might have been making love to a stone.

264

Someone shouted, the train began to move, and Iain came to his senses. As he jumped back, Phaedra slammed the door and waved.

He stared after her, raising his hand stiffly in salute. Then he took a handerchief from his pocket, wiped his forhead, and turned away. A close shave that. He'd regained his sanity not a moment too soon.

By the time he reached the barrier, the train was out of sight.

Phaedra watched his back until she could no longer see him. Then she sat down, ignoring the curious gaze of a small woman in a hat across the aisle, put both hands over her face, and didn't look up again until the train pulled in to her station.

She couldn't face the world just yet. Maintaining her composure in front of Iain this morning had been the hardest thing she had ever done in her life. But she had known the moment she got up that it was the only way she could get through the last few painful hours they would spend together.

Resisting that kiss had been the worst part. But she had known if she responded it would all start again. And later Iain would remember she was Phaedra and leave again.

She couldn't have borne that.

Now it was over, and she could go back to being who she was. Sensible, reserved Ms Pendenning who didn't give her heart the chance to rule her head.

As the train shunted to a halt, Phaedra picked up her suitcase, stepped briskly on to the platform and squared her shoulders. She had used up all the time she could allow herself for grieving. Now she had a life to get on with.

Only one thing had changed.

She ran a finger over her lips, remembering all the places Iain had touched her, knowing that however much it hurt to live without him, what she had told him last night was the truth.

It *had* been worth it. She had a memory to take with her down the years.

CHAPTER 12

'What time are you expecting Phaedra?' Angus hitched up the knees of his perfectly pressed trousers and seated himself in one of the two overstuffed armchairs that, along with a small oval coffee table and a television, were all that could be fitted into the glorified cupboard that passed for Esther's sitting-room.

'I'm not sure.' Esther wrinkled her forehead. 'She'll go up to the house first, I should think. But she's coming on here for supper. I do wish I had room for a proper tree.' She gestured at the foot-high artificial Christmas tree perched on the edge of a table already overburdened with biscuits, teapot, milk, sugar and two white china cups with gold trim.

'You don't need one, my dear. Not when we're all spending Christmas Day at Chy an Cleth.' Angus gave her the annoyingly soothing smile he had been in the habit of bestowing on his wife.

Esther poured milk into the teacups. 'I suppose you're right. But Christmas doesn't seem the same without a proper tree. Not that anything's been the same since Charles died.'

'Hmm.' Angus cleared his throat and helped himself to a biscuit. 'Feel the same way myself sometimes. Allison wanted me to go all the way up to Yorkshire for the holiday, but I couldn't face the journey at this time of year. Or the noise. I'm partial to my grandchildren, but they don't know the meaning of quiet. Decided I'd rather spend the day here with you – and those two long-haired misfits Iain has permitted to take over his house. Odd business, that. Can't understand it at all.'

'Angus! Those long-haired misfits were kind enough to ask you for Christmas dinner. And they're friends of Phaedra's. A nice enough young couple, even if they don't dress like the rest of us.'

'That may be so.' Angus pursed his lips, plainly unconvinced. 'I still think Iain should marry Phaedra. Then the two of *them* could move in to Chy an Cleth. Much more suitable. My old friend, Charles, was right for once.'

'Rubbish.' Esther was fond of Angus, but sometimes his old-fashioned prissiness got on her nerves. 'Iain and Phaedra know what they're about.'

'My dear Esther! That may be so, but I hardly think –'

'No, no, of course not. You're quite right.' Esther wasn't sure what he was right about, but she knew he meant well. It wasn't kind to quarrel with him. She picked up her cup, then changed her mind and put it back in its saucer. Tea wasn't the same without a cigarette. 'The truth,' she explained, giving Angus a conciliatory smile, 'is that I'd like to see Phaedra and Iain marry as much as anybody. But I don't think it's likely to happen.'

'Pity.'

'Yes. Yes, it is.' Esther glanced hopefully at the window, but the empty flower-boxes blocked her view of the courtyard. Even if Phaedra was on her way up, she wouldn't be able to see her. And she did wish Angus hadn't chosen this afternoon to invite himself to tea. If he stayed much longer she would have to ask him to stay on for supper, and tonight she wanted her daughter to herself.

Angus said, 'Well, well. Must be getting along,' as if he sensed that his presence was superfluous. But he didn't get up, and Esther knew he was hoping she would tell him he didn't have to leave.

'Yes, I think you *had* better be going,' she said firmly. 'I have one or two things to see to before Phaedra comes.' She hadn't. Everything had been ready for hours. But she really didn't want to share her child with Angus. Not tonight, when she hadn't seen her for two months.

Reluctantly, Angus levered himself out of his chair. 'Will I see you at church tomorrow?' he asked, smoothing his thinning hair and giving Esther what she thought of as his hungry beagle smile.

'Maybe.' She wasn't much of a church-goer, but she had gone a few times lately just to please him. Perhaps that had been a mistake.

'I'll look for you,' Angus said, as she hustled him out the door.

Esther nodded absently. She was wondering if she had time for a quick cigarette before Phaedra came.

In fact she had smoked two before the long-anticipated knock sounded on her door. She flung open her bedroom window, closed the door, and hurried to let Phaedra in.

'Oh, Mum,' Phaedra cried, enveloping her mother in a frantic hug. 'It *is* good to see you.'

'Mmm.' Esther patted her shoulder and turned her face to the light. 'You look pale.'

'Mum, it's winter. Of course I look pale.'

'And your eyes are too bright.' Phaedra had lovely eyes, but they tended to glow rather than sparkle. When they sparkled, it was a sure sign she was trying to conceal something. 'Is anything wrong?'

'No, of course not. Come on, Mum, how about a cup of tea?'

Something *was* wrong. Her quiet daughter sounded positively hearty.

'I've got something stronger than tea,' Esther said. 'You look as though you could do with a pick-me-up.' Ignoring Phaedra's dismissive shrug, she went into the kitchen, took out the bottle of sherry she'd been saving, and filled two crystal glasses to the brim. 'There.' She handed one to Phaedra. 'Happy Christmas, dear.'

'Happy Christmas.' Phaedra took the glass and sat down at the kitchen table. 'How are you, Mum?'

'Not too bad. Usual aches and complaints of advancing years. Nothing serious.'

Phaedra looked pained.

Oh dear. That had been the wrong thing to say. 'Just a joke,' she said quickly. 'I'm fine. In fact, according to Angus, I'm in my prime.'

Phaedra smiled. 'How is Angus?'

'Oh, all right. But I'm afraid he's going to ask me to marry him.'

'Afraid? I thought you liked him, Mum?'

'Yes, of course I like him. I'm just not sure I want to marry him.'

'He'd be company. Take your mind off things.'

'Things?'

'Well, you know . . .'

Esther wondered why her daughter was wriggling her shoulders and refusing to meet her eyes. 'I *don't* know,' she said, with a little more starch than she intended. 'I'm finding I quite enjoy my own company. I've had my share of catering to a man's needs.'

'Yes, but this is different. You weren't married to Charles . . .' Phaedra broke off abruptly. 'I expect it sometimes felt that way though, did it?'

If only it had! 'Yes,' Esther agreed, rubbing the back of her wrist across her nose. 'Yes, I expect it did. Sometimes.'

The two of them were silent, gazing into the rich brown liquid in their glasses.

'How's school?' Esther asked after a while. 'Have you had a good term?'

Phaedra smiled wryly. 'Oh yes. We had an out-break of chicken pox, Jennifer Reilly fell over her own feet and broke her ankle – the left one this time, two of the seniors tried to seduce the gardener's assistant behind the gym, and we had several cases of drunk and disorderly in the dorms. It turned out Nancy Ingles was brewing dandelion wine in a bucket in one of the rose beds. But on the whole it wasn't a bad term.'

Esther laughed. 'Never a dull moment from the sound of it. And you? Have you been all right?'

'Of course I have.'

Esther decided it was time to be blunt. "Iain," she said. 'I know he's spending Christmas in London with friends, but have you heard from him since he drove you back to London? He was down here a week ago, you know.'

Phaedra picked up her glass and held it in front of her nose. 'Yes, I know. He left a message to say he'd checked on Jade and Lloyd and decided they could stay until the spring. Generous of him,' she added.

Esther didn't miss the sarcasm. 'That's all?' she asked. 'All the message he left?'

'Not quite. He also said he'd opened a bank account in my name. But you must have heard that from Angus.'

Oh. *Now* she knew what was eating away at Phaedra. That and the prospect of a Christmas without Charles *or* Iain. As she had said to Angus less than an hour ago, it didn't look as though there was much hope of Charles's matrimonial machinations bearing fruit.

'No,' she said. 'Angus said nothing about it. He can be very discreet when he wants to be.' She took a quick sip of sherry. 'What are you going to do about the bank account? I assume it has money in it?'

Phaedra shrugged. 'Plenty. And I haven't decided. Try to give it back to him, I suppose.'

'He won't take it.'

'No. He wants to *buy* Chy an Cleth from me.'

'Then why don't you let him? That's why you married Charles, isn't it? So Iain could inherit the house.'

Phaedra shrugged. 'Yes. Maybe you're right.'

Esther frowned. That listless, uninterested response didn't sound like her Phaedra talking. She seemed so defeated, so uncaring. 'Have some more sherry,' Esther suggested, getting up to bring the bottle to the table. 'It'll do you good.'

Phaedra didn't argue, which only deepened Esther's concern. A bad sign, that. Her daughter usually objected on principle to anything prescribed as a tonic.

Esther sat down again. 'You still care for him, don't you?' she said.

'Care for him?' Phaedra laughed, an ugly sound that made her mother feel like crying. 'Yes, I suppose I do. But I'm trying not to.'

'It takes time,' Esther agreed cautiously.

'I know. A lifetime,' Phaedra said.

'Nonsense. You're still young.'

When Phaedra said nothing, Esther got up and began to poke at the fish pie in the oven. A lifetime? Dear God, please not again! Please don't let my daughter waste her life on a love that will never be returned. Don't let a Trebanian break her heart.

273

She closed her eyes, put her hands together and gazed beseechingly at the unresponsive ceiling.

'Mum? What are you doing?'

Esther jumped, and went back to poking the fish pie.

'Would you like some more mock turkey, Mrs Pendenning?'

'No, thank you, Jade. I've done very well.' Esther smiled bravely. 'The brussels sprouts were especially delicious.'

Phaedra buried her nose in her wine glass to hide a smile. Jade's tofu turkey with all the trimmings was not going over well with the older members of the small party of five gathered around the table.

'Mr Cooper?' Jade turned to Angus, who was dabbing at the corner of his lip with a red paper napkin.

'No, no. Thank you. Most kind. Not much appetite these days, I'm afraid.'

'Oh, but you've had so little. You want to keep your strength up,' Jade urged him, spearing a pinky-grey slab of something circular and soft, and waving it on the end of a fork.

Angus held up his hand. '*Most* kind of you to invite me,' he said. 'So sorry I'm unable to do it justice.'

Phaedra removed her nose from the glass and fixed her gaze on the window. A few flakes of sleety snow were falling from the grey blanket that formed the Christmas sky. Anything was better than allowing herself to catch her mother's eye. She knew that if she did, she was likely to dissolve into howls of helpless mirth.

Jade had done her best. The table was festive with holly and crackers, and she had taken the trouble to dress almost conventionally in jeans and a red chiffon blouse that, by chance, contrasted colourfully with Phaedra's sober black and white sheath. Lloyd had even been persuaded to trim his beard. But there was no way either Esther or Angus Cooper could be convinced that tofu was any substitute for real turkey. Phaedra had tried to warn them, but they hadn't believed her.

She didn't mind mock turkey herself. It saved a lot of fiddling with bones.

Lloyd, who hadn't wanted to trim his beard, said with just a shade of belligerence, 'This is a lot better for us than eating some unlucky dead bird full of pesticides. Don't you think so, Mrs Pendenning?'

'Oh, call me Esther, please,' Esther said, deftly avoiding Lloyd's question.

Well done, Mum. Phaedra cheered silently and went on watching the snow, which was starting to fall in big wet flakes. Her mother had had plenty of practice at not answering inconvenient questions in the days when she had looked after Charles. It was good to see she hadn't lost her touch.

Jade said, 'Well, if everyone's finished . . .'

Phaedra hadn't, but she polished off the rest of her meal in record time and stood up to help Jade clear away the plates.

This Christmas that she'd been dreading hadn't been so bad after all. At school she had managed to anaesthetize her emotions with work. But back in Porthkelly, where Iain was in the very air she breathed, she had expected all the pain to come flooding back. So far it hadn't. The bittersweet memories were sad, but not overwhelming. And poor Angus's face when he'd first caught sight of the alleged turkey had been more than enough to lift her spirits from any tendency to brood.

Phaedra Pendenning, stop that at once, she admonished herself as she walked past the big tree in the hall that Jade had decorated with home-made ornaments in shades of pink and red. Just because *you're* not brimming with Christmas spirit is no reason to take pleasure in an old man's disappointment.

'Iain Trebanian, you've got a lot to answer for,' she muttered, opening the kitchen door with her hip.

'Huh?' Jade lifted a steaming plum pudding from the oven and paused with it halfway to the counter. 'What did you say?'

'Nothing,' Phaedra said. 'Nothing important.'

'Oh.' With a last suspicious glance at her friend, Jade upended the pudding on to a platter, soaked it in brandy and set it alight. Phaedra dumped her load of dishes on the draining board and followed her hostess back to the dining room.

'Ah, that looks more – that looks very nice.' Angus nodded with relief as Jade placed the flaming pudding on the table.

Phaedra smiled. Knowing Jade, this wouldn't be any standard Christmas pudding. But, with luck, Angus wouldn't know the difference.

He didn't, and when Jade offered him a second helping, he accepted. The meal ended on a note of cordiality with the pulling of crackers and the donning of paper hats.

Afterwards Jade hustled a willing Angus and a reluctant Esther into the drawing-room to relax with their new Christmas books while she and Lloyd got on with the washing up.

'You, too, Phaedra,' Jade said. 'You're supposed to be on holiday.'

'Oh, no, thank you. I'd rather help.'

Lloyd nodded approvingly and sidled towards the door. 'Think I'll just fix that leaky tap in the upstairs bathroom.'

'Hold it,' Jade said. 'I need you to . . .'

But Lloyd had already disappeared.

His wife shook her head. 'Sometimes I think he sabotages taps and other things just so he can have an excuse to fix them.'

Phaedra laughed. 'Maybe he . . .' She paused. 'What was that? Are you expecting someone? I thought I heard a car pulling up?'

The doorbell rang before Jade had a chance to answer. She and Phaedra were still staring at each other in surprise when it rang again.

'Someone's impatient,' Jade said, scraping the rejected remains of Angus's tofu turkey into the bin beneath the sink.

'I'll get it,' said Phaedra. 'Probably just some lost soul looking for directions.'

But when she opened the door, it wasn't a lost

traveller she found drooping on the doorstep in floods of tears.

It was Joan.

'Joan! What is it?' Phaedra cried. 'Oh, do come on in. You look frozen.' She seized Iain's sister by the sleeve of her snow-covered black coat and dragged her into the dubious warmth of the hall. A moment later Jade emerged from the kitchen drying her hands on a red and white towel.

'Hi,' she said to the newcomer. 'Who are you? Oh, I remember. You're Iain's sister, aren't you? Listen, you've missed Christmas dinner, but . . . oh.' She moved a few steps closer. 'You're not in the mood for food, are you?'

Joan shook her head vigorously, spraying Phaedra and the tree with a shower of melted snow.

'What is it?' Phaedra repeated. For no reason, fear, unreasoning and overwhelming, had welled up inside her and was making her feel sick. 'Iain –'

'Iain's fine. As far as I know.' Joan pulled a handkerchief out of her pocket and blew her nose. 'Oh, Phaedra, it's Anton! We've had the most terrible fight! I don't think he loves me any more.' She dissolved into a fresh paroxysm of weeping.

'Of course he does,' Phaedra said, in the bracing voice she automatically used on tearful girls whose parents hadn't arrived to pick them up. 'Now then, you take your coat off, and we'll talk.'

'Brandy,' Jade said, and disappeared.

Esther and Angus appeared in the hall together just as Phaedra was carrying Joan's coat to the cloakroom. 'We thought we heard . . .' Esther began. She broke off. 'Joan! What are you doing here? Whatever's happened? Oh, my dear, not that I'm not pleased to see you.' She bustled across the floor and caught the shivering Joan in her arms. 'My dear child, it can't be as bad as all that.'

'It's worse,' Joan howled, wrapping her arms around Esther's plump neck. 'Oh, Pendy . . .' She burst into loud, gulping sobs.

Phaedra, coming back from the cloakroom, heard the phone ring, but Jade, arriving with a large glass of brandy, reached it first.

'Hello? Yes, this is Jade. Who – oh, yes, of course. Yes she is. Phaedra . . .' She handed the receiver to Phaedra. 'It's our landlord.'

'Iain?' Phaedra took the instrument as if she expected it to blow up in her face. 'Hello? Happy Christmas.'

'I have a feeling it isn't,' he said. 'Is my sister with you?'

'Yes. She's just arrived. She's upset because she and Anton had a fight.'

Joan, hearing her husband's name, chose that moment to let out another wail. Startled, Jade dropped the glass of brandy with a crash. Esther gave a cry of pain as Angus, trying to help, side-stepped the shattered glass and landed on her foot.

'What the . . .?' exclaimed Iain on the other end of the line. 'Phaedra, what's going on? Is Joan all right?'

'I think so. She's just a little upset. Don't worry, we'll look after her.'

'How could he?' Joan was crying on Esther's shoulder. 'Oh, Pendy, how could he? I'm so desperately unhappy. How can I possibly live without Anton? What am I going to *do*?'

'Is she hysterical?' Iain asked.

'Borderline. She'll be all right in a minute.'

Joan gave a howl like a tone-deaf dying diva, and Iain said, 'Good God. Happy Christmas,' and hung up.

A few seconds later Lloyd came wandering down the stairs, screwdriver at the ready, in search of something to fix.

'Put that down and light the fire in the living-room,' Jade said to him at once.

'Yes, sergeant.' Lloyd saluted and went off to do as he was told.

It took them a good fifteen minutes to get Joan calmed down and settled in front of a glowing fire with a fresh glass of brandy. By that time Phaedra was reluctant to set her off again by asking what the quarrel had been about.

Jade had no such qualms.

'Did he hit you?' she demanded. 'Because if he did –'

'Anton? Oh, no.' Joan looked shocked. 'He wouldn't do that. But he – he . . . I think he's having an affair with Ida Byrd.'

Lloyd cleared his throat, picked up his screwdriver and made a beeline for the door.

'Anton? He can't be,' Phaedra exclaimed. 'She's old enough to be his mother.'

Joan tucked her chin into the collar of her black, polo-neck sweater. 'Only just old enough. And she doesn't look it.'

Phaedra had only met Ida Byrd once, at Joan and Anton's wedding. And she had to agree the woman was young for her years. But not *that* young. And Anton had never had eyes for anyone but Joan.

'You must be mistaken,' she said firmly. 'Anton wouldn't –'

'That's what I thought.' Joan, over the worst of her panic, was wrapped in gloom. 'But I caught them with their heads together. *Whispering*. And when they saw me they jumped apart, and Anton started talking very fast. He always does that when he's feeling guilty.'

'Could mean anything,' Angus interrupted in his best judicial voice. 'Not necessarily guilt.'

'But he wouldn't deny it when I accused him. He said I was a suspicious little cat who didn't deserve –'

'Didn't deserve what, dear?' Esther asked gently.

'I don't know. I wouldn't let him finish. And he shouted some awful things at me and walked out. He was going back to Ida. I know he was. So I took the next plane to London and came here. I thought I'd find Iain.'

'Iain's spending Christmas in London,' Esther said.

'Oh.' Joan sniffed, and pulled a handkerchief out of her sleeve.

'Where actually *is* Anton?' Phaedra asked.

'Paris. He's in Paris. With Ida.'

'Scum,' muttered Jade.

'He's not scum,' Joan objected contrarily.

Angus coughed, looked at his watch, and stood up. 'Time we were leaving,' he said.

'Don't be silly, Angus. I can't leave Joan like this.'

'I'm all right,' Joan said. 'You mustn't worry about me.' She glanced at Phaedra and then at Jade. 'Is it all right if I just go to bed?'

Good, Phaedra thought. The worst is over.

Joan had always had the ability to curl up like a cat and go to sleep whenever the woes of her world became insupportable.

'Your room's all ready for you,' Phaedra said. 'Isn't it, Jade?'

'I guess so.' Jade jumped up, as if eager to escape Joan's doleful presence. 'I'll just go and check to make sure. Mrs Pendenning, you and Mr Cooper mustn't leave. I'm going to make tea in a minute.'

At the mention of tea, Angus sat down again.

Another hour had passed by the time he and Esther finally took their leave, and by that time night had fallen and the snow was an inch thick on the ground.

Phaedra went upstairs to check on Joan, and found her lying fast asleep and fully clothed on top of the bed. Shaking her head, she took a blanket from the linen cupboard, draped it across her sleeping friend and started down the stairs again to see what Jade was doing.

When she reached the hall, she heard the sound of stamping feet outside the door.

What on earth . . .? Not another unexpected guest. Who could be out there at this hour? She put a hand to her mouth as a key clicked into the lock. Then, before she could move, the front door flew open and Iain stalked in accompanied by a blast of swirling snow.

Behind her, the decorations on the tree shivered and tinkled in the wind.

CHAPTER 13

'Iain!' Phaedra's vision blurred. Attempting to steady herself, she grabbed a branch of the Christmas tree and hung on. It felt soft and rubbery instead of prickly. Her grip tightened as Iain, his dark hair frosted with snow, shrugged off his overcoat, slung it over his arm and walked towards her. His shoes left damp prints on the polished floor.

'Don't tell me you're surprised to see me?' He started to smile, then seemed to change his mind. 'You must have known I'd come?'

'No.' He was standing too close, and he smelled of fresh snow and warm man. 'Mum said you were spending Christmas in London. With friends.'

'I was until Anton phoned. He caught me just as I was leaving.'

'Oh. Is he still in Paris?'

'As far as I know. He sounded in something of a panic. I don't think he realized that when it came to the crunch there was never much doubt my sister would turn up here – in spite of her disdain for the country.'

'She only came because she thought she'd find *you* here.'

'Ah.' Iain's gaze shifted to the stairs. 'I can't imagine why. I haven't spent Christmas Day at Chy an Cleth in years.'

'Perhaps she thought things would change – now that your father's gone. Did you let Anton know she's all right?' And why was she standing here trying to pretend this was an ordinary conversation, when the man she loved was behaving as though she meant no more to him than any other casual acquaintance. Or a useful pair of shoes. Phaedra bit her lip and tasted salt.

Iain's eyes didn't quite make contact. 'Yes, he knows. I called him back as soon as I'd talked to you. He's coming to fetch her tomorrow.' He pushed a hand through his hair as its frosting of snow began to melt. 'Phaedra, why are you torment-ing that tree?'

'I didn't know I was.' She released her branch reluctantly and smelled the faint scent of pine on her skin. 'You got here amazingly fast.'

'There wasn't much traffic on the road. Now where's my sister?'

'Upstairs. Asleep.' Phaedra's reply was as abrupt as the question. It had to be. As usual, all she really wanted to do was fall into his arms.

Iain raised his eyes to the ceiling. 'I might have known. What you're telling me is that I drove all the way down here to prevent her from jumping off the cliff before Anton arrives to toss her over it tomorrow

– and all the time she's been in bed, peacefully sleeping off her fit of pique?'

'I told you we'd look after her. And it wasn't just pique –'

'Frankly, I don't care what it was. I've a good mind to wake her up and give her a good reason to have hysterics.' Iain half-turned towards the stairs.

'Over my dead body.' Phaedra planted herself squarely in front of him. 'You ought to be glad she's asleep.'

Iain stared at her for a moment, then gave her a crooked smile and shook his head. 'You're right, of course. I can safely leave that sort of thing to Anton. How was she then? Before she fell asleep?'

Phaedra noticed that his overcoat had started to drip on to the floor. Wherever it touched him, his dark blue pullover and wool trousers were soaked to the colour of ink.

'Give that to me,' she said, holding out her hand. 'I'll hang it up.'

Iain didn't move. 'I asked how Joan was.'

'She's upset, naturally. And furious with Anton. But she'll be all right in the morning. Now – are you going to give me that coat? It's wet.'

Iain handed over his coat with surprising meekness, and she hurried off to hang it in the cloakroom, glad of any excuse to get away from its owner. Being near him, yet unable to touch him, was a torture she could only bear in small doses.

She hung the saturated overcoat on a hanger, and the smell of damp wool became inextricably mingled

286

in her mind with the smell of the aftershave Iain always used.

With a soft groan, she wrapped her arms around the wet garment and buried her face deep in its folds.

Iain found her there when he came to see what was taking her so long.

'Phaedra?'

The touch of his hand on her shoulder, a gentle reminder of happiness gained and now lost, ripped away the paper-thin scar tissue that, over the last few weeks, had begun the slow process of healing over her heart.

With a gulping sob, she tightened her grip on the sodden coat and clung to it – her only hope of survival in a surging sea of her own frustrated longings.

'Phaedra! For God's sake . . .' Iain's big hands closed over hers, pried her loose from the clammy, wet cloth. Then she was enfolded in his arms with her cheek pressed against the soft, blue wool of his pullover. Through it she could feel the steady beating of his heart.

They stayed like that for some time, while Iain murmured encouragement and gently massaged her back and neck. But when she finally gained the courage to raise her head, she saw nothing in his face to give her hope.

What was she doing? Was she crazy, allowing Iain to hold her, to stroke her – to promote the illusion that she mattered to him?

'I'm sorry,' she said, disentangling herself from his embrace. 'I don't know what's the matter with me. I ought to be full of Christmas spirit –'

'I don't see why. I'm not.'

'Aren't you?' She hadn't expected that.

'No. In my opinion Christmas spirit is a myth put about by advertisers and shopping malls. And I should know. Half Trebanian's revenue comes from the Christmas season.' He gave her a lopsided grin that she guessed was costing him an effort. 'I'm usually exhausted and thoroughly bad-tempered months before the actual day comes around.'

'With an attitude like that, I'd say it's lucky for your friends you didn't get there.' She managed to keep her tone light.

'I expect they'll think so too. Jacko and I were at school together, but these days he has a wife, in-laws, two hairy little creatures he assures me are his children, and a cat. A houseful, in fact. So I shan't be missed. Except, perhaps, by the cat. We get along rather well.'

Two of a kind, Phaedra thought. All the same, you'd be missed if you were *my* houseful. What she said out loud was, 'I suppose you haven't had any dinner.'

'I had a sandwich on the way down.'

'There's cold turkey. Sort of,' she said, thankful to have something practical to do. 'I'll cook up some fresh potatoes and . . . Oh.' She broke off as Jade's startled face appeared in the doorway.

'Phaedra! What . . .? Oh. Sorry. I didn't see you had company.' She looked from Phaedra to Iain, then back again.

'She hasn't,' Iain said. 'Only me.'

'There's no one in the library.' Jade ignored him and turned to smile slyly at Phaedra. 'Much more intimate for entertaining. No boots or wet coats either.'

Not for the first time, Phaedra was glad she wasn't given to blushing. 'Thanks, but Iain hasn't eaten. I was about to raid your fridge.'

Jade nodded. 'Help yourself. Lloyd and I are about ready to hit the sack.'

'Happy Christmas,' Phaedra said, as her friend began to back into the hall. 'And thank you. It's been a lovely day.'

'Yeah,' agreed Jade. 'It's been a blast.'

'Your friend has a colourful way of putting things,' Iain observed as Phaedra led the way to the kitchen.

'Mmm. She has. She's nice though. I'm glad you said they could stay on.'

'What choice do I have?' Iain spoke in the kind of voice that made Phaedra wish she'd kept her mouth shut.

'Not much,' she said quickly, as she dragged a platter of leftover tofu turkey from the fridge. 'If you want a leg, there isn't one.'

'It doesn't matter. I'll eat whatever you put in front of me.'

If he only knew what he was saying! Yet that was something she had always liked about Iain. He had a healthy appetite, wasn't fussy about his food, and never seemed to put on an ounce of extra weight.

Today was no exception. He ate the heaping plate of leftovers without comment while she sat across from him and nursed a glass of red wine. It had been a long, emotionally draining day, and now, almost too tired to feel, she was content to sit quietly and watch him eat.

It was as good a way as any to end her first Christmas at Chy an Cleth without Charles.

She wondered if Iain was missing his father, who had always said 'Humbug' if anyone made the mistake of wishing him a Happy Christmas. Phaedra, the delighted recipient of a number of generous gifts from Father Christmas, had privately thought Charles was the humbug.

'You must be tired,' she said to Iain when he had finished. 'I'll just go and make sure your room's ready –'

'No.' He caught at her hand as she brushed past him. 'You've done enough. I'm quite capable of looking after myself.'

Phaedra stared down at the hand wrapped around her fingers. A current passed between them, swift and devastating. Could she – *should* she tell him there was no need for him to sleep alone tonight? She looked up hopefully, but the darkness in his eyes made her hesitate.

Iain turned his head away and dropped her hand as if he'd picked up a lighted match. Yet she couldn't rid herself of the notion that if she asked him into her bed, he would come.

She didn't ask.

'Goodnight, Iain. I hope you sleep well.'

'Goodnight,' he replied.

The bleakness in his voice reminded her of the man standing alone on the rocks on the day of his father's funeral – and she wanted to comfort him, to tell him that time would one day conquer whatever demon was currently consuming him. Only she wasn't sure she believed it.

In the end she left him sitting alone at the table with the wine, a manadarin orange and a bright green Christmas cracker. When she reached the bottom of the stairs she heard the cracker pop.

The following morning she found Iain still seated at the table, in the same position and wearing the same clothes, but without the wine.

'Don't tell me you haven't been to bed!' she exclaimed, collapsing against the doorframe.

'All right, I won't,' he said, scowling at her. 'I couldn't sleep, so I got up.'

'On the wrong side of the bed from the look of you.'

'Watch your tongue or I won't let you drink any of that.' He waved at a carafe of steaming coffee on the counter.

'You made coffee?' Phaedra sniffed approvingly.

'Do you see any elves lurking under the table? Of course I made it. I'm the only one up.'

'Heaven be praised! Is that coffee I smell?' a hopeful voice trilled from the passage.

Iain, who had been stirring sugar into an empty cup, raised his head at that and said, 'Ah. Sleeping Beauty awakes. And no, it's not coffee, it's a damned

291

flower garden. What the hell kind of scent are you wearing this time?'

'Iain!' squealed Joan, squeezing past Phaedra and hurling herself across the kitchen at her brother. 'Oh, Iain, I thought you were in London.'

'I'm beginning to think I should be.' Iain removed his sister's arms from his neck, kissed her on the cheek and sat her, none too gently, in the nearest chair. 'What the devil's this all about, Joan? Your unfortunate husband was almost out of his mind with worry until I called him and told him you were here.'

'*He* was out of his mind! How do you think *I* felt when I caught him making cow's eyes at the Byrd?' Joan slapped her hands on to the table, causing Iain's cup to rattle merrily in its saucer.

'Wrong farm.' Iain was unimpressed. 'You mean sheep's eyes, don't you? And he wasn't. He was asking Ida's advice on a suitable anniversary present for you. But as usual you jumped to conclusions.'

'What?' Joan raised her arm and touched the back of her hand theatrically to her forehead. 'He couldn't have been.' When her brother merely looked at her without comment, she asked suspiciously, 'How do *you* know? They were *whispering*.'

'Of course they were whispering.' Iain might have been speaking to a particularly dimwitted child. 'It was meant to be a surprise. And when Anton tried to explain, you wouldn't listen. He said you dashed off in such a state he was afraid you'd harm yourself.'

When Joan, in a rather pleased voice, said, 'Did he think I was going to throw myself under the Metro?'

Phaedra decided she was well overdue for her daily dose of caffeine.

'Something like that,' Iain said. 'And don't look so damn satisfied with yourself. You've caused us all a great deal of trouble.'

Joan had the grace to look sheepish. 'I didn't mean to.'

'No. You never do. In any case, Anton will be here to fetch you this afternoon – and if I were him, it wouldn't be any present you'd be getting.'

Joan shrugged. 'Don't be such a grouch. Anton will forgive me. He always does.'

'You mean this is a regular occurrence?' Iain shook his head. 'Remind me not to get married.'

'Huh! Who'd have you?' Joan snorted.

Phaedra, who was standing with her back to them pouring coffee, thought, *I would* – and immediately singed her knuckles on the hot plate.

'Ouch,' she muttered, trying not to call attention to her clumsiness.

But Iain was already on his feet. 'Don't try to cook yourself,' he said. 'Toast will be sufficient.'

Phaedra was still trying to come up with a suitably smart answer when he strode over and turned on the tap.

She watched the cold water swirl down the drain as he held her wrist under the cold-running flow. She felt no pain now. Only a kind of numbness of the mind. At first she wasn't sure what had caused it. Then she realized it was hearing Iain repeat what she already knew – that he didn't plan to marry again.

Damn. This mustn't be allowed to happen. She couldn't, *mustn't* allow herself to go through the hell of learning to live without him every time some unexpected crisis brought them together.

'It's all right now,' she said, pulling her hand away and making for the door. 'Thank you.'

'My pleasure,' Iain drawled. 'May I ask where you think you're going?'

'Out. To get some air.'

'You haven't drunk your coffee. Or had breakfast.'

'Oh.' Phaedra went back to the counter and swallowed her coffee in three gulps. 'I'll eat later.'

As she hurried out of the kitchen, she was vaguely aware of Iain's face – hard, square-jawed, as if he was trying to rein in an incurable urge to tell her what to do.

The snow had stopped some time during the night, and when Phaedra went outside the cool rays of the sun were already up and dancing on a carpet of whiteness. Not much traffic had passed, and only a thin layer of grey lined the sides of the road as she ploughed her way doggedly into town, boots crunching the frozen surface as she walked.

She went right past her mother's flat, past the Spotted Dog where Letty waved from the door, and didn't stop until she reached the town's sheltered harbour. There, leaning on the battered sea-wall, she breathed in the familiar smell of oil and salt and watched the seagulls scrabbling for scraps among the rocks. Greedy things, grabbing what they wanted and never thinking of sharing with their neighbours.

But she liked watching them. Sometimes sharing caused more trouble than it was worth.

Eventually, when the cold began to penetrate her coat, Phaedra made her way back up the hill to her mother's flat. By the time she got there, the snow was already dripping from the eaves. If it got any colder there would be icicles by morning.

Esther had been enjoying her mid-day cigarette. Phaedra could smell it the moment she stepped through the door. But she didn't say anything because her mother seemed a little out of breath – no doubt from scurrying to open the windows.

Esther took one look at her and said, 'Is Iain back?'

Phaedra laughed for the first time that day. 'Oh, Mum. Is it that obvious?'

'I'm afraid so. I suppose that means nothing's changed?'

'No. I thought it had until I saw him again.'

Esther sighed. 'I know. That's the trouble with Trebanians. Come and have some lunch.'

It was mid-afternoon by the time Phaedra made her way back along the cliff to Chy and Cleth.

In her absence, Anton had arrived to fetch his wife. As she walked up the driveway, Phaedra could see the back of him protruding from the boot of an unfamiliar car. Joan, radiant in red, was standing on the steps watching him load in their suitcases.

'Peter phoned,' she called. 'You just missed him.'

'Good,' Phaedra said.

Joan laughed. 'And you missed Iain as well. He's gone back to London. But he was in one of his black moods, so you didn't miss much, believe me.'

Phaedra did believe her, but she couldn't prevent her heart from taking a nosedive to her knees. She managed a smile for her friend, but couldn't think of anything to say.

Joan, gazing fondly at her husband's muscular backside, asked, 'Did you and Iain have a fight? Or something?'

'No. Not even "or something".'

'I get it. You wanted to get away from him. I know the feeling.' She grinned. 'How did he take it when he found out you'd given him the house?'

'Not very well.'

Joan smiled ruefully. 'We Trebanians must be a great trial to you. You're always so sensible yourself. But Iain and I go off the deep end over nothing.'

Phaedra didn't think she was sensible. Nor did she think the small matter of the house called Chy an Cleth was nothing. But she knew what Joan meant. Iain's sister might not be what anyone would call reliable, but she'd never been anybody's fool. She also knew exactly what she wanted and how to get it.

As if on cue, Anton straightened, sauntered over to his wife and gave her a leisurely kiss. 'Time for us to go, little one,' he said when he was through. 'I must be back in Paris early tomorrow.'

'But you haven't said hello to Phaedra.'

'Hello, Phaedra.' Anton bowed with the old-style courtesy that was his trademark. 'I am most happy to meet you again.'

'But now you and Joan have to go,' Phaedra said, making it easy for him.

'Alas, yes.' He gave her an even more elaborate bow, and Joan said, 'Do get your nose out of the snow, Anton. Phaedra's not impressed.'

'I'm very impressed,' Phaedra contradicted her. 'Speaking as one who can't even touch her toes.'

Joan shook her head and said she didn't believe her. Minutes later, as Phaedra waved the two of them goodbye, she remembered what Joan had said about Trebanians. Yes, they were certainly a trial to those who loved them. But life without them was an even bleaker prospect.

She rubbed a fist across her eyes, stamped the snow from her feet, and went into the suddenly quiet house.

School was over for the day. Phaedra was combing her hair in front of a small mirror propped on her solidly functional chest of drawers when the knock came on her door.

'Come in,' she called, unnecessarily as it turned out, because the door had already opened to admit Jennifer Reilly.

'Hello, Jennifer. What is it now? No more broken bones, I hope?' She tugged her comb through a particularly obstinate tangle.

Jennifer looked important. 'No, Ms Pendenning. Miss Carter sent me to tell you you have a visitor.'

'A visitor?' Phaedra put down her comb. She never had visitors. None of the staff did. Only Miss Carter had a private sitting-room suitable for entertaining. The rest of them went into town when they wanted to meet family or friends, and then it was usually a matter of tea and toast at the Old Mill Hotel or scones at the Bluebell Café.

Phaedra looked at the digital alarm clock clicking away beside her school-issue bed. Four-fifteen on the last Friday in January. Who on earth could be calling on her now? Surely not her mother . . .

'Where is she? I mean, where did Miss Carter get her to wait?' she asked.

'Wait?' Jennifer, a hard-working pupil but never brains trust material, looked blank.

'My visitor,' Phaedra explained patiently.

'Oh. She's not a her.' Jennifer's brown eyes bulged with curiosity. 'She's a he.'

Phaedra peered into the mirror to study a possible spot on her nose. 'My visitor is a *man*? Is that what you're saying?'

Jennifer nodded vigorously. 'Yes. A young one. He's – he's actually quite nice looking. Oh dear.' She put a hand to her mouth. 'Excuse me, Ms Pendenning, I didn't mean –'

'That's all right, Jennifer. Where did you say *he* was?'

'I didn't, but Miss Carter said to put him in the staffroom.'

'Oh. Yes, of course. Thank you. Would you mind telling him I'll be down in just a minute, then?'

'Will do, Ms Pendenning.' Jennifer lumbered around, bumped into the doorframe and limped off in the direction of the stairs.

Phaedra pinned her hair in a quick twist, smoothed down her navy blue skirt and hurried after her.

A young, nice-looking man waiting for *her*? Iain? Not likely, but who else could it be? And what was he doing here? Was something wrong at home . . .?

By the time she reached the staffroom her heart was thumping like a one-woman rock band. But whether her nervousness was due to the thought of seeing Iain again, or to the possibility of trouble in Porthkelly, she wasn't sure. Both, perhaps.

In the end it didn't matter, because it wasn't Iain who sat drinking tea on a narrow pink chair set between Mme Henriette Duschesne from the French Department and a giggling Barbara Bingley-Smith from Domestic Science.

It was Peter Sharkey.

Phaedra's heart stopped thumping and returned to its regular plodding beat. Peter Sharkey! Of all people. At least it couldn't be bad news – except in the sense that Peter was always bad news.

'Peter.' She spoke his name quietly, as if she were reading from a list.

Peter put down his teacup and rose, beaming, to greet her. 'Phaedra, my dear. You look ravishing.'

Barbara Bingley-Smith gave another giggle. Phaedra couldn't blame her. In a severe navy skirt, white blouse and shapeless cardigan, she knew she was no more ravishing than the average cabbage.

'Thank you,' she said, injecting several thicknesses of frost into her tone. 'What are you doing here, Peter?'

'I came to take you away from all this.' He waved at the collection of rigid-looking armchairs pushed against the walls, the scratched walnut table in the centre of the floor, and the collection of horsey prints that, according to Miss Carter, added 'just the right touch' to the room. Touch of what? Phaedra had never quite got around to asking.

Henriette Duschesne began to giggle too.

'Don't be ridiculous, Peter,' Phaedra said in her best classroom voice. 'Do you have a reason for being here?'

Peter, seeing which way the wind was blowing, became businesslike. 'Yes, of course I do. I hoped to discuss it with you over dinner.'

'I'm on duty at dinner time.'

He summoned a particularly ingratiating smile. When that brought no response, he said, 'Tea, then. I've come all the way from Porthkelly just to see you.'

'You shouldn't have.'

'Oh, go on, Phaedra,' urged Barbara Bingley-Jones. 'Give the poor man a chance.'

'Barbara is right. It is not kind to say no,' Henriette agreed. 'You must hear what this man has to say.' She crossed her legs to display an elegant length of nylon-sheathed thigh.

Peter licked his lips.

Damn the both of them, Phaedra thought. They weren't particular friends of hers, yet she had no special wish to appear ungracious. And if she turned Peter down absolutely, the story, with embellishments, would be all over school by tomorrow. It would anyway, but a casual departure with a man from her home town would be less cause for gossip than a full-fledged scene in the staffroom while Peter used up his repertoire of greased blandishments in an effort to make her change her mind.

'All right,' she said. 'I'll have tea with you. Just wait while I go upstairs and fetch my coat.'

Did he *have* to look so smug? she wondered irritably as she shut the door on his smiling face.

Ten minutes later she was seated in Peter's flashy silver car as they sped along the road in to town.

It was a dreary sort of day. Not raining, but grey and misty, and the bare branches of the trees as yet offered no promise of the green Eden that would come with the spring.

Peter, as she had known he would, chose the Old Mill Hotel over the Bluebell. It was modern and pretentious, and all trace of the old mill had long since been obliterated by fake teak panelling and tasteless murals of the countryside as it had been in years gone by.

'Not bad for an old-fashioned town like this one,' Peter said, as they took their seats by a plate-glass window overlooking a small, fenced garden filled with plaster rocks and green plastic frogs.

Phaedra didn't answer. She couldn't think of a single thing to say.

'Well, now,' Peter said, after the waitress had brought tea and a selection of sticky buns. 'Isn't this better than that dull little staffroom at your school?'

'It's a change,' Phaedra admitted. Peter was, after all, paying for the tea.

'I knew you'd like it.'

If he was waiting for more effusive praise, he wasn't going to get it.

'To business, then.' He offered her a bun.

Phaedra took one and put it on her plate. 'What business?' They might as well get it over with at once.

'Chy an Cleth for one thing. I understand it's rented.'

He knew perfectly well it was rented. Porthkelly was a very small town. 'Yes,' she said.

He took a careful bite of his bun, but a speck of sugar clung to his upper lip. 'I was thinking – you can't be making very much in rent.'

'Not much, no. We don't want much.'

'We?'

'Iain and I. Technically we both own the house. At least, I think we do.' She might as well make that clear at once. Nip any further attempts to purchase Chy an Cleth in the bud.

'Ah. But if I offered you a suitable sum, and you took it, Iain might be quite amenable to selling his half. Don't you think so?'

'I doubt it. Anyway, I wouldn't take "a suitable sum".'

Peter smoothed his lip and wiped away the sugar. 'I thought you'd say that. No matter. That wasn't the real reason I came to see you.' His fleshy smile would have been obsequious if it hadn't suddenly turned salacious.

Phaedra began to munch her bun. She wasn't hungry, but she needed something to do to take her mind off the way he was looking at her. 'What *was* the real reason, then?' She would have to know sooner or later. Peter wasn't the type to be distracted once he'd set himself on a particular path.

He leaned forward and said confidentially, 'You know I've always been fond of you, don't you, Phaedra?'

'No,' she said. 'I don't know that.' She made the mistake of putting down her bun, and Peter immediately reached across the table to take her hand.

'Don't you?' he said earnestly. 'It's true, though. And neither of us is getting any younger.'

Phaedra extracted her fingers from his grasp. 'That may be so, but I don't see –'

'Wait.' He held up his hand. 'The thing is, I've been thinking about you a lot lately. Any chance you've been thinking about me?'

Phaedra said, 'Not on purpose.'

'Ah. Well.' He blinked, and smiled cajolingly. 'I hope that means that, when you're least expecting it, I do sometimes pop into your head?'

'To be honest, no,' Phaedra said. 'I hardly ever think about you.'

Peter, in pursuit of a goal, was about as easily put off as a tank. 'But now that we're here, together, you *are* thinking. Aren't you?'

What Phaedra was actually thinking was that there was too much artificial sweetener in the bun, and that if Peter didn't soon get to the point, she would have to leave. That large plastic frog beside the puddle that was supposed to be a pond was starting to ogle her.

'I think it's time you said what you came to say,' she told him candidly.

'Yes. Very well, then.' Peter steepled his fingers beneath his chin and leaned across the table, at the same time pasting on to his face what she supposed he fondly imagined was a charming smile. 'You and I – it's time we settled down. As I said, I've always been fond of you.'

Phaedra gave him a blank look. 'Thank you.'

'The thing is – I'm asking you to marry me,' he finished in a rush.

Phaedra choked into her tea.

'Of course, I don't expect you to give me an answer right away.' He reached for her hand again. 'All I'm asking is that you think about it.' When she only stared at him, speechless, he said, 'Well? What do you say?'

'No.'

'What?' His plump palm tightened around her fingers.

'No. I said no.'

'I think you misunderstand me. I only want you to think about it, Phaedra dear. I know it's too soon –'

Phaedra took a deep breath and succeeded in regaining her fingers. After that she hid both hands under the canary yellow tablecloth. From the corner of eye, she saw their waitress with her mouth hanging open, watching them.

'I understand you perfectly,' she said. 'But I don't want to marry you, Peter.' His face fell, and to soften the blow she added, 'I don't want to marry anyone. And I don't think you want to marry me. It's Chy an Cleth you're really after, isn't it?'

Peter clasped both hands on the table. 'No, no. Of course not. It's a nice property, certainly. But there are others just as suitable. It's you I want most, my dear Phaedra. I've realized that for some time.'

Phaedra started to say 'No' again, but Peter stopped her.

'Don't say anything. Please. I won't expect an answer just yet. Maybe in a month or two you'll feel differently – better able to make a sensible decision.'

God, was he serious? It *was* possible. Just.

She leaned back in her chair to avoid his drifting breath. It wasn't malodorous exactly, but cloyingly sweet. As if he were breathing out cheap aftershave. 'Look,' she said. 'I won't feel differently. But I'm honoured that you asked me.' She wasn't, but it didn't hurt to say it. A thought occurred to her. 'This came up very suddenly. You never gave any indication . . .'

'I tried to at half-term, if you remember. And I phoned at Christmas – but you were out. Just as well, really. People talk. Better to leave a decent interval between husbands. Gossip's bad for business.'

'Oh. I see.' Phaedra ran a finger round the sugar on her plate, relieved that he still put business before his heart. She didn't like Peter, but that was no reason for inflicting unnecessary hurt. All the same, when she saw that he was about to reach for her hand again, she put it quickly back under the table.

'I'd better be going,' she said. 'I'm due back at school in half an hour.'

'Of course.' He sprang up to help her out of her chair with such bouncing gallantry that he almost knocked her over. 'You will think about what I've said, won't you?' he pleaded.

This man didn't take no for an answer. Didn't even *hear* no. Which was probably why he was so successful in his business.

She wasn't business. Especially not Peter's business.

'Yes, of course I'll think about it,' Phaedra said. How could she *not* think about it? 'But it won't make any difference.'

Peter took her elbow with a proprietory smile, and looked around to see if anyone was impressed. 'Let's wait and see. I'm not a bad bargain, you know.'

'I'm sure you're not,' Phaedra agreed faintly. What was the use? Somewhere between Charles's funeral and today, Peter Sharkey had made up his mind to acquire a new property. Unfortunately, this time *she* was the property. And it wasn't likely she'd heard the end of his latest project.

Peter was nothing if not persistent.

Phaedra had a raging headache by the time he delivered her back to school.

CHAPTER 14

Iain curved a gloved hand over the wheel of the Porsche. If that jerk in the van with the dice and the dolls in the windows, and 'He Who Hesitates is a Damn Fool' emblazoned across his bumper, attempted to play chicken with him just once more, he might soon find out what it felt like to be roasted.

The game had been going on since Salisbury, and Iain had had enough. He valued his paint and his chrome as much as the next man, but not to the extent of allowing some bearded idiot to run him off the road. Besides, he'd had enough of bearded idiots for one week. His already ferocious scowl deepened. Beards reminded him of Lloyd, and Lloyd was part of the reason for this unscheduled trip to Cornwall.

A week ago, in a moment of sheer frustration, he had phoned Phaedra to ask why the account he had opened in her name had not been touched.

'Because I haven't accepted it,' she said.

'I see. You don't think this nonsense has gone on long enough?'

'Yes. As a matter of fact, I do.'

Cool as a cucumber and twice as maddening. Iain set his teeth. 'Phaedra, I want this business of the house settled. Soon. And permanently.'

'In that case,' she replied sweetly, 'I'm afraid you'll have to settle it yourself – because Lloyd just phoned to tell me that Jade has gone back to Colorado. Her father had a heart attack, and both her parents are elderly and ill. Lloyd plans to follow her as soon as he's wrapped up their business in England. So the house will be empty,' she finished, with a complacency that made Iain wish she wasn't out of reach.

'I don't want it empty.'

'Then live in it yourself. Or find a caretaker.'

'I will. When's Lloyd leaving?'

Phaedra hadn't known, so he had phoned the house himself and got no answer. When he tried Esther instead, she told him Lloyd would be spending his last couple of weeks in England on a friend's sailboat.

'He'll be out of the house before Easter,' she said. 'To make it easier for you to find someone else.'

'I see. But Phaedra will be there, won't she? Over the holidays?'

'No, Iain, she won't.' Esther's tone was precise and unrevealing. 'She and one of the other teachers are taking a group of girls to France.'

'But –'

'She'll be here for a couple of nights before school starts. If that helps.'

It didn't. Iain swore, then recollected himself, and apologized. Pendy, bless her heart, only laughed.

'Chy an Cleth will survive quite well until you get new caretakers,' she assured him. 'A week or two with no one living there won't hurt. It's survived nicely for over two hundred years.'

That, Iain thought, as the jerk in the van beside him made another feint across the centre line, was the whole point. Two hundred years ago vandalism as a Saturday night sport hadn't reached the epidemic proportions it had today. Nor had Cornwall been crawling with curious tourists who thought any building that was old, large and picturesque was public property.

The bearded idiot rolled down the window of his van and shouted an obscenity. This time Iain, already doing a slow boil, didn't even think about ignoring him. As the van swerved his way again he swung the wheel to the right, and this time it was the idiot who was forced to veer away. Iain caught just a glimpse of his face as, with a squeal of brakes, he barely avoided crossing the median and locking bonnets with an oncoming Volvo.

There was no doubt about who was the chicken now. The man was terrified.

Iain grinned malignantly. A little healthy terror wouldn't do a twerp like that any harm. Yet as the van dropped back, and his blood pressure sank to its normal healthy level, it occurred to him that the driver of the Volvo might be less amused. His grin faded. What kind of a macho fool was he turning into? The mature response to a juvenile challenge like the one he'd just overreacted to would have been to pull off the motorway and use his cell phone to alert the police. But no – he'd been in a foul mood in the first place at the disruption of his plans for the weekend – which had included a pretty journalist he wanted to get to know better – and instead of behaving sensibly, he'd responded like a knee-jerk adolescent.

He looked in his rearview mirror and saw that the van was nowhere in sight. That, at least, was something.

'You're a fool, Trebanian,' he muttered. 'A first-class cretinous blockhead. And you know who's the cause of it, don't you?'

A young woman in a Volkswagen thought he was cursing at her, and raised two fingers.

Iain laughed and began to feel better. Yes, he knew who was the cause of his ill-humour – as well as the cause of this unplanned trip to Cornwall. Not Lloyd, but Phaedra Pendenning. Nothing had gone right since that dark-eyed sea-witch had reappeared in his life. He had even lost an advertising campaign he'd thought was in the bag. No disaster, but something that didn't normally happen.

Phaedra . . . Iain glanced at the line of daffodils growing in sunny profusion along the side of the road. At least he could be thankful she wasn't in Porthkelly to interfere with his choice of caretaker yet again. And yet . . . he hadn't been thankful at Christmas when she'd suddenly disappeared. He'd been bored and frustrated and had gone back to town the moment Anton arrived to cope with Joan.

Frowning, he glanced at his watch. Three o'clock on a mellow April afternoon. No reason he shouldn't be there before dark. So maybe, with a bit of luck, by the time Easter rolled around he would have a new and reliable caretaker in the house. One of his own choosing this time.

He'd paid Phaedra fair and square. If she refused to see it that way, that was her problem. He trod on the accelerator, passed the woman in the Volkswagen, and waved.

As it turned out, an accident just outside Exeter slowed him down, but it was still well before dusk when he pulled in to Porthkelly. The sun was only just beginning to turn from glaring yellow to the burnt orange fire of a Cornish sunset as he drove the Porsche around to Chy an Cleth's garage.

Iain got out, stretched, and made his way at a leisurely pace towards the front of the house.

He was home. There was nowhere else in the world where he experienced such an instant feeling of belonging. Yet London was his home too – had been for years – and he loved the pace of city life and the rush of excitement that came with closing a deal or starting a fresh campaign. Perhaps, in order to be whole, he needed the best of both his worlds. But then who didn't want to have his cake and eat it as well? It went with the human condition.

Iain shrugged off a fleeting sense of gloom and took a deep breath of clean, salty air before turning his key in the lock and stepping into the hall. He paused to absorb the familiar yet elusive scent of home.

Nothing had changed.

Or had it? Wait a minute! He lifted his head and sniffed the air. Lemon polish and – surely that wasn't *raspberries* he smelled? It was too early for raspberries. Unless . . . He frowned. What was that sound? Was someone in the house after all? He listened, and from a distance heard the faint but steady murmur of voices. Lloyd? Was he still here then? According to Pendy, he was supposed to have left last week.

Some instinct honed by years of staying ahead of the competition stopped Iain from announcing his presence. Quietly he moved through the hall and along the passage to the kitchen. There was no one there. He reversed back the way he had come and paused to listen again.

Ah. The voices were coming from the conservatory, which on his last visit had been cluttered with easels and a collection of shapeless rocks that Phaedra had assured him were destined to become sculptural masterpieces – once Lloyd ran out of things to fix around the house.

This time, as he approached the open door of the conservatory, Iain saw that the masterpieces had gone. In their place were the wicker tables and chairs that had been there in his father's and grandfather's day.

When a woman's voice said, 'Peter, I can't,' Iain put a hand on the wall of the passage and stopped dead.

So . . . Phaedra wasn't in France.

She was seated with her back to him in one of the wicker chairs, her glorious hair tumbling over its back.

Leaning over her, with his hands gripping the left arm of the chair, was Peter Sharkey.

'Of course you can,' Peter was insisting. 'It's just a matter of saying "yes". There's no one else, is there?'

After a long pause, Phaedra said, 'No.'

'Then what's the problem?'

'I just – don't want to. Please, can't you understand?'

Peter moved suddenly and put both hands on her shoulders. Now he was almost directly facing Iain, but he had eyes for no one but Phaedra. The orange rays of the sunset striking his head through the glass turned his thick hair the colour of molten copper.

Like the damn devil overseeing the fires. Iain scowled and shifted his shoulder against the wall.

He made no attempt to hide himself, and he was so absorbed in the scene taking place before his eyes that it barely crossed his mind that he was eavesdropping. Not that it would have made a difference. He would still have listened. His hands doubled into fists against his jeans.

'Peter, please,' he heard Phaedra saying. 'I told you the last time I wouldn't change my mind.'

The last time? What last time? Iain discovered he was grinding his teeth. He clamped them tightly together.

'How do you know you won't?' Peter said. He took a firm grip on her upper arms and, as Iain took a half-step forward, dragged her up out of her chair.

'Really, Peter! What do you think you're doing?' demanded Phaedra in her schoolteacher voice.

That was exactly what Iain wanted to know. Instinctively he looked at his watch as the grandfather clock in the drawing-room chimed the hour.

'I'm trying to change your mind,' Peter said.

'Well, you're not going to do it by mauling me. Would you please take your hands off my arms.'

Peter complied by moving a hand round the back of her neck.

Iain felt the small hairs on the back of his own neck begin to rise. He took a another half-step forward.

'Peter,' Phaedra repeated, 'I said take your hands off me.'

Iain bent his legs into a sprinter's crouch.

'In a minute,' Peter said. 'There's something I want you to try first.'

'Try?' Phaedra lifted her arms as if to push him away. But his grip only tightened until Iain could see the white bulge of his knuckles.

'I've never kissed you, have I, Phaedra?' Peter said softly.

'Of course you haven't. We're not – I'm not . . . Peter, *let me go*!'

Instead of letting her go, Peter put an arm around her waist, and hauled her, struggling, against his chest.

Phaedra twisted sideways and raised her knee. It didn't have time to find its mark.

The sea outside was roaring in Iain's ears as without thought, without acknowledging the possibility of thought, he launched himself down the passage and on to Peter Sharkey.

He heard the satisfactory sound of ripping cloth before Peter crashed to the varnished floorboards beneath his weight. He raised a fist, aiming for the solid bone of the other man's jaw, anticipating retaliation. But as his arm came down he recognized just in time that the face below him had turned the colour of paste. The fleshy lips were literally quivering. And Iain smelled the rancid scent of fear.

He dropped his arm and rolled sideways. Beside him, Peter gave a moan of relief. Without taking his eyes off his adversary, Iain rose swiftly to his feet.

For a moment he was blinded by the glow from the dying sun. Then the body on the floor came back into focus and began to squirm.

'Out!' Iain said. 'Out. And don't come back.'

Peter's throat muscles were working visibly as he pushed himself up.

'Out,' Iain repeated. God, the man was a wimp. Wetter than an overcooked noodle. He flexed his forearm and deliberately examined his fist.

Peter made a small yelping noise and scrambled on to all fours. 'Don't – don't worry,' he gasped, as he staggered up. 'I'm going. Didn't – didn't know you and Phaedra were an item. No need to . . .' He blinked, as Iain took a threatening step forward. 'OK, OK. Sorry. I said I was going.'

Iain watched him scurry down the passage like a dustball blowing in the wind. The roaring in his ears subsided and his heartbeat slowed gradually to normal. He closed his eyes, rotated his shoulder muscles and turned to look for Phaedra.

She wasn't there, and the chair she had been sitting in was lying forlornly on its side.

'Phaedra!' he shouted. 'Where are you?'

No answer. But he could hear water running.

His shirt had come out of his belt in the course of his skirmish with Sharkey. Quickly shoving it back into his trousers, he straightened his leather jacket and strode off in pursuit of the woman who had caused him to act like a brawling schoolyard bully for the first time since – well, since his schooldays.

Phaedra was standing at the kitchen sink, splashing water down her blouse and on to her face. She heard Iain's footsteps pounding down the passage and turned to face him as he blazed across the threshold in black jeans, black boots, and black jacket.

No civilized executive here today. More like the Black Prince demanding his reward after rescuing the Fair Joan from the unwelcome advances of some lesser knightly suitor.

She put a hand up to her mouth to hide the reluctant smile tugging at her lips. Even suited up in the best armour, she couldn't see Peter Sharkey as a knight.

'What's so bloody funny?' Iain growled.

Phaedra stopped wanting to smile. The Black Prince had probably loved his Fair Maid of Kent. Iain didn't love her.

'Nothing,' she said. 'What are you doing here, Iain?'

'That was supposed to be my question. What are *you* doing here? You're meant to be in France, not scuffling with that little toad, Sharkey.'

'The trip was cancelled. Jennifer Reilly caught chicken pox and started an epidemic.'

'Hmm. That doesn't explain Sharkey.'

'Do I have to explain him – since you and I are *not* an item?'

Iain, who had been lounging in the doorway, advanced into the kitchen to face her across the table. 'Yes, you do.'

'Why?'

'Because I want an explanation, that's why. You knew what he was like? Why did you let him in?'

'Haven't we been here before?' Phaedra resisted the temptation to meet his belligerence head on. 'Since you refused to accept Chy an Cleth as a gift, it's entirely my business whom I choose to let in. And by the way, who invited *you*?'

She knew the question was illogical but, dammit, in spite of his bossiness he was doing it to her again. Just when she thought she was getting over him. For a few seconds there, when he'd burst into the conservatory like Superman on pep pills, she had been foolish enough to hope he'd changed his mind. Besides, he had no business looking so damn sexy.

'I don't need an invitation, remember?' Iain leaned towards her, mouth hard, jawline aggressively squared, 'You ought to be thankful I turned up.'

'Why on earth should I be thankful?'

And why was it that in the space of a few seconds Iain could turn her from calm, sensible Ms Pendenning into a screaming harpy with murder on her mind?

'Because the toad was mauling you, that's why. You said so yourself. I heard you.'

'So what? I could have handled him without your help. And anyway, why should you care? Peter, at least, wants to marry me.'

She sagged against the sink, watching him with a feeling of disconnection, as if she were observing a play in which she had no part. Iain, to her confusion, put his fists on the table and bent his head. Was he praying, or getting set to charge?

She pinned her gaze on the blue-black gleam of his hair and waited for what would come next.

Following so quickly on anger and action, the silence should have been deafening. Instead it was alive with sound.

The tap behind her dripped steadily. She turned it off, but immediately the fridge began to hum. The clock chimed again, and a board creaked somewhere upstairs. Outside, the sea beat its ceaseless rhythm against the rocks, and a small night animal squealed in fear.

The atmosphere was so tense that Phaedra had almost reached the point of screaming by the time Iain raised his head to speak.

'You're right,' he said. 'I *don't* care, of course. It seems old habits die hard.'

Phaedra nodded. Her heart felt as if he'd taken it in his hands and squeezed it dry. But she understood what he meant. He was talking about his habit of coming to her rescue. After all, he'd been doing it since before she could remember.

'Are you going to marry him?' he asked.

'What do you think?' Phaedra wrapped her arms around her chest, instinctively defensive.

Iain took his time about answering. 'Judging strictly from the scene I just witnessed, I'd guess you're not.'

'Bullseye.'

'So why did you let him in?'

'You don't care. Remember?'

'Right. I don't. Which doesn't mean I want him worming his way into my house.'

'It's my house too. I wanted it to be yours, but you wouldn't take it.'

Iain's shoulders slumped as if they bore an impossible burden. 'Dammit, Phaedra, I *paid* you for it.'

'And I didn't accept your payment. Iain, we're going round in circles.'

He closed his eyes. 'Yes. So we are.'

Phaedra watched with an air of detachment as he rammed his hands into the leather pockets of his jacket. She went on watching as, without another word, he turned on his heel and slouched out of the kitchen. Even slouching, she'd never known a man who looked as appealing as Iain did from behind.

When the front door slammed, and footsteps crunched down the gravel in the driveway, she was still staring at the place where he'd disappeared.

After a while, when the only sounds were the hum of the fridge and the murmur of the waves in the dusk, she lowered her arms and went to look out of the window. It was almost dark now. Where had Iain gone? Where did he plan to stay the night? And, more importantly, why did she care?

He didn't. He had said so.

Phaedra laid her head against the glass. It felt cold against her skin. 'Oh Iain, Iain. What's happened to us?' she whispered. 'What's happened to make you so hard? I know you want me to forget you. But I don't know if I can.

'You have to. You *can* do it. By keeping your mind on your work as you've always done – and remembering not to remember.'

When it dawned on her that she was talking to herself, Phaedra hurried into the cloakroom to grab a coat. If Iain came back, she didn't want him to find her standing in a corner performing Ophelia's mad scene from *Hamlet* to the hall table.

Iain stood at the top of the cliff path staring into blackness. It was a warm night for April, and the small breeze barely lifted his hair. There was peace in the stillness of the night, and the sound of the waves he couldn't see went some way towards easing the turmoil in his mind.

What had he done back there in the house? Why had he reacted like a man possessed to the sight of

Peter Sharkey with his hands on Phaedra's supple body? She hadn't thanked him for his intervention. Not that he wanted her thanks. He wanted *her*. But since he'd chosen not to have her, why should it matter . . .?

Who was he kidding? Of course it mattered. Peter Sharkey and Phaedra? It didn't bear thinking of.

Iain kicked at the turf at his feet and stubbed his toe. He swore. And why had he told her he didn't care? He *did* care. Had always cared. She was Phaedra. But that didn't mean he wanted her for his wife. He didn't want any woman for his wife.

Glowering into the darkness, he bent down to pick up a stone and hurled it as far out to sea as it would go – too far for him to hear it hit the water. What he did hear, coming from the direction of the house, was something that could only have been the slamming of a door.

What the hell? Surely Phaedra wasn't going out alone at this hour? Even in sleepy Porthkelly things could happen.

With an uneasiness he convinced himself was merely irritation, Iain walked briskly back the way he had come.

She had looked so stricken when he told her he didn't care. Those beautiful eyes of hers had given her away as they always did. He had hurt her. Hurt her unkindly and unnecessarily because the very suggestion that she might marry Peter Sharkey had made him want to lash out. At her, at Sharkey, at the world. And at that moment she had been the only one available.

How could he have walked out on her like that? If Sharkey was a toad, that made him an even less attractive creature. He quickened his pace. After all Phaedra had done for him, he had to put things right. Had do what he could to mend the hurt. He couldn't, *wouldn't* marry her. But he could apologize for behaving like the arrogant bastard he undoubtedly was.

Iain was practically running by the time he neared the house. But when he opened the door and shouted, 'Phaedra!' there was no answer. No elusive tang of raspberries tickled his nose.

He called again. Still no answer. He looked in the kitchen, the library, the dining-room. After that he searched the house from top to bottom and even went out to search the garden. But when he was through he was forced to admit what he'd sensed from the moment he'd walked through the door.

Phaedra, with a fearlessness that did her credit, and a foolhardiness that did not, had taken it into her head to vanish into the night.

CHAPTER 15

Esther sat in her favourite armchair with her stockinged feet propped on the coffee table. She was watching *Casablanca* for about the twentieth time, but familiarity in no way bred contempt. At the fog-shrouded airport, Humphrey Bogart was stoically taking his leave of Ingrid Bergman. Esther mouthed the words along with the actors as she dabbed at her eyes with one of the tissues she had stockpiled on the table. Any second now, the lovers would part bravely and forever. She sniffed, waiting for Humphrey Bogart's immortal words, 'Here's looking at you, kid.'

They were drowned out by the sudden ringing of the phone.

Esther, tissue at the ready, took a few seconds to return to reality. The ringing continued. A moist-eyed Ingrid Bergman walked through the fog towards the plane that would take her forever from her love. Esther wiped away a tear. Humphrey Bogart was saying to Claud Rains, '. . . I think this is the beginning of a beautiful friendship.'

It was over.

With a sigh, and another sniff, she pushed herself out of her chair and thumped irritably down the short passage towards her bedroom. 'I'm coming, I'm coming,' she muttered as the phone continued to demand her attention.

Just as she reached to pick it up, an urgent knock sounded on the door. Now what? This was supposed to have been a pleasantly peaceful evening.

'Who is it?' she called.

'Mum, it's me.'

Phaedra? Again? Her daughter had already spent the day with her and wasn't due back until tomorrow.

'Hold on.' Esther picked up the phone. 'I won't be a minute. Hello,' she said into the mouthpiece, doing her best not to sound as irritated as she felt.

'Pendy, it's Iain. Is Phaedra with you?'

'No, but she will be once I open the door. I'll just get her for you —'

'That's all right. Thanks. Sorry to disturb you, but it's dark out. I wanted to make sure she was OK.'

He hung up before Esther could ask him what he was doing in Porthkelly.

What was the matter with everyone tonight? 'Peace and quiet. What a hope,' she muttered, fumbling to release the chain across the door. When she finally managed it, Phaedra darted across the threshold, bringing with her a blast of cold air.

'What's happened?' Esther asked, her maternal alarm system instantly on alert. 'Are you all right?'

'I think so. I just didn't want to stay in the house alone. In case Iain came back.'

'Iain just phoned. He was worried about you.' Esther shut the door hastily. 'What brought him to Porthkelly?'

'I'm not sure. We didn't get around to that. I think he thought the house would be empty.'

'Probably. I told him you'd be in France.'

'Oh, Mum.' Phaedra peeled off her coat. 'I wish you hadn't. Can I make us a cup of tea or something?'

'If you like. I was planning to go to bed soon.' Devoted as she was to her daughter, Esther couldn't help thinking wistfully of her bedtime cigarette.

'Oh. Yes, of course. Sorry, I expect you're tired.'

'Not that tired.' She wasn't an old woman yet. Esther straightened her shoulders and attempted to look lively.

'Mum . . .?'

'Mmm?' She refastened the chain. Damn thing was more trouble than it was worth, but Angus was such a fusspot about security . . .

'Would it be all right if I stayed the night? I know it's a squash, but I could curl up in one of your chairs . . .'

Esther put a hand to her back, feeling a sneeze coming on. What could she say? Phaedra looked desperate. 'Of course, if you want to. But why not curl up in your own bed? Iain's an honorable man. He won't bother you.' The sneeze came, and pain stabbed at her spine as it always did.

'Bless you,' Phaedra said automatically. 'Mum, Iain bothers me just by existing. And anyway, he's in a horrible temper because Peter Sharkey was there when he arrived.'

'Isn't that a good sign?' Esther had given up being overly optimistic about the situation between her daughter and Iain. But if he objected to Phaedra entertaining Peter, surely that meant there was *some* sort of hope.

Apparently there wasn't. Phaedra was shaking her head emphatically. 'There aren't any good signs, Mum. Look, if you don't mind, I think *I* need that cup of tea.'

'Of course you do, dear. I'll make it.' Esther bustled into the kitchen. When she saw Phaedra watching the stiff movements of her fingers, she turned her back so that her fumbling wouldn't be as obvious.

Angus wasn't the only one who fussed.

'Where did Iain phone from?' she asked, once the two of them were seated at the table with cups of tea.

'I don't know. He walked out when I told him Peter wanted to marry me.'

'He's a fool then. He should know you better than to think you'd settle for that Sharkey.'

'Yes. He should. Would you believe he knocked Peter flat on the floor?' Phaedra put a hand up to her mouth.

Esther fixed her with a deeply suspicious eye. Was her daughter laughing? It wasn't like her to laugh at another's affliction. And she had always despised violence.

'He did what?' she asked, just to be sure.

'Knocked Peter on to the floor. In the conservatory.'

Esther pressed her fingertips to her temples which had suddenly started to throb. 'Am I hearing right? He knocked Peter down? Because of you?'

'Because of something.'

'Trebanians,' Esther muttered. 'They have to be the stubbornest, most perverse human beings in the world.'

'Yes, but I don't think they mean to be.'

'Hmm. The trouble with them is they have a well-developed sense of right and wrong, but very little knowledge of their own hearts. And they're far too stubborn to take the time to learn.' She frowned into her tea, stirred it reflectively, 'Mind you, I'd say there's a better chance for you than there was for me.'

'What? Mum? Are you talking about . . .?' Phaedra's voice lost its certainty as she put down her cup and leaned across the table.

'Trebanians,' Esther repeated darkly.

'Yes, but . . . Oh. Oh, I see. You mean you and – well, Charles?'

Esther looked up quickly. What had she just admitted? Phaedra didn't know . . . Or did she?

'What about me and Charles?' she asked, affecting an unusual interest in the state of her neat nails.

Phaedra sat back and fidgeted with the handle of her cup. 'When we were clearing out Charles's desk, Iain found . . .' She stopped, took a quick gulp of tea and clasped her hands around the flowered china cup.

'Found what? What are you talking about?'

'A picture. Iain found a picture. Of you and Charles.'

'Did he? I should think there must have been quite a few pictures taken at Chy an Cleth over the years.'

Why did Phaedra look so uncomfortable? To the best of her knowledge she had never posed in the nude.

'This one was taken in Paris,' Phaedra said.

Oh. Paris. For a few seconds Esther's mind froze.

'Paris,' she repeated, for the first time in years allowing her mind to travel that painful path. Funny. It wasn't so painful any more. She was growing old, of course, but in those days she'd been young, bursting with emotion and need. And yet . . . now that she had finally faced up to those memories she found them more nostalgic than painful. Bittersweet. That was the word.

After all this time she could think of that week in Paris with something approaching peace. Or even laughter.

It hadn't ended as she had expected or hoped. But, if nothing else, she had learned to respect the power of love.

'Mum? Are you all right?' Phaedra was bending towards her, looking worried.

'Yes. Yes, I'm perfectly all right. You reminded me of something, that's all. Phaedra . . .' She reached out to take her daughter's hand. 'Phaedra, if things don't work out between you and Iain –'

'*Mum –*'

'No, let me finish. However much it hurts you at the time, it *will* get better. I don't suppose you believe me now, but –'

'Oh, I believe you,' Phaedra interrupted. 'Before I came home this time, it was getting – well, maybe not better, but *tolerable*. Only now I've seen him, and it's started all over again. It always does.

'Trebanians do know how to love,' Esther said, absently stirring her nearly empty cup.

'Do they? Iain doesn't.'

'Don't be so sure of that. I remember . . .'

Oh dear. She ought to be concentrating on her daughter's problems, not reliving her own youthful memories.

'What do you remember?' Phaedra asked.

Perhaps it was time to tell her. Perhaps, now that Charles was dead, she had a right to know.

'That picture,' Esther said, making up her mind. 'I didn't know Charles had kept a copy too. I was certain he'd thrown it away.'

'Can you tell me about it?'

'If you like. It's not a long story.' She fixed her eyes on the white face of the clock. It was less disturbing than watching Phaedra's face.

'It was taken early in May,' she began. 'Iain was at school, and you and Joan were staying with the Coopers. Charles and I closed up the house and sailed on the ferry from Dover . . .'

Until they had actually set foot on the deck of the ferry, she hadn't dared to believe it was really happening. In all the months the two of them had been together at Chy an Cleth, Charles – her handsome, stubborn Charles – had given no indication that she was any more to him than a friend and a housekeeper. And she had watched him, worked for him, and dreamed dreams. Until the night when she had slipped on the stairs and sprained her ankle.

Charles had picked her up and carried her to her room. Her arms went quite naturally around his neck, and when he laid her on the bed she didn't immediately let go. Their eyes met, a message was sent and received, and he kissed her.

After that things were different. He kissed her often when the children were out of sight, and she kissed him back with all the love and passion that had been growing in her heart during the long, lonely months since Phaedra's birth. But Charles never once told her he loved her. Then one day, out of the blue, he asked her to go to Paris with him.

She had agreed without hesitation. He hadn't offered marriage, but she believed he would in the fullness of time. She had been so sure . . . so naïvely, pathetically sure. And so in love . . .

'Mum . . .?' Phaedra's low voice broke into her memories. 'Mum, I didn't mean to upset you.'

'You haven't.' It took no effort to smile. 'You've reminded me, but I'm not in the least upset. Not any more.'

'You and Charles were lovers, weren't you?'

It wasn't an accusation, but none the less Esther asked quietly, 'Would you mind if we were?'

'No,' Phaedra answered without hesitation. 'Why should I mind? If it made you happy?'

If only it had. Esther sighed. 'We weren't lovers. If we had been, Charles would have married me.'

'That's what I thought.' Phaedra nodded slowly. 'He was like that. The picture then –'

'We meant to be lovers,' Esther explained. 'But Charles wanted it to happen away from Chy an Cleth. He said it was because of you children, but I think the truth was that he couldn't bear the memories of his wife. So we went to Paris.'

'And it . . . and nothing happened?'

'Oh, a lot happened.' She smiled ruefully. 'We had a wonderful week enjoying the sights of Paris, doing all the things young lovers are meant to do. All except the one thing that meant commitment. Charles kept putting that off. At first because we'd had a long journey and I was tired. Then he ate some snails and said they hadn't agreed with his English stomach. Then he had no protection. Then he decided we should get to know each other better –'

'Didn't you think it odd?' Phaedra asked.

'Yes, I suppose I did. But I was in love. Whatever Charles said must be right. He was quite a lot older than me, more experienced, and I thought he was leading up to the big moment so it would be even more wonderful when it happened. And he was. The only trouble was that when it came to the point, he couldn't bring himself to – um, well, to perform. He liked me, you see. Was genuinely fond of me. Maybe even loved me in a way.' She took a sip of tea, and discovered it was cold. 'I wouldn't have been his first since Helen died, but I would have been the first one he cared about. And he discovered he couldn't make love to me without offering me the benefits of marriage. I think, at one time, he did mean to propose. But he couldn't. Because of Helen.'

'So . . .?'

'So he couldn't make love to me without marriage, and wouldn't marry me without love.'

'Oh, Mum.' Phaedra's expressive eyes swam with sympathy. 'How awful for you.'

Esther pulled an old, grey cardigan from the back of her chair and wrapped it around her shoulders. It was warm for April, but she shouldn't have turned off the heat. 'The picture,' she said. 'It was taken on the street on our last day in Paris. When I still believed that night would be the night. Only it wasn't. Charles tried. But he couldn't . . .' She blew her nose briskly. 'I think he saw it as a betrayal of Helen. Because he *was* fond of me. If he hadn't been it would have been all right.'

'Oh, Mum,' Phaedra repeated, reaching across the table to squeeze her hand. 'So all these years . . .' She paused. 'I don't understand. How could you *bear* to stay on as his housekeeper after that?'

'It was hard at first. Charles told me he wouldn't blame me if I didn't stay. But we were friends, you see. Had been for years. And being near him was better than nothing. Besides, Chy an Cleth was my home, and I'd always loved his children. Even though it nearly broke my heart, I had to respect

332

the love he bore his wife. I think, in the end, it was that respect that gave me the courage to stay on. Because I know he respected me too.'

'And you never thought of leaving again? Never loved anyone else?'

Esther recognized the intensity in her daughter's voice for what it was, knew exactly what she was asking – and she wanted to lie, to say she had recovered from her passion for Charles. In a way, she had. As they both grew older, the passion had faded somewhat. But the love hadn't.

'No,' she said. 'No, I never did.'

'Not Mr Cooper?'

'Angus? No. I'm very fond of him. We'll always be friends. But I had to tell him I wouldn't marry him. You see . . .' She hesitated, not sure she wanted to admit the truth to a daughter who was suffering from the very same malaise.

It came out anyway. 'After loving a Trebanian, I couldn't bring myself to marry a Cooper.'

Phaedra nodded, understanding completely, as Esther had been afraid she would. 'I know. I think the same thing's happened to me. Well, almost the same. Iain and I did . . . once . . . but only once. He won't let it happen again. Because he doesn't want to marry me.'

The room wasn't cold after all. Esther felt her body start to overheat, not from any post-menopausal flash, but from a wave of anger directed at the young man she had raised almost as her son. How *dare* Iain put her daughter through this hell? How dare he ease his bodily needs with Phaedra and then callously toss her away?

'Iain needs a good swift kick in the right place,' she said. 'And if he turns up here tonight I'll see he gets it.'

Phaedra, to her relief and amazement, burst out laughing. 'Oh, Mum. You know he wouldn't let you. Not any more. And anyway, he won't turn up here. He only phoned because he felt responsible for me.'

'Then you should go back home and try to talk some sense into his head.'

'It's not a matter of sense, Mum. He doesn't love me.'

'He thinks he doesn't, you mean.' Esther stood up, opened the fridge, decided there was nothing there she could pound or puree, and slammed it shut. 'It's Charles all over again,' she grumbled. 'Old fool had to be dying before he admitted he knew what he'd given up. Men! Especially Trebanian men.'

She thumped herself down in her chair, felt a familiar spasm travel up her spine, and winced.

'Careful, Mum,' Phaedra warned. 'You know you're supposed to take it easy.'

'It's too hot in here.' She got up again to open the window.

'I could have done that,' Phaedra said.

Esther wasn't listening. She was staring at the moon.

There had been a moon that last night in Paris. She remembered how it had shone on Charles's hair as he turned his back on her.

'Trebanians,' she muttered. 'Damn them all.'

Phaedra got up to stand beside her. 'Will it be all right if I stay the night, then?'

Esther put an arm around her waist. 'Of course it will. We'll manage. If I hadn't put on so much weight you could share my bed.'

'I'll be OK. I can always pull your two armchairs together and turn them into some sort of bed.'

'Yes, I suppose you can.'

It took some shuffling and rearranging, but eventually the small sitting-room was transformed into a makeshift bedroom. Then they said goodnight to each other, and Esther retired to her room.

In the morning there were dark bruises beneath Phaedra's eyes.

Esther hadn't slept much either. At first she had been too busy thinking up ways of administering that well-placed kick to a vulnerable part of the man who was causing her daughter so much grief.

Later, she couldn't stop remembering.

Phaedra left her mother's flat immediately after a hasty breakfast of tea and toast. She had bolted from Chy an Cleth in such a hurry the previous night that she hadn't even stopped to pack a toothbrush, let alone clean underwear or jeans.

If she was lucky, she could sneak back to her room, grab a change of clothes, and be out of the house before Iain even noticed she'd returned. If she was unlucky, and he tried to confront her – well, the

335

confrontation wouldn't last long. She'd make sure of that.

Luck wasn't with her. She reached the gate just in time to see Iain walking out the door.

Phaedra stiffened, ready to do battle, waiting for him to open fire. But Iain wasn't interested in warfare. As she stood with one hand closed over the gate and her breath trapped tensely in her throat, he raised an arm in salute and headed round the side of the house.

Phaedra placed her hands on her hips and released her breath. Of all the . . . No. She caught herself in mid-explosion. There was no point bursting a blood vessel just because the man she wanted to avoid had avoided her. On the other hand, she didn't much appreciate being treated like an odour from the harbour during fishing season. She didn't put up with rudeness from her pupils, and she certainly wasn't putting up with it from Iain.

A breeze came up from the ocean and curled around her neck. Phaedra turned up the collar of her old navy jacket and started after him. She didn't pause to analyze her actions, or to wonder why she was suddenly in hot pursuit of a man she definitely didn't want to talk to.

Iain, as she had expected, was striding along the clifftop like a storm cloud bent on destruction. He always walked like that when he was troubled – with a loose-limbed violence that frightened her not at all. She paused for a moment, watching the wind lift his hair against the brilliance of the sky.

What an extraordinarily bright and balmy day it was for April. Too balmy to suit the turbulent mood consuming Iain.

He was walking so fast she would have to run to catch up with him. The question, of course, was did she want to? The whole idea had been to grab a few clothes and get back to her mother's before he saw her. So why should one dismissive wave of his hand be enough to change her mind?

Phaedra tripped over a stone as she came to the edge of the path along the cliff. It was only a small stone, but she let out a grunt of surprise.

Iain heard her and swung around.

He was wearing the same thick fisherman's pullover he had worn on the day of his father's funeral, and his glare was so fierce that Phaedra decided all he needed to complete the picture was a cutlass clamped between his teeth.

She said so.

Iain shrugged and relaxed. Marginally.

He didn't move though, so Phaedra took it upon herself to close the gap between them. When they were only a foot or so apart, and he hadn't yet stirred a muscle, she stopped.

He did move then, but only to thrust his hands into his pockets. 'Why did you leave?'

Not the words she had expected. 'I decided to sleep at my mother's. Why?' She pushed at her hair which, as usual, had come loose from its clip and was tangling around her face.

'You didn't leave a note.'

'I didn't think you'd mind.'

His eyes were set deeper than she remembered, smudged by shadows that came from – sleeplessness? Or an unquiet mind?

'I've always minded. You know that.'

She nodded. 'Yes. I suppose I know that.'

'Phaedra . . .' He took his hands out of his pockets as if he meant to touch her, then allowed them to fall against his sides. 'It isn't enough, is it? My minding?'

She dragged her gaze from his face, fastened it on the pale grey horizon. 'No. But it's not your fault.'

'What happened in London was my fault. I shouldn't have touched you.'

'I wanted you to touch me.'

'But now you don't?'

Phaedra watched a small bird, a duck of some sort, skim across the surface of the water. How could Iain not know she still wanted him? And how could she tell him she did if the wanting wasn't mutual?

Still pretending to watch the bird, she replied with deliberate ambiguity, 'Not necessarily.'

When Iain didn't answer, she forced herself to face him again. He gave her a thin smile and held out his hand. She took it, hesitantly, and after that neither of them could pretend the flame they had lit that night in London wasn't once again on the verge of becoming a three-alarm fire.

'Let's walk,' Iain said, jerking his head at a point along the cliff where a narrow path through the short, scrubby grass led to a steep trail down to the beach.

He didn't wait for her answer, but began to tow her behind him as if he imagined she ran on well-greased wheels. Phaedra didn't attempt to stop him. She knew why he wanted to walk – if you could call it walking – and what he was afraid would happen if they didn't keep moving.

She wasn't willing to go through that again any more than he was. Because without a doubt it would end the same way – with Iain saying he was sorry, but he couldn't make a commitment, and that she deserved commitment whether she wanted it or not.

Charles and Rosie Sharpe had a lot to answer for.

The stones on the beach made walking slow, but Iain ploughed on with her hand clasped tightly in his until they came to a tall, free-standing rock that jutted up from the sand like a giant's finger pointed at the sky. The tide was coming in and waves were lapping hungrily at its base . . .

Without warning, Phaedra was transported back to a day seventeen years ago when her childish adoration of Iain had turned to something else – when she had felt for the first time the subtle stirrings of a true and lasting love.

'Amphitrite's rock,' she murmured, as Iain pressed on, head down, determined to keep moving.

'What? What are you talking about?' He stopped, and when he let go her hand she felt as if she'd lost her anchor to reality – as if, without him to hold on to, she would drift away into the void that lay ahead.

'Don't you remember?' she said. 'You rescued me from that rock when I was little. The sea came up. If you hadn't got me down I could have drowned.' She felt as if she were drowning right this minute.

The ghost of a smile lifted Iain's lips. 'Hmm. Yes, now you mention it, I do remember. You scared the hell out of me. I was ready to drown you myself.'

She responded guardedly to his smile. 'Wouldn't that have defeated the purpose of the exercise?'

'I suppose it would. Phaedra . . .?'

'Yes?' She waited. A seaplane droned overhead, a gull squawked in protest, and a wave, more adventurous than the rest, broke into foam only inches from their feet. 'Iain?'

He shook his head as if he needed to clear it. 'Phaedra, I'm sorry.'

'You said that a long time ago.'

'No, I mean about yesterday. I had no right to tell you who you could, or couldn't, invite into the house. And I suppose . . .' He turned away so she couldn't see his face. 'You could do worse than to marry him.'

'Marry who?' Surely he wasn't suggesting –?

'*Sharkey!*' Iain snapped the name out like a bullet.

Good Lord! He *was* serious. 'Not much worse,' Phaedra said.

'What?' Iain stared at her. She stared back, and after a while he said quietly, 'I have no business to be glad you said that.'

'Are you glad?' she asked, clasping her hands behind her back to stop herself from reaching up to touch him.

He took her shoulder and pulled her back from the sea as it surged around the rock. 'Yes. God help me, I am. But it doesn't change anything. Phaedra, I want you to know that last night, when I went back to the house, I intended to tell you I didn't mean a word of it, that you were welcome to entertain Captain Hook if you chose, to marry whom you damn well pleased . . . But you'd already gone.'

'Only to my mother's.'

'I know . . .' The plane droned back overhead, drowning out his next words. When she could hear him again, he was saying, '. . . bloody little fool. Don't you know better than to go prowling around Porthkelly in the dark?'

Her hackles rose at once. 'I wasn't prowling. And I *can* take care of myself, Iain. I took a course in self-defence just last year.'

Iain's eyelids snapped up. 'Did you, by God? Judo?'

She'd surprised him. Phaedra allowed herself a small smile. 'Mmm. Like to take me on?'

'Not in the least. You'd probably lay me flat on my back in the sand.'

'Not an unappealing thought,' Phaedra murmured. 'Except that I happen to know you have a black belt in karate.'

'Hardly a skill I'd use on you.'

'Wouldn't you? How gallant. In that case why don't I try?' His lips twitched, and she added, 'I seem to remember that you're not unattractive on your back.'

Funny, she felt relaxed now, almost light-hearted. The sun must be going to her head.

341

'Phaedra –' Iain spoke her name as if it hurt him '– can't you understand? It's over.'

She blinked at him, still dazed, admiring the way the wind lifted his hair.

Iain tipped his head back and, without looking at her, said, 'For God's sake, Phaedra – no, for *your* sake – go and get on with your life and out of mine. Marry Sharkey. Marry anyone. I'll even dance at your wedding. Just don't – don't waste your time, or your generosity on me.'

Phaedra wanted to tell him she wouldn't dream of wasting her time, or anything else, on a man as afraid of love as he was. But she made the mistake of looking at him, and after that she couldn't say it.

A single tear had escaped from the corner of his eye and was running unattended down his cheek. He made no effort to wipe it away, and neither did she.

She knew then that although Iain might be afraid of loving, that didn't mean he didn't bleed as much, or more, than other men.

'Yes,' she whispered. 'I mean no. I won't waste – time. I . . .' She couldn't think of anything more to say.

There was no answer to wait for, so she stumbled away across the sand and up the rocks as if the ghosts of all Iain's ancestors were after her. But no one was behind her and when she looked back, he was no more than a dot in the distance.

By the time she reached the top of the cliff she was gasping for air and her shoes were filled with sand. A pain like hot needles stabbed her side.

At last she allowed herself to rest.

She waited for the needles to reach her heart. But they didn't, and as she walked back to Chy an Cleth she felt calm, not quite at peace, but peaceful.

The pain, she knew, would come later.

CHAPTER 16

Iain balanced his hip against an outcrop of rock and brushed the back of his hand across his eyes. It came away damp. He shook his head. What in hell was the matter with him today? Was he catching a cold? It wasn't raining, and surely the wind wasn't strong enough to make his eyes water.

He watched the erratic approach of a boat with blue sails. It wasn't a bad day for sailing, but it ought to be. This was April, the spring equinox, when the southwesterly winds could so easily veer to the north and blow unwary craft on to unseen rocks beneath the sea. Iain shuddered, although he wasn't cold. Days like this triggered memories – memories that, under normal circumstances, had long since ceased to haunt him.

The boat heeled suddenly, and he kept watching until he was sure all was well. Rosie had died on a day very much like this one – or so he'd been told. Clear and mild, with a deceptive May breeze that had suddenly turned violent. Add to the mixture two inexperienced sailors more interested in sex than in sails, and you had a classic recipe for tragedy.

He hadn't been in Cornwall when it happened. He and Rosie had had one of their frequent rows over money, and she had stormed off home to her sympathetic family, expecting him to follow with apologies. Poor Rosie had been a slow learner. By then she had been married to him long enough to have noticed that he rarely apologized – especially for rows *she* had started. When he hadn't followed her, she'd gone off with Peter Sharkey's cousin just to spite him. It was a familiar pattern.

Phaedra was different. Iain bent down to pull a strip of seaweed from a pool among the rocks. He should have found a kinder way to convince her to go away. She had looked like a wounded puppy with her big eyes and wide, mobile mouth. Lord knew he hadn't meant to hurt her. He *never* meant to hurt her. But, dammit, she *had* to see it wouldn't work. He dragged the slippery seaweed through his fingers. If only she didn't care so much. If only she had been the gold-digging bitch he had once thought her, instead of the loyal, steadfast, pig-headed, unbelievably passionate woman he knew she was.

Iain tried, unsuccessfully, to snap the seaweed in half, then tossed it back into the pool with a muttered oath.

No, Phaedra wasn't anything like Rosie, who, as far as he could tell, had been immune to all but the most superficial hurts – a child easily placated with treats or expensive baubles which in those days he'd been in no position to provide. She'd been a sexy little piece though. They'd had their moments, he and Rosie . . .

She hadn't deserved to die.

It was Pendy who had phoned to tell him. Not his father. Afterwards he had asked why, and Pendy had said Charles was in the library drinking whisky and chewing the heads off anyone who came near him. She had thought it better for Iain to hear the news from her.

He had been in the middle of a meeting crucial to the advancement of his career when an anxious secretary had called him to the phone. He had chewed *her* head off for interrupting.

Iain picked up another strip of seaweed and tried to snap it. But it was wet, like the first one, and it slipped unbroken through his fingers.

Rosie hadn't broken either. Her body had been pulled from the sea by the horrified crew of a passing sailboat. But he had been the one who identified her. He remembered looking down at her lifeless, once-beloved body and feeling . . . The fact was, he no longer remembered what he'd felt. Regret, certainly, for dreams that had died too fast. And pity for the senseless loss of life. Blind fury towards the man who had brought about Rosie's death – not because his grief was unbearable, even then, but because the other man had stolen something that was his. He hadn't been able to stand the sight of a Sharkey since.

Yet looking back on it – hadn't there also been a shameful feeling of relief? Iain folded his arms and allowed his chin to drop on to his chest.

Rosie's death had solved a lot of problems.

The breeze spattered a dusting of sand across his boots. He kicked it off. What was it they said about the sands of time? Something about not getting them in your lunch . . .? Which reminded him . . . He looked at his watch and saw that he had spent the entire morning on the beach – first with Phaedra, and then remembering Rosie.

Funny, he didn't often think of her these days. In fact the only woman he thought of with any kind of consistency was Phaedra. Oh, he'd taken a few others out over the past months – wined them and dined them, thanked them for their company, and returned them chastely and politely to their homes. Gloria had given up on him. She said he was losing his sex drive.

If only that were true. Iain squinted up at the sun, which was almost directly above him now, and started back across the beach. If he were losing his sex drive, he wouldn't feel as if his loins had turned to lava every time he saw Phaedra walk up the stairs ahead of him or bend down to pick up the morning post. Or smile that wide, sweet smile that was uniquely hers.

Her smile was the most seductive of all. And if he didn't have her again soon he would go mad.

He stopped in mid-stride. So startling was this unacknowledged truth that he almost fell over two small boys throwing stones at an unperturbed seagull perched on the edge of Amphitrite's rock.

'Watch where yer goin', mister,' shouted the one with a runny nose and several missing teeth.

'Yeah, you watch it,' parroted the other, who sported a bruised nose and a grimy bandana wound around his head.

Iain's urge to box their dirty, pointed ears subsided almost as quickly as it arose. Aside from the dirt, there had been a time when he hadn't been unlike these two himself – aggressive, surly, angry with a world that had stolen his mother and left him with a father who had forgotten that children weren't miniature adults. Only Pendy had really understood. And Phaedra sometimes, in her childish way.

'No, *you* watch it,' he said to the astonished boys. 'Seagulls aren't for target practice. They're living creatures, just like you, and if you disturb them they're likely to fight back. Ever been bitten by a seagull?'

The boys shook their heads. 'Seagulls don't bite,' said Runny Nose. 'They peck.'

'So they do,' Iain agreed. 'But it hurts just the same. I know, because I had to go to hospital once when a seagull bit me. They stuck six needles in my arm.'

'They never,' chorused the unappealing pair.

'They did,' Iain lied. 'Scout's honour.' He'd never actually been a scout. The scoutmaster at school had refused to have him.

He left the boys with their mouths hanging open as they scuffled among the rocks looking for shells. At least he hoped they were looking for shells – not used condoms or further weaponry with which to torment the wildlife. He wasn't convinced his scare tactics

348

had worked. No doubt Phaedra would have handled them quite differently.

Phaedra. Why did everything always come back to Phaedra? There was no getting away from it – he wanted her with a passion he had never experienced, hadn't counted on, didn't want and had no idea how to conquer.

He kicked irritably at the remains of somebody's sardine sandwich. The seagulls would make short work of that.

The worst part was that he knew he could have her any time he chose. She wouldn't refuse him. *He* was the one holding back, the one insisting that without commitment there could be no consummation.

So obviously he had to be insane. He paused briefly, his gaze on the boat with the blue sail, then walked on as a new and, up until this minute, inconceivable idea occurred to him.

What was to stop him marrying Phaedra?

Who was he to deny her what she – what they *both* wanted? Was commitment wholly out of the question? Plenty of marriages happened without love – and Phaedra was nothing like Rosie. If he married again, there would be no blinkers on his eyes. Or on hers. She knew he didn't love her. His first marriage had failed mainly because of false expectations. But if he married Phaedra, they would both know exactly what they were getting into. Bed. At once. And often.

Not a wholly hopeless basis for a marriage.

Fantasies of Phaedra, naked, eager and waiting for him, made Iain quicken his pace across the sand. Was he rationalizing? Probably. And what had caused this sudden reversal of principle after all the agonizing months of unholy abstinence?

That, of course, was easy to answer. But did it matter? At this moment he didn't know and didn't care.

What did matter was that without his realizing it had happened, Phaedra had become the focus of his life. He wanted her, wanted her now, immediately, as much as she said she wanted him. If the price he had to pay for that wanting was marriage – well, so be it. His father could have the last laugh for all he cared. *He* would have Phaedra, exactly where he wanted her.

Why in hell had it taken him so long to get the message?

Eager now to tell Phaedra he'd had a revelation, Iain hurtled up the cliff path as if he'd sprouted wings. He wasn't even out of breath when he reached the top, but somehow the air seemed colder. Was it his imagination, or had the weather started to change?

There was no one in the hall when he arrived. Thinking he heard a noise at the back of the house, he hurried into the conservatory.

Everything was just as it had been on his last visit. Even the wicker chair that had been pushed aside when he landed on Peter Sharkey remained in the exact spot where it had fallen. He picked it up.

Where was Phaedra? Not here, obviously. In the kitchen making lunch then? In her bedroom? Yes, that would be it. She was unhappy. He would find her lying on her bed with her face pressed into her pillow . . . and he would go to her, sit down beside her, touch her hair and run his hand slowly down her spine – over the sweet, seductive mound of her bottom . . .

Iain took the stairs two at a time. Next he would lift her up, take her in his arms . . . and she would turn to him, curl up on his lap, wrap her arms around his neck, and her legs around . . .

He pushed open the door to her bedroom.

She wasn't there.

OK. He took three long, sanity-restoring breaths. So much for fantasy. His never had worked out the way he'd hoped. Next stop the kitchen.

He headed back down the stairs. She would be standing at the cooker, perhaps, her long hair breaking loose from that restraining clip he always wanted to remove and stamp on . . .

Hmm. No. Not in the kitchen. Damn.

At this second setback, Iain paused to consider his options.

So absorbed had he been in erotic dreams fuelled by months of unnecessary abstinence, that he hadn't stopped to consider what he would do if he couldn't find Phaedra. In fact, it hadn't occurred to him that she might have taken his words to heart and left the house.

God, he was a fool. An arrogant fool at that. He glared at the brand new white cupboards installed above the sink. More of Lloyd's handiwork, no doubt. What had been wrong with the comfortable oak cupboards that had been there forever?

The phone started to ring, and Iain stopped glaring and strode into the hall to pick it up.

'Yes? Trebanian here.'

'Hello, Trebanian,' Esther's voice said drily. 'My daughter said I could give you a message if I liked.'

'Yes?'

'She'll be gone for the rest of the day. She didn't think you'd care, but I thought you might.'

'You were right. I do. Thank you.' How could a day suddenly seem like a week? 'Will she be spending the night with you again?' he asked as casually as he could.

Esther cleared her throat. 'No, she'll be spending it at Chy an Cleth. I managed to persuade her that you wouldn't either try to steal her virtue – not that she seemed as worried as she ought to be on that score – or attempt to have her for breakfast with toast and jam.'

Iain laughed, but it came out more like a groan. 'Don't count on it, Pendy. But thanks for the vote of confidence.'

'Don't thank me. I've grown used to my privacy, you know.'

Not to mention your cigarettes, Iain thought sympathetically. Years ago he had almost got hooked on the dreaded weed himself. 'Is Phaedra with you?' he asked.

'No, she's gone sailing. On the *Morvoren.*'

'On the what?'

'The *Morvoren*. It's Cornish for mermaid. Lloyd's been living on her for the past few days. She belongs to a friend of his.'

'Yes, of course. Phaedra mentioned it. Did you say she'd gone *sailing*? At this time of year? Does she have the faintest idea what she's doing?'

'Not much, I think. But she went with Lloyd, who does.'

'Rubbish. He's out of his mind.' Iain remembered the boat with the blue sails that had made so little headway in spite of the brisk breeze and steady seas. Then he recalled that he was talking to Phaedra's mother, and said guiltily, 'Still, it's a nice day, isn't it? They'll be all right.'

He wished he believed that. What in the world had possessed that fool Lloyd to take Phaedra, his Phaedra, to sea off the North Coast in April? Who did they think they were? The Owl and the bloody Pussy Cat?

'Thanks for letting me know,' he said to Esther, in what he hoped was a suitably calming tone. 'Give me a call when they get back.' He hung up before he could communicate any more of his anxiety to Phaedra's worried mother. After that he wrapped his hand around the phone cord and considered pulling it straight out of the wall.

Eventually, when that vengeful and pointless impulse wore off, he did what he had always done when his violent urges got the better of his common sense.

He went for a walk along the cliffs.

It beat giving the sack to the nearest luckless employee, which was the best he could usually do in London.

By the time he got back to Chy an Cleth, red-rimmed clouds had begun to gather in the sky and the breeze had become, if not a gale, certainly a lively wind.

He hoped Phaedra and her blasted companion had had the brains to set sail for home.

They hadn't.

As soon as he walked through the door the phone began to ring. It was Esther again.

Phaedra, who had been due back two hours ago, hadn't phoned her mother as she'd promised.

'Is she with you?' Esther asked, her voice filled with a hope Iain hated to dash.

'Are you saying she *hasn't* phoned you?' he asked.

'No. I mean no, she hasn't. *Is* she with you?'

'No, I'm afraid not. Pendy, what possessed that bearded fool to take her out?'

'Phaedra said it was her idea – that she talked him into it.'

'But why, for God's sake? She grew up on this coast. Surely she's bright enough to know better.' In his heart Iain knew the answer to his question. But he wasn't ready to face it just yet.

'I don't know,' Esther said. 'She mentioned something about needing a good, brisk wind to clear her head. Iain, do you realize it's getting rough out there –?'

'I know. It's also getting on for dinner time. They'll have put ashore somewhere. Don't worry.'

'I suppose you're right. Iain . . .?'

'Yes?' He wanted to snarl and snap his teeth. But this was Pendy. He had to remember he was no longer in the dog-eat-dog jungle of the city.'

'You'll phone if she goes to you first. Won't you?'

'Of course. No, on second thoughts, *she* will. All right?'

'All right. Thank you, Iain.' Her voice was colder than usual, and Iain had an idea it wasn't all due to worry about her daughter. She probably blamed him for this fiasco. And how could she not when he blamed himself?

Esther hung up, and Iain was left glaring at the mouthpiece.

Phaedra was missing in action with bloody Lloyd.

He slammed the phone on to its cradle and made his way back to the kitchen. This promised to be a long and deadly evening. He might as well fortify his body with sufficient sustenance to get him through it.

Peering into the fridge, he wondered how Phaedra would fancy a nice dose of arsenic for breakfast. Lloyd too. How dared an experienced sailor take such risks with Phaedra's safety?

At ten o'clock Esther phoned again.

'She's not here,' Iain said.

'I know. I've reported them missing.'

'What?' Iain tightened his grip on the receiver. 'Why did you do that, for heaven's sake? They're probably having dinner somewhere.' Or dancing. Or enjoying some activity more stimulating than either.

With Jade out of the picture, the bearded ape was probably feeling deprived. Iain fastened his gaze on a narrow path of moonlight on the floor. Not that Phaedra was the type to encourage him, but alone in a small boat at sea . . .

'No.' Esther's insistent voice penetrated his dismal reflections. 'No, Iain. She would have phoned. Haven't you seen how rough it is out there?'

Iain forced his mind from a nightmarish vision of Phaedra sprawled in the cabin of a boat somewhere, her long, white limbs entwined with Lloyd's. Pendy was right. He had been deluding himself. Phaedra would never intentionally distress her mother – even though she might not be averse to distressing *him*. So if she hadn't phoned, it could only mean . . .

'Phaedra?' he groaned, forgetting Esther could hear him. '*Phaedra!*' A shaft of cold, white fear snaked through his belly, followed by a wash of self-recrimination. What was the matter with him? Why hadn't *he* had the sense to call the coastguard? Or the police? Phaedra was missing at sea in a spring storm. And he had left it to Pendy to do something about it.

'Are you alone?' he asked Esther, attempting to sound a great deal calmer than he felt.

'No. Angus is with me. He's going to stay until we get some news.'

'Good. That's good. Are they – are the coastguard people searching? Were you able to give them any idea where to look?'

'No. Phaedra didn't say where they were going. Lloyd's an experienced sailor and I didn't think to ask. But no Mayday call has come in. The man I spoke to said they man the line twenty-four hours a day, so –'

'Are you saying Phaedra has a VHF radio on board?'

'I don't know. They should have.'

'Of course they should have. They also should be safe on shore. Jesus, Pendy, don't they have flares with them either? Distress rockets? *Anything*?'

'Maybe. I suppose so. But no one's seen any signs.'

'Aren't there always lookouts along the coast?'

'Not since 1978, the man said. Now they rely completely on radio.'

'Which those two idiots aren't using or don't have. Sorry,' he added, as Esther murmured a protest. 'Sorry. Of course it may not be their fault at all.'

'That's what I'm afraid of,' Esther said.

Iain heard the click of a lighter being fired up and could almost smell the smoke coming down the line.

'Can't the coastguard do *anything*?' he asked.

'They'd launch a lifeboat, probably from Padstow, if they had a signal. Or even ask for a military helicopter if they thought it would help. But without a signal all they can do is get their auxiliaries to check along the coast.'

Iain swore, and didn't bother to apologize. 'It's not enough,' he said. 'I'll see what I can do to get some action.'

Fifteen minutes later, after an acerbic conversation with the coastguard co-ordinator in Falmouth, it

357

began to dawn on him that there was very little he could do. The *Morvoren*, he was told, had an engine. But the sea was rough, and getting rougher – as he'd see for himself if he looked.

'Frankly,' the man added, 'if they're wise, they won't try to come in too close. Shore conditions are likely to be worse.'

'Thanks,' Iain said.

The man explained patiently that without radio contact or any other signal there was little chance of spotting the missing pair. Was he *certain* they were actually still at sea?

Iain had the impression that the man in Falmouth was not entirely convinced they had a genuine crisis on their hands.

'Dammit, this is an emergency,' he shouted. 'You can't just sit there filing your nails while –'

'Sir,' said the voice on the other end with commendable but maddening control, 'we understand your concern, of course, but isn't it possible the young lady went ashore some hours ago. If she was with her boyfriend –'

'She was *not* with her boyfriend,' Iain roared. 'And if you think she would put her mother through this kind of worry deliberately, then you don't know Phaedra Pendenning.'

'No, sir,' agreed the unflappable voice that Iain longed to choke. 'We're doing everything we can in the circumstances. If you could try to keep calm –'

Iain crashed the phoned back on to its cradle. 'Calm! I'll give you calm,' he growled at the squat black box. 'It's not *your* woman who's missing. She's . . .'

He sat down hard on the carved Chinese chair beside the phone. He had been going to say, 'She's mine.' But Phaedra wasn't his. He raised a hand to his forehead as the ache that had been grinding at his temples since morning intensified into a rampaging, throbbing torment. What was the matter with him? Of course Phaedra wasn't . . .

'Don't be a bloody fool, Trebanian.' In the sudden silence he heard his own voice echoing off the walls. 'Of course she's your woman. Always has been. Even before she was one.'

He groaned, as the knowledge he had fought to shut out from the moment Phaedra opened the door to him last summer, burst over him in anguished remorse. She had looked so lovely, so wild and sweet that day. 'Hello, Iain,' she had said. 'Won't you come in?'

From that moment on he had been lost.

'Phaedra!' Unable to remain still one second longer, Iain surged to his feet, lifting his arms above his head in an agonized gesture of supplication. 'Don't die, damn you. Phaedra, I love you. I've always loved you. You can't leave me now. Don't you dare . . .'

The clock in the drawing room chimed the half hour, and Iain allowed his arms to drop back to his sides. He bowed his head.

Phaedra couldn't hear him and there were no gods out there to listen, or to care. Even if there had been, she wasn't one of them. She was a real, live, modern woman with almost as many faults as he had, God help her. And he loved her for her faults as well as for her virtues. But now, because he had refused to accept the truth that had been staring him in the face all along, he was going to lose her.

No! Iain fixed his gaze on a heel-mark on the polished oak floor. No. He couldn't give up yet. It might be true there was nothing he could do. But that didn't mean he had to spend the night sitting uselessly by the phone waiting for a call that might not come. Not while Phaedra was out there, in trouble, probably frightened, with no one but Lloyd to protect her.

He didn't have much faith in Lloyd.

Pausing only to grab a jacket, Iain strode through the conservatory, into the garden and up on to the rockery his father had built for his mother long ago.

He had to keep watching. Somewhere out there in the night, amidst the blackness and the wind and the waves, the woman he loved might need his help. If she called to him he had to be there. No matter that the wind would steal her voice. No matter that she had sailed away with another man. Just so long as she stayed alive . . .

When the first pale light of morning rose above the misty horizon, Iain still stood on the rockery with his arms crossed and his eyes focused out to sea. The wind had died down and the waters were relatively calm again, but no slender young woman waved gallantly from the deck of a battered small boat called the *Morvoren*. Apart from a flock of small birds, the ocean was empty for as far as his eye could see.

Iain dropped his head into his hands. It had happened again. History, as always, had repeated itself. He looked up, brushed the hair from his forehead and searched the horizon without hope.

Rosie had died on a boat with another man. Why had he allowed Phaedra, whom he loved more than he had ever loved Rosie, to suffer the same undeserved fate? Why had she paid the price for his obstinacy?

He raised his eyes to the green-tinted clouds that were emerging in pale whisps from the night. 'Please,' he begged. 'Don't let Phaedra die. Let it be me instead.'

He knew there was no one there to hear. Providence, fate, call it what you will, had offered him a second chance at love.

And he had blown it.

Head down, shoulders hunched against the cold, Iain scanned the horizon one last time and trudged back into the house. It was morning. If the boat had survived the night, the searchers would find her now.

It wasn't until the persistent ringing of the telephone jolted him out of his stupefied misery, that Iain realized his skin was beaded with damp and his body frozen nearly to the bone.

'She's all right,' Esther said when he finally lifted the receiver. 'Iain, I think she's all right. They've sighted the *Morvoren* and she's on her way in. One of the searchers saw her first from the shore. The man I spoke to said they probably waited for high tide before attempting to come in. Oh, Iain, isn't it –?'

He cut her off. 'How long before they dock?'

'Not long. Angus and I are going down to meet them.'

Iain supposed he must have made some sort of answer. Afterwards he couldn't remember, because the next thing he knew he was revving up the engine of the Porsche. Then he was flying over the hill, turning on to the steep road winding down to the harbour. It didn't occur to him to walk, although it would have been almost as fast. All he knew was that he had to be there, waiting, when Phaedra's boat came in – so that when she stepped ashore he could take her in his arms and ask her – no, *tell* her – to marry him.

It didn't matter that she would be with Lloyd, didn't matter that he would, ironically, be keeping the promise his father had craftily exacted on his deathbed.

He had been given another chance to make Phaedra his lawfully wedded wife, for better or for worse, for as long as forever should last. That was all that mattered.

Iain was grinning as he spun past Esther's flat. The sun striking the pink archway made him blink, so that he didn't, at first, see the child in the sea-green dress run out of the doorway of the sweet shop and dart into the middle of the road.

When he did see her, it was already too late.

He was going to hit her.

NO! a voice roared in his head. Turn the wheel. Run up the pavement. Climb the wall . . .

White stucco filled the windscreen. Someone screamed. The sound of a crash reverberated through his eardrums. Glass shattered to silver in front of his eyes.

He felt no pain when he lost contact with the world.

CHAPTER 17

Only another five minutes and they'd be back on dry land. Phaedra leaned forward, her body swaying along with the rolling swell of the ocean as Porthkelly's familiar stone seawall came in sight.

They'd been lucky, she and Lloyd. Last night they had suffered more than a swell as they lurched towards the sheltered bay that Lloyd said was their best hope of survival – once they realized they had left it too late to outrun the sudden storm.

'The radio,' Phaedra had cried. 'We do have a radio. Don't we?'

Lloyd said they did, but he'd already tried it and the batteries were dead.

'Flares?' Phaedra suggested with dwindling hope. 'Rockets?'

Lloyd shook his head. 'Nope. Sorry.'

It was too late for apologies, too late for blame. Surrounded by towering waves and a savage sea that threatened to engulf them at any moment, it had been a matter of staying afloat and doing the best they could.

Phaedra shuddered, remembering the wild buffeting they had endured on their way to the comparatively calm waters of the bay. According to Lloyd, it was one of the few places along the coast that didn't dry out at low tide, leaving desperate sailors at the mercy of the rocks – as the wreckers of old had known only too well.

They spent a wretched night in the cramped, creaking confines of the *Morvoren*'s cabin with its two narrow bunks, doll-sized galley, and sanitary facilities in which no normally built person could turn around. She and Lloyd even took turns playing at sleep, but both of them were too much on edge to let down their guard while the wind wailed hungrily around the mast, and the endless motion of the waves denied all hope of useful rest.

She had felt safe enough once they dropped anchor. But her stomach had rebelled at the constant pitching and rolling. So had Lloyd's, and it had been a wan and exhausted pair who dragged themselves up the ladder to welcome the pink benediction of dawn.

The question of raising the blue sails hadn't arisen. The wind was still brisk, but Lloyd said they could make it back to Porthkelly as long as they kept an eye on the tide. When the time was right he'd started up the motor and set a course for home. He hadn't spoken to her after that, and she knew he was angry with himself for allowing her to persuade him to set sail. He'd wanted to be persuaded though. Lloyd loved sailing, and it was certain he wouldn't have much opportunity in Colorado.

They were about three-quarters of the way back when they were intercepted by a coastguard vessel whose captain, after ascertaining that they were seaworthy, had accompanied them most of the way in.

Phaedra glanced over at Lloyd as he held grimly on to the tiller. He was glaring at the dock as if he expected it to disappear if he didn't keep an eye on it.

Whatever had possessed her to beg him to take her to sea? She knew the dangers well enough.

When she stumbled up from the beach after leaving Iain, she had been surprised to find Lloyd at the house. But it turned out he'd only come back to pick up a few tools he'd forgotten. If they had left it at that, things might have been all right.

Unfortunately, he had mentioned the *Morvoren*.

Phaedra had immediately suggested he take her sailing, though she wasn't sure why any more. It had probably had something to do with getting away from Iain – or with the need to feel the wind in her hair and on her skin, banishing, at least for a little while, all thought of those last painful minutes with her love.

It had worked all right. There had been long periods during the night when she'd had neither the time nor the inclination to think of anything but the likelihood of their surviving the night.

Lloyd, still clinging to the tiller, tossed the hair out of his eyes and pointed the *Morvoren* at the dock. 'We're almost there,' he said. 'I think I see your mother.'

'Yes. Yes, you do. That's Mum.'

How could his beard possibly have grown longer and scruffier overnight? And what had happened to the buttons on his stained khaki jacket? Half of them were missing. Phaedra sniffed delicately. He didn't smell any too sweet either. But then she supposed she didn't exactly smell like a rose bush herself.

What a picture they would present to their friends and family gathered on the shore.

Was Iain among them? She scanned the dock, not sure whether she was sorry or relieved that no dark-haired figure stood waiting. In fact it looked as though only two people awaited their arrival.

Iain hadn't been worried about her, then. That was good, of course. Her mother, who must have been frantic, was definitely there. She recognized her cornflower-blue scarf that matched the sky. And the bald-pated man beside her could only be Angus.

As Lloyd cut the motor and pulled the boat alongside the dock, Phaedra's eye was caught by a flurry of unusual activity on the street winding up from the harbour. Clusters of townsfolk stood about talking and gesticulating. When anyone new appeared on the scene, their attention was immediately directed to something, or someone, which remained frustratingly out of sight around the corner.

'Phaedra?' Lloyd spoke with a trace of impatience.

She started, and realized he wanted her to throw a rope up to Angus who was waiting with his hand importantly outstretched.

A moment later she was in her mother's arms.

'Oh, Mum,' she cried, laughing as she pulled reluctantly away. 'Are you sure you want to touch me? I probably smell like rotten cabbage.'

'No, you don't,' Esther said. 'But you could smell like a whole compost heap for all I care. I'd still swear on the Bible it was the sweetest scent in town.'

Phaedra smiled. 'I'm sorry, Mum,' she said softly. 'The worst part was knowing you'd be worried.'

'I'm all right,' Esther said.

An unusual huskiness in her mother's voice caused Phaedra to examine her more closely. She had taken off her scarf and was pulling it through her fingers in an uncharacteristic show of nerves.

Something was wrong. Something unconnected with her recent harrowing night or loss of sleep. Phaedra switched her gaze to Angus. He was standing right behind Esther with his head bowed and his hands folded as if he were praying. In his dark suit and sober grey tie, he reminded Phaedra of an anxious undertaker.

She turned her attention to Lloyd, who was smiling sheepishly at Esther and apologizing for the worry he knew their absence must have caused her.

When Esther attempted to answer, he said hastily, 'I hope you'll excuse me, but I think I'd better clean up the cabin,' and beetled below decks before anyone had a chance to argue.

'He's feeling guilty,' Phaedra said, casting a puzzled glance around the unusually deserted harbour. There was an element besides Iain missing from this scene. Dr Polson – along with an ambulance, police and, quite possibly, the fire brigade as well.

It wasn't like Esther to arrive at a scene of potential disaster involving her daughter without a full crew of medics plus a rescue squad in tow. Not that any of them was needed. But she knew her mother when it came to the welfare of her one and only child.

'Mum, what's wrong?' Phaedra asked with sudden foreboding. Unreasoning fear tied a knot in her stomach.

Esther's quick smile lacked conviction. 'I'm all right. Really. Now tell us what happened to you and Lloyd? Were you caught in the storm? Yes, of course you were. Silly question.'

Her mother was positively fluttering. Something *was* wrong.

'We found a safe anchorage,' Phaedra said quickly. 'I would have let you know, but the radio was dead. Lloyd didn't expect to go sailing, and he forgot about it. I think he's worried about Jade.'

'Careless, very careless,' muttered Angus.

'It was my fault as well,' Phaedra said. 'I shouldn't have rushed him.'

Her mother gave her a sharp look and said nothing. A dozen or so seagulls circling overhead began to shriek at them. The pungent smells of the harbour drifted up her nose. Why was she afraid, on this clear and glorious April morning? What was this feeling of darkness closing in? And why did she want to return the breakfast she hadn't yet eaten now that the ground beneath her feet was no longer heaving?

'Mum? Something's happened. I know it has. Is it . . .?' She couldn't finish. There was no reason why whatever was wrong should have to do with Iain. But she knew it had.

'I'll explain in the car,' Esther said with obvious reluctance. She put an arm around Phaedra's shoulders. 'Come along. Time for a nice hot bath.'

'Just a minute.' Phaedra moved to the edge of the dock and shouted, 'Lloyd, we're leaving now. Are you OK?'

Lloyd's muffled reply indicated that he was.

She hesitated. After the night they had been through together it didn't seem right to leave him alone cleaning up the mess. But she guessed he was embarrassed and wanted her to go. In the end, she did.

'See you later then.' she called. 'Look after yourself.'

Esther tugged at her sleeve, and she followed her mother into Angus's ancient but well-maintained Fiat.

The moment he switched on the engine, Phaedra leaned forward and said pointedly, 'Well?'

Esther swallowed and waited until the car had begun its slow climb up the hill. 'You mustn't take it too hard, dear,' she said, still in that peculiar, husky voice. 'I wasn't able to find out any details, so he may be all right.'

'Iain?' Phaedra whispered.

'I'm afraid so. But I understand he was breathing.'

Phaedra wanted to scream, to insist she be told the worst at once. But she managed to hold her peace and wait for Esther to explain in her own way.

She was still waiting when they turned the corner by the Spotted Dog.

'Don't look,' Esther said quickly.

She was too late.

Iain's beautiful white Porsche lay on its side across the pavement in front of the sweet shop, its left side flattened like a tin destined for recycling. The bonnet was squashed up against the wall. Glittering diamonds of glass dotted the pavement. But it was the door on the right that held Phaedra's attention. It hung half off its hinges, and where the window had been, all that remained was a gaping hole surrounded by jagged slivers. A dark, sticky substance stained the seat.

Two solid-looking policemen stood in the road taking notes. Behind them the citizens of Porthkelly shuffled about as if hoping for further drama.

'Ghouls,' Esther muttered.

As Angus drove quickly past the scene, a tow-truck braked at the top of the hill.

Phaedra clutched at the buckle on the belt holding up her jeans. Its sharp corners dug into her palm. 'What happened?' she asked.

Her voice sounded normal. How strange. She didn't feel normal. Her mind seemed disconnected, severed from the rest of her, all bodily sensation on hold.

'I don't know exactly,' Esther said. 'We heard the crash, but didn't realize it was Iain until Letty from the pub came by and told us. She knew we'd gone down to meet you.'

'When we arrived they were lifting him into an ambulance,' Angus explained in his most precise tones. 'He was unconscious. There was nothing we could do, so we went back to wait for the *Morvoren*.'

'Yes. I see. Would you take me to the hospital, please.' Phaedra pinned her gaze on the short hairs springing from the back of Angus's wrinkled neck.

'Perhaps you should have a bath and some food first,' Esther put in quickly. 'I don't suppose they'll let us see him yet.'

'No. I have to go the hospital. Now.' How could anyone think of food while Iain lay fighting for his life? If he was fighting. If he wasn't already . . .

She refused to finish the thought.

Angus glanced at her over his shoulder. 'Very well. That's where we'll go, then.' He spoke as if he were soothing a fractious child.

Phaedra discovered she could feel after all. Her body was cold. Icy cold, in spite of the frantic pumping of her heart. And her mind was crying, Iain! Iain, don't die! You can't die on me. It doesn't matter if you don't love me. Just don't make me spend the rest of my years on earth knowing you are nowhere – nothing. Please . . .

She didn't realize her hands were folded in prayer until the tips of her fingers touched her chin.

When they reached the small, redbrick hospital on the outskirts of town, they were told Iain was still being treated in surgery.

Phaedra couldn't speak, and it was Esther who asked, 'Will he be all right?'

The receptionist glanced at her computer screen. 'We have no information yet. Are you family?'

'Yes.' Esther lied without batting an eyelid. 'His stepmother and his fiancée.'

Angus shuffled his feet. Phaedra looked at her mother and said nothing.

The receptionist nodded. 'If you'd like to wait . . .'

'We'll wait,' Esther said.

The waiting room contained hard, pond-green chairs with chrome legs. The walls were hospital green and smelled of disinfectant. The round white clock on the wall read one-fifteen.

When the big black hands reached two o'clock, Phaedra got up and went back to the receptionist.

'Dr Polson will be with you shortly,' she was told.

She went back to the waiting room. Angus was pretending to read a magazine on Cornish gardens. Esther was twisting her pretty blue scarf into a perspiration-soaked rag.

'No news?' she asked, after taking one look at Phaedra's face.

'No. No news.'

At two-thirty Dr Polson bustled in. He raised his eyebrows. 'I understood Iain's family was here. His sister . . .'

'Joan? She's in Brazil, Doctor,' Esther said. 'We're all the family he has in Cornwall. Please – how is he?'

'Could be worse. Ought to be worse. Slight concussion, bruises and abrasions, a number of cuts that needed stitching. Broken leg. Nothing that won't mend. He'll be back making life difficult for his office staff in no time.' Dr Polson ended his phlegmatic recital of Iain's injuries with an unprofessional chuckle.

Phaedra closed her eyes. Hadn't Iain said something once about Trebanians never dying in hospital? 'Thank you, God,' she whispered.

Dr Polson cleared his throat.

'And thank *you*, Dr Polson,' Esther added. 'Can we see him?'

'Not all at once. Too much for him. But if *you'd* like to go in, Esther . . .'

'No. Not me. Phaedra.'

'Ah.' Dr Polson frowned at Phaedra as if he wasn't sure he approved. Then he cleared his throat and said, 'Very well, then. They'll be taking him up to the ward in a few minutes. I'll let you know.'

A few minutes turned into half an hour, then forty minutes. Phaedra spent the time gazing blindly at the clock and trying not to think about the future. Iain was all right. The doctor had said he wasn't going to die. That was all that mattered. Nothing had changed since yesterday, but . . . in a way everything had.

Now she had a reason to go on living.

Dr Polson finally arrived to take her up to Iain. He had a room to himself, as she expected, but when she got there, instead of looking at him, Phaedra found herself concentrating on the details of his room. A cupboard, cream walls, two of the pond-green chairs and a bedstand. All the standard hospital features.

Iain made no sound, and she finally mustered the courage to look at him.

The first thing she took in was the white, bandaged protrusion suspended like a fat white slug from a contraption at the end of his bed. She stared at it while she gathered strength to move her eyes to his face. What she could see of it.

His forehead was swathed in a bandage. Below it jutted the pale, swollen bulge of his nose. His cheeks and chin were a map of fine scratches and cuts, and a plastic tube protruded from his arm. His eyes were closed. She could hear his breathing in the silence.

'He's asleep,' Phaedra whispered to Dr Polson.

'Like hell he is.' Iain's voice was as strong and decisive as it had ever been.

Phaedra's hand went to her mouth, and then her body sagged and she started to laugh as relief rolled over her like yesterday's waves. Iain was still the tough, peremptory, unyielding man she had come to love.

She closed her eyes and sent a silent prayer of thankfulness to the Deity who had listened to her pleas. When she opened them again, she saw that Iain was taking the opportunity to examine her minutely – from the top of her head to as far as his eyes could travel from his supine position. For a man reportedly recovering from concussion, his examination was astonishingly thorough.

'Phaedra,' he said.

She swallowed and found her voice. 'Yes. How are you?'

His smile, stretched across the scarred wreck of his face, was as wicked and sexy as ever. Seeing it, Phaedra choked back a sob – and Iain opened his arms. The movement made him wince. She hesitated, and at once his battered features darkened.

Oh, Iain. Don't misunderstand me, her heart cried silently. Don't shut me out again. Not now.

He moved his head as if he understood, and with a soft cry she moved to the edge of the bed. At once he took both her hands and pulled her forward until she was close enough for him to stretch an arm around her waist.

'Be careful,' she whispered. 'Iain, your leg. You mustn't –'

'You're nowhere near my leg. I want to hold my woman, and no one had better tell me I can't.' He slid his hand under the back of her sweater.

Phaedra, gazing at his battered but still beloved face, knew that at last she was where she belonged. In Iain's arms. Even if he did smell like a hospital dispensary.

Behind them, Dr Polson murmured, 'No one is telling you anything, Iain. Experience has taught us all it's a waste of time. But if you don't give that leg a chance to heal, *you're* the one who's going to regret it.'

Oh dear. With a pang of guilt, Phaedra removed Iain's hand from her waist and sat down in one of the green chairs.

Dr Polson nodded. 'That's better. Don't stay too long now. Can't have my patient getting over-excited.'

'I'll be a lot more excited if Phaedra tries to leave,' Iain assured him. 'In fact, I'll unhook myself from all these ridiculous tubes and pulleys and fetch her back.'

'On one leg?' Dr Polson asked drily.

'On my stomach if I have to.'

'Ten minutes.' The doctor was smiling as he left them.

'Not long enough,' Iain called after him.

Dr Polson ignored him. They could hear his feet slapping the polished floor as he marched off down the hall.

Phaedra turned back to Iain. His dear face was so bruised and battle-scarred. But it was still his face. This was still the man who had, all unknowingly, kept her from loving any other man. The bruises would fade, and the cuts would heal with time. She reached out to touch him, then thought better of it.

'Iain, what have you done to yourself?' she whispered. '*Why?*'

He reached for her hand and held it against his cheek. 'I was in too much of a hurry to haul you off that damned boat and shake you silly for going off with Lloyd,' he admitted. 'The result, or so I'm told, was that I had a serious disagreement with a wall.'

'The wall won, obviously.'

'Not for long.' Iain's grip on her fingers tightened. 'I thought you told me the bearded one had left town.'

'No. I told you he'd left Chy an Cleth. He's not joining Jade until after Easter.'

Iain let her hand drop on to the sheet. 'So you spent the night with him? On the boat?' He sounded no more than mildly curious.

Phaedra wasn't for a moment deceived. She stood up and moved to the end of the bed.

He made no attempt to stop her.

'I suppose you could put it that way,' she agreed. 'We were caught by the storm. It came up very suddenly, and there wasn't a chance of making it home before it broke.'

'How convenient.'

'What?' Was she hearing right?

'I said, "how convenient".'

So there wasn't anything wrong with her hearing.

'Iain!' she said. 'If you weren't sufficiently battered already, I'd be sorely tempted to slap your face for that. You know there's nothing between me and Lloyd. He's married. To Jade. Who is my friend.'

'That never stopped Rosie.'

Phaedra forgot about staying out of his reach, forgot about everything except that she had a burning desire to kick his very presentable, if unavailable, backside.

'I – am – not – Rosie,' she said, sounding out each word with fierce precision, and leaning over him so that her face hung just above his swollen nose. 'I am Phaedra. And I don't sleep with the husbands of my friends. The only man I have ever slept with is you – and to the best of my recollection, there wasn't much sleeping about that.'

Instead of snapping back at her, Iain raised a hand to his mouth to cover what looked suspiciously like a slightly rueful grin. 'I'm sorry,' he said. 'I'm a jealous fool who ought to have his ass kicked.'

Before Phaedra could mention that she would bear that in mind when he was better, she felt his other hand curve around her bottom – or around as much of it as he could get at from his less-than-advantageous position. He was stroking it purposefully, and with every sign of proceeding to further and more intimate explorations, when a scandalized voice exclaimed from the open doorway, '*Mr* Trebanian. This is a hospital, I'd like to remind you. Not a brothel.'

'And I'd like to remind you, Nurse Nosebottam, that this is my fiancée, not a –' He stopped suddenly and sniffed, as if he were a greyhound scenting a trail. 'On second thoughts, my sweet, you do smell a bit – exotic. Been fermenting the turnips again, have you?' He gave her a light pat and ceased his ministrations.

Phaedra scrambled to her feet, embarrassment effectively putting paid to the instant arousal his practised touch inspired. She pulled awkwardly at the hem of her black sweater.

'I haven't had a chance to bathe yet. It was rough, and both of us were sick. Do I really . . .?'

'No,' said Iain, his voice unusually soft. 'You don't. I was teasing. You shouldn't make it so easy for me.'

Phaedra smiled ruefully. 'It's a habit, I think. I . . .' She broke off. What was that he'd said? About her being . . .

'Iain, did you call me your – your *fiancée*? Because –'

Nurse Nosebottam, if that really was her name, didn't give her a chance to finish. 'You'll have to leave,' she said. 'Visiting hours are over, I'm afraid.'

'Nonsense.' Iain waved a dismissive hand. 'I'm the one occupying this bed, and visiting hours are over when *I* say so. Would you leave us alone now, please?'

Phaedra began to see why Trebanian Advertising was so phenomenally successful. Iain didn't take prisoners.

The nurse drew a sharp breath and sailed out of the room with starch in her spine. Phaedra decided it was as well Iain wasn't hooked up to anything crucial to his survival.

'For a man who's supposed to be recovering from concussion, you're disgracefully bossy,' she told him. 'And I suppose you realize she'll be back with reinforcements in a minute. You shouldn't have done that, Iain.'

'Why not? I'm damned if I'm having an audience while I propose to the woman I love.'

Phaedra lowered herself back into the chair. There seemed to be something the matter with her legs. They felt like spaghetti. She pressed a hand to her throbbing head. She *wasn't* Iain's fiancée. Was she . . .?

'Phaedra? Did you hear me?'

No, she hadn't heard him. Had he said something? 'No,' she admitted. 'What?'

'I said, "Will you marry me?" But on second thoughts I'll rephrase that. *When* "will you marry me?"'

His eyes were very bright. Was he feverish? 'Do you mean that?' she asked.

'Of course I mean it. I'm not in the habit of asking women to marry me just for something to do.' He smiled, and even though his mouth was surrounded by bruises and stitches, it was the most beautiful smile she had ever seen. The same smile that had stolen her heart from the beginning. Just as now it had stolen her voice.

When she didn't answer, Iain said softly, 'I'm sorry, Phaedra. Sorry it took me so long to see what was under my nose. I should have known, at least since that night in my flat. But I was so sure I could never love again, so convinced that anything my father wanted must be wrong, that . . .' He stopped, and she watched the muscles working in his throat.

Why was he finding it hard to speak? Was he more seriously injured than he wanted her to know?

'Iain?' she said, fighting to keep the panic from her voice. 'Iain, are you all right?' She bent over him anxiously.

'I don't know.' He took her hand again. 'Have I left it too late? Have you changed your mind about loving me? Because if you have –?'

'It could never be too late.' Joy filled her being, warming her heart like sunshine after snow. Iain loved her. He wanted to marry her. 'No,' she whispered, drawing his fingers to her lips. 'I haven't changed my mind.'

'Then, yes . . . I am most definitely all right. As all right as I've ever been in my life.' He placed a hand on the back of her neck. 'Would you believe I can even tolerate the thought of children if they're yours?'

'Oh, Iain.' Phaedra was so overcome she could barely get the words out. 'I do love you.'

'As I love you, Phaedra mine.' He slid his hand under her hair, and after a moment said pensively, 'I suppose it's been done before.'

Helpless desire shuddered down her spine. 'What has?'

'Making love in a hospital bed.'

'With a broken leg?' Phaedra sighed regretfully. 'It probably has. But it's not going to be done again today.'

'Hard as nails,' Iain said. 'I've fallen in love with an iron lady.'

Phaedra smiled. He was teasing her again, just as he had done in the old days. And he loved her. There really was a place where dreams came true. She just hadn't guessed it would be a hospital room with Nurse Nosebottam breathing fire down the hall.

'Kiss me,' Iain said.

'I can't. Your poor face –'

'Needs kissing better,' he finished for her.

Phaedra leaned forward and brushed her lips very lightly across his mouth. His thumb teased the sensitive spot just below her left ear.

'Again,' he said. 'That wasn't a kiss.'

'Maybe not, but it's all the kissing you'll be getting tonight, young man.' Dr Polson's voice was friendly but firm. 'Phaedra, I'm sorry to break up the party,

382

but if you want him to get better you'll be off now. Nurse Nosebottam refuses to come back until you've gone.'

'A bonus,' Iain said. 'Phaedra, don't you dare leave me. That woman likes sticking needles into me just to pass the time.'

Dr Polson shook his head. 'A big fellow like you shouldn't be afraid of a few needles. Phaedra –'

'I'm going,' Phaedra said. 'Be good, Iain. I'll see you tomorrow.'

'There'll be nothing left of me to see after that woman's through with me.'

'There'll be plenty.' she said, waving from the doorway. 'It will take more than needles to vaporize you.'

'Just you wait till we're married,' Iain growled. 'Just you wait, Phaedra Pendenning.'

Phaedra blew him a kiss. 'I will,' she said. 'But it won't be easy.'

Iain's reluctant laugh followed her down the hall.

No, waiting wouldn't be easy. But she'd waited this long. She'd survive another few weeks – at least until he had his cast off.

Nurse Nosebottam, on the other hand, might not.

EPILOGUE

The joyful melody of church bells sang clearly on the wind. The last time Iain had heard those particular bells, exactly one year ago today, they had rung in sorrow for the passing of his father. Now they pealed in celebration of his marriage to Phaedra.

He couldn't take his eyes off her as she walked gracefully beside him down the aisle – not, for once, in a practical skirt or jeans, but in an ivory silk dress of classical simplicity that did for her what frills and bows could not. Today the housekeeper's daughter looked like the princess she was. His princess. Iain placed his hand over hers where it clung to his arm. She was smiling, not at him now, but at the small crowd of wellwishers who had been invited to celebrate with them in the weathered old church above the cliff.

Perhaps sensing his scrutiny, at that moment Phaedra turned the smile on him.

Iain caught his breath. He had known for a long time how much she loved him. But only now, seeing that love shining from her eyes, did he truly understand what he had almost thrown away.

'I love you,' he mouthed silently, as they came to the ancient stone arch at the front of the church and walked together into the sun.

Phaedra squeezed his arm, and it was all the answer he needed or wanted.

God, she was beautiful, this Cornish rose of his. Obstinate to a fault, just as he was, but as sweet and as frighteningly generous as any woman he'd ever known.

He bent down to press his lips to hers, ignoring the laughing group gathered at the bottom of the steps.

Time passed without his being aware of anything but the taste of her, the feel of her breath on his cheek and, in the background, the eternal murmur of the sea. Then his sister's voice cried, 'Hey! Hold it for the honeymoon, children. Iain, you're not the only one who wants to kiss the bride.'

Reluctantly, Iain released her. Immediately Anton, resplendent in dramatic black and red, swept her into his arms and kissed her cheek. He was followed by Angus, who had given her away, and Esther, who was crying unrestrainedly over her smart blue, mother-of-the-bride suit.

'Oh, my dear child. I'm so happy,' she sobbed. 'I've waited so long for this day. Charles . . .' She couldn't go on.

Phaedra gave her mother a hug. She understood that Esther was crying not only for her daughter's happiness, but for the Trebanian she herself had loved and lost.

'There now, there now.' The ever-faithful Angus drew Esther away, patting her gently on the shoulder. 'You haven't lost a daughter, you know. You've officially gained the son you always had.'

Esther sniffed and dabbed at her eyes. 'I know, I know. And I have you too, Angus. You'll always be my very dear friend.'

Only Phaedra noticed the wistfulness in the little solicitor's eyes as he nodded and said of course he would be her friend.

When the breeze lifted her veil so that it flew up behind her head like an angel's halo, Iain laughed and suggested it was time they all went back to the house.

A great sense of timelessness and peace descended as they wound their way through the old churchyard between the graves of generations of Trebanians and Pendennings. She and Iain would be moving to his London flat for the time being, and she had already found a part-time teaching job in town. But Chy an Cleth would always be here, waiting for them, when they needed time to rest and revitalize their souls. Both of them knew that years from now this was the place where they would come to end what was left of their days.

When they came to Charles's last resting place with its modest white headstone saying only, 'Charles Trebanian, loving husband of Helen,' and giving the dates of his birth and his death, Phaedra caught at Iain's arm and said, 'Wait. Let the others go on.'

Esther looked over her shoulder, saw them standing there, and nodded in understanding. Spreading her arms wide, she shooed the rest of the guests ahead of her through the gate.

'You know,' said Iain, putting his arm around Phaedra's waist and pulling her close, 'when you first said we should marry on the anniversay of my father's death, I thought it was a bad idea.'

'I know. But it wasn't, was it?'

Iain shook his head. 'No. Mind you, if he knew I'd asked Anton to be my best man, he'd probably make a point of coming back to haunt us.'

Phaedra smiled. 'I don't think so. I don't think he'd mind any more.' She raised her arm and pointed at the impossibly blue July sky. 'You know, I have a feeling he's watching us today – and chuckling with triumph up there somewhere.'

'Or down there somewhere,' Iain murmured.

'Iain!' Phaedra pulled away from him and took an indignant step backwards. Then her features softened. 'You don't mean it, do you? You don't care that he's got his own way.'

Iain took her hand. 'Not a bit,' he admitted. After a moment he added with a grin, 'My wicked old father has finally succeeded in getting me to do as I'm told. And I wouldn't have it any other way. Hard to believe, isn't it?'

'No. Not really. You're both Trebanians.'

'Why do I think that's not a compliment?' Iain ran a finger gently down her nose.

Phaedra wrinkled it at him. 'It is, really. I've

always had a great affection for Trebanians.'

'So I should hope. Now how about showing me some of that affection.'

Phaedra raised her arms and wound them around his neck, showing him so satisfactorily that they might have missed the reception altogether if Esther hadn't sent Joan to remind them that they had a houseful of guests.

A warm gust of wind pursued them as they left the churchyard. It rustled leaves on the bushes and whispered through the grass with a curious rasping noise – remarkably like the sound of an old man's satisfied chuckle.

**THE EXCITING NEW NAME
IN WOMEN'S FICTION!**

PLEASE HELP ME TO HELP YOU!

Dear *Scarlet* Reader,

As Editor of *Scarlet* Books I want to make sure that the
books I offer you every month are up to the high standards
Scarlet readers expect. And to do that I need to know a
little more about you and your reading likes and dislikes. So
please spare a few minutes to fill in the short questionnaire
on the following pages and send it to me.

Looking forward to hearing from you,

Sally Cooper

Editor-in-Chief, *Scarlet*

QUESTIONNAIRE

Please tick the appropriate boxes to indicate your answers

1 Where did you get this Scarlet title?
Bought in supermarket ☐
Bought at my local bookstore ☐ Bought at chain bookstore ☐
Bought at book exchange or used bookstore ☐
Borrowed from a friend ☐
Other (please indicate) _____

2 Did you enjoy reading it?
A lot ☐   A little ☐   Not at all ☐

3 What did you particularly like about this book?
Believable characters ☐   Easy to read ☐
Good value for money ☐   Enjoyable locations ☐
Interesting story ☐   Modern setting ☐
Other _____

4 What did you particularly dislike about this book?
_____

5 Would you buy another Scarlet book?
Yes ☐   No ☐

6 What other kinds of book do you enjoy reading?
Horror ☐   Puzzle books ☐   Historical fiction ☐
General fiction ☐   Crime/Detective ☐   Cookery ☐
Other (please indicate) _____

7 Which magazines do you enjoy reading?
1. _____
2. _____
3. _____

And now a little about you –
8 How old are you?
Under 25 ☐   25–34 ☐   35–44 ☐
45–54 ☐   55–64 ☐   over 65 ☐

cont.

9 What is your marital status?

Single ☐ Married/living with partner ☐
Widowed ☐ Separated/divorced ☐

10 What is your current occupation?

Employed full-time ☐ Employed part-time ☐
Student ☐ Housewife full-time ☐
Unemployed ☐ Retired ☐

11 Do you have children? If so, how many and how old are they?

_____

_____

12 What is your annual household income?

under $15,000	☐	or	£10,000	☐
$15–25,000	☐	or	£10–20,000	☐
$25–35,000	☐	or	£20–30,000	☐
$35–50,000	☐	or	£30–40,000	☐
over $50,000	☐	or	£40,000	☐

Miss/Mrs/Ms _____

Address _____

_____

_____

Thank you for completing this questionnaire. Now tear it out – put it in an envelope and send it, before 31 January 1998, to:

Sally Cooper, Editor-in-Chief

USA/Can. address
SCARLET c/o London Bridge
85 River Rock Drive
Suite 202
Buffalo
NY 14207
USA

UK address/No stamp required
SCARLET
FREEPOST LON 3335
LONDON W8 4BR
Please use block capitals for address

HIFAT/7/97

Scarlet titles coming next month:

THE MARRIAGE CONTRACT Alexandra Jones
Olivia's decided: she's not a person any more . . . she's a wife! She's a partner who's suddenly *not* a full partner because of a contract and a wedding ring. Well it's time her husband, Stuart, wised up, for Olivia's determined to be his equal . . . in *every* way from now on!

SECRET SINS Tina Leonard
When they were children, Kiran and Steve were best friends, but they drifted apart as they grew up. Now they meet again and Kiran realizes how much she's missed Steve . . . and how much she loves him. But before they can look to the future, she and Steve must unravel a mystery from the past . . .

A GAMBLING MAN Jean Saunders
Judy Hale has secured the job of a lifetime . . . working in glamorous Las Vegas! Trouble is, Judy disapproves of gambling *and* of Blake Adams, her new boss. Then Judy has to turn to Blake for help, and finds herself gambling on marriage!

THE ERRANT BRIDE Stacy Brown
What can be worse than being stranded on a dark road in the dead of night? Karina believes it's being rescued by a mysterious stranger whom she ends up sharing a bed with! But better *or* worse is to come, when Karina finds herself married to Alex, her dark stranger.